Praise for Michael Malone

"A masterful storyteller."
—*Booklist*

"Michael Malone has the true narrative gift, the true eye for character in action, and a fluent prose, wrought carefully and well."
—Robert Penn Warren

"Malone...delights the reader with his witty eye for the kind of detail that proclaims with humor and confidence, 'This is true!'"
—*Los Angeles Times Book Review*

"To get to the bottom of one of Malone's books is always a searing experience, like plumbing a well and finding oneself looking at the faces of the stars."
—*Chicago Sun-Times*

"Michael Malone is the most generous of writers: his booming narrative voice is full of good humor, and his feelings for his characters—sometimes amused, nearly always passionate—seem paternal, in the best sense of the word."
—*New York Times Book Review*

"Perhaps the best novelist of the New South..."
—*Guardian*

"A superbly stylish author whose books deserve the widest audience."
—*New Yorker*

"One remembers Mr. Malone's idiosyncratic creations the way one remembers those of another brilliant social caricaturist, Charles Dickens...."
—*New York Times Book Review*

The Delectable Mountains
or, Entertaining Strangers

by Michael Malone

The Delectable Mountains
or, Entertaining Strangers

By Michael Malone

SOURCEBOOKS LANDMARK™
AN IMPRINT OF SOURCEBOOKS, INC.®
NAPERVILLE, ILLINOIS

Published by Sourcebooks, Inc.
P.O. Box 4410, Naperville, Illinois 60567-4410
(630) 961-3900
FAX: (630) 961-2168
www.sourcebooks.com

Library of Congress Cataloging-in-Publication Data
Malone, Michael.
   The delectable mountains, or, Entertaining strangers / by Michael
Malone.
      p. cm.
Originally published: The Delectable Mountains. New York: Random House, 1976
   1. College graduates—Fiction. 2. Summer theater—Fiction. 3. Young
men—Fiction. 4. Colorado—Fiction. 5. Actors—Fiction. I. Title:
Delectable mountains. II. Title: Entertaining strangers. III. Title.
   PS3563.A43244 D45 2002
   813'.54—dc21

                                        2002006927

Printed and bound in the United States of America
          POD   10 9 8 7 6 5 4 3

ACKNOWLEDGMENTS
My grateful thanks to Kelley Thornton,
Jacquelyn Posek, Amy Baxter, and
Megan Dempster for all their talented help
in preparing this edition of
The Delectable Mountains.

To Cervantes'
Restaurant

Mrs. Booter's
Boarding
House

Police
Station

Kennedy
Campaign
Headquarters

Rings
Morelli's
Cabin

Tacos

Art
Gallery

Japanese
Restaurant

Porno Store

Austrian
Sportswear

MAIN STREET

Morrelli's
Dance Hall

Tanya's Cabin

SLOUGH LANE

Navajo
Jewelry

Western
Outfits

ARCADE

Shooting
Gallery

Hade's
Buick

Streetcar Diner

Danish Toys

Nixon
Headquarters

Floren Par

Trout
Fishing

*SHRINERS'
BANNER*

Summer, 1968

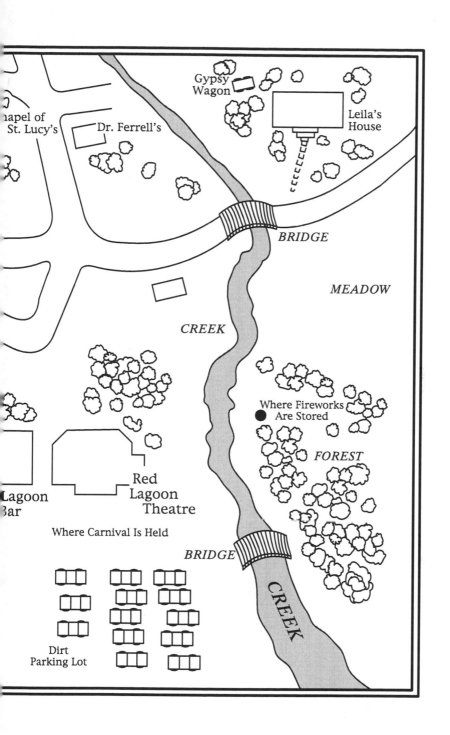

Gypsy
Wagon

Leila's
House

Chapel of
St. Lucy's

Dr. Ferrell's

BRIDGE

MEADOW

CREEK

Where Fireworks
Are Stored

FOREST

Lagoon
Bar

Red
Lagoon
Theatre

Where Carnival Is Held

BRIDGE

CREEK

Dirt
Parking Lot

the people

Devin Donahue	The protagonist, twenty-two years old, just graduated from Harvard, and out of schedule
Verl Biddeford	Devin's childhood friend and moral guide

THE PLAYERS

Leila Dolores Beaumont Thurston Stark	Devin's first love and the force behind the summer stock company, Red Lagoon Players
Mittie (Mitchell) Stark	Leila's melancholy actor husband, founder of the Players
Maisie (Madeline) Stark	Leila's four-year-old daughter, canny and sweet
David Stark	Leila's two-year-old son, curious and playful
Amanda Sluford Beaumont Thurston	Leila's indomitable and garrulous mother
Nathan Wolfstein	Lonely, aging and ailing guest director; once famous, now forgotten.
Joely Finn	Company stage manager, with fiery red hair and politics, Devin's summer roommate, and his partner in many bizarre adventures
Sabby Norah	Shy but gifted actor with slavish devotion to the theater and to her fellow Players
Pete Barney	Plump piano player for the Red Lagoon Theatre

Margery Dosk	Talented actor, impregnated by fellow player Marlin Owen, soon to be a Canadian
Marlin Owen	Actor who gets Margery Dosk pregnant and flees the draft in Canada
Ashton Krinkle	Actor, gothic and pretentious
Seymour Mink	Actor with great voice who also runs the box office
Suzanne Steinitz	Snobbish actor who somewhat resembles Devin's former girlfriend.
Jennifer Thatcher	Actor who wishes she'd been alive to play Scarlett O'Hara
Ronny Tiorino	Actor with a glass eye and a Brandoesque style
Buddy Smith	Actor who never showed up because he was sent to Vietnam

FLOREN PARK LOCALS AND VISITORS

Spurgeon Debson	Crazed artist and activist
Bruno Stark (Boris Elijah Strovokov)	Mittie's rich, unpleasant father
Calhoun Grange	Cowboy movie star who drops in and dazzles them all, and who may be Nathan Wolfstein's long-lost son
Sheriff Gabe Booter	Entirely too full of himself
Mrs. Booter	The sheriff's widowed sister-in-law, runs the boarding house
Deputy Jimmy Maddox	The sheriff's officious and unmotivated assistant
Dr. Calvin Ferrell	Floren Park general practitioner

Bonnie Ferrell	Dr. Ferrell's fifteen-year-old daughter, dating Ronny Tiorino
Lady Red Menelade	Adds a discotheque to the Red Lagoon Bar to liven things up
Tony Menelade	Red's uxorious husband, manager of the Red Lagoon Bar
Kim	Sad, overweight dancer at the Red Lagoon Bar, wants to get to California someday
Cary	Kim's son, helps pack up the theater
Rings Morelli	Runs the porno store, friend of Lady Red's, dates Kim the doughy dancer
Dennis Reed	Verl's shallow seductive friend with the pickup
Tanya (Carlotta Sirenos)	Runaway wife, dancer at the Red Lagoon Bar, sleeps with Devin
Al Sirenos	Tanya's husband, slugs Devin
Vic Falz	Spurgeon Debson's artistic backer, an affluent hippie
Saul Fletcher	Floren Park's mortician, kept busy this summer
Eddie Hade	Wealthy car dealer eager to spend money and impress anyone, especially Leila
Professor Aubrey	Devin's affected Harvard mentor
Mr. Bipple	Inspector from the Department of Safety Regulations, has a clipboard
Mr. Edgars	Mr. Stark's employee
Mr. Edmunds	Mr. Stark's employee

BACK HOME

Mama	Devin's mother, mostly deaf, known as the Rock of Gibraltar by her five children
James Dexter "J.D." Donahue	Devin's older successful brother
Jardin	Devin's old girlfriend, now about to marry his older brother, James Dexter.
Fitzgerald Donahue	Devin's younger brother, a politician and a pack rat
Colum Donahue	Devin's other brother, who with a broken leg is leading a "soft life"
Maeve	Devin's sister who married Harnley II and is mother to Harnley III
Harnley II	Maeve's husband, away at ROTC camp
Harnley III	Maeve's son with boiled feet

LEILA'S FAMILY TREE

Arvid Andrew Sluford	Leila's great-great-grandfather
Buford Sluford	Arvid Andrew Sluford's son
Kurbee Sluford	Buford Sluford's son
Leila Rickey Sluford	Married Kurbee Sluford, a vegetable heiress and a literalist
Esther Sluford	Leila's aunt, gorgeous and slow
Gene (Genesis) Sluford	Leila's uncle, found God in the most unusual way
Nadine Sluford Clyde	Leila's aunt

Ethan Clyde	Leila's maternal uncle who married Nadine then retreated to the basement with his rabbits and rye whiskey, very kind to Leila
Brian Beaumont	Amanda's first husband, Leila's father, irresponsible
Mr. Beaumont	Brian Beaumont's father, loved Leila and tried to make a family for her
Jerry Thurston	Amanda Thurston's second already-married husband

Contents

Perche non sali il dilettoso monte ch'e principio e cagion di tutta gioia?

"Why don't you climb that delectable mountain
which is the origin and the source of all delight?" said Virgil
to Dante, just before he took him down to hell.

The Sequel of My Resolution

When summer started in 1968, I awakened to find that at twenty-two I had run out of scheduled program and the rest was going to be up to me.

Until then, I'd gone where I was expected to go—school, sports, clubs, dates, and political rallies.

My parents had named me Devin William Butler Donahue. Courtesy of my father, I could move in and out of Irish blarney with the grand imperturbability of a champion Chinese checkers player. Courtesy of my mother, I was accustomed to regarding this tendency as evidence of creative imagination rather than of moral turpitude. Thinking that way was what got her married to him in the first place. A cliché (as all southerners are), my mother was a lady teacher of English literature who played the piano in the evenings; she married him on Yeats's birthday, eloping in a green Ford, which she had bought him with the money she had gotten for selling her piano.

Mama thought she was joining up with the Playboy of the Western World, which, considering his abrupt departure (in a later model Buick) some nine years later, may have been a testament to her perspicacity. Among the things he left behind him were his recordings by John McCormack, a sizable bill at a clothing store, and the five of us. We celebrated St. Patrick's Day with a flourish even after he left us. (Maybe it was with a vengeance then, but if so, only Mama knew it.) She read us all about Cuchulain and the Easter Sunday Uprising, just as she'd named us all out of Irish poetry. Devin means poet, and W.B. is for William Butler Yeats, so I suppose I was baptised to tell my story: Poet Poet Donahue.

Modern novels are supposed to be about writing modern novels, they say, since all the stories have already been told—but not by all the storytellers.

part one

The Land of the Leopard

chapter 1
I Make Another Beginning

Like the country, I was really fouled up when summer started in 1968. The whole family was. When I say the whole family, I do not include (1) the father who had departed on a trial separation eighteen years before (the trial was ours), or (2) the eldest son, for reasons that will become apparent. Apart from them, there were five of us, and these five comprised the unit I refer to as the whole family. We were all fouled up. Mama was sick. My brother Colum had broken his leg by sliding it into a medical student in the semifinals of the softball intramurals. He had been lying on the living room couch for weeks now.

Our sister Maeve was home with her two-year-old son, Harnley III, while Harnley II was away at ROTC camp. She had been staying at his parents' home in Richmond, until she found their cook, Thelma, boiling Harnley III's feet in a pan of pot liquor (which is turnip-green juice) as a purgative or curative against his walking on his tiptoes, which after that he didn't do for some time. Harnley's parents asked Thelma to apologize, but she said she was not changing her ways for a child that was having children of her own, leastways out of books, when she (Thelma) had raised seven of her own, all of which was doing just fine, to the glory of the Lord. But Maeve couldn't find pot liquor in Dr. Spock, so she strapped Harnley III in his car seat, his gauzed and taped feet sticking straight out in front of him, and headed home to us. It was the habit of Mama's family to live in Earlsford, which is why she brought us back there from Clemson after the divorce. Her folks told her divorce's what happened to people who moved away in the first place.

The youngest and tallest of us was Fitzgerald; Mama told everyone to stop accenting the first syllable, but no one remembered. He was the only one at home with any money. At sixteen, Fitzgerald wore a three-piece seersucker suit and carried his textbooks in an attaché case. Having gotten himself elected to whatever was available since he was six, he already held the governorship of the state gleaming before him like a Rotary Club Loving Cup. Meanwhile, he was after the presidency of Earlsford High School.

The oldest and shortest, James Dexter, lived in New York City, but managed, even from up there, to reach down into my life and louse things up. We did not really think of James Dexter as being in the family any more. He had his own life. J.D. was a grown-up. And successful. Apparently he'd been both since shortly after he was born. He was more grown up than Mama, who was capable of silliness. She'd talk to a hamster for half an hour. She'd drink too much wine and flip a spoonful of mashed potatoes onto the ceiling. She'd put a plastic banana in my lunch box. None of these things James Dexter would have done even if delirious. He had control of his life, seemed to understand what it was supposed to be about. He had directions, and achievements, and programs for success. This was more than the rest of us, even Fitzgerald, could always claim. Instead, life had a puzzling way of getting on top of us, and we often found the basic mechanics of manipulating it a mysterious skill beyond either our capacity, or our inclination, or our mastery. We made it only to the semifinals.

So we all admired James. We admired his cleverness and talents, the image he had of himself. He wore beautiful clothes and won lots of awards. I suppose we even came to admire his being a little ashamed of us. His taste was very refined.

He went to Cornell. So I went to Harvard. I felt better for a while. Then at the end of my freshman year, Mama wrote me

that James had won a Rhodes scholarship. That summer I carelessly stuck my hand into my friend Lampie Frederick's power
mower.

When he came back from Oxford, James Dexter went to
work for an advertising agency in New York City. At home,
Mama, Maeve, and Fitzgerald sat like robots in front of the
television set, constantly switching the channels out of fear
that they might miss one of J.D.'s three commercials one time.
TV *had* been a real pleasure of mine. On St. Patrick's Day, he
flew from New York into Raleigh with shopping bags full of
store-wrapped packages. "They charge a dollar to wrap them
like that," Fitzgerald told us. One visit he brought Mama a mink
stole, which she wore to the airport when he left and then had
stored at the cleaner's. On three consecutive Christmases, he
gave me the same set of Beethoven's Nine Symphonies.

Then, in my senior year, I fell in love. Her name was Jardin,
and she was studying the violin. I took her to New York to meet
my big brother the New York Advertiser. He treated us to dinner
in French and took us to a special small showing of large paint-
ings at the Guggenheim. In April, they got engaged. They even
drove up to Cambridge in J.D.'s Alfa and took color slides of me
in Harvard Yard "to show the family." That was the end of May,
1968. They offered me a ride home, but I took a Trailways bus.

On the night of May 30th, I was thinking about whether to
shoot myself before, after, or during their wedding. (J.D. hated
a scene.) We were all sitting in the living room of the stucco
house. Mama, Maeve, baby Harnley, Colum, and I. It was the
eighteenth house we'd rented since I was born, for we were
always being evicted because of our animals or loud records, or
because the landlords thought Mama might be a communist.
Or Mama would say we weren't going to stay there any longer
because of a conflict in principles, or because the plaster fell out
of the bathroom ceiling on her head while she was in the tub
reading, or because she had to kill a rat by throwing a can of
Campbell's soup at it (which Colum and I admired enormously,
as we were then with the Little League). So we moved a lot.

We remembered each house by a system of architectural referents: the Ugly Green House, the Rat House, the House with a Basement, the Upstairs Apartment, or the Stucco House, which is where we were then. For a week, all of us had been pretty much living in the front room there because it had a little air conditioner that Mama's brother Norwood had lent her. Winter is a much better time to be grief-stricken, so naturally now it was in the high nineties and so humid it was like breathing cotton fuzz. (What I mean is, you look sadder in a gray overcoat with a scarf around your neck than you can in tennis shorts and sneakers, with your skin gummy from the heat.)

I was in Mama's chair (its new upholstering material, to cover the places Colum's dog had chewed, flung across it and shoved down in the corners), reading the sonnets Dante Gabriel Rossetti had on first thought buried in his wife's coffin, and on second, dug up and published. Nobody said much to me about J.D.'s wedding, but I'd found out from a look at the invitations that it was going to be on August 2nd in Charleston, Jardin's hometown. J. Dexter was there now, taking snapshots of the silverware. So I didn't mention it either, except to Colum, who offered to have a girlfriend of his get James summonsed on a paternity charge August 1st. Colum always took a legal approach to life.

"Well," he mumbled at me from the couch, where he was scratching his toes with a long plastic stick, "maybe he'll send us all mink coats to wear. Mink hats too."

"What was that, Colum?" Mama asked.

"Nothing," Maeve turned to me, "Would you like some cantaloupe, Devin? Shut the door, Fitzgerald, you're letting out the air conditioning!"

As he went by, Fitzgerald announced quickly, "Mama, I'm going over to Jackson Frederick's. I'll be back in a little while, okay?"

"Fitzgerald!" Maeve yelled after him, "Will you please shut the front door?" She was afraid Harnley III was going to get a heat rash under his bandages.

"Where did he say he was going? It's after eleven," Mama asked us.

Mama couldn't hear. Sometimes we took advantage of this handicap by insisting we *had* told her where we were going. The telephone in particular put her in a very vulnerable position since she couldn't read our lips on it and would usually say, "Yes, yes, all right," just so she could hang up. That's how we got our television set; Colum had told the appliance store manager that Mama was definitely interested in buying a set on time if they went on sale, and the guy called her up about it. She had just bought a secondhand piano, and as we hovered in front of *The Lone Ranger* and *The Cisco Kid*, her dreams of a Rubenstein gathered dust on the other side of the room. She hated the telephone. Still, her deafness was the footstool to the throne of her serenity. Simply turning off her hearing aid had enabled her, as we bragged, to read the works of practically everybody while raising five children. (It was our great disappointment that we couldn't persuade her to go on a quiz show and win us a real house, for she even knew all the major league batting averages.) She wore her hearing aid clipped to her bathrobe pocket.

I gave up on Rossetti's sonnets; given the opportunity to bury some of my poems in Jardin's casket, I was sure I'd leave them there. "Listen, I think I'll go up to South Campus." We lived only a few blocks from Earlsford University, where, at fifteen, I had strolled about pretending to be an undergraduate.

No one said anything. Weren't they afraid I'd jump in front of a truck?

Stepping out into the thick, still air, I walked to the stone wall that protected Earlsford University from the tobacco town that had built it, and sat there for a while remembering easier summer nights. Colum and I used to hide behind that wall to throw dirt clods at passing vehicles. One day three college guys jumped out of their car right in the middle of the street and charged after us. I got away by climbing up the fire escape to the roof of the language building. But Colum crouched down inside an empty garbage can in the alley below me, and his dog, Perry

Mason, stood right outside the can barking until the college guys got there and shook Colum out. How big and terrifying they had seemed to us. Now I was all the way through college; now I was older than they were. And people were still big and terrifying.

Walking back, I hadn't even noticed the beat-up yellow Triumph outside the house, that's how bad off I was, so I didn't know Verl was inside until I saw everyone grinning, exhilarated with surprise, and him standing there, tall and much too thin, smiling at me.

"Why don't you ever answer my letters, you lazy bastard?" he greeted me.

We had been friends since the second day of the tenth grade, when he came to Earlsford High from Shreveport and got put right away on the basketball team. He played the trumpet too, and became head of the National Forensic League. I admired first his height, then his brains, and finally, I guess, decided that the main thing about him was that you sensed he had the key to something, a way of being that you wouldn't mind having too, if you could figure it out. A sort of inside order he felt sure of, that let him know what the meanings were. At various times we planned various futures. We wrote an opera together about the assassination of President Kennedy that wasn't accepted for the senior play. When I went to Harvard, he went to Columbia; he planned to go on to divinity school not to preach, he said, but to teach. He was a Quaker. We'd meet in New York City, where we'd ride back and forth on the ferry and debate the world. Then Verl became a conscientious objector, took a bus to Wyoming, and went to work in a national park. He would startle you that way every now and then. Like when he socked me for eating in a restaurant when there was a sit-down strike there. He'd always loved American folk songs, and at first I figured the western lyrics had gotten to him; I predicted he'd be back before long. But he said he liked being around mountains, and he took a job with a paper in Boulder, Colorado.

Now he said he had a plan, but that he'd save it until morning. Was it about me and my situation (James and Jardin)? I had the feeling everyone had been telling him about it while I was gone, but when we finally went to bed, no one had mentioned a thing.

Off and on until morning, I heard Colum's crutches clomping to the bathroom. Mama always told him not to drink so much Pepsi because they used it to clean johns in the navy and it was going to corrode his stomach, but he said it was never in there long enough to do much damage. I was pleased to discover I had insomnia, for I knew from literary experience that blighted suitors lost their appetites along with their beloveds, and so I'd been a little disturbed by the amount of food I had been able to absent-mindedly consume subsequent to my third full meal, when (according to Mama) I had ingested a leftover pork chop, a banana split, half a cantaloupe, a bowl of popcorn, a bowl of chicken noodle soup, and two cold slices of pizza. But I could only assume that anguish leads to excess as well as to deprivation.

chapter 2

The Emigrants

The next morning, after what Mama called "eating off our laps" but Maeve said was a "breakfast buffet," Verl and I walked up to look around Earlsford High, last site, as he quipped, of our sense of unlimited importance to the world.

Then he told me his plan. "I didn't want to bring this up in front of your mama in case you felt with her being sick you shouldn't leave. But I've got to start back to Colorado tomorrow, and I figured maybe you'd like to come along. It looks like you don't have much planned here."

"I never do," I agreed.

Verl stopped at the old water cooler. "The thing is, on my way back east, I stopped off in Floren Park a couple of weeks ago and saw Leila."

"Leila! Does she still have that theater out there?"

"Yep, and she asked me if I'd let you know she'd like you to come on out there and design sets for her and Mittie. She wanted to know if I could bring you out. Sounded like she's been sort of worried about you, you losing touch and all."

"What's she worried about?"

"I don't know. Maybe somebody wrote her you were kind of down."

"Well, how do you expect me to act?" I was alarmed by Verl's insensitivity. He still hadn't asked me about the Jardin situation.

"Listen, Devin, if you don't mind my saying so, I think you're letting things get bent all out of shape. You know how you do. But, come on, *I was there*. Sure. You really liked Jardin. But, frankly, I don't remember any talk about how madly in love you were until after she started going out with James Dexter. Good Lord, man, you were dating other people."

I walked off.

"And this whole thing," he threw out, "has got more to do with your big brother, and your big brother's got more to do with your damn father, than it does with Jardin, anyhow, and you know that's true."

"Stop analyzing me."

"Okay, okay," he caught up with me and put his hand on my shoulder. "But what good does it do sitting around here like a lost soul, giving your mother something else to worry about. Why don't you let me take you on out there? You've never been west, really. Look, you'll be doing yourself a favor and helping Leila out at the same time. You'll get room and board. Most of all, you'll be doing something productive."

"Look here, Verl. I'm no James Dexter. And I'm not Fitzgerald. I don't especially want to be productive." He gave me one of his looks.

But I thought it over as we walked on through the old halls. I had to do something. I knew Mama was worried about what she was going to do with me, especially when everybody went down to Charleston for the wedding. Taking off westward with Verl would show them all I was okay and, at the same time, suggest to Jardin that I was indifferent to her betrayal—or that I found being in the same half of the country with her too painful to be borne. Both ways, it had an appeal. And I ought to be able to do the work too; after all, I'd won a state prize for my *South Pacific* set in the drama club competition. Besides which, going out to Colorado might actually be—I wasn't prepared to say "fun"—but at least a distraction from misery.

And seeing Leila. That sounded good. Leila. Leila, née Beaumont, stepfathered Thurston, married Stark. "My old flame."

For that is who she was. Leila, my first flame, my original carnal knowledge, my first eternal love. Warmth flushed through me as I floated backward into the past. Oh, I had been happy then. Leila and I moonfully in love. Until her mother, Mrs. Thurston, had clamped Leila away in a Catholic girls' school (St. Lucy of the Pines, hundreds of miles away in Asheville's mountains) midway through the twelfth grade; this cloistering occurring immediately after her mother accidentally came upon and unforgivably read a sonnet sequence I had written in which her daughter was rather extensively described.

Locked away in a hilly convent where medieval nuns read her mail and kept the door keys to the dormitory rooms, Leila became to me even more erotic than she had been up in the lighting booth of the high school auditorium during study periods. Barriers to love are bonfires. Love became a mystic exercise. My passion in my pen flamed across the state to her secret downtown post office box, and I hoarded my allowance for Trailways tickets. For four months we gloried in our hardship. Then one night my vigil was broken in the back seat of Judy Field's father's Lincoln, and Leila subsided from the present of my mind. Yet, over the following years, she had settled down somewhere close to the center of memories. Looking back now, I thought, those had been good days. Leila my girl, Verl my friend. And they had liked each other. Still did.

Leila. I would go and see her. She had probably never gotten over me. Her mother and I hated each other, but her mother wouldn't be there.

Even before I had a chance to talk to Mama, she suggested that maybe I could ride out to Colorado with Verl. Familial clairvoyance was an unnerving habit of hers. As I was sliding my fingers into that power mower, she had dropped a six no-trump hand and rushed home from her bridge club to find me howling in Lampie's front yard. But on this occasion she admitted she'd just had a letter from Leila.

She also suggested that we take Fitzgerald with us because he'd been wheedling her for the money to go to the Young

Democrats Conference in Salt Lake City, and she had decided that if we could get him as far as Denver, then she could manage bus fare the rest of the way. That afternoon, Fitzgerald had returned home from his last day at school, his hair tousled in tribute to Bobby Kennedy, and announced that he had carried 63 percent of the vote for next year's presidency; he had predicted only 61 percent. Verl said sure, he could come along.

And so that night we packed; I stuck my framed picture of Jardin in between my socks and pajamas. The next morning was May 1st. After the bags of new clothes Mama had charged, and the boxes of cold food Mama had cooked were loaded into the Triumph, and after Fitzgerald had made about thirty phone calls delegating interim political authority, he, Verl, and I squeezed into the car, and Mama and Maeve went around it to hug us good-bye. From inside the living room window, Colum waved a crutch at me. Mama gave us a list of written instructions and a lot more verbal ones about happiness, hygiene, and courtesy. And three twenty-dollar bills, which Fitzgerald examined all the way to Greensboro. Then she and Maeve stood in the maple-arched summer street and waved until we were around the corner. Maeve held Harnley III up for us to see. He could already bend his legs a little better, and the bandages would be coming off soon.

So out on the highway set forth we three, following the trail of McDonald's westward to Leila and my destiny. Verl and Fitzgerald in front, and me in the luggage hole, brooding on my despair and hanging my legs over the back to catch a tan.

In Nashville, the left front tire blew. Fitzgerald took a picture of it. We forgot to put the canvas car top back in the trunk with the jack. So all the way across Kansas we were rained on, despite Fitzgerald's Theory on the Relation of Motion and Gravity, which argued that if we went fast enough, the rain would go sideways around the car and miss us. We still used the windshield wipers, but a spring was broken somewhere, so whoever in the front seat wasn't driving had to keep pulling the wipers back and forth with one of Verl's old ties. He no longer wore ties for he considered them symbols of former false and constrictive values.

Fitzgerald clearly thought of the trip as an Experience to be Related in the Future and, for that reason, was seriously engaged not only in taking photographs of road signs, but in garnering proofs of visitation like some suspicious Cortez. Our Triumph was gradually filling with local newspapers, rocks, tourist information leaflets, and regional soil samples collected in empty cigarette packs. He would fill up one large green plastic garbage bag with booty, and then start on another. When the rains came, he transferred all of these to the space left in the trunk by the car top, which we had forgotten in Nashville.

But Fitzgerald's preliminary passion was to transverse as many states and as many miles as quickly as possible. As we went, he traced our route on a fold-out map in red magic marker. Once a state was touched by our front wheels, he colored it in yellow. Humoring his enthusiasm for acquisition, we drove quickly in and out of Tennessee, Indiana, Illinois, then across Missouri and into the Kansas rain.

THE LONG WAY UP THE MOUNTAIN

Cursing the canvas car top sitting dry somewhere in Nashville and spitting out the water that sprayed into our mouths, we drove through the squalls, and out of the plains, and climbed toward Denver, where Fitzgerald sent his first bulky installment of memorabilia back home C.O.D. By the time he finally got on the bus for Salt Lake City, where he was going to meet with other future leaders of a Democratic Society, his clothes were almost dried out and only slightly mildewed. While Verl and I mugged peace signs at him through the window, Fitzgerald got interested in unscrewing the notice about seat positions off the back of the seat in front of him. He was slipping it into his plastic bag when the bus pulled out.

Meanwhile, someone had lifted both hubcaps from the curbside of the Triumph and, presumably as a caprice, the top half of the antenna.

"The less you want, the less they can hurt you with," Verl intoned. "You have to will for yourself what the gods will."

"Verl," I told him, "you'd sit down next to Epictetus and let them saw your leg in half too, just to show them your integrity would be intact. Maybe it would, but you'd be walking lopsided. The less they can hurt you with, the less you got."

"Awh shit, all that means is an itch for things." Verl was scared of possessions the way a mountain climber would be leery of a dead body hanging at the end of his rope.

We argued values just like in the old days—push-ups for the brain—then we tired out and started singing all the songs we could think of with a girl's name in the title. Then we did cities. Then states, like, "Carolina in the Morning," "Moonlight in Vermont." I was trying an Al Jolson finish on "Carry Me Back to Ol' Virginny," when we saw the sign.

WELCOME TO FLOREN PARK. HAVEN OF HAPPINESS.
COME AS A STRANGER. LEAVE AS A FRIEND.
UNKNOWN
POPULATION: XXXXXXXXXXXXX
UNKNOWN
ALTITUDE: XXXXXXXXXXXX

The Elks Club had noted that they had donated the sign, but apparently somebody else had scratched out all the particulars.

It was nearly sunset when we circled the mountains and sloped down into the valley. And then, there it was: pines and forests of aspens, squares of meadows yellow with dandelions, blue with periwinkle, purplish weed like heather; the town and fields all walled in like a medieval fortress by the ring of green mountains.

In a field across the highway galloped toward us a young girl on a roan horse. Her hair swirled copper in the sunset. As she sped closer we saw that she held a big black transistor radio pressed against her ear.

"*Et ego in Arcadia*," I laughed. "The voice of the turtle is heard in the land."

We stopped the car and walked down past the shoulder into the meadow and squatted down and picked at some tufts of grass.

Verl brought out some apples and a sack of ham biscuits. We ate them while we watched the sun going slowly down behind the mountain ring, big and close and familiar as the moon in North Carolina. Verl stretched out, but I was feeling all of a sudden too exuberant for serenity, so I did some knee bends and jogged and talked about how somebody ought to write an article on the disappearance of the father from American television series. Because of my own experience, it was one of the things I felt good about generalizing on.

"Americans," I expounded, "have rejected all the fathers. All the kings and popes. We're a land of dadless men." I'd read Leslie Fiedler that year and was quite taken with his theories. "Like your father, Verl. He walks around your house invisible. Inaudible. People walk right through him. It's your mother that's directing the show."

I lobbed my apple core up in the air, and it rolled down the grass into a little bunch of aspens. Verl put his in the paper sack and put that in the litter bag under the dashboard.

We drove on down into the town to find Leila.

chapter 3

I Look About Me and
Make a Discovery

Floren Park was a tourist town, the ticket booth of the
Rocky Mountains and its national park, where people rented
knotty-pine bungalows for a week or whole houses for whole
summers, safe from riots and robberies, and set out from them for
fishing creeks, riding stables, and natural walks. Other residents
had retired there in rabble-free alpine A-frames or been born
there in Victorian gingerbread three-story houses. And both
these sets of "locals" avoided the center of town on inherited
principle.

Downtown Floren Park was bright, noisy, and confused;
confused because each building in it was disconnected by
origin and temperament from its neighbor. Impermanencies
clashed like the living rooms filled with imitation furniture of
different styles—a colonial armchair, a modern coffee table, a
provincial couch. Along the main street, TACOS flashed in neon
next to cocoa-carpeted art galleries where handsomely framed
mountain landscapes were sold by handsome proprietors for
handsome sums. Austrian sportswear was housed beside Navajo
jewelry beside a Japanese restaurant where you watched your
food dangerously prepared beside a pornographic book store
beside Western Outfits beside folk dancing nightly beside

children's toys from Denmark. This summer there was also a Republican campaign headquarters and a Democrats campaign headquarters. For different fees in Floren Park you could have your portrait pasteled, your body massaged, your palm read. You could angle for indifferent trout in a plastic bin, shoot at targets for prizes, play bingo for a painted punch bowl. All the old-fashioned pleasures.

Monday night, June 3rd, both sidewalks of the main street were solid with crowds shoving to move in one direction or the other. I was surprised to see most of the men there wearing red fezzes. Verl pointed up at a huge banner strung over the street, on which the town provided an explanation for this phenomenon. A convention was climaxing.

FLOREN PARK WELCOMES SHRINERS MAY 31–JUNE 5

There was no point in trying to drive the Triumph any further into the main thoroughfare. We were like two polite tourists struggling to maneuver their Hertz through a flea market in Istanbul.

The Shriners had spilled noisily out of buildings, over the sidewalks, and were loudly pushed from behind by their fellow Shriners into the street. We honked the car over to a curb finally, and parked it there. Immediately, a dozen middle-aged faces leaned down into us, black tassles twitching between their eyes. One, running to and beyond fat, breathed on us strongly.

"Get out of that yellow matchbox," he ordered us, "and I'll buy you a drink. I don't care who you are."

"I tell you, they're Artie's boys," the man next to him said. "I bet you money. This one looks just like him. How much you want to bet?"

The fat one's sportive companion, who seemed so certain of my paternity, jabbed at my face to show his friend its similarities to Artie's, and being rather haphazard about it, nearly put out one of my eyes. He was wearing, besides his red fez, a Hawaiian shirt with daffodils on it, a button reading "Nixon's the One," yellow Bermudas, and yellow knee socks with white loafers. The overall effect was a little like a sudden attack of jaundice. Meanwhile, his wife (or so I assumed from her matching yellow outfit) kept pulling at the back of his Bermudas and repeating in a stentorian whine an urgent litany of complaints and instructions.

"Come on, Saammm. Let's go do the polkahhh. You promised me. Lois is waiting for us. Come oinnn. You promishhhed! She's holding the big table beside the band."

"Go tell her to put it down!" roared the fat man in my face. Fortunately, I got my head turned away from the fumes. He squeezed his eyes so tightly shut in his amusement at his own remark that he had trouble getting them unstuck. The fat of his cheeks had completely covered them over, and he had to raise his eyebrows up and down several times before his eyes popped open again.

Sam's yellow-matched mate seemed, however, to miss the fat man's joke.

"You're a pig, Bobbie," she remarked. "The lousy way you treat Lois. God knows why she married you. Come on, Saammm."

Sam took his probing hand out of my face and said, "ALL RIGHT, Shirley, all right! We'll all go do the stupid polka. But first! Everybody's gonna have one more little drink. My treat."

"Christ! I wish I'd stayed in the motel," was Shirley's response to her husband's suggestion. "I wish I'd stayed in Boise."

Verl and I shook our heads, also in the negative, which left only Sam and Bobbie enthusiastic about the drinking plan. They lurched off into the crowd of bobbing red thimbles. Shirley, forced to choose between them and us, decided in favor of familiarity and took off too, calling after the jostled yellow meadow walking away from her, "Just you wait, Sam Midpath. Just you waaait!"

The street noise grew into a jangle of drunk and jovial and grouchy voices. I stood up on the car seat to look around. Abruptly, three shots rang out of the jangle, followed by high screeches and a basso, "Goddammit! What the FUCK was that?"—a remark which, having misjudged the noise level, came out after everyone else had quieted down, so that the speaker (Sam's friend, the fat Bobbie) was laughed at by his immediate neighbors. Perceiving his miscalculation, he turned first the color of his fez, then consumingly nonchalant.

In the middle of the street, four cowboy desperadoes, each in a motley of western styles, were firing revolvers at each other without regard to verisimilitude, ingeniously discharging at least twenty bullets from each six-shooter. As each one was hit, he leapt into the air, gracefully spun about, and flamboyantly died on the pavement. After all four had been pronouncedly dispatched, a bright-badged and rather busty sheriff, followed by a somber young man in a stovepipe hat that rested loosely on his ears and had JUDGE painted on it, marched ceremoniously up, and with some superfluity, clamped handcuffs on two of the slain gunslingers. These and their two former enemies promptly rose like phoenixes from the asphalt and were applauded by the bystanders. The judge then handed each of the cowboys a large poster on a stick, which he took from a box lying near him on the sidewalk. The posters said:

!!! 8:30 TONIGHT !!!

THE BELLE OF BLACK BOTTOM GULCH

FAMILY FUN ** CHILDREN ONLY $.50 **

OLD-FASHIONED MELLERDRAMMER

! #! #! #! # DON'T MISS IT! #! #! #! #

!! RED LAGOON THEATRE !!

NEXT TO THE CREEK

The western troop paraded about the street with their posters and then moved into the crowd, grinning and handing out playbills. A red-haired desperado stopped from time to time to twirl his pistol for the onlookers.

"Red Lagoon. That's Mattie and Leila's theater," I shouted at Verl.

Then I saw her on the other side of the street from us, laughing up at someone tall and bearded, someone who was not her husband, Mattie Stark. She had on a very short blue dress that looked like it had once been a long blue shirt. Leila made her own clothes, and she always made them out of something that used to be something else—being a recycler long before it became fashionable. She also experimented in lifestyles. This time she looked like a hippie: she was wearing a lot of silver jewelry—hooped earrings, dangling bracelets, and loosely designed rings. On the sidewalk beside her was a huge leather pocketbook that came up to her knees and could stand alone. On her feet, the soles of former shoes were tied to her ankles and toes with blue leather thongs. Leila was blonder than anyone I had ever seen, and her eyes were the same blue as I had always figured lapis lazuli must be.

"LEILA! LEILA!" Verl and I yelled and flagged our arms at her a while, but couldn't get her attention.

So we locked our stuff in the trunk and headed across the street, going against the flow and making very little progress, for we were swept back by the tide of Shriners onrushing to meet old friends. I kept my eye on the buoy of Verl's black curly hair, following it until it rose as he stepped up on the other curb and I joined him there.

"Oh!" Leila laughed, "Devin! My God, you're already here! This is wonderful. Good Lord, you look just the same."

I hugged her back and forth comfortably, then I thought about what I was doing, got self-conscious, and stopped.

"Boy, I'm glad to see you, Leila."

"I'm a wreck." she said, tossing her head back in a spray of sunburst. "Hello, Verl." She kissed him. "Thanks for bringing him. This is Spur. Spurgeon Debson. Spur, Devin and Verl. Aren't these Shriners insane? Grown men!" She laughed. I had always loved to see her laugh; she was the only real person I'd met who had teeth like movie stars have.

Spurgeon was large and very well built. He wore soft, pale blue jeans and a sleeveless khaki shirt. His hair was long and dark, with a few streaks of gray glimmering in the black, circled with a leather headband. Around his neck, he had a silver chain with the same kind of random design as Leila's rings. The most immediate thing about Spur was his eyes, which were deep-set with lined circles under them. They were insistent and almost frantically light white-blue like a whale's eyes. And his whole face had the pale fervor of a prophet.

We offered him our hands, but he picked up Leila's remark instead, the one about the Shriners. His voice lifted in a marching singsong, louder and fuller, into an evangelist's rhythm.

"Somebody should exterminate them. Look! Typical example of the fucking American asshole mentality. Our FATHERS! Morons! Cretins! Living off the labor of better men. Looking down their thick hairy nostrils at the rest of the world. You realize! They are all on the payroll of General Motors, Washington, D.C. Every one of them! Scrape and slobber to the slime of the military industrial complex. Grovel in the blood. *Murderers!* They butchered the Indians. *And* the Jews! Now they're practicing genocide on Blacks and Vietnamese. Read Marcuse! Read Cleaver! Read Sinclair Lewis!"

It was doubtless the most striking introductory remark anyone had ever made to me; people generally limited themselves to, "Nice to meet you," or other bland formulae. I didn't learn until sometime later that Spur's outbursts were repeated nearly verbatim whenever he was addressed on any topic whatever, and that they continued at high volume until he was stopped by your excusing yourself to go to the bathroom or any other emergency you could come up with. By the end of the month, I had involuntarily memorized a portion of this set piece and moved my lips along with him as he screamed.

I noticed that Leila didn't appear to be paying much attention to what Spur was saying. Verl looked displeased but I was fascinated by such abrupt fervor.

"I'm a poor one-armed son of a bitch," he continued.

This was upsetting until I saw that he was shaking two quite healthy-looking fists at us and that therefore the phrase had to be a rhetorical rather than a medical one. Actually, it was a quotation, Leila told me later, from Spur's father, for whom it had not been rhetorical—the father having been retired by that mishap from his position as brakesman for the New York

Central, and his son raised in venom on his reaction to being unjustly pensioned-off.

Spur talked on. "I don't have power. And why? Why don't I have power? Because I don't have bread. Money's their power! Their balls are sacks of silver dollars! Their pricks are rolls of dimes! But I wipe my nose on their money. I wipe my ass on their bonds. They can put me in prison. Leave me there to rot. GAS ME! They do it every day. MURDERERS! SLAUGHTERHOUSE!"

Spur may not have had power, but he certainly had lungs. A crowd was gathering. One Shriner threw a quarter into Leila's pocketbook. Spur sprang up on the hood of a yellow Lincoln Continental parked next to us.

"BABYKILLERS!" he yelled.

"Hey, you! Get down off my car!" a voice yelled from across the street. It was Sam Midpath, the daffodil field, our old but brief friend. Spurgeon ignored him and began kicking at the windshield of the Lincoln with his cowboy boot.

"How many poor slobs," he intoned, "how many Dachau prisoners broke their backs building this pile of shit so you and your fat-ass wife"—he had presumably never met Shirley, but visionaries (and such Spur certainly was) have prophetic insight—"so you two can drive around, run over Black kids in the ghettos?" he asked Sam.

"Listen, you freak. You shut up and get down from there before I call the cops," Sam replied.

At that moment, Shirley came squeezing up through the crowd, apparently all polkaed out.

"Call the pigs, you motherfucker!" Spur challenged him.

"Goddammit! You can't talk to me like that in front of my wife," Sam expostulated. As he did so, he grabbed at Spur's leg, either to stop him from kicking out the windshield or to encourage him to get off the car. Spur booted Sam in the face the way a kicker would a football. It was a seven-foot punt. Sam landed shoulders down, flipped over, and stretched out peacefully, just like the four desperadoes had. Startled into affection by her husband's suffering, Shirley set off in his ear an impressive imitation of an ambulance siren. We rushed over and helped Sam to his feet.

"*Shut up, Shirley!*" were his first words.

Spur had disappeared into the crowd, and as the Midpaths didn't seem to connect him with us, our solicitude was well received. Finally, Sam and Shirley decided against bothering with the police and went off for another drink, if not a dance. Leila thought we should have a drink too. She appeared completely unremorseful about her friend Spur's behavior.

"Oh, Jesus. I'm sure he didn't mean to hurt that guy. And maybe there's a truth in the things Spur says. He's just not very well socialized, the way he says them. Spur's a little crazy sometimes,"

"A *little* crazy? Leila, he's crazy as a loon!" I pointed out.

She looked upset, so I let it drop.

• • •

The Red Lagoon Theatre (formerly a rollerdrome) was next to the Red Lagoon Bar, the manager of which owned both buildings and leased the bigger one to Mittie for his stock company. They were both large, red wooden barn structures backed by pine forest and fronted by a wide dirt parking lot. Beside the theater ran a rapid and broad creek, deep enough in places to be called a river. Leila wanted to build a windmill there and call the theater the Moulin Rouge because once, after seeing the movie, she had fallen in love with Toulouse-Lautrec in, she said, a Jane Avrilish sort of way. For Leila found handicaps irresistible the way some people find long eyelashes or a French accent.

Like the wounded chickens. Years ago, in Earlsford, she used to ask friends of hers who had cars (Verl, for instance) to drive her along behind the truck that brought chickens every morning to the town produce market. A crate of fowls occasionally bounced off the back of the delivery truck and, as the drivers never stopped to retrieve them, Leila would collect the maimed and angry chickens and take them home with her. There, collected into a large pen, she eventually housed at least thirty highway victims, some with splints on their legs, some with bandaged wings, some with beaks bent sideways, or an eye missing. All of them were given names—Socrates, Bessie Smith, Helen Keller—christened with the triumphs of other embattled spirits, though they never answered when called. And now she collected broken people the same way.

When we squirmed through the customers into the Red Lagoon Bar, it seemed even fuller and noisier than the street outside. But few of these people were wearing red fezzes; perhaps it was a local sanctuary for anti-Shriners. The jukebox shrieked and thumped, the lights were red. We were quickly pressed up against a bar designed to represent a red coral reef. Everybody was talking.

"So I told my old man, 'Who are you to tell me?' You know? 'Do you think you've been any kind of a shining example yourself?'"

"Yeah, I've seen her around. Why? You think you can make her?"

"Well, Bobby isn't getting my vote. I don't trust him. And I didn't think much of his brother either. What do people like that know about real life? Millions! And ten kids! Millions! It's disgusting."

"Who's that singing?" someone near us asked.

"It's a guy named Tom Jones, like in the movies," her escort replied.

"Oh, yeah, I read about him. He's an Irish Negro."

"Is that a fact?"

"Well, they said so. I don't know why they'd make it up."

It took us some time to squeeze our way over to a booth. Leila seemed to know everyone in the place. People would call to her, grab at her arm, even hug her as we pushed along. She smiled at them. A buzz of panic circled my head. She seemed to know so many people. Where was I in relationship? Maybe some of them were involved with her; maybe she'd slept with them.

What did I really know about Leila? After all, her life was here now, here and in Los Angeles, where she lived in the winters. For the past five years, I'd seen her only at Christmas vacations when, on her annual trip to her mother's for the holiday, she'd drop by to visit Mama.

What was Leila's life like now? What did she care about? Who? I realized I didn't know; she could be anything at all, and I thought, Why the hell did I do a stupid thing like coming out here? Why did I let Verl and Mama talk me into it? I was angry at both of them.

Then a strong proprietorial feeling flashed inside me. Why was I being forced to stand about with a vacant smile while strangers gabbled at Leila as though she belonged to them? I'd known her practically all our lives. Longevity had rights.

"What's the matter with you?" Verl asked when we finally sat down in a red oyster-shell booth and ordered our drinks.

"I'm just thinking," I told him.

"Well, Devin, for Christ's sake, talk," Leila said as she took the cigarette out of my mouth to light hers. "I've missed listening to you talk."

"I thought you were going to give up smoking three years ago," I talked.

"I did, but I'm really incredibly oral, and last week I broke off the stem of my pipe prying open a paint can. As a matter of fact, guess what? I won a prize in a pipe-smoking contest at the Memorial Day Street Festival. I smoked forty-seven minutes on one match." She offered this information as a child a first poem, with the shy, tentative smile with which she always called attention to her private successes, uncertain they would be believed, much less praised.

"Are you kidding? Almost an hour?" I was deliberately impressed. In secret, anyhow, I did envy Leila the multiplicity of achievement with which she renewed herself, for, personally, I felt the loss, which I attributed to the James-Jardin debacle, of any capacity to juvenate myself with fresh talents, however inane.

Leila ordered more drinks. "So, Devin," she said, "when are you going to write realms and realms of scholarly books and become a famous professor and tutor Maisie and Davy?"

Leila had enormous respect for education, a nineteenth-century German merchant's awe of *Herr Professor*. To my continued surprise, she also had two children, and in an imagined future, I was to lead them both ceremoniously to the fountain of knowledge. Now Maisie (Madeline) was four and David was two. I had briefly encountered Maisie three times, and Davy once— only, however, as an alteration in Leila's figure. I remembered now that seeing her thus maternalized had provoked an unsettling excitement in me. I had forgotten that.

"Who knows?" I answered, and ordered another drink. "I don't really know what I want to do. Why don't you choose for me? One thing's as good as another, considering it's all irrelevant, right?" I wasn't sure I believed this, but it was my style with Verl and Leila. They were both so sure and serious.

"Christ," she laughed, as I expected, "are you still waiting around to get focused?"

Verl said, "Devin's just a little ole blotter. Just soaks it all up. Hell, ma'am, haven't you noticed the western walk he's developed since he's been in Colorado two whole hours? Pure Alan Ladd. *Shane.*"

"Pure negative capability. Keats," I told them happily; few things pleased me more than having people criticize me affectionately while I was there. Verl and Leila did this a lot.

He shook his head. "You don't want to bother figuring out who you are."

"That's why I say I'll never trust you again as far as I can throw you," Leila said. "You're emotionally fickle."

"How can you say that?" I looked hurt. "I'm here, aren't I? I met you when we were fourteen. Nine years later, and here I sit. What counts for fidelity?"

"Being faithful," she said.

"Oh, God, we were practically prepuberty; that doesn't count." Leila had often razzed me, rather obsessively, about Judy

Field and her father's car. She rarely missed an opportunity to remind me of this sliver of ancient history.

'You think you aren't 'real' when you're fourteen? You think you aren't capable of love? You think you can't get hurt?" Verl asked in that Quakerish style that had led him to consider divinity school and which really irritated me. I turned to Leila.

"I hope you're not still hanging on to that grudge, Leila. How long are you going to keep on blasting me for something that happened in the eleventh grade, for Christ's sake? I'm not even the same person."

"I am" she said quietly.

Somebody said, "Oh, here you are. Hello."

We all looked up. Leila's husband, Mittie, was standing there, beaming at us with a trained smile that slipped back toward his natural diffidence before he could lock it in securely. I almost didn't recognize him. The last, which was the third, time I had seen Mittie he had been very heavy—I think Leila said he had tried to eat his way into character parts—and his weight gave him the impression of a kindly stability. Now that he was thin, all his mannerisms had speeded up into a cluttered nervousness. Only his thick black mustache still had solidity. Leila introduced Verl; everyone said hello.

Mittie Stark, as he often explained himself, was a scared and sad person. Only one thing sustained him above the pit he saw gaping open beneath his feet—and that one thing was his love of acting. He was not especially good at it, but not suspecting that fact at all, he was never troubled by the realization. His stock company at the Red Lagoon Theatre was therefore the perfect setting for Mittie's affair with his craft. Since he (or more precisely his father) paid for the playhouse, he was spared the vagaries of casting directors and the disappointments of not being preferred to others. Any part in any play was his for the choosing at the Red Lagoon.

"How did Mittie get this place?" I had asked Leila when she pointed out the building to us as we were going into the bar.

"The Big Man gave it to him," she said. She did not like Bruno Stark. "He's some kind of lousy steel millionaire." Money was suspect to Leila.

Mittie sat down with us and ordered everyone more drinks. Then he asked us politely about our trip, and talked to me enthusiastically about the theater. I quoted him everything I could remember from the one book I had ever read on the subject of set designs, the one that had won me the *South Pacific* prize. For that apparently was what I had been brought there to do. All the while, he watched Leila tentatively. I thought her knee was brushing against my leg under the seat of the oyster shell; it was so crowded I couldn't be certain, but in case it was, I tried to keep casually still. After a while, my leg went to sleep from the effort and I had to jiggle my foot, which I tried to do in time to the music on the jukebox.

For some reason Mittie gave me an impatient feeling, and I was relieved when he announced that he had to go next door to get made up for the show. Verl said he was sorry he wouldn't be able to see the play. He had to drive to Troy, sixteen miles south, where he had his cabin, but he promised to bring a new friend over to meet me the next day. Mittie left, and the three of us had another drink. Leila wasn't in this opening play, a holdover from the previous summer; she had been in Oregon visiting the Starks with Maisie and Davy then.

As we drank, she told us a little more about the father, and thereby a lot more about Mittie. Bruno Stark had once been Boris Elijah Strovokov, born in Kiev, from which he had fled with his mother across several continents to his uncle's junk shop in Portland, Oregon. Mrs. Strovokov brought her brother two assets, neither of which he had an opportunity to appreciate, since he died four months after their arrival when he suffered a heart attack while trying to deliver a secondhand safe to a new customer. Those assets were (1) her own indomitable insistence on life, and (2) her will genetically growing inside her son, Boris.

When Boris was twelve, he drove the junk wagon and peddled its goods. When he was sixteen, he traded it for a large lot of wrecked automobiles. When he was nineteen, Boris Strovokov bought a small foundry and changed his name to Bruno Stark. At twenty-one, he was a decorated hero in the Second World War. At thirty-five, Bruno Stark owned a large factory. The Pacific Valley Country Club nonetheless declined his request for membership. The following year, Stark married the only daughter of Oregon Metal Works, and his application was reconsidered. Mrs. Stark, having fulfilled her immediate function of insuring her husband's applicability, spent the remaining long years of her life attending civic club meetings, tending her flowers, reading tales of romantic espionage, and being intimidated by Mrs. Strovokov's domestic authority. She was also a little frightened of Mr. Stark, to whom she puzzledly presented one child, which was followed by a hysterectomy.

Stark named his son Mitchell for his father-in-law and Lionel for his heirdom. When Mitchell (our Mittie) was eighteen, he knew he wanted to be an actor. He changed his name, following a family tradition in reverse, to Isaac Strovokov. He sold his graduation present, a Corvette, and went to work in a theater company in Israel. Half a year later, Israeli authorities advised Isaac to go home to Oregon, where he could get help with his drinking problem. Back home, he changed his named to Misha, which was what his grandmother Strovokov had always called him anyhow. Everyone who knew him after that called him Mittie.

While Mittie was getting help after his Israeli deportation, Mr. Stark sent away for the application forms to several colleges. Subsequently, he drove his sole son and asset down to Palo Alto, where Misha Mitchell Lionel Isaac Strovokov Stark sat through four years of standard courses at Stanford. He brought the diploma back and set it down on his father's glass desk. He brought back the new trunks of new clothes.

"I still want to be an actor," he said.

Stark flew him to New York, where several of Mittie's friends, whom he pretty much supported, eventually became successful. Mittie did not. After a year and three months of failure, his father stopped the checks and wired his son a plane ticket to Portland. He took him into his office at the factory. The Stanford diploma was framed on the wall.

"Mitchell," he said, "you want to be an actor? Okay. I bought you a theater. It's in Floren Park, Colorado. It's a good place there, a summer resort. So go be an actor."

"I was planning on trying Hollywood."

"Okay. Try Hollywood in the winters," the father replied, and turned his attention back to the papers on his glass desk.

Bruno Stark knew how to be patient. He endured the acting; he endured its failure. The next assault was Leila; he endured her as well. Mittie had met and married Leila the first summer he went to Floren Park. She was eighteen, and not at all what Mr. Stark had planned. But their son, David, might be. David Beaumont Stark, now two years old, had Leila's blond hair and blue eyes. Bruno Stark set aside a college fund for his grandheir and waited.

In the Red Lagoon Bar, people left and came. My tired-ness went away, and I waxed eloquent under the influence of exhaustion and drink about a Professor Aubrey at Harvard, who had saved me from suspension in a dark hour. His admira-tion for me grew as I spoke, until Leila abruptly said we should go. On the way out, she told the manager to charge our drinks; it was the younger Starks' arrangement to have them added to the rent bill, which went to the elder Stark. The manager's attitude toward Leila combined obsequiousness and lechery in what I considered an unattractive balance. I elaborately ignored him.

Next door, on the stage, the Belle of Black Bottom Gulch was already considerably fatigued when we looked in on her from the lobby doors. From later performances, I learned why. In the first act, she was robbed, seduced, foreclosed upon, aban-doned, nearly raped, practically frozen, and almost bifurcated by a cardboard buzz saw—all to the rapid tempo of a red upright piano energetically pounded in the pit by a plump and pimply young man who wore flowered armbands and a bowler hat. The Belle, however, continued to hold up, being youthful and sturdy, remarkably resembling, in fact, the sheriff we had seen on the street earlier in the evening.

Mittie had decorated his lobby to resemble a nineteenth-century western saloon, with a row of gaslights hung above the red felt concession stand. Later on in the week, I suggested that we paint Leila's face in the middle of the barroom floor, and Mittie thought it a fine idea, though I had meant it as a joke, so we oiled her in and covered her with varnish to keep the customers from leaving heel marks on her.

That night the house was packed full. Half of this audience was "under-twelves" who, being encouraged by the actors to join in, screamed and hissed enthusiastically when the villain, played with an endless sneer by Mittie, was chased off the stage and then around the aisles by the hero and the local law officials. Mittie gave us a sweaty wink when he galloped past us and turned the far corner on one foot to head back to the stage.

Leila had gone backstage to check on someone who wasn't feeling well. While we were waiting for her, Verl and I watched a little of the play, and then studied the photographs of the company hanging across one felt wall of the lobby. One girl reminded me a lot of Jardin; her name was Suzanne Steinitz. There was a huge picture of Mittie in the center of the group; it was surrounded by eight-by-tens of everyone else, including Maisie and Davy and myself (a blow-up of my high school graduation picture, which I was grateful to learn Leila had kept).

Eventually she came back out with an armful of spangled rags on her arm. These I saw the next week stitched onto the chorus line of the musical we were then putting on. Gradually I came to see, and then to experience, the complex connections of this world I'd come into, but for a while yet, I noticed only colored bits unrelated to each other, isolated from their functions. Spangles, a bag of nails, a soprano, a paid-for ad.

Leila went into the box office, where a taciturn, frail young man was twisting his wiry hair into a Dairy Queen cone on top of his head as he added up columns of figures on the back of a playbill. I recognized him from one of the photographs.

"How was the house, Seymour?" she asked him, rubbing his back.

"Two hundred seven dollars and fifty cents," he announced, as though he had personally arranged it, and done so only to please her.

Ceremoniously, he handed Leila a gray tin box, which she dropped down into the recessed cavern of her huge pocketbook. I had difficulty thinking of real money in relation to all this playing. Two hundred dollars in a night?

"Devin Donahue, Verl Biddeford—Seymour Mink. He's got the best voice here," Leila told us, referring, I assumed, to the stock company at large, rather than the four of us. She had no succinct definitions of Verl and me to offer Seymour in return, so we talked a bit about his singing. He was just doing it because he liked to. He was going to be a doctor.

Seymour was to be driven home with us, for he lived in Leila's basement with several other members of the company. The rest, I learned, barracked in arbitrary coupledom on one whole floor of a downtown boarding house. We got into Leila's car outside the bar; it had once been a small school bus, now it was painted red and labeled RED LAGOON THEATRE. She did pretty well with the gears and steering, although she was simultaneously smoking, drinking Chablis from a half-gallon bottle she kept under the driver's seat, and turning around to talk to us over the volume of the radio, which she had up as high as it would go. It came at us full blast as soon as she turned on the ignition. She was hoping, she said, to hear a favorite song of hers by Aretha Franklin that sounded like religion in her mind.

For most of the drive she talked about "the plight of the Mexican and Indian migrant farm workers" with Verl, who also seemed to know a lot of statistics about their situation. Leila said she hoped I was not buying any nonunion lettuce. I told her I had never bought any lettuce.

She drove Verl and me to the Triumph, and then we followed her bus through the still-carnivaling main street over to a quieter area of town, and finally up a gravel road. Leila's house was large and sprawled among spruce and pine clusters. A steep path of loose bricks led up to a full porch, half screened in, the other half walled up to make a room, Mittie and Leila's. Behind the porch was a living room of miscellaneous resort furniture and a wide stone fireplace, over which there was a large photograph of Leila holding Maisie and Davy in her lap, with candles in front of it like an altarpiece. Four doors led off to the rest of the house.

To the left were the kitchen and the children's room. She opened their door so that we could see them. They were sleeping on two small mattresses on the floor; stuffed animals, books, baby bottles, wooden farms, schoolhouses, airplanes, merry-go-rounds lying beside them. For some reason, I took a secret and personal pride in their beauty, a perfection of form I had never before realized, almost as though I were their unacknowledged father. Leila kissed them while I stood back in the doorway and watched her.

On the right were a bathroom and the bedroom of a Nathan Wolfstein, a man who had once taught drama at an excellent eastern academy, who had once been well-known in his field, who had met Leila at a Los Angeles community theater production, and who had soon afterward agreed, just for fun, to come to Floren Park as a consultant and guest director. He went to bed early and was not to be disturbed, for, Leila said unspecifically, he had a number of diseases, and overstimulation aggravated them.

We discovered a pallid young girl asleep on the couch before a dead fire, her glasses slipping down her nose and her mouth open in a sputtering sniffle. A paperback copy of *The Prophet* lay open across her Red Lagoon sweatshirt. She was Sabby Norah, baby-sitter as well as company apprentice, whose love of the theater was such, Leila told us, that she had to be forcibly kept from scrubbing the Starks' toilet bowl daily, simply out of the fullness of her adoration. She also lived in the basement, sleeping there celibately across the boundary of a table from Seymour Mink, whose room she shared, and deriving from the situation a stimulating, though entirely theoretical, sense of decadence.

Leila informed me that I as well was assigned to half a basement room. I responded with confused indignation to this discovery. For while I had not previously thought about where I would be bedded, to be boarded thus among alien and adolescent apprentices had not been a possibility even subconsciously considered. In retrospect, I suppose I imagined myself in the master bedroom.

After we unloaded my things, Verl left us for the night. Leila woke Sabby, told her that she had talked to Mittie about the second lead, and he had said okay, we'll give her a try, received from Sabby for this news a look melted as that of a Magus at the manger, gave Sabby the armful of spangled shreds, and sent her off to bed beside the silent Seymour.

Then Leila poured Chablis into a coffee mug and a Chinese tea cup. She soon seemed to me rather flushed from the wine. I guess because she was unusually fair, her face, to her chagrin, always translated the immediate state of her soul, mind, or body into various shades of rose. She blushed more quickly than anyone I'd ever known.

"God, I'm tired," she yawned. Those were not the opening words in private I had heard in my head while driving across the Midwest. But then she said, "This is so nice, Devin. Like old times. Like family."

However, the connection "family" started her on more questions about Mama, Maeve, and the others—about whose current lives she seemed to know more than I did anyhow. Nothing at all was asked, and therefore nothing offered, on the more relevant tragedy of myself, J. Dexter. and Jardin. Assuming she wished to respect the solitude of my grief, I reciprocated with bland inquiries as to the well-being of Mittie (who was the same as ever—depressed) and her mother, Mrs. Thurston (who was, for Christ's sake, not to be talked about).

After that, she talked of Maisie and Davy. I took the gauge of my importance from her willingness to share with me (and I felt certain, intimately with no other) the closest secrets of how she felt—love, anger, pride, fear, and frustration—about her children. Then in the midst of describing her breathing exercises for natural childbirth, she yawned herself into sleep, leaving me holding the past, the mug, and the cup of wine. I sat still for a while, but as she showed no signs of reviving, I tried to accidentally shift my place on the couch in order to move her out of her comfortable slump against my arm, and thereby wake her up. However, I succeeded only in sliding her further down my side onto my thigh, which she nuzzled into smoothness as though it were sand beneath her beach blanket. The thought that she had done it deliberately excited me, adding to the discomfort of my position.

The screen door slammed. I scurried out from under Leila's head and to my feet, leaving the cups on the couch behind me. But even this abrupt displacement failed to rouse her.

"Hello there, cracker."

It was the gun-twirling desperado from the street show. A chunky young man about my height with firetruck-red hair pointing outward all around his head like on the Statue of Liberty. Behind his round, rimless glasses, he shined at me eyes as brown and glossy as two M&M's.

"Hello, I'm Devin Donahue," I whispered.

"Hi. Joely Finn. How you doing? Just get in?"

"About six hours ago." It surprised me to realize I was such a comparative newcomer to the Red Lagoon world; I also felt that it put me at a disadvantage. "Why do you call me 'cracker'?" I asked him.

"Oh, somebody said you were from the South, from Leila's hometown, right?"

"Yeah, but we're Tarheels. Aren't crackers from Georgia?"

"That so?" He considered this a moment and then grinned at me. "I didn't know it was so specific down there. I'm from Chicago. South side."

"Leila's asleep," I pointed out, in case he wondered why I was whispering.

He leaned over the back of the couch to look at her. "Yep. Conked out again. One of the few Americans alive who feel zero

guilt about sleeping. You must be ready for the sack too. I guess
you'll be staying in my room. Glad to have you. Doesn't look like
much, but it's okay downstairs. Especially since you're usually
so wiped out anyway when you hit the mattress, you don't give
a damn where you are. And other times, nobody's ever in their
rooms. My bunk's the one by the window. Grab whatever you
need. That's the john down the hall there."

"I know," I told him.

"Well, I gotta get back. Drove over. Mittie forgot his solder-
ing kit. Lights are acting up again. See yuh."

I had thought of asking him what we should do with Leila,
but had decided against sharing the decision with him. His
proprietorial tone annoyed me. After he left, I soothingly shook
Leila by the shoulders.

"Leila, you want to get up and go to bed?"

"No. Please," she murmured. "Just let me sleep here a little
longer. It's so peaceful."

I was aggravated. If I was going to be treated as a stranger
and have the location of the bathroom pointed out to me by
strangers, then at least I should be given the benefits traditional
to guests. As things were, I was dispossessed of both a sense of
belonging and of hospitality.

So, somewhat testily, I found my toothbrush in the corner
of my suitcase where Mama had packed it wrapped in a paper
towel, used the alien bathroom with deliberate carefulness, and
then noisily carted down to the basement my summer's worth of
clothes and talismans.

My room was the one with the door open. I could immediately tell that Joely Finn cared little for personalizing possessions.
There was nothing on his dresser top but change, screws and
bolts, matches, a copy of *Catch 22*, and a pair of grayish boxer
shorts. On the other bureau I lined up my miniature busts of
Shakespeare and J.F.K., my daily journal bound in leather, six
felt-tip pens, my picture of Jardin, my paperbacks (I brought with
me fourteen books I had always intended to read at Harvard),
and my loose collection of foreign coins.

Newly pajamaed and in an inappropriate bed, I fervently wished I had never left North Carolina, and consoled myself with a rhythmically sonorous speech I heard myself making to Jardin in the Charleston church vestibule over the muted strains of the fugue from Beethoven's Third, which James Dexter had funereally chosen in place of the traditional Wedding March.

The timeless time I gave to this reverie ended when a raised voice from upstairs intruded on my climax. The voice was Mittie's. "And don't think I'm such a schmuck I don't know what you're doing, you bitch! The stud's back, right? Right? No more finger stuff with the little boys in the dressing room now. So nobody wanted his lousy play? So he's back to pushing that lousy art-fart jewelry on the streets? What did you do, buy out his stock for the day so you could jerk him into the nearest alley before lunch? Bitch! Bitch!"

Leila's voice was quiet, almost bored. "Just go to bed, Mittie. You're drunk."

Mittie kept on talking. After a while, I thought maybe he had started crying. Then he sounded as though he were trying to apologize, but I couldn't hear distinct words anymore. That gave me time to let my share in their shame subside until it was quiet and I could think about what this revelation meant. Obviously there were things going on in the Red Lagoon Theatre of more immediate moment than my arrival.

Leila was having an affair. With Spurgeon Debson. How rotten to Mittie. But on the other hand, it implied that their marriage was already in trouble. Collapsed even. And though I'd seen Mittie for perhaps a total of six hours, I felt ready to agree with him that in a lot of ways he was a schmuck. But Leila and Spurgeon? Spur was *insane*. What was the matter with Leila anyhow? Of course, maybe Mittie was mistaken. Paranoiac jealousy.

Who were these boys in the dressing room? Joely Finn? Seymour Mink? She had rubbed Seymour's back. I decided I disliked them both, and when, shortly after the Starks quieted down, Joely came into my room, I pretended to be asleep so he wouldn't speak to me. But he just stripped and flopped into his bed without turning on the light anyway. The noise of his turning and breathing was an irritating intrusion that made me want to choke him. It was a personal affront.

Finally I grew drowsy. As I slid toward sleep, I determined to take charge of Leila's honor against the misplaced desires of others, or her own indiscreet disregard, or the delusions of her husband's fears. Having so pledged myself, I felt a lot better. In which state I fell asleep, saying good-bye to Mama and Maeve and Colum, and hello to the rich flat fields of middle America, and then to the mountains, and Fitzgerald boarding the bus, as my body drove along the wide highway west until it climbed to a stop in the sudden red jostle and noise of Floren Park.

chapter 4

Some Old Scenes and Some New People

The next morning was Tuesday, June 4th, the second day of my tenure as scenic designer to Mittie Stark; with it, I was brought fully into all the new people and things going on in the Red Lagoon world I had been joined to. And so they and not Leila, who had gathered me into that world and who mattered more than the other people and things, were what made up my time, the way we let new things do.

I was awakened by subterranean knowledge of an appraising stare. It was Leila's daughter, Maisie. She stood silently across the room from my bed, watching me, when I opened my eyes, puzzled to find myself in the wrong bedroom, in the wrong state.

Maisie had her father Mittie's black curly hair and thick eyelashes and her mother's blue eyes, and she knew at four that she was beautiful. She wore a long purple negligee, which probably belonged to Leila, for it hung off her shoulders and circled the floor around her small, bare feet—the toenails of which I was startled to see painted red.

"You sleep a lot," she said, twisting a strand of big, red glass beads into loops on her wrist.

"No, I don't," I told her. "I went to bed late."

This justification did not impress her. She pursed her mouth in apparent disapproval of my lethargy. I noticed that Joely Finn had already left.

"I go to bed when I like," she told me, "and I don't ever have to go to sleep."

"Do you stay up all night?" I asked her.

"Sometimes I do and sometimes I don't." With that, she changed the subject. "I'll be five soon. How old are you?"

"Twenty-two." I felt younger.

"My mother's twenty-four. You used to know her when you were little. My father's twenty-eight. Some people get gray hair before they're even old, but I'm glad they didn't. You didn't either. I hope I don't."

"You have awfully long hair for someone your age," I threw out. I was trying to keep up my end of the conversation, but had the feeling that I was being inane. I was distracted by a strong urge to relieve myself. It was my habit to head for the bathroom immediately upon waking, and I was discovering through these recent disruptions that I was a creature of habit.

She walked over to the bed. "Yes," she agreed. "It's never been cut. I won't cut it. Ever. See? It's down this far."

She turned her back so I could see it. Then she stopped talking and continued her thoughtful examination of my suitcase, my bureau top, and me. I was curiously embarrassed. There didn't seem to be anything definably childish about her eyes; they were, in fact, disconcertingly conscious and seemed to imply that she knew a great deal more about herself and about me than I would ever know about either.

Suddenly I remembered the fight I had overheard the night before between Leila and Mittie about Spurgeon Debson. The whole Stark family ambiance was beginning to make me uneasy.

"It's time to eat," Maisie broke our silence, delivering the message she had presumably been sent to deliver. "Breakfast is ready. Can I have one of these pens?" She picked it up from the bureau top.

"Sure, okay, just one. You go tell them I'll be right up."
Though I reminded myself that she was only four, I wanted her
to leave, even at the price of a pen, before I changed into my
clothes. Gathering up her long gown, she ran over to the door,
paused, swirled around, and said, "I'm pretty tricky, you know."

"I believe it," I assured her.

Upstairs, people at a big wooden picnic table in the kitchen
were finishing up the morning meal. It consisted of strange runny
food, tacos, and beans. Mama had accustomed me to eggs and
bacon, pancakes and sausage, ham and biscuits, corn flakes and
orange juice, and I was unprepared to accept so radical a divergence
from my expectations. Here was yet another instance of Leila's
reluctance to nurture my needs, a reluctance that I was becoming
unpleasantly used to. I might as well have stayed at home.

So, politely, I refused nourishment other than a cup of coffee
and sat down. Seymour, Sabby, and Joely Finn were just finishing their tacos and preparing to leave for the theater. There was
another person at the table. A pale, emaciated man, elongated
as an El Greco saint. He was in his late sixties, with a tuft of
speckled graybrown hair high swept off his high forehead, with
a narrow beaked nose on a long thin face, and with long thin
arms and legs like a crane's. Leila introduced him as Nathan
Wolfstein—the director she had mentioned the night before,
the one who slept in the private room.

Mr. Wolfstein wore a brown suit, a western string tie, and
high-heeled cowboy boots that made him even taller than he
already should have been. He was pouring bourbon into a cup of
coffee and smoking an unfiltered cigarette; these two morning
rituals required his entire concentration. His hands trembled
spasmodically, his head jerked in a persistent tic, and it seemed
inevitable that he should sooner or later spill the coffee and
swallow his Camel. A calamity made more predictable by his
being also periodically shaken by abrupt spasms of coughing.
Since Leila had told me that Mr. Wolfstein was the victim of
a number of diseases, I speculated on whether tuberculosis or
cerebral palsy were among them.

But despite his obvious discomforts, Mr. Wolfstein was very courteous to me and spoke with a quiet and steady intelligence. He seemed to me a dissipated distortion of Mr. Aubrey, my teacher at Harvard. At his request, I brought him quickly up to date on my history, education, tastes, and futures. I didn't want him to classify me with the other apprentices. Then he turned back to a conversation with Leila about a trip he had once taken to Australia with a repertory company. It was clear to me from his eyes that he was infatuated with Leila, for reasons undefined (and probably undefinable) to himself. He seemed, in fact, not even to know that he was infatuated at all. The realization saddened me for him. The *Blue Angel* ailment, on top of all the others.

Mittie, they told me, had gotten up early and driven to Denver, where he bought our theatrical supplies and where he would be staying that evening to see a road company production of *Damn Yankees,* a favorite show of his. The Red Lagoon Theatre was always, as they put it, "dark" on Tuesdays, so his presence would not be required in Floren Park, at least for professional reasons, until the next morning's rehearsals, and he wouldn't be home until after midnight. I noticed I was glad to hear it.

But Wolfstein had called a reading of the following week's musical, and as Leila was playing the lead, her attendance was required there. She wondered if, during that time, I would mind keeping an eye on Maisie and Davy. I did in a way, but said I wouldn't mind at all. Serving as a day care center seemed rather far removed, however, from the function I had been hired to perform. I was supposed to be a scenic designer, and the ease of this functional substitution was a little humiliating.

We left the leftovers for lunch, helped Wolfstein up, and all piled into "the Red Bus," as the Starks called their school van. Davy sat on my lap and was, in comparison with his sister, refreshingly childlike. As we drove to town, Joely teased Seymour and Sabby about pretended noises he had heard coming from their room until the early hours of the morning. Sabby blushed, and Seymour told him he wasn't funny. In the right front seat, Wolfstein was effortlessly bounced around by Leila's acceleration on the curves, and I began to think there were no actual bones beneath the long, flapping brown suit he wore—and little flesh. I still felt as if I were in North Carolina, and all this was happening to someone else.

As everyone tumbled out at the theater parking lot, Leila mined a battered copy of *The Fantastiks*, our next play, from her mammoth pocketbook. She advised me to read it, since the rehearsal sets would be needed within the next few days.

Then all of them went inside the theater and left Maisie, Davy, and me behind. So the three of us sat down on the bank of the creek that ran beside the building and talked for a long time, largely about their interests, and on my part, in reply to their endless questions about miscellaneous phenomena, such as Why doesn't the water stand still? and What's a hophead? Davy "meowed" quite a bit and licked my face. I told them about Huckleberry Finn and his raft trip. Maisie said she did not believe that somebody could go the wrong way on a river and not even know it. She said it sounded like a story.

As we talked, it became very important to me to win them to my side. From whose side other than mine, I did not specify to myself, nor could I have articulated for what purpose they were to be won. So we spent the next hour constructing wooden boats with paper sails to be floated down the creek's maze of currents, which eventually, I promised, would take our boats all the way to the sea, though I couldn't answer Maisie's question, "Atlantic or Pacific?" We were right in the middle.

A little before noon, the wind got to be unignorably chilly, especially for Maisie, who had on only a thin shawl over the purple negligee which she had insisted on wearing as a party dress. Finally Leila came out of the theater to retrieve us. The plump and pimply piano player was with her; she kissed him on the cheek, and he went back inside.

Despite the cold cloudiness of the weather, she was wearing very short lederhosen that day; she also had on the large round sunglasses with one stem loosely rewired to the frame that she wore throughout the summer.

For the rest of the afternoon, I sat with a strong sense of purpose in the supplies storeroom, which I was calling my office, and designed sets for *The Fantastiks* in my new sketchbook— minutely elaborate edifices on revolving platforms with flyable walls. I wasn't sure they could be built. Around me, the theater was quiet. Everyone else seemed to have somewhere to go.

I was getting bored when one of the apprentices, a big muscular guy (Marlin Owen, I later learned) stuck his head in the door without knocking and said, "Hi, you Devin?" I remembered him as the hero in the play last night.

"Yes," I jumped up to be introduced, but all he said was, "Some friends of yours outside looking for you," and shut the door again.

In the parking lot, Verl stood beside an old pickup equipped for snow with a broom and wide shovel stuck upright behind the cab. Next to him a tall, lanky blond guy leaned cavalierly against the side door. I shook hands with Dennis Reed. He offered to take me for a ride.

In and out of the winding dirt roads of the circling mountains, he drove us for hours, drove gracefully, as if his truck were not a machine but a dance partner. And squeezed comfortably into the cab, I felt for the first time since I'd come there the fineness of the place. A fine place to see from a truck. At dusk, we came to a rambling white stucco building sheltered by crab apple trees. It was a Mexican family's restaurant called Cervantes's, and it had a windmill painted on the front by, I was told, a friend of Dennis's. So, while the owners lingered affably around us serving more and more strange food, we talked of philosophy, and the war in Vietnam, and the revolution of the young, and sexuality, and all the limitations of the human condition. I was having a wonderful time.

We argued politics. Verl thought we were going to win, that what people like Danny the Red were doing in France to De Gaulle, that what we had done to LBJ, that what Robert

Kennedy would do for us, all meant we could believe again that maybe everything could work—the way we had believed in 1960.

"But who do you think got us into Vietnam in the first place?" I asked. "A Kennedy. I think it's all over. Everyone should just go home and grow his own roses."

"You're a cynic," Verl smiled.

"I'm a southerner."

"I thought all southerners were sentimentalists," Dennis said.

"That's when they're reading Look Homeward, Angel. After that they go to Harvard and study cynicism," Verl told him.

"And look around for Quentin Compson's bridge," I said. Dennis laughed. I was glad that Verl's friend liked me. I ordered the fourth bottle of wine. By the time we finished eating, I was sure that (next to my family and Verl) there was no one in the world I could like more than Dennis Reed. He was so good-looking he might have been intimidating, but part of his charm was a natural easiness whose sincerity you had to accept. In the john, Verl told me that Dennis knew Greek well and was a drama enthusiast, but I guess he was too modest to mention either subject during our talk. He didn't mention what he did, either, except that he had refused to go to law school because he had no use for his father, who was a judge.

By the next time I came back from the bathroom, four more people had joined our party. Then Dennis borrowed the proprietor's guitar and sang songs that they all seemed to know. Chain gang songs, and union songs, and laments about cornbread and beans, and a ballad involving the tribulations of a Miss Cornelia, resident of a New Orleans bordello, who suffered from pernicious anemia, who was visited and graphically cured by Our Lord Jesus Christ, whom she then charged two dollars for the house call.

"I'm glad I came to Colorado," I told everyone there.

On the ride home I stuck my head out the window to feel the tingle. My face had gone slightly numb, and the words to the songs we were still singing kept having trouble with my tongue. Then all at once we were pulling up in front of the Starks' summer house, and my new friends were saying good-bye to me.

Dennis anointed my head with oil. "You're all right, Donahue. Why don't you give up the grease paint, come over, and stay with us? You play *Scrabble?*"

My cup ranneth over with fellowship. "Sure. Listen, I may just do that. Anyhow, next time you guys get over here, we'll play some in the bar. Okay? And thanks a lot, hear?"

I started up the steps to the house.

"You all right, Devin?" Verl called after me through a tunnel.

"Sure, fine. See you," I yelled.

"Okay. I'll be in touch. Take care of yourself."

"Jesus, you're such a mother hen," I told him. "Come back soon. See you."

They drove away.

The wind was really blowing now; pine needles flew out of the trees and stung my face and arms. The clouds were whirring about in blacker and blacker spirals. Van Gogh brushstrokes, I thought. It made me heady in the straight-from-the-stomach way a Ferris wheel does when you go over the top.

My spirit expanded. The air held that sustained suspension of a storm's imminence just before its letting-go. I would meet it. "Oh, to live each moment at this height, this enlarging of the faculties until they are at one with the unconquerable forces of nature," I thought, or something like it.

Then I thought again of Leila. How, one immemorial day at the high school water cooler, I had rescued her from that narrow ignorance that lashed her to the masts of hillbilly music, majorette practice, the cloddish attentions of the football defensive line. How I (a younger, smoother Henry Higgins) had led her gently by the mind into the bright, still chambers of Art (the Impressionists), Music (Rachmaninoff and Wagner), Literature (beginning with *Wuthering Heights* and *Sanctuary*), and Drama (beginning with securing her, through my influence as president of the theatrical club, the lead in the junior play, *Anastasia*).

Had I not given her a soul capable of feeling grandeur? Had I not proven that by our love and my literary enlightenment, we could reach that pure rare empyrean, the eternal trysting place of those who set no bourn but new heaven, new Earth? Had we not felt as they felt, shared their company up there, cut out in little stars? Dido and Aeneas. Paris and Helen. Tristan, Isolde. Lord Nelson and Lady Hamilton. André and Natasha. Madame Bovary. Sayonara.

"But, soft! What light through yonder window breaks?" I thought. It was the bedroom and Leila was awake. In itself a presentiment. As I climbed the steps, I took one last full breath of fire and air. My baser elements I gave away. They slipped on the loose bricks, and I tripped. Righting myself, I went softly inside the house.

chapter 5

My First Dissipation

Inside the living room, I sailed on a weave to the fireplace, where I threw on some old newspapers, pine cones, Sabby Norah's copy of *The Prophet*, two logs, and half the box of magic color flames. With one match they took fire. Then I went to Leila's bedroom, knocked, and opened the door.

She was lying upon her bed. It had a brass headpost, one she had found in the back room of a Salvation Army store. She had stripped off its layer of blue paint and now transported it with her wherever she went in her small wooden trailer that was now parked in the backyard. She called it her gypsy wagon.

What I could see of the room by the light of a blue bulb in a purple tasseled shade was not very neat. The closet was just a chain strung across the window, with hers and Mittie's clothes hanging from the loops. More clothes were piled in two director's chairs labeled "Mittie" and "Leila," others flung over the dresser; clothes carpeted the floor along with play scripts, shoes, empty Chinese food cartons, and the children's toys. A shop window full of silver jewelry hung from cuphooks on one wall. Pictures and posters of the Starks were tacked onto the others. And over the bed was a poster of Robert Kennedy and a nude sketch of Leila drawn from the rear (white pastel on rose paper, unsigned).

Below, the original Leila lay upon tangled sheets handsewn of blue silk jersey. Uncovered pillows striped behind her, she was watching the California presidential primaries on a portable television that had a coat hanger for an antenna. Leila followed all the campaigns assiduously, for she held strong and wide-ranging political opinions—espoused simultaneously, in fact, the policies of the French Revolution and the sentiments of Victorian philanthropists.

She looked up. "Where have you been, Devin? You missed supper."

"I missed you," I smiled, sitting down on the bed and staring at her nightgown. "That's very pretty," I commented with a larger smile. The gown was shimmery and white.

"It's my Jean Harlow dress," she said. "I got it for my audition in *Rain*...Well, I found it. Somebody threw it in one of those collection bins Goodwill Industries puts up. Can you believe that?"

I said I couldn't.

Then, pulling my smile to a close, I spoke in gentle earnest, "You know what, Leila? You know what you have? You have *fineness*. This is what...what I want to say. You've been the very best thing in all of my life. You and Verl. And Dennis. And Jardin. And Mama. But what I mean is, you're the very...the finest center of my being. That's the truth, Leila. That's really true."

"Are you okay?" Leila asked me.

She got up and turned off the television. When she looked at me, she started laughing. "Where have you been? You're snockered!"

I fell back upon the pillows from where she had arisen and found them warm.

"I've been talking with some good friends, talking for hours, trying to figure it all out, what it comes down to, what lasts and what shimmers. The readiness is all, Leila."

"Good," she said, "I'm ready to take a shower." I had never really gotten Leila to respond correctly.

Having gathered her apparel, she left me while I was still trying to decide what the difference was between the readiness and the ripeness. It seemed vital. Looking down to the floor at the side of her bed, I noticed a blurred and bouncing record player stacked with Aretha Franklin albums and the soundtracks of *The Fantastiks* and *Damn Yankees*. I took these off and put on Rachmaninoff's Second Symphony, which I found at the bottom of a pile of albums under the dresser. It was the very copy of the symphony I had given her six years ago, inscribed 'Here will we sit and let the sounds of music creep in our ears; soft stillness and the night become the touches of sweet harmony.' With love forever, Devin." Ah, she had treasured it. I sank back, buried my head in the pillows of my fair love's ripening breast. (*"Sweet" love's?* Which was it?)

"Devin! Are you crazy?"

Leila had returned. She stood in the door, wrapped in a towel. It was also inscribed: "Howard Johnson's Motor Lodge." Harshly she advised me, "Turn that damn thing off, you idiot! You're going to wake everybody up."

When, slowly, I protested, she rejected Rachmaninoff herself and went back to the bathroom. I followed. In the living room, my fire had gone out, miraculously consuming *The Prophet* on a stake of untouched logs.

Reaching the bathroom, I continued my testament while Leila turned on the shower, stepped behind a bilious plastic curtain, and handed me her towel.

I began, "You know, love's not hereafter. Is it? Let's ball our sweetness up. Let's…" I began again. "Look, Leila, all of us just go 'round and 'round our pasts forever trying to get back home. A just circle. Ends where it begun. Began. That's why, without you in my life, I couldn't keep on being me."

She stuck her head out at the front of the curtain. Her shower cap had blue umbrellas on it. It made her ears stick out. That bothered me. "What?" she asked.

"*I said, without you in my life, I couldn't keep on being me.*"

"Oh," she smiled and withdrew behind the curtain. Having to shout over the water was a handicap; it was difficult to enunciate in a wistful tone. I was beginning to get depressed.

"*You are me,* Leila. Do you remember when Cathy and Heathcliff said that? You're the only haven I can go to that will take me back to who I need to be."

"Devin, I'm sorry. I can't hear you. What did you say?"

"*I SAID...*" I leaned forward to put my right foot on the toiletbowl lid. It happened to be up at the time, so my leg went through as far as the knee.

"Oh, C-h-r-i-s-t," I whispered.

She stuck her head out again, turned off the shower faucets and laughed. The indifferent laughter of Olympus above and around me. I was shaking my leg up and down like a dog come out of the rain.

"What did you do?" she laughed.

Despite the superfluity of her question, I brought myself to respond with a head-tilted Tom Sawyer grin. It was the right approach. Clumsiness, if artfully manipulated, can be as effective as suavity, since nothing, I had concluded, flames more swiftly to the erotic than the maternal.

"Take off your shoes and pants and put them out on the back porch," she sweetly enjoined. A proposal indirectly promising. In addition to my as-yet unpeeling Tennessee tan, I had on one of the new pairs of baby-blue shorts Mama had hurried out to buy me for the trip—along with four undershirts and four pairs of socks so that if worse came to worst, I could be hospitalized in clean underwear. Our hygiene-for-disaster mentality, she called it.

I wrung my pants out over the toilet bowl, took off both shoes and socks, and shiveringly carried them out to the back porch, where I was immediately reminded of the storm, no longer imminent, but fulfilled. Rain was squalling down. Leila's directive struck me as less practical than I had at first thought it, but rather than return for alternate instructions, I hung my pants and both socks over the rail. My shoes, I left in the kitchen.

Meanwhile, my pants blew off into the yard and were swept here and there by short gusts of wind. Up on a bush, wrapped around a tree, down among the leaves. I chased after, circling in the rain, but the wind kept grabbing them, slapped me in the face with them, so I gave it up, almost in tears now at the pity of the whole soggy situation. My new red-and-white-striped shirt had become a solid pink body shirt. My shorts were soaked. My nose was running. I was depressed.

Slushing back to the bathroom, I found Leila thoughtfully appraising her face in the medicine chest mirror. She studied it as one would a familiar object to determine its continued serviceability, like a family armchair or an old party dress.

She mused, ignorant of my distress, "If I can learn to live without makeup now, maybe I'll be able to stand getting old and looking like my mother."

With her face washed naked, she was blond everywhere, the Leila of my adolescent room, where she had undressed one Sunday afternoon when Mama and the others were away visiting Uncle Norwood. Leila Dolores Beaumont. Leila D'Or. Seductress of Sorrow, I used to call her. Dolorous Delilah, weeping barber. Gold Mountain, Leila of old.

Behind her I said, "You know, I would have thought that without your eyes made up you'd be defenseless, more vulnerable. But you're not. You're more protected. More you. And you'll never look like your mother."

This was observation now, not strategy, for I had given up on Cathy and Heathcliff, was feeling world enough in time.

"Just not as flashy, you mean?" she asked, then turned. "Devin, you're soaking wet!"

Shivering all over the Holiday Inn floor mat, I rather ashamedly muttered, "My pants flew away. Out in the backyard. It's raining out there."

She smiled, biting softly on her lower lip. It was the old indulgent smile, which rushed the years backward so we both could feel them give way. I kissed her.

Water was dripping down from my hair around my nose, making it itch, and in between our mouths. I was wondering about the possibility of moving my left hand from her back to scratch my nose and then touching her right breast, when she turned her head enough to say, "You want to fuck me, don't you?"

I was startled by the profanity.

All of a sudden, I felt a lot younger than Leila. In the past we had always used more generalized terms like go to bed with, sleep with, mess around with, make love with. I was afraid she might notice my embarrassment if I didn't make a reply, but a simple "yes," though to the point, felt too blunt and wouldn't come out. Hyperbole was inappropriate. My tendency was to return the question to her ("Would you like me to?"), but I could conjecture how evasive and juvenile that might sound. I felt like saying I didn't know what I wanted to do, now that things had gotten so real. For I hadn't planned on her leaping in front of her own capitulation to memory this way, and I needed a moment to adjust.

I didn't say anything. Jesus, I thought, maybe I'm going to cry. Leila took my hand and led me into her bedroom.

Warm, damp, under her tangled sheets and a quilt of blue velvet that she pulled from beneath a mound of clothes at the bedfoot, I turned to her and kissed her, kissed all the felt memories of shadow, curve, light, gesture, odors, weight, kissed my first kiss, touched my first breast for the first time, again.

Oh, God, I thought, maybe this is really true.

"OH, GOD, GOD!" someone screamed from the back room.

I soared to attention. Scurried for a pair of Mittie's pants.

"THEY'RE ALL OVER THE PLACE!" the scream continued.

It was Nathan Wolfstein's voice.

Leila rose as well, all white-robed. We reached the living room just as Wolfstein, looking like a pajamaed Ichabod Crane, roared flapping out of his bedroom.

"BUGS! BUGS!" he screeched. "THEY'RE ALL OVER THE PLACE!"

"Nate! Nate!" Leila tried to stop him. "What's the matter? What bugs?"

He stared past us with the blind horror of the damned. "BED! Bugs crawling! Bed bugs!" was what I made of his mumblings.

Then he rushed on past in a roar of wheeze, flinging off his pajamas as he went, clawing at his white bony frame in a frenzy of panic. We ran after him to the bathroom, where he was already in the tub with the shower going full blast. After five seconds there, he jumped out, jerked the towel from my waiting hand, fled into his bedroom, came out pulling on his pants and sweater, and stomped his feet into his cowboy boots all at the same time.

Ignoring our inquiries, our assurances about nightmares, he streamed outside, got into his old Austin, started it up, and ran it into the nearest pine tree. The horn went off.

I ran down the walk, slipping in rain puddles, opened the car door, and pulled Wolfstein off the steering. His mouth was cut and his face was blue. He didn't appear to be breathing.

"Call a doctor." Assuming the worst, I yelled up to Leila, "I think maybe he's killed himself."

She ran back inside. By now, Joely, Sabby, and Seymour were hurrying out of the basement in various styles of night garb.

Collectively we argued about whether or not to move the body until Dr. Calvin Ferrell arrived. He was the Floren Park general practitioner, a youthful, tousled man who proved disturbingly jovial about both life and death.

By the time Ferrell reached the car, the corpse inside it was conscious. We carried him up the steps and returned him to his bed, once I had inspected it for insects and declared it safe for slumber. After the doctor put a bandage on his cheek and provided a sedative for his soul, Wolfstein sank to peace. So we adjourned our vigil at his bedside and stood outside the door. Then Joely, Sabby, and Seymour went back downstairs to bed.

"That man ought to be dead," Ferrell told Leila and me. "And not from any car accident, either. His body's riddled with ill health. Cigarettes, booze, nerves. I'd make him do something for himself or else get him out of here before you have to pay to ship the body home." He cheerfully snapped his bag shut.

Leila offered Ferrell a drink of scotch, which he annoyingly accepted. He aggravated that rudeness by sitting down and amiably reminiscing with Leila about the medical calamities of previous summers. Finally he got up to say good night. Leila was unabashedly yawning, offering a hint.

"Well, see you, Leila. Things sure do pick up for me when you get to town."

She saw him to the door. I went down to my basement room, changed into some blue jeans and a T-shirt, and returned with Mittie's slacks to Leila's bedroom. Once again, I found her lying upon her bed. This time, however, she was sound asleep. The speed, ease, and frequency with which Leila landed in the arms of Morpheus was enough to make a younger suitor jealous. As she failed to respond to either vocal or physical promptings, I folded Mittie's pants neatly over a chair back, then thought better of it, mussed them, and dropped them on the floor where I had found them. I left her with one backward look at her wondrous (though not as far as I was concerned, wonderful) capacity to relax.

At that moment, a lumpy gray mattress beside Joely Finn in the basement would undoubtedly have led to an unattractive self-pity. So I stretched out on the living room floor, relit my fire carefully, and stared at it. And then, remembering her, though nothing is worse than such memories when you're miserable, I fell asleep, "Jardin, Jardin," ringing like a sweet bell in my brain. The great waste of life expended in the living of it weighed on my heart and sank me into a sorrowful slumber. Stuporous as the dead.

chapter 6

I Fall into Disgrace

I awoke, dank, cold, and achy. Mittie Stark was standing over me. Oh, shit, I thought, he knows. He glowered high over my head, swaying back and forth in a tower (I assumed) of Othelloean rage. We stared at each other mournfully across the vertical distance of his height, which made me even more apprehensive. So I stood up to alter the angle, to face the blow directly. But to my surprise, he offered me not a choice of weapons, but a proposal.

"'Lo, Deshin. You wake? Les go. Don' wanna go in there." He pointed vaguely toward Leila's room. "Not yet. Not sleepy. Les go for drink. You me. Oookay?"

The fondness I felt toward Mittie for not knowing I'd tried to have sex with his wife was such that had he asked me to walk back to Denver with him, I would not have refused.

"Sure," I sighed in relief, "I'll be glad to go with you, but are you sure you wouldn't rather go to sleep? You look sort of unsteady." I didn't want to be judgmental, but he was staggering about on a raft at sea, and I had heard the tales of his past "problem."

"Am unsteashy," he agreed, and tapped the side of his head significantly to indicate the area of disequilibrium. "Thas why les go."

Assuming that he knew his own antidotes better than I, I pulled on my boots and we weaved, arms on shoulders, in a fraternal embrace out into the rain.

By then the storm had slowed to fat, soppy drops of rain, which thunked down on us perpendicularly. The wind was gone, and the air was heavy. Mittie insisted on driving the Red Bus, and after a series of unnecessary horseshoe curves executed on perfectly straight-stretched roads, we slid to a halt in the mud field that had been earlier the Red Lagoon parking lot. Stepping out of the bus, Mittie lost his footing, stumbled, and threw me face forward into the mud. He promptly fell on top of me and relaxed, giggling. In an attempt to help each other rise, we danced about in a bear hug for a while, evidencing in the execution of splits, spins, and flips, acrobatic agility I had not known myself capable of. Finally I caught hold of the running board and then pulled us both up by a door handle. I felt like an idiot. After a brief rest, we made our way over to the bar; our shoes sucked in, slurped out of the sticky mud.

"SHIT," Mittie said. "Debson! Naturally!"

He was pointing, however, not at Spurgeon Debson, but at a monstrous dog, a Great Dane, skulking about the bar entrance. Aroused perhaps by this mention of his master's name (for it was, I deduced, Spur's dog and not Mittie's metaphor), the animal leapt forth, flattened us both once more into the mud, and took to biting us about the ankles. Paralyzed as I was both by position and anxiety, I was able to remember that I still had in my jacket pocket two enchiladas wrapped in wax paper, which the Mexican proprietor had pressed on Verl (who never finished his dinners) and which Verl had pressed on me. I squeezed them out of my pocket and flung them over into the mud field. The dog scrambled off in their direction. We slid off in the opposite, ran through the door of the bar, and slammed it behind us.

The consternation of our rout and arrival at the Red Lagoon provoked some of the regulars near the door to welcome us in with undue attention.

"You two fellows been fighting over a greased pig?"

"Naw. They's a couple of rooting hogs themselves."

We ignored these random pleasantries and slid into a booth.

Mittie ordered us tequila, which I had never tried before. The manager, Tony Menelade, brought it over personally, and joined us. Mittie and he then explained to me the inviolable ritual of drinking tequila by demonstrating on the two drinks before them. First the salt on the flesh between the thumb and forefinger, then the liquor in one quick motion, then the lemon squeeze.

After my lesson, the manager went back at Mittie's request and returned with a whole bottle and a whole lemon. We drank and talked. Tony told us he was apprehensive because his ex-wife, whom he referred to as "Lady Red," was back in Floren Park. He didn't know why yet; she'd offered no explanation. But since, originally, she had signed all the legal papers, the whole place was actually, by court law, hers, every stick of it, down to the booth we were sitting in and the saltshaker in his hand. As she was sneaky and nasty-tempered as a cat in heat, there was no telling what tricks she was planning to pull. All he knew was he had a physical weakness for her he just couldn't recover from, much to his (confidential) shame, and the only thing for him to do to keep from just handing the whole place over to her was just to stay away. I couldn't understand why he was telling us this. Finally he sighed, brushed away our commiseration for his weakness, and slid to his post behind his threatened bar. People in Floren Park seemed to be having trouble with their spouses.

So Mittie and I were left by ourselves with every intention of good fellowship, but nothing very much to say to each other. As I practiced flipping salt into my mouth during the lull, I caught a side glimpse of Spurgeon Debson coming out of the men's room zipping up his pants. He stalked through the bar and then through the front door. I also saw that Mittie had seen him.

"Know who that is?" Mittie asked.

"No. Who?" I replied, as I thought it wiser not to mention my previous meeting with Spur since Leila had introduced us.

"A shit-eating cocksucker," Mittie answered, just as though he had said "the guy who runs the butcher shop down the street," or "tackle for the Green Bay Packers."

"You don't like him?" was my next question.

Mittie's eyes narrowed into a wary watchfulness, "Know any reason why I should?"

I truthfully couldn't think of a one and said so.

"He thinks he's a playwright. He's not. His plays are garbage. Know what they're like?"

I shook my head.

"One ass stands center stage and spits on the Establishment for three hours. That's what."

It sounded quite probable, judging from what I remembered of my first encounter with the author when he had punted Sam the Shriner across the street.

Mittie proceeded to almost articulate further objections to Spur. "He spits on the Establishment, and *then* he brags about his lousy M.A. he got from some fart-ass school. Can you beat that?"

I said I couldn't and asked, "How old is he?"

"Thirty-four! A bum. A leech. Won't get a job. Against his principles. Makes jewelry and diddles teenage girls into buying it. Son of a bitch."

"What's he doing in Floren Park?" I asked.

Mittie gulped his drink. "Trying to put it up my wife," he answered. He paused to let this statement take effect. I was very uncomfortable. At that moment the manager came over with a bowl of pickled hard-boiled eggs, which he assured me were the best thing to eat with tequila. They were, at least, a thankful diversion. He went away. I offered an egg to Mittie; he ignored me. I ate three myself in six quick bites.

Mittie went on. "That's why he's here. Probably done it already too. Him and his lousy Great Dane both. Probably slid the lousy dog between her legs. Shit, she's had everything else there."

Why, I wondered, don't I tell him to stop, tell him he had no right to talk about her like that? He was making me sick. And my silence was a betrayal of Leila, wasn't it? But then, hadn't I, like the disgusting Spur, wanted to betray Mittie? Should I confess that? Even if I hadn't succeeded, hadn't I tried? I ate another egg and let him talk. It was undoubtedly helpful for him to get it off his chest. He had finished with Spur and turned to Leila.

"Bitch. Just can't have enough. Kill you. It's never enough. Suck you up. Right?" He leaned into my face, his breath was thick and bitter. "You know, don't you? Here we sit, and we've both had it up her. What a joke. You were the first, weren't you? I think that's what she told me. Maybe not. Who knows? I don't think you're so great-looking. Anybody can be smooth…Bitch! Her and my old man. It's never enough, is it?"

Mittie ought to have help. My ears were throbbing with a flush of jammed blood. I ate two more eggs and washed them down with tequila. Mittie kept on. The tequila had no taste, and I kept drinking.

My stomach heaved on the seventh egg and I made it to the sink in the men's room with my hand holding vomit in my mouth. When I finally could look up, my visage in the broken mirror over the sink almost made me retch again. I scrubbed my face with paper towels and tried to scrape some of the mud off my clothes. Across the mirror someone had written, "Kim will suck your dick like a candy stick." I stared at the words while I waited for my stomach to let me know if it was finished. Who was Kim? Hey, I saw your name on the lavatory wall. Who was that? Temple Drake, wasn't it? And where was Leila's name and number? I smeared the words across the mirror with my hand.

As I carefully led myself back to our booth, a fat hand reached up and grabbed my sleeve. "Hey! I know you from somewhere. Sit down! I'm buying."

It was the fat Shriner from yesterday. (Yesterday! Could that be true?) "Bobbie," Sam and Shirley had called him. So the woman with him now must be his wife, Lois, the long-suffering Lois who had been left holding the big table at the polka hall.

"I beg your pardon," I mumbled, as I tried to walk on past his table.

"Don't tell me," he warned. "I'll get it." He pointed a barbecued sparerib at my face. "Yes, sir! Artie's kid! Sam knew you. Got it! Have a seat, sonny." There was a paper platter of gnawed rib bones in front of him, and his fat fingers were sticky with red grease. At the sight, my stomach tightened in protest, and my face broke out in a sweat.

"Excuse me, but I'm afraid you've made a mistake. I don't know anyone named Artie." I wrenched these words out between my teeth, my sleeve slid from the grasp of his fat red fist, and I walked away.

"How do you like that?" I heard him say behind me. "Snotty little prick. Try to be nice. They're all like that. Deny their own father. Country's gone to the dogs, Lois. Pure and simple fact. It's been a downhill slide since Ike. We ought to go to Australia. Ought to just get out and let the freaks and the fairies have the whole damn place!"

If Lois agreed to emigration, I couldn't hear her.

Mittie was not at our booth. Frankly, I hoped he had gone home without me. I would have preferred a walk in the rain to more of his accusations. But he hadn't. He had in fact gotten his second, his tenth, wind of the evening. He had moved over to the bar, where he stood in a thick clump of men for whom he was offering to buy drinks.

"Wans tobias uh shot," one of the bystanders informed me with satisfaction. But a barrel-chested man in a plaid sports jacket protested. *He* would buy the drinks. He would buy the Red Lagoon. He would buy any damn thing he wanted.

chapter 7

A Little Cold Water

"My name is Hade. Eddie Hade. Order anything you want. Everybody." He swept us all into a wave of his gaudy arm; a cuff link glared. "Made it hard. Spend it easy. Right?" We nodded. "Money's a powerful thing, it's like a good-looking woman," he snorted. "You can't shut it up in a vault and stare at it. You got to treat it right. Take it out and flash it around."

A chorus of toadies standing near him echoed:

"You're damn right!"

"Can't take it with you, that's for sure."

"Might as well."

"Damn government will grab it if you don't."

The manager whispered to Mittie and me, "He can afford to throw it around. That's Ed Hade. Owns the biggest car dealership in the state. Listen to them suck up to him. He could paper the Grand Canyon with dollar bills if he wanted to."

"He reminds me of my father," Mittie said sorrowfully.

"Me," Menelade went on, "I gotta be careful. If I didn't stick it away, where would I end up? You gotta think of the future."

"You remind me of my father too," Mittie told him.

On the other side of Mr. Hade, leaning away from him, was a Marine, Black, about six-foot-four, who turned, gave Hade one long evaluative look, and then stepped sideways, smoothly, and put more distance between them. Hade was sucking the ice cubes from his glass into his mouth and noisily chewing them. As more drinks were pushed onto the counter, he swept a chunky wallet of alligator tan from his breast coat pocket. He flipped it open and spilled out a long streamer of credit cards. Then he fanned a semicircle of fifty-dollar bills at his guests like a card dealer. Everyone gasped their admiration. He squeezed them closed with a grin and stuffed them back in the wallet.

There was a smirk from the toady standing immediately to the left of Mr. Hade, a smirk of rebellion, or presumption of his host's good humor, or support of the surrounding toads. "How far did you have to chase a nigger for that Harlem billfold, Ed?"

Before we had a chance to see how Hade would respond to this question, the Black man reached across him and laid his huge hand firmly on the toad's arm, at the same time asking, very quietly, "What did you say?"

Hade laid his hand on the Black man's hand, which he removed from the toad's arm. "I don't think I heard anybody talking to you, Roscoe."

The Black guy flicked Hade's hand away and shoved him backward into the toadie. The toadie fell down. At this point the manager tried to mediate by offering advice to both parties: "Let it go. He didn't mean it," and "Come on, Hade, he'll kill you."

Hade didn't listen. Instead he lunged, swung, caught the Black man in the stomach with his first blow, glanced a soft jab off his shoulder with the second. That was all. The Black Marine knocked Hade full in the face three times and full in the paunch four. Hade sank down in a lump. Meanwhile, the toadie had clambered up the Marine's back in order to get a chokehold around his neck from the rear. The Marine reached behind him, the way you would pull off a shirt, grabbed the toadie, lifted him over his head the whole long length of his arms, and pitched him sideways into the bar window. The crash started people screaming.

By this time Hade had stumbled back to his feet. He came at the Marine, head down, his face red, his hair flat with sweat, and the Marine slammed Hade's skull five or six times into the side of the bar. When three other toadies began taking swings, Mittie and I went for them. Mittie jerked at someone's arm; the guy ploughed into his stomach and flattened him. I tackled someone beneath his knees, was kneed in the chin.

Tony Menelade ran around in front of the bar. "Okay, okay," he yelled. "Cool off. That's enough. Get the hell out of here. All of you. I'm calling the sheriff. I'm calling Booter, Hade!"

It was quiet for five seconds. Hade grabbed his wallet out of his pocket, his face on fire, his mouth open panting. He took five of the fifty-dollar bills out, stuffed them in the manager's shirt pocket, pushed him aside, and swung a wide left hook at the Black man, who side-stepped it. Half the people in the bar started in, kicking, cursing, spitting, grunting, and swinging at each other. The other half rushed to the exit. I pulled Mittie to his feet, and we were swept outside in the stampede, shoving and slipping our way through the mud.

Just then a bolt of lightning sharked down the sky with a clipped retort of thunder. It startled Mittie, and he lurched backward into the man who was pushing at him from behind. It was fat Bobbie the Shriner. Mittie had inadvertently elbowed him in the nose.

"Why don't you watch where you're going?" snarled Bobbie. "Dumb Jew."

Mittie whirled, his nostrils flared open, but Bobbie stiff-armed him into the side of the building. Mittie cracked his head against the wall, slumped to the ground, and Bobbie passed on with the rest of the crowd. Mittie and I were left alone. The rain hurt, hitting hot sweat, and a rancid smell steamed from my jacket.

I was suddenly achingly exhausted. I wanted more than anything to go home, any home, and fall in any bed. I had been in Floren Park less than thirty-six hours. And too much had happened, too much to worry over, deal with, see, too much food and drink. Too many people.

But Mittie refused to get in the Red Bus or even to step inside the theater to be out of the rain. He had the keys to both so I was handcuffed, especially since Spurgeon's Great Dane still guarded the other end of the parking lot, and any retreat back to the Red Lagoon was cut off by a patrol car that had screeched up unbearably loud and bright to the entrance of the bar; two policemen were standing in the doorway pushing people out.

So I walked over and sat beside Mittie on the bank of the creek, where he had decided to lie down for a while. The black water was rushing past us, furious, insane, slapping at the rocks and siding, almost up to the edge of the bank, so high that it hit against the bottom of the wooden bridge that spanned the creek about twenty feet up from where we were sitting.

"Look how high that water is! The bridge is going to go," I said, hoping to arouse him.

Mittie didn't answer. A cut on his cheek had opened, and rain washed the blood down, red-black through the caked mud, into his mustache. My mouth tasted salty; my tongue hurt from where I had bitten it. My head ached, so did my neck, arms, legs, and back and heart. I stared at the water.

Finally Mittie sat up and spoke. "What's the use?" he said. I agreed. He went on, "Everything I touch turns to shit in my hands. Did you see what that guy did to me?"

"Which one?" I asked. The toadie who had flattened him in the bar, or Bobbie who had slammed him into the wall outside, or Spur, or me?

"Does that to me, and what do I do? Take it! Lie down and *suffer*. The suffering tribe! I hope he burns in hell. Shit."

Listening to Mittie talk embarrassed me, made me ashamed for him and of him and of myself.

Suddenly a car with one headlight screeched into the lot behind us. It was Wolfstein's Austin Healy, now the shorter for a crushed front end. Leila got out of it. How did she know we were there? Spur? The manager? Oracles, visions, crystal balls? She had on a beat-up raccoon coat over her robe and some silver boots, probably relics of old majorette days. I stood up and called to her. Mittie grabbed my arm.

"Why did you do that?" he hissed at me. "I don't want her to see me."

He pushed up off my shoulder, digging into a bruise, vaulted to his feet, and started running along the bank, away from Leila's approach, toward the bridge.

"STOP HIM!" Leila called, and I obediently took off after him. He got to the bridge, ran halfway across, then climbed the side rail, poised himself, and just as I caught up with him, jumped. I threw myself at his back, but missed him.

"Oh, Christ, Mittie, for Christ's sake," Leila called.

Straddling the side rail, I leaned over to get a closer look at the foaming chum I was going to have to dive into in order to rescue my employer, my drinking pal, my rival. But before I jumped, Mittie's head appeared. Then his shoulders. Then his gleaming belt buckle. The water was only waist high.

We could see that he was clutching his left arm, hugging it with his right. "YUH-OWWWHH!" he cried.

Scrambling back from the bridge, I rushed to the point on the bank closest to Mittie. There I skidded down and out into the current. From shore, Leila tugged at me, and I stretched out to tug at Mittie. Slowly we landed him.

"I think I've broken my arm," he screamed.

"Well, Mittie," Leila said softly. She looked at the arm, felt it, moved it, "It looks like you've broken your watch too."

This time we did not ask Dr. Ferrell to make a house call, but drove to wake him up at his office-home instead. We found he had not been sleeping.

"I hate life," Mittie mumbled as we helped him up onto the examining table. His arm was not, after all, broken—merely bruised. He had, however, pulled a muscle, jammed a finger, and crisscrossed his legs with nicks and cuts. We told Dr. Ferrell that Mittie, slipping in the mud, had accidentally fallen into the creek. But he must not have believed us, for when we were leaving (cleansed, braced, and bandaged), he put his hand on Mittie's shoulder and spoke to him cheerfully, "I know it's enough to make you think it's not worth it, to drive you mad. I mean, if the world's that crazy, then nothing makes any sense. Kind of puts our problems in a sort of perspective, though."

We looked at him puzzledly. "What do you mean?" Leila asked.

"Kennedy." He rubbed his forehead with his hand.

"Did Bobby lose the primary? Oh, he couldn't have!" Leila moaned. The Kennedys received from her a fidelity unwavering; more absolute, it struck me, than more immediate passions.

Ferrell stared at each of us. "Where have you been? I thought you'd heard. Some maniac shot Bobby a couple of hours ago. He's not expected to live."

part two

The Land of the Lion

chapter 8

Depression

We of the Red Lagoon world survived. And even, after a while, stopped talking about the loss of Robert Kennedy too. And settled into the frenetic, yet rather enjoyably exhausting routine of performing daily before a live audience, whose critical and financial favor we courted, in the reverse order.

Two weeks went by, filled mostly with onstage dramatics, as opposed to the in-the-wings variety that had so crowded my opening days with the company. Sabby Norah got poison ivy and Mittie shocked himself sticking a screwdriver into a live socket, but otherwise routine prevailed. To my relief, I even discovered I had an actual flair for set designing, and having been complimented on my modernistic approach to *The Fantastiks* (a style arrived at by the genius of ignorance and consisting largely of the chairs and tables used during rehearsals), I felt optimistic about taking on the construction of a "real set."

With this confidence in mind, I checked out the three books on stage production, carpentry in the home, and working with wood owned by the Floren Park Public Library. These I conspicuously read over lunch and dinner. Meanwhile, I had other duties. I painted local advertisements on our drop curtain, varnished Leila's face on the barroom floor, sat with an eager smile in the box office, assisted nervously in the light booth, drove to the supermarket to buy supplies for the concession stand, and baby-sat for Maisie and Davy. At Mittie's request, I also agreed to act the part of the sheriff in the street-canvassing pantomime, though, feeling like an idiot, I was rather stiff in the role. The previous sheriff, having risen to stardom as the Belle of Black Bottom Gulch, refused to continue in the part, or more particularly, in the outfit. Her name was Margery Dosk, and she was, according to Joely Finn, heavily involved with Marlin Owen, the burly fellow who played the heroes in our mellerdrammers. It was their second mutual summer. Maisie had already told me that Marlin had a "sex book" and "smoked drugs." As usual, she was right about both, being uncannily canny for a four-year-old. She also told me another of the guys had a real glass eye.

The fact that both children seemed to take pleasure in my company during those weeks was always flattering and only occasionally annoying. I spent a lot of time with them. Together we constructed forts, painted people and places, collected interesting objects like dead beetles and strips of tire treads, made-believe, and watched our surroundings. Maisie was an excellent cardplayer (Go-Fish and Concentration being her best games), and without my detecting her in any acts of legerdemain, she consistently beat me at both. Davy was a less complicated child than his sister: open, easily happy, easily hurt. I found myself liking them.

Weekends at the Red Lagoon were much like other days, except that on two Saturday mornings, Leila got us all up at dawn to drive fifty miles somewhere to put on a puppet show at a camp where city projects children were brought to spend a week of their lives in natural surroundings. They were always glad to see her.

As for the rest of my leisure time, Verl and Dennis drove into Floren Park every once in a while. We went fishing and played *Scrabble*, and Verl talked to me; he somehow seemed to get me connected with what was going on inside of me, and I would have missed him more had I not begun to become good friends with Joely Finn, who shared with Verl some of that weight that always acted on me like ballast to a skittery craft. Joely was less hopeful, though, and angrier.

Meanwhile, Mittie and Leila had apparently signed at least a temporary moratorium on their disagreements. However, except in a business way, they appeared to see little of each other, and I, partly by design, saw less of both. I found out it had been Tony Menelade who had called Leila about Mittie, apparently who got drunk and into fights there all the time.

Nathan Wolfstein was still alive and functional, despite Dr. Ferrell's prediction, as well as his admonitions. While blocking in a scene, he would sweep and stalk around the stage, cigarette in one shaking hand, a cup of bourbon in the other, looking like a heron with the d.t.'s. His directing techniques, nonetheless, impressed me as more professional than anything else I'd seen connected with the Red Lagoon. Understanding, in a very fine, precise way, the individual limitations of his material (the company players), he still managed to elicit from them skills that surprised even the actors involved. An autocrat by intent, he was a midwife in strategy; by wheedling, coaxing, flattering, nudging, and frightening them, he delivered very good performances from very inexperienced people, while leaving them the satisfying impression that they had given birth to their own dramatic Muses. I enjoyed watching him work; it was like watching a good pitcher.

Wolfstein directed the "real plays," which were presented on Wednesday and Thursday nights when there were fewer vacationers wandering in Floren Park. Mittie remained in charge of the melodramas. The latter were our moneymakers, therefore offered to the public on Saturday and Sunday matinees, Saturday, Sunday, and Monday nights. The "real plays" were primarily for the private pleasure of the company (since few people came to see them), as well as for the education of the "apprentices." Mittie, after all, advertised the Red Lagoon Players as a "training school" for young actors, and since each apprentice paid $400 in advance for this vocational program (on his father's advice, Mittie estimated $900 per pupil per summer, awarded each a $500 scholarship because of his or her special qualifications, and asked that

76 • michael malone

the remaining $400 be mailed to him by check or money order before their arrival), it was incumbent on the teaching staff to offer instruction in more aspects of The Theater than simply that perennial favorite *The Belle of B.B.G.*

The teaching staff was composed of Mittie, Leila, Wolfstein, Joely Finn (who was a graduate student at the U.C.L.A. film school in the winters and stage manager of the R.L. Players in the summers), plus any apprentice who had been there more than one summer. The second-run apprentices were Marlin Owen, who had graduated from Ohio State and lived with his widowed mother in Dayton; his girlfriend Margery Dosk, the Belle from Indiana; and Seymour Mink, who stayed with his grandparents in Newark, New Jersey, and wanted to be a doctor. There for the first time this summer were Sabby Norah, who had just graduated from a small Nebraska high school; myself; Ashton Krinkle, a delicate young man who had a 1-Y classification, wore a black cloak, and read—or was purported to read—Swinburne in his room; Pete Barney, who was overweight and had asthma and played the piano in a bowler hat; Suzanne Steinitz, who claimed to know the Strasbergs and claimed to be from Manhattan, though all her mail came from Delaware; Ronny Tiorino, who really was from Manhattan and thought he was Marlon Brando; and Jennifer Thatcher, who was from Alabama and had sung in all her school plays and whose aching grief was that she had been born too late to try out for Scarlett O'Hara. There was one other picture on the castboard: Buddy Smith, who had never come because be had been drafted in May; Mittie left it up. I wasn't sure I wanted to spend time with any of them except Suzanne, whom I took to the movies from time to time; she hated bars, and there were no coffeehouses in town. Together we kept up with what was going on in New York.

The third week in June, Wolfstein was directing *Hedda Gabler*, and Leila had the lead. Since she had recently played the lead in *The Fantastiks* too, the Starks were charged in the suggestion box (by Suzanne) with rank nepotism. Actually, Leila kept held the latter part only two nights, before Mittie—without the slightest twinge of uxoriousness—had given it to her understudy, Jennifer, who lacked some of Leila's physical appeal, but did manage to sing on key. Regarding Leila, a guy had once yelled from the audience, "Christ! Is she going to sing *again?*"

Meanwhile, I had been diligent with a T-bar and No. 3 pencil up in my studio. And I was confident in my mastery of scenic skills. I now knew how to build a flat, making tall screens of frame and canvas, coupling them side by side into a miraculously standing wall. I now knew how to scumble, spatter, sponge, roll, trim, trip, strike, and fly. I now knew the meaning of flippers, and wagons, and two-folds, and toggle-rails, and brace cleats, stage pegs, boomerangs, tormentors. I now knew the meaning of ellipsoidal reflector.

And like the walls of a De Mule Jericho reversed, the walls of Hedda Gabler's house, complete with windows and doors, were up a good half-hour before the curtain rose on June 21st. Onstage was a drawing room smug with rummaged Victorian furniture, behind which, by opening some double doors, one could walk a few feet into a small sitting room upstage center. And then, my favorite effect, a garden cultivated stage left, with assorted trees blooming in paper-mâché on a painted backdrop, and with a white garden bench, all visible to the audience whenever Hedda chose to draw back the rich drapes that covered my paneless glass French doors.

For these triumphal edifices, I anticipated laurel; instead, I was handed birch switches by the malign fates (and by several members of the company).

First of all, my flats did not seem to fit together as well on the stage as they had in my new sketchbook; arithmetic was always my weakest subject. Instead, they tended to buckle and gape rather unbecomingly. Next, the side sections were so long that when we attached them to the back wall, there was no room left behind it for the sitting room no matter how we squeezed the furniture together. We couldn't pull the sections forward because of the permanent flats which extended from either side of the proscenium to mask the wings from the spectators' view. So our only recourse was to jockey the sides at wider angles. This took care of the depth problem, but left the back wall a half-foot too long on each end so that we couldn't lash it to the sides frame-end to frame-end in the normal secure manner, but were forced simply to lean the flats against each other, brace them, and run a rope around the back of all three sections—above the door and window lines—and hope it held them.

In addition, the individual flats (four to a wall) proved to be of rather varying heights, and gave the overall impression of a graph of the monthly stock market report. We passed it off as expressionism, but frankly it was not what one would expect in the drawing room of an upper-middle-class home.

As I stapled the last lilac, the curtain rose on these slight imperfections only fifteen minutes late. Because it was raining and both the movie houses in Floren Park happened to be showing *The Absent-Minded Professor*, our house was larger than it usually was for one of our Wednesday night classics. Forty-three accidental patrons of the arts were therefore treated, as Joely Finn cruelly noted, to the surprise drawing room comedy of the summer season.

At 8:45, having done my best by my sets, I hurried over to the lighting booth, where I was to assist Seymour Mink at the control board. The first act moved along reasonably close to the text. Only one really noticeable slip occurred, when the large portrait of Hedda's father, General Gabler, slipped off the wall and onto the head of her visitor (an elderly aunt played with the sniffles by Sabby Norah), knocking the tea from her hand and the lines from her head.

Our real difficulties did not begin until the first intermission; they continued, however, uninterruptedly, past the final curtain. Hedda Gabler (played with the smolders by Leila) had distinctly stated in Act I that she planned to remove her piano from the drawing room into her (offstage) bedroom. A writing table, she said, would be put in its place. Sadly we discovered that because of the elaborate way we had tied the set together, it was impossible to get the piano off without dismantling the walls. So we were forced to leave it onstage covered with a tapestry and to place the writing table in front of it. This cut down considerably on the acting area and hampered the actors' movements, for now they could sit on the sofa in the center of the stage, and at the same time, scribble at the writing table, which was presumably set against the far wall. Home had a cluttered look

We solved a related problem (that Hedda was supposed to go offstage from time to time to play this same piano) by scurrying around to locate a record player and a classical record, and setting them up in the wings. (Our original plan, dependent on the piano's being off in the bedroom, was to have Ashton Krinkle actually play the Chopin Nocturne he knew on it.) Unfortunately, the only classical record Pete Barney, not an aficionado anyhow, could find in the theater happened to be a symphony rather than a solo piano piece. Hedda's resulting musical virtuosity (as she walked into her bedroom and performed, alone, Beethoven's Fifth), probably caused our audience to wonder why she had not chosen a career on the concert stage as a clear phenomenon, rather than settling for the drudgery of housewifery that she so obviously despised.

Next, in Act II, Hedda attempted to walk through the French doors out into her garden, where it was her custom to get in some morning target practice with her dueling pistols. By arbitrary mischance, I had hinged these doors so that they opened inward rather than outward. However, they did not, when pulled upon, open inward either, because of the curtain rod, from which the handsome handsewn drapes were hanging: it was in the way. After tugging at the doorknobs long enough to give the audience a clear sense of her passionate nature, Leila/Hedda exited through the rear sitting room and *appeared* in the garden, allowing the viewer to deduce that there were simply other legitimate ways of getting there.

We raised the curtain rod during the next intermission and felt safe, for we knew the other double doors, those upstage center, would not jam in that way. They didn't. In fact, so far from jamming were these particular doors that when Hedda's husband (played with his mellerdrammer sneer by Mittie) swept them open, they came flying off in his hands and sent him bottom first over the sofa, upon which he executed a brisk back flip, to the applause of our now most enthusiastic audience.

In Act III, Hedda pulled back the drapes to let in the morning light from her garden, but let in instead the sight of Sabby Norah (still dressed as the elderly aunt except that she was barefoot) lying on her stomach on the bench reading *Rosemary's Baby*. Hedda's reputation for heartlessness was presumably enhanced by this intimation that she was callous enough to leave her aged, coatless, and shoeless relative outside for the night like the family cat.

But the worst climaxed, as all good dramas should, in the final act. About five minutes before the play's conclusion, Joely ran into the lighting booth to get Seymour to take over for him as stage manager because his own energies had to go into an effort to control Spurgeon Debson, who had shown up backstage, high, as Joely said, on something heavy. He was clearly upsetting the company, particularly Mittie, who had to deal tonight with playing Leila's husband onstage as well as off.

My reaction when told to take care of the lights by myself was self-effacing terror. Seymour patted me on the shoulder and quickly whispered his instructions.

"Look," he assured me, "it's simple. You don't have anything to do 'til the end. Then it's a full blackout. Just jerk down the master switch. The signal light will go on. That's your ready sign. When it goes off, pull the switch. On again, get ready. Off, push the switch up for the curtain calls. Got it? On, standby. Off, go."

And he was gone. I stared intently at the signal light for two minutes, but then the stage began to compel my attention. As the drama drew to its exciting close, a voice, not originally written into the script, could be indistinctly heard from the wings, chanting in a distant crescendo that I seemed to recognize.

"Bloodsucking… lishment! … ilitary.. . dustrial… plex! ill! Kill! KILL!!!"

Obviously, Joely and Seymour had not completely succeeded in controlling Spur's rhetorical fervor. But (as though oblivious to what might be taken as the cries of a disgruntled mob of Scandinavian proletarians outside the windows of the wealthy) the actors onstage ignored these intrusive remarks, raised their own voices, and persisted in their own world.

Hedda, profoundly disappointed by the imperfections of life (and there had been even more than she had counted on this evening), took one of her father's dueling pistols, went into the rear sitting room, and shut the rehinged doors behind her. At this point, a shot was supposed to ring out, the sound of suicide. It didn't.

Sabby Norah, who was designated to fire the fatal blank, had retired to her dressing room in tears following her mortifications on the bench in Act III. So after an uncomfortably silent wait, the three characters onstage waiting for the "BANG" jumped to their feet anyway and rushed the sitting room. Leila just had time to throw herself lifelessly into a chair as Mittie screamed, "Shot herself! Shot herself in the temple!"

At that instant, Sabby (rushing back from her hiding place to perform her duty) fired off the belated shot, and at the same instant, my signal light came on. The combination of sight and sound unnerved me, and I pulled the master switch. The theater went abruptly and completely black.

"For Christ's sake!" the apparently resurrected Hedda Gabler yelled.

What happened next was recounted to me later that evening by Joely Finn. As he'd been chanting his sermon, Spurgeon Debson had been absently unwinding some rope that connected the sections of my set together. When the lights went out, he let go, and so did my sets.

So when I jerked the lights back on, which regrettably I did before Joely could get the main curtain down, the stage was set not for the curtain calls, but for the finale of Samson and Delilah. Mittie was holding the back wall up over his head as though he were posing for a statue of Atlas. Leila was laughing on a chair in the sitting room, the ineffective pistol in her hand. Margery Dosk and Ronny Tiorino, the other two actors onstage, were crawling about under the side walls. Perhaps most fitting of all, my two sets of double doors still stood, tall and glorious as Victor Mature in the midst of a world in ruin.

Spurgeon, finding himself for the first time in his life with a sizable audience before him, seized the opportunity by running center stage, unzipping his pants, and defiantly exposing himself, as he screamed to the now screaming audience, "Can you take reality, you rich bastards, you corpses, you gassers of genius, you BABYBUTCHERERS?"

Mittie dropped the back wall down on Spur's head and silenced him.

There was one more line in the play, the final one. It was Ronny's, and he was determined to get it in. The line was, "Good God! People don't do such things!"

And that brought down the other house.

chapter 9
Somebody Turns Up

Leila drove Spurgeon to Dr. Ferrell's office. Suzanne Steinitz was sympathetic enough to attend Hedda Gabler's wake with me in the Red Lagoon Bar. But it was so crowded that I was eventually squeezed into the narrow tip of a conch shell by others rudely joining us. Pinned, I was subjected to the hollow mirth of Joely Finn and his following among the apprentices—Ronny, Pete, Jennifer.

"They jest in bars that never smelt a wound," I told them. Suzanne patted my arm.

As yet I wasn't prepared to laugh at the way somebody had turned the wine of my set designing into the brackish water of defeat.

"We sure smelt that bomb next door," Joely unfeelingly persisted. "Oh, boy. If you're gonna build Rome in a day, you know. Oh, boy, why didn't I have a camera? What a decline and fall was there! Oh, boy!" and so on.

His jocular hoard japed with him until, during a brief lull in the laughter, Sabby came by and asked me if I had picked up my mail. Usually the mail delivery figured with eager preeminence in my morning schedule. In fact, I was so often on hand for its arrival that the postman and I had developed a chatty familiarity with each other, and were accustomed to exchange weather predictions the way people do who have no basis for relationship except encounter. This postman had an apocalyptic hunger, which was continually frustrated by the mild climate of Floren Park. For as he only worked summers, he never had an opportunity to complete his rounds through rain, sleet, snow, nor dark of night, and felt misled by the job's promise of such adventure.

But my infatuation with the postal service—which is really a passion for possibility—had been superseded on that particular day by the building of a temple for Hedda Gabler. Now that Spurgeon, himself the vociferous jawbone of an ass, had brought the house down around everyone's head in his fury against the Philistines, I could turn my attention back to the possible arrival of messengers with news of home. For though I was certain that Jardin had no intention of writing to me, I insisted every day on confirming my chagrined hypothesis at the earliest opportunity. Meanwhile, I had unilaterally written to her once since coming to Colorado, just to assure her that her actions had been forgiven and forgotten.

So, extricating myself from our conch shell, I walked next door to the theater. Late-leavers were still standing about, still laughing. In the box office mail basket, three letters and a package lay waiting for me, imperturbable and composed. Nothing from Jardin, but still the best day I had had all month. The package contained four pairs of socks and a dozen very dry brownies from Mama, who never got the aluminum foil around anything properly. She had also written a long letter.

Her letters had always been long, but up in Cambridge, I had enjoyed getting them, even the ones without checks, because they were like reading books, not at all like the letters the other guys got from their parents, and that made me proud of her. Jane Austen, I would boast, could have written those letters. Typically, the news came in the first few pages; the next ten or so were observations and speculations. In this one I learned that baby Harnley was walking again (flatfooted); that Detroit might take the pennant, but not the series; that Colum had met a nurse in physical therapy who had come over for dinner and was very pleasant, despite holding rather vigorously to a "postural" view of salvation: the slumped would be damned; that having just reread *Jude the Obscure*, she thought it should be more so; that she herself was feeling intermezzo; that in regard to the awful grief of Robert Kennedy's death, America took a smug satisfaction in the way its great symbols graciously fulfilled their myths by dying off in sudden, Greek-like fashion so that they could be indulgently mourned over rather than dealt with or tired of; that Fitzgerald, who had been visiting friends in Laramie since his convention, would be arriving in Floren Park on June 25th (at Leila's invitation) and that I was to keep an eye on him to prevent him from selling uranium stock to the tourists or getting elected to some city office that would prevent his getting back to Earlsford by early August; that with regard to the pain of loss that I was feeling about Jardin…and here followed five pages of hypotheses on the attainment of personal peace.

Next I opened a letter from Verl, wishing I had him there to talk to instead. He wrote, in part: "I know you're upset about this thing with Jardin. Nobody's denying how you feel. It's just that (mind if I preach?) I think there's probably an awful lot of complicated and very ambivalent emotional motives going on in all of us, and sometimes we don't pay enough attention to parts of it. Are too lazy. I wish there were something I could do to make you feel better. Meanwhile, be glad at least to offer an ear. Be back over in a couple of days. Take it easy, okay? And you know, there's no good reason why you can't come down to Boulder one of these days. Catch a breath of serenity."

This letter was a comfort. Also a surprise, as it had since slipped my mind that in a moment of depression the previous week, I had written him a rather gloomy appraisal of my misunderstood emotional state. But now, what with the play and everything, I was depressed again, so Verl's response was a timely succour. I thought for a minute about why I didn't want to go to Boulder, didn't want to leave Floren Park; it wasn't just that there was enough new in it to last me a while; it was like a ritual. I had this almost mystic feeling that by staying, something was going to be figured out.

Verl and Mama had cheered me up enough so I could open the other letter. It was a brief note from my older brother and had his name engraved across the top of the page all in little blue letters: "james dexter donahue," with an address under it so that anybody who cared to could get right back in touch with him.

I looked it over; the message was typed, and it was signed in black ink with a bunch of thin loops and gyres. In the first paragraph, he advised me to grow up. In the second, he suggested that I was inconsiderate and selfish. In the third, he mentioned that if I wrote to Jardin again, the letter would be returned to me unopened. In the last, he assured me that the above three paragraphs should not be taken harshly, but in the spirit in which they were intended, with everyone's best interests at heart.

I decided to keep J.D.'s memo; it would be handy to have around as documentation of his character if Jardin ever came to her senses.

Feeling better, I went back to the Red Lagoon Bar. It was still crowded inside. A large-boned woman with copper hair loosely twisted up on top of her head was ringing the cash register behind the bar. Joely told me that she was the manager's wife, Lady Red. So she *had* come back to claim her estate, as Mittie and I had been gloomily warned. There were rumors she was going to change the place, maybe put in a dance floor; she liked things lively. Suzanne was gone; I sat down and watched the manager watch his wife. Menelade was right about his weakness; he looked moist with a sort of doting pleasure he seemed to take just in her simple physical reality. I watched him keep staring at her as though she might stop *being*, like one of Bishop Berkeley's trees, if he ever took his eyes off her. Then he walked past her from behind and floated his hand across her rear as he went by. She tucked in her buttocks by tightening the muscles and went on punching more buttons on the register. I recalled seeing Mittie try to touch Leila in that unacknowledging, and unacknowledged, way.

Joely was talking about the problems of being his father's only son; there were five girls in his family. And suddenly,

Nathan Wolfstein sat up from the corner of the booth. He had been so slumped into his seat that I hadn't noticed him there before then. It looked as though he might have drunk quite a bit of bourbon, but because of his shakes, only about half of each of his drinks got to his mouth, so you really couldn't judge his condition from the number of accumulated glasses.

"I have a son too," Wolfstein said. "I never met him. He doesn't know who I am."

We were surprised when Wolfstein said he would tell us the story. Twenty-seven years ago, he had had an affair with a Hollywood script girl. Though she became pregnant, she had declined to marry him. He was Jewish and she was Catholic, or maybe she simply didn't like him. His son was now Calhoun Grange, the cowboy star. Five years ago, this information had been given to him by Calhoun's mother (whom he had traced down), but she had told him only under pressure and with his promise that he would never make himself known to the boy. He didn't explain to us why he had agreed to this promise.

"I'm glad I know, though. Otherwise I wouldn't know if he were dead or alive. A child dead or living." He shook a drink over his suit and to his lips and was finished.

I wasn't sure whether I believed him or not. There had been a picture of Calhoun Grange in a magazine in the bathroom at the house. In the article he said that if his draft number had been chosen, he would have been proud to go to Vietnam; maybe that put the name in Wolfstein's head. Maybe it was true, maybe reading that would make a father want to talk to someone about his son. I supposed my knowledge of what fathers might do had always been rather limited.

Wolfstein knocked a drink over, and Joely asked him if he didn't want us to drive him home. He dropped his cigarette on the table, and I stuck it back between his fingers. After staring at each of us in turn, as if he were deciding whether or not to trust us, he finally nodded yes. We slid him out of the booth, walked him to the door, and he pointed us in the direction of his battered sports car.

Back at the house, we found Sabby Norah at her baby-sitting post again, finishing up the book she had started on Hedda Gabler's garden bench.

"Where're Leila and Mittie?" I asked her.

"Oh, didn't they tell you? They went to Denver. Leila's mother's come to visit."

"Leila's mother?"

"Leila' mother. I think it was unexpected." She went back to her book.

"Now, that ought to be something," Joely smiled.

"More than you know," I said. "We don't like each other." Leila's *mother*. Amanda Sluford Beaumont Thurston. I told him the story.

Then we went downstairs to our room and talked of America until we fell asleep.

chapter 10

A Retrospect:
The Story I Told Him

Leila's mother.

To explain Leila, just to talk about her at all, means going back beyond my own knowledge, even beyond that mother, for Leila had a past, as Southerners can and Westerners cannot. But Leila, even more than most of us.

Leila Dolores Beaumont Thurston Stark. Born of her mother's line to a repeatedly vanquished heritage, Leila's family was the paradigm (to my firsthand knowledge) of Gothic ancestry. For I knew, in synoptic telling form, the sequential defeats of her perishable forebears; nor ever thought to question them, though outlanders (I realized) suspected the stories were only anecdotes told to comply with their preconceptions about crazy Southerners.

These were Slufords.

Arvid Andrew Sluford. Her great-great-grandfather. The first, to our factual certainty, of her traceable ancestors. Mistakenly shot for a Union scout while, without prior announcement or permission, borrowing C.S.A. rations from a neighbor's tent outside Manassas.

His son Buford (Buford Sluford, out of his father's rhythmic instinct). Who drowned in the big pond in which he was convinced (by his careful reading of the one letter his father, Private A.A. Sluford, sent home—in which he emphasized wishing he could see the old pond again) that, before his departure for the War of the Confederacy, his father had sunk his mother's silver candlesticks and some ready cash in gold.

Buford had been right, not about the *whereabouts* of the cache, but about the impulse to conceal treasure. For they found, while digging his (the son's) grave—having, the next morning, fished him out of the pond where he had drowned while seeking the gold—a buried burlap sack, repository of more valuables than even Buford had predicted.

Enough to enable *his* sole son and recipient of his posthumous, or rather humus, estate, Kurbee Sluford, to implement a vision. Which he did, following it out of the scrub mountains to a small rural village in the south piedmont of North Carolina.

Kurbee Sluford. Whose dream was one of environmental pragmatism, whereby the two Carolinian contributions to the world market, the produce of alternating growth in the hard red soil, fused their separateness in an epiphanic vision granted to Kurbee. He began to manufacture cigarettes of 40 percent tobacco and 60 percent cotton. His brand, King Cobacco, was undestined, however, to rival Bull Durham. Unfortunately, no matter whether the leaves and bulbs were joined in the making or were grafted upon each other growing, people simply failed to take to the taste.

In his disappointment, he married the heiress to twelve acres of mixed vegetables, Leila Rickey.

Leila Rickey Sluford. Our Leila's grandmother and namegiver. Herself, like her husband Kurbee, a visionary, but her epiphanies increasingly sky rather than earthbound. She cared as little for the grafting of King Cobacco as the lilies reportedly care about their raiments.

The first Leila had not always been so celestial. But she had always believed in Truth, and had an awesome faith in the hierophantic powers of language to articulate that truth, even in fact to call it into being. When she was a child, this faith rested, without sophistication, in her persistent literalization of other people's metaphoric communications. So profound was her belief in the word, indeed, that when her mother found their dog gobbling up an unguarded side of bacon in the kitchen and said he ought to be hanged for all the mischief he'd caused, Leila knew as absolutely as St. Joan what she must do, and that afternoon her mother found the dog hanging by its leash from a barn rafter. Six months later, the family cat was drowned in a washtub out of the same conviction.

Ultimately, the Rickeys developed an almost Jesuitical care with the spoken word, watchfully avoiding hyperbolic throwaways like, "If we don't get some rain soon, I swear I'd just as soon be dead." But after an evangelist-inspired religious conversion at fifteen, words to Leila Rickey became The Word and Otherworldly, and the Rickeys sighed in relief for the continuation of their livestock as just that.

Once married to Kurbee, Leila now Sluford bore witness at each revival camp meeting and tent show that was reachable first by mule team, then by a Ford purchased from the canning of her inherited vegetables solely to serve as her chariot to the house of the Lord. Returning home at night in the fervor still fevering her from the laying on of sanctified hands, she conceived seven children, bore them, and left them to Christ's protection. Despite which, the three middle ones did not endure; dying respectively at five, three, and one. For some reason, the four others (two from each end of the sequence) insisted on surviving.

These were her firstborn son, Genesis, called Gene. Her firstborn daughter, Nadine. And her twins, Esther and Amanda (who was our Leila's mother).

Nadine Sluford. Embittered from infancy, begrudging and begrudged. Who concluded in the crib that life did not intend to treat her well (which it didn't) and who disliked it accordingly.

Amanda Sluford. Who was not so much angry as prudent, for she knew herself to be sane, and therefore an anomaly in her family. Whose sense, she was well aware, was simply a lucky fluke, whereby the few sane genes bequeathed her (perhaps by her paternal grandfather, Buford Sluford, who had at least realized the fact of the buried treasure, if not the site) had happened to come together in a rare stable combination. Prudent because she thought herself continually vulnerable to hereditary contagion and lived in a daily plan of quarantining her mind and body from the others until she could escape the farm and acquire the immunity of a college education.

Esther Sluford. Amanda's ripened twin. Whose acknowledged good looks our own Leila had inherited, and whom Leila compared, after I had given her the book, to Faulkner's Eula Varner, who was uneducable by lack of need and unambulatory by choice.

In all possible ways, Esther differed from her embryonic sibling. Amanda was for *doing*. Esther was, one supposed, for *being*. Not that she couldn't, or refused to do. If they yelled into her dream and instructed her, pushed her in the direction of a chore, she would carry it out. But then she would sit back down in her rocking chair on the front porch, in which she swayed contentedly, stared at by passers-by, the subject of gaped double-takes from whichever male walked past the house for the first time. And thus the object of Nadine's bitter chagrin, Amanda's social indignation.

Nadine believed Esther would disgrace the family sooner or later simply by the fact of her physical attributes, and that belief, like most of Nadine's other dour predictions, brought her, by its imminent fulfillment, Cassandra's sullen comfort—the right to remark in the midst of catastrophe, "I told you so."

It could be claimed, however, that Nadine's phrasing of her prophecy was misleading in the sense that Esther (or more simply, Esther's looks) proved to be only the inactive recipient of the disgracing action. Genesis, his mother's first creation and her chosen favorite, was the causal agent. Or, rather, the predetermined proximity in time and space of how Esther looked and how Genesis responded.

Genesis Sluford. Shared with his mother that indomitable fevered thirst for ecstasy that comprised and defined Mrs.

Sluford's integrity. It was sublunary in him, however, and honed toward earthly milk and honey, of which Genesis realized (in his congenitally granted epiphanic moment) that his then fifteen-year-old sister, Esther, was the true incarnation.

He made no plans; he just believed that he knew where the incarnate godhead lay. This certainty grew upon him for the full fasting year of his novitiate, through which his mother coddled with sugared treats, this chosen of her brood; and during which Esther (allowing fried pork rinds to dissolve in her mouth) ripened further on the front porch, swaying in her chair.

Then the moment that came to Saul on the road to Damascus came to Genesis. One July evening, sent on a chore to the barn, he found Esther there lying drowsed on a hay rick, three apple cores beside her, for she had been directed some hours previously to bring back a basket of apples to the kitchen. Esther was not sullen or uncooperative; she would go if asked and do if watched. Otherwise she simply came to a stop, being unable to retain instructions in any mechanism of memory, and waited with a somnolent patience until retrieved by a member of the family.

When he saw her there, Genesis knew himself ready for union with the host, and rushing to the fragrant golden altar with as much certainty as his mother had swooned to the platform of a revival tent, he reached for the wafers of that spirit-containing flesh, grabbed the chalice, and gulped it down. His capacity to find the actualized objective correlative (Esther) to fit the symbol (the host of the Lord) was yet another of the mother's gifts to her son. This particular act, however, was a pure apostasy, for Mrs. Sluford had given Genesis a strictly Protestant upbringing, and it had been over this very issue of transubstantiation that his ancestors had broken with the Pope centuries ago.

Esther, the manna in question, had not been made wise by the apples in her womb, but somehow this assault had at least brought her to the realization that she had a self to be assaulted. And she spoke out of that knowledge. And she began to scream, "SSSS-STAUUPPIT, GENE, STAUPPPP!" And she kept on.

Their mother, tired of holding supper for them, and coming out to select the apples herself, was given to witness this communion ritual at the instant of *consummatio*, whereupon without thought, she reached for the long-deceased Arvid Sluford's rabbit gun hanging in the tack room and shot the communicant. With which salvo, she fired Genesis out of temporal bliss and into eternal, so that he died unabused of joyful belief.

Later opinions differed as to Mrs. Sluford's motivations. Most people believed that she had failed to recognize her son and had maternally shot a presumed intruder. A few (Nadine) thought, quite in opposition, that Mrs. Sluford had not failed to recognize her son and had jealously shot a betrayer. Those who had known her as a child (the few surviving Rickeys) wondered whether there had been time or opportunity for anyone in the vicinity to have said to her, "The simple truth is any boy who would defile his own sister like that ought to be shot!"

Unfortunately, Mrs. Sluford's own comments were not available accessories to clarification, for while she spoke a lot afterward, she spoke in tongues unintelligible to the secular from whom thereafter she wholly distinguished herself. As a matter of fact, from the instant of that shot (unpremeditated, but reverberate with the doomed mischance of all the Slufords), she never said another word in Southern Americanese or in any other branch of the IndoEuropean root.

Instead she rose from the dead (after pulling up his overalls, which she neatly buttoned) and ascended into garble.

Genesis was buried in the family plot without further unearthing of treasure deposits. A deputy sheriff accompanied the small funeral cortege led by the father, Kurbee Sluford (more bewildered now than by the failure of King Cobacco to become a household word), followed by the deflowered victim of outrage, Esther (possessed of a self but bereft of a brother), and by her two sisters, Nadine and Amanda—neither of whom expected to be able to hold up their heads anywhere in the county again. This expectation decisively grew in them when their mother rose to her feet midway through the Baptist

minister's eulogy (commending Genesis for his regular attendance at Sunday school), and insisted on delivering the funeral
oration herself, perhaps (though no one present could translate
it) taking as her text, "The mother gaveth, and the mother
tooketh away."

That in any case is what the deputy sheriff did with Mrs.
Sluford. And after a long and presumably unsatisfying interroga-
tion, she was charged by the state to be taken on the thirtieth
day of July to the place of institution and there to be deranged in
the head until she was dead. And they did, and she was.

Nadine, the following year, met and married, largely to
punish him for being innately good-natured, a mild salesman
of pharmaceutical supplies. They moved to Earlsford, North
Carolina, where over the years, his disposition not so much dark-
ened as contracted to two solaces, both of which he kept in the
basement: a collection of pet rabbits and a collection of rye whiskey—the latter of which diminished as the former increased.

Esther, burdened with an identity now, relieved herself of
its weight by bestowing it with developing frequency on the
town's yeomen, knights, and landed gentry. But her democratic nonchalance in this matter so appalled Amanda that she
(Amanda) felt only relief when Esther ran off with a man who
said he owned a nightclub in Baltimore and who promised to star
Esther in his floor shows; relief even though she (Amanda) felt
quite certain that the man's terminology in regard to clubs and
shows was highly euphemistic.

Amanda, valedictorian of fourteen graduating seniors, was
awarded an Elks' scholarship entitling her to study home economics at the state agricultural college, accepted it, took the
family's sole remaining suitcase (her mother, Nadine, and most
recently Esther had made use of the other three), and telling her
father to use his head for a change, left home.

She studied with diligence and prospered in knowledge,
worked as a waitress, made her own clothes, kept herself aloof
from the frivolities of her peers, and in her second year received
a cable from her mother's sister:

COME HOME. YOUR PAPA'S TROUBLES ARE OVER. CAUGHT IN
TOBACCO MACHINE. HOPE AND PRAY HE DIDN'T SUFFER LONG.
GONE TO HIS MAKER. ALL SYMPATHY IN HOUR OF LOSS. YOUR
AUNT, LUCEEN.

But now, just when one would think she had escaped infec-
tion (by the death, incarceration, or departure of all her blood
except Nadine—least likely to mortify her), Amanda herself
came down with the Rickey-Sluford fever for ecstasy which she
had so assiduously avoided for nineteen prudent years. She fell
in love.

Brian Beaumont was a senior and now at his sixth college
in seven years. He might actually have graduated this time had
events gone otherwise, for he was inherently a bright young
man, and now he had Amanda to settle him, encourage him to
attend a few of the more important classes, write for him on time
the papers he undoubtedly would have eventually gotten around
to himself. More than quick, Brian was handsome. Blond, but
unlike all the Slufords except Esther, not the bleached eyes and
skin of the paradigmatic southern towhead; no, Brian sparkled
with bright northwestern blondness. Someone had told him
once that he resembled F. Scott Fitzgerald, and from then on,
he modeled his appearance, as well as his drinking problem, on
the analogy. However, unlike the writer, Brian never suffered
a moment's remorse—not that anyone ever heard of or saw,
at least. He was always joking, laughing, talking in a patter of
bright, quick sparkle.

Amanda had erected protective walls so far outside herself that, never expecting anyone to smile his way inside her
defenses (nor anticipating her own vulnerabilities), she had
planned no tactics for battle *within* the fortress. Outmaneuvered
by Brian's surprise assault on her heart, or whatever muscles,
nerves, chemistry she preferred to think it, she managed only to
insist on a ceremony with a South Carolina justice of the peace
the afternoon prior to her final capitulation. That in itself was
no slight achievement for one of her youth and inexperience.

But it ultimately proved a Pyrrhic victory, this through no fault of Amanda's tactics, but as the result of a technicality: a prior, uncanceled marriage of Brian's at an earlier university insisted on by an earlier young woman strategist. This very important information Amanda did not even receive until she might have predicted it anyhow, being an authority by then on the subject of Brian Beaumont's perfidies. Which misdeeds included impregnating Amanda and leaving seven months later unencumbered by either diploma or his heavily laden illegal bride.

Amanda, despite having suffered these assaults upon her dignity, reasoned that Brian's misconduct resulted purely from insanity (a disease she knew to be prevalent) and that steps had to be taken by someone responsible, i.e., herself. Not steps to recover Brian (whom she dismissed as one would a lapsed illness), but steps to insure her own diploma, that certificate of immunization she had stupidly almost forfeited.

Learning Brian's father's address from an unopened letter in his dresser, she wrote to the elder Mr. Beaumont, who immediately took a train from St. Paul, Minnesota, all the way to her side, full of indignation at his son (whom they later learned had traveled overseas courtesy of the Canadian Air Force) and full of warm support for his new daughter-in-law. Mr. Beaumont was a widower, lonely and alone, except for his housekeeper. Amanda would come and live with him. So two months later, our Leila was born, not in the South at all, but among the alien corn and wheat of her alien father's fatherland.

Six months after Leila's birth, Mrs. Amanda Beaumont (as she preferred to call herself) informed her husband's (as she preferred to call him) father that she was returning to school and that, in all justice, *he* should meet the costs, since had he not been initially and directly responsible for the mendacious Brian's existence, she never would have lost her Elks' scholarship in the first place.

He agreed. And, having loved Leila before she was born and knowing himself enthralled once he held her in the expansive crook of his arm, he also agreed—more than willingly—to keep the child. For it was clear that Amanda would not be able to manage a bachelor of arts hood and motherhood simultaneously.

In fact, in his efforts to make things right, Mr. Beaumont went so far as to marry his housekeeper, and Leila lived for six years in St. Paul, Minnesota, believing this quickly assembled and adoring elderly couple to be her mother and father.

Meanwhile Amanda graduated, received a small sum from her mother's death, bought a car, and drove it to Norfolk, Virginia, where she took a position as the purchasing agent for a V.A. hospital. There the fatal genes of Gene and the other, as she called them, fools of her bloodline caught up with her again. She met a man.

Jerry Thurston, an outpatient at the hospital, was suffering from periodic arthritis. The result, he told her, of seventy-four hours in the North Sea, where he had been shot out of his carrier. This ordeal had been followed by two years in a damp P.O.W. camp.

Thurston was dark, quiet, and without sparkle. Amanda at least knew enough not to repeat an *identical* mistake. He was an older man, thirty-eight. He told her he was on the verge of several million-dollar real estate deals in Daytona, Florida. How could she know otherwise, having only her agricultural college knowledge, which had little to say about the economics of speculative magnates? She had only been out of her native state twice in her life prior to coming to Norfolk: once, to the superfluous justice of the peace in South Carolina, and once, pregnant to St. Paul. How could she judge such possibilities? She had only her rural world's myth that Florida was a magically rich place. So she believed him. So she married him.

Mr. Thurston's enterprises remained on the verge as long as Amanda knew him. And she (who believed so firmly that education was the key to safety) was the victim again of lack of knowledge. Imagine, then, her deepened sense of injustice when she subsequently discovered that Jerry Thurston, like the distant Brian before him, was already married. To a Florida live bait stand owner. It really was enough to give Amanda Nadine's

gloomy attitude toward life to learn that she, so humble a sup-
plicant to respectability, should find always a bigamist, never a
groom. Her single consolation was that no one need ever know
of her unsanctified status, not even Nadine: in fact, especially
not Nadine. The world, Amanda discovered, asked for certificates less often than she had anticipated, though—just in case—
she still kept her high school and college diplomas and both her
marriage certificates (which appeared as substantial and proper
as anyone could ever ask of pieces of paper) in her top dresser
drawer, along with her savings account book.

Then Mrs. Amanda Thurston (as she preferred to call herself now) journeyed to St. Paul, and to the bewilderment of the
happy family there, claimed her six-year-old child. She would
soon have a home for Leila, she announced, a home with a daddy
in Daytona Beach, Florida. Leila belonged to her, she told the
elderly Beaumont couple, she had never signed any documents,
as they well knew, renouncing her legal rights. And they would
have to accept that, because should they try to prove otherwise,
she would be forced to go to court, which would of course be
a traumatic experience for the child. Whom, she added, Mr.
Beaumont had meanwhile spoiled rotten and allowed to practically ruin her teeth by a poorly balanced diet.

Mr. Beaumont was too old, too mild to fight. He acquiesced
in relinquishment, yielded to what he was told were the natural
rights of the natural mother. He did not want Leila hurt by a
battle. He let her go, settled his estate on her, and went back
to being lonely and alone, except for his housekeeper. He died
three years later.

In the few photographs of Leila taken after she left St. Paul,
the surprised look of the unexpectedly betrayed (first seen by her
grandfather when he told her that Mrs. Thurston was taking her
to Norfolk, and later saddening my mother when Leila brought
her the pictures to look at as they talked) never quite left her
eyes. How, she wondered the rest of her childhood, did I fail him
that he should let me go? In what way was I inadequate? What
is the matter with me?

She watched Mrs. Thurston with a shy wariness through their first year together. And she tried, she told me, to construct hypotheses to explain these confusing adult relationships that apparently were always so abruptly to change her own life. Had Mrs. Thurston been married to her daddy (but no, he was her grandfather) and left him because she liked Mr. Thurston better? Mrs. Thurston was her mother, but Mr. Thurston told her distinctly he was not her father and never would be. She spent a great deal of her time with him, watching him, for while his deals were still on the verge, he stayed at home, dealing out poker hands, and Mrs. Thurston kept her job at the V.A. hospital. Leila knew that Mr. Thurston disliked her, although she did not know why he felt the way he did. Nor why he took such pleasure in inflicting pain on her by surreptitious pinches and slaps and jerks on her hair or arms when no one else was around. Or why he did things that he then told Mrs. Thurston Leila had done—things like scrawling on the walls with crayons or pulling the plants out of the window boxes. Leila was punished by her mother for these transgressions, and since she was punished further for saying that her stepfather was the real culprit, she stopped saying it, and accepted the unreason of life as it continued to be presented to her.

Finally, Mrs. Thurston discovered her husband's sabotage for herself, once returning home early to find him wiping huge blobs of mud on her pink flowered rug. She sent him to a psychiatrist; by now she was a devout believer in the scientific efficacy of psychoanalysis practiced by diplomaed, and thus expensive, professionals. But Thurston having shown no diagnosable progress at the end of four years (the magnanimous time limit she had mentally set him), Amanda "divorced" him, which is to say evicted him, deprived him of room in which to play cards, and of board of far more snacks between meals than her salary could really afford. Snacks of kippered herring and sardines, whose cans he then used as ashtrays for his cigars and as repositories for the numerous orange peels he accumulated over a day of solitary seven-card stud.

Commanded to go, Thurston departed sorrowfully (after phoning in one last grocery order to tide him over on his long bus ride to Florida). His revealed destination, that magic land he was always to take her to, was by then a source of neither suspicion or regret to Amanda, for she had years ago developed so pervasive a cynical skepticism in regard to Florida land sites that she scarcely believed the state to exist physically at all, even as a swamp.

Thurston's farewell speech to the ten-year-old Leila, plenished with tearful lamentations at their forced separation and with lofty advisory warnings concerning what her future would be like deprived of him, left Leila confused. He seemed so sorry to leave her that she wondered whether perhaps he had loved her all along and whether she had loved him too, and was sorry that he, like her grandfather, was to be removed from her life without satisfactory explanation. She missed him. She even wrote to him in Florida, wrote him for two years, though she never received a reply.

Mrs. Thurston (she kept his name and a framed photograph of her second "wedding" for future verification) then, in an economy measure, transported her goods, self, and Leila down to Earlsford, North Carolina, for there, Nadine and her husband, Ethan Clyde, the pharmaceutical supplies salesman, owned a small but respectable duplex. They lived in the larger half. Amanda would get a job and rent the other side. However, finding in Earlsford no immediate position commensurate with her qualifications (educational and experiential), she was forced to take a temporary post, which she held for the next twenty years, as assistant office manager of a dry cleaning plant, whereby, she reasoned, they would at least have freshly laundered clothes on their backs.

Leila loved her uncle Ethan. She spent her early evenings in the basement with him, where they fed lettuce to the rabbits, played checkers, and hid from the calls of Amanda and Nadine as long as they dared. There Leila attempted, though without much success, to substitute her affection for Ethan's alcohol, for she knew that when he had drunk so many glasses of rye whiskey, which he kept in an old dismantled washing machine, the progressive results were fuzziness of speech, carelessness of movement, and the incurrence of his wife's (her aunt's) anger.

Leila loved but did not like her Aunt Nadine, whose housekeeping she was charged with doing as her contribution to the rent. Nadine, now quite plump, still begrudging, but unbegrudged (to her face at least) by Ethan, Amanda, and Leila, spent most of her day lying on her living room couch with her flowered heating pad, her boxes of dietetic candy, her collection of drugs for her nervous condition—supplied by her husband, the pharmaceutical supplies salesman—and her current copies of *Redbook* and *Popular Medicine*. When not reading, she watched the daytime television shows or listened to the radio serials, her favorites being those whose characters suffered year after year in a domino tumble of diseases. She would call to Leila to take time out from her dishwashing or dusting or vacuuming to come into the living room and change the stations for her.

Leila told the few of her school acquaintances with whom she forced herself to converse during recesses occasionally, (acquaintances, not friends, for she acknowledged none, nor was asked to do so), that her father had been lost in the war. Which was true in the most literal sense, since no one had ever heard of Brian Beaumont again. Then when her uncle Ethan from time to time began to stop by the school building to accompany Leila on the walk home to the duplex, she implied to these same few acquaintances that Mr. Ethan Clyde was the lost father previously referred to—now miraculously recovered and restored to the arms of his family. She told me she was unable to determine whether they received this new information with compliance, indifference, or skepticism. On the whole, she kept herself apart, in self-imposed isolation from the tribe, out of fear of hurt, out of self-deprecatory acceptance of her difference. The neat certitude with which her peers mentioned incontestable and confirmable fathers, mothers, grandparents, siblings, friends, possessions, skills, values, and preferences confused her and defined her only as alien.

So Leila's childhood passed while she dreamed of an adolescence that must of necessity be an improvement. Her uncle Ethan died. She was not surprised. Since she had loved him, his departure was to her already an inevitability. Her Aunt Nadine sold the rabbits to a grocer, and in arbitrary memoriam, never again made use of the overhead lights. Instead she kept burning two electric lamps of pink flowered glass globes, which Leila was obliged to dust daily. The widow's one other obsequy was biweekly attendance at the neighborhood Baptist church, which Amanda and Leila were therefore also pressed to frequent.

Then at fourteen, by the hormonal miracle of pubescence, Leila gained a sense of her, at least, external worth. She began in bodily form to resemble her personally unknown, but at home much discussed, Aunt Esther. At the same time, she began to command the attention not only of the male half of her peers, but of four-, five-, or even six-year male elders.

A motorcyclist (loosely associated with that awesome, distant structure, the senior high school) now substituted for her uncle Ethan and waited for her after the three o'clock bell. He was Link Richards, who, with one revolution of his Harley-Davidson, vanquished rivals before they even dared enter the ring, much less reach up to cuff his face with their gauntlets. Link was before his time in personal rebellion against the orthodoxy as to, for example, hair style, dress, and subservience to rules other than those that he himself formulated. He was the third person whom Leila had allowed herself to believe genuinely cared for her—the other two being her grandfather Beaumont and her uncle Ethan, both deceased. And so, in return for Link's affection, she was more than willing to perform those at first inexplicable manual and oral rites that he asked of her, though she already knew instinctively not to mention them to the girls who were for the first time desirous of her company at lunch and on the playground, but who were (she also knew) banded in an unadmitted tribal hostility toward her, not selfhood perhaps, but body. Nor did she mention to them that Link came to perform the companionable rites on, for her, and that she came to enjoy, to desire them.

But eventually Link himself was routed from the victor's circle by Leila's need for acceptance *inside* the tribe's citadel. He was, after all, an outlander, a barbarian. There were smoother, smaller gentlemen who sneered at his leather jacket and even at his most potent weapon, the chrome-gleaming motorcycle—which, after all, he couldn't use to storm the bastions of clubs and cliques, nor to ride in triumph on around the gymnasium during the half-time of basketball games, nor during the intermission of proms.

And in the meanwhile, eleven years previously, my own life had come to Earlsford and adapted itself happily to furnishing its own niche as one of those same smoother gentlemen.

So on an October 7th, everything former and accumulative of Leila's foundations (now fully hypothesized), beginning with her great-great-grandfather Arvid Andrew Sluford's death by mistaken password, was ready to be joined to my foundations (ending with my mother's return to Earlsford, her ancestors' home, following a nine years' Irish fling). Both our pasts had moved from their antipodes of origin and were now ready to be led inexorably by the chance impurposefulness of the gods to their inevitable conjunction.

On that day, I, hurrying from an eleventh-grade Latin class toward an American Literature class, saw Leila leaning over a water cooler in the high school corridor holding her blond hair back from the spigot with one hand, her notebook carved with innumerable initials in the other, wearing a red nylon sweater, a plaid skirt, and Dickey Brown's, the fullback's, going-steady ring fashionably beaten out of a new quarter.

And it took all that I have told (Buford's drowning, the failure of King Cobacco, Esther's burden of identity, the undisclosed marital status of Brian Beaumont and Jerry Thurston, the fall of Link Richards), and all that Leila told us of herself, and endlessly uncountable other decisions, coincidences, the probably infinite spinning tumbler of flukes, to bring Leila and myself to that water cooler at that moment.

And from there by more involutions and twined progressions out to a gray June morning in 1968 to find myself lying in a bed in Floren Park, Colorado, tapped on the shoulder by the four-year-old daughter of Leila Beaumont Thurston Stark (granddaughter of Boris Strovokov, great-great-great-granddaughter of Private A.A. Sluford, C.S.A.).

"Grandma's upstairs," Maisie said.

"Does she know I'm here?"

"She says you ought to get a job."

The reason Mrs. Thurston had flown so unexpectedly to Colorado, when she did not trust the airlines and when, as she said, this trip had already cost her more than she could afford, was that she had some bad news to deliver and needed family to deliver it to. Her sister, Nadine, had departed this mortal life. And on her own prerogative, which was the worst part of the whole thing, as far as Amanda was concerned.

For Amanda was a Catholic now and knew, she informed us, that people had no right to fly in the face of the Higher Being by killing themselves because it was for Him to give and to take away, and not something for us to decide. According to her, the Sluford family had always displayed a careless disregard of the privileges of the One Above, as evidenced by their willful insistence on disposing of themselves and their kin whenever and however they pleased. The position of the Church regarding such behavior was quite explicit and not subject to interpretation.

Ironically, it was Nadine herself who had led Amanda down the road to Rome, making her the first Sluford to travel that way since the Reformation. For Amanda had intensely disliked being obliged to walk her sister up to attend the Baptist church twice a week, as Nadine felt compelled to do in the post–Ethan Clyde days. She, Amanda, found the parishioners there so déclassé that, as she said, she frankly would be surprised if the minister himself had a college degree, much less there being another in the whole congregation besides her own.

After a particularly benighted Sunday school class in which someone suggested that there was no such thing as mental illness, just devils, Amanda quit the flock. Such ignorance was intolerable to one who believed as strongly as she did in the reality of insanity.

After that, she began taking lessons from one of the priests at the single Catholic church in Earlsford—a handsome modern structure nearly half-filled when every Catholic in the county, plus several dozen curiosity seekers attended Mass together. So they were pleased to receive Mrs. Thurston into their fold. And she was pleased with them. They knew how to do things. Properly. They were gentlemen. Why, her instructor knew Latin and three other foreign languages. She could talk to him. It wasn't like being with those Baptists who were downright illiterate, or might as well be, for all they ever got out of a book. Amanda, on the other hand, had last year read a library book every three weeks of her life, including the complete works of Mr. Thomas Costain.

So she often invited this priest to dinner and was, in general, so willing to bestow attention on him that, as Leila told me, the poor man would cut across the lawn to the rectory whenever he saw Amanda heading down the steps toward him after Mass. It was he who had recommended St. Lucy of the Pines for Leila's education and salvation for me.

Thus, because of her new faith and theories, Amanda found Nadine's suicide particularly upsetting. But by paying a late evening visit to the rectory after she found the body and by making six subsequent phone calls to the priest, she came to feel a little better. She told us why at breakfast the morning after her arrival in Floren Park.

The priest, a Father McGray, had given her the hope that her sister might have been insane. Amanda had interjected at once that such had been her suspicion for some time. Now, suicide, if deliberately chosen of one's own free will, was a mortal sin. But *insane* people could not be held morally responsible for their actions since they lacked the free will to choose good or evil. This possible loophole provoked a mixed reaction in Amanda. On the one hand, it was comforting to think that as a result of their quite evident insanity, her mother, father, brother Genesis, sister Nadine, and brother-in-law Ethan were now in heaven, where they had been, or eventually would be, joined by her husbands Brian Beaumont and Jerry Thurston and by her sister Esther. On the other hand, she rather resented it that everything, even heaven, came so easily to lunatics when *she* had to bear all the heavy responsibilities that went along with being sane.

Sitting there, I felt certain that Mrs. Thurston liked me as little now as she had the day six years ago when she came across that sonnet sequence I had written fully describing Leila's earthly delights. Sending Leila to a Catholic boarding school had cost her more than she could afford, and I could tell that when she looked at me she saw the sum total of those expenses branded on my forehead. However, now she pretended that bygones were bygones and even told me not to think she held the past against me because I was only a child then and didn't know what I was doing, whereas she was an adult and the guardian of her daughter's soul, and so she had had to do what she'd done in order to save that child from her own foolishness. But despite these disclaimers, I knew that she wasn't overjoyed to see me there. My suspicions were confirmed by a suggestion she made to me as we sat together that first morning. Or as I sat, and Mrs. Thurston scrubbed the table. She was thin, pale, blonde, and very, very thin.

"Devin, honey," she said, "a young man like you, with a college education behind you, why, you ought to be out there seeing the world, not sitting in a little dinky place like Floren Park painting on play-acting sets. You ought to be doing something exciting. Why, like teaching in a war zone! Someplace like Vietnam, where things are happening to change the very world we live in. You know, I read where the government has special jobs for young people like yourself who want to do something to help the less-privileged little ones and give them an opportunity to better themselves and seek an education."

I thanked Mrs. Thurston for this advice and kicked Leila under the table to keep her from laughing.

Leila did not seem unbearably upset about her aunt Nadine's death, although she said she was sorry that any human being should apparently have been that unhappy.

Her mother explained that Aunt Nadine had bequeathed Leila the two pink flowered glass globe lamps that she had for many years required her to dust daily. Mrs. Thurston had brought them out on the plane wrapped in newspapers in a big cardboard box. Laughing, Leila placed the lamps on the mantelpiece and said she would enjoy watching them getting filthy dirty. She gave me the newspapers, as I was eager to have some recent copies of the *Earlsford Herald* to read; I thought I might find a wedding picture of Jardin in one of them.

"Well, Leila darling," Mrs. Thurston said as she shifted one of the vases on the shelf to make them perfectly equidistant, "it's more than Nadine left to me, her only living blood relation."

Leila stopped stirring the giant pot of leftover chili still simmering on the stove for our supper.

"What about Esther?" she asked her mother. For though she had never met her other aunt, Leila still felt a deep empathy with and a strong affection for her. From periodic Christmas cards, they knew that Esther had traveled from Baltimore and the "night club" to St. Louis to New Orleans to New York, where she was presumed to be living with a man in express violation of the Holy Scriptures as well as the city ordinances.

Nadine's husband, Ethan, had in fact written to Esther once and told her that she had a niece. After that, she began sending Leila presents—a gaudy tea set, a stuffed bear, a fake ermine muff. And though Leila was fifteen when these gifts started arriving, so that the red kimono fit the bear instead of her, she treasured each present as a mystic bond between herself and the unmet aunt. She kept them all with her. The bear and tea set were now in Maisie's room.

"No, darling," Mrs. Thurston replied in her slow, precise, imperturbable southern accent. "We ass-ume your aunt Esther is still alive. If you can call the way she has chosen to con-duct herself leading a human life."

"Oh, for Christ's sake, Mother," Leila said as she sat down, threw her feet up on the table, and lit a cigarette.

"Now, Leila Stark, I have asked you many times not to use that manner of language with your mother. And I think if you will analyze your subconscious motivations, you will have to admit that you only say such things just to shock people."

Here she paused to smile at the rest of us and to direct a remark to Nathan Wolfstein. His attention at the time was more fully focused on efforts to move his cup of coffee and bourbon from its saucer to his mouth than on listening to Mrs. Thurston's conversation, but she had isolated him as the only other adult available to her, and went right on.

"You know how it is," she reminded him. "Young people have to de-fy the teachings of their elders so they can establish their own i-denti-ties. They have to think simply nothing at all of everything we ever said to them, in-cluding the importance of civilized manners!"

With that, she daintily shoved Leila's feet off the table, and removing the cigarette from her daughter's mouth, soaked it under the sink faucet and dropped it in the trash can.

chapter 11

Our Housekeeping

After dinner, I ventured to ask Mrs. Thurston what had happened to Mrs. Clyde's house.

She put down her coffee cup and touched her napkin to her lips. "I will tell you that, Devin, and you will simply not believe what Leila's aunt, my own sister, did with that duplex. Though, of course, she was not a well woman at the time she made up her testament, as her later desperate action showed only too well. But, honey, she left that entire duplex, ow-er home, to the First Avenue Baptist Church, lock, stock, and barrel. Now, that is the truth. And they are *'kindly'* allowing me, her own flesh and blood, who nursed her in those last sad years when she just lay in bed with those nervous headaches of hers, they are *allowing me* to stay on at the same rent for three months. Stay *on*. For three months! And then they are going to *sell* that duplex to the city for some undisclosed purpose."

She paused to let the impact of this protestant perfidy take effect. She nodded her head at me as I grasped the horror. The chances of her ever renouncing Catholicism and returning to her first faith seemed increasingly remote.

"That's awful, Mrs. Thurston," I told her. "What are you going to do?"

Leila gave me a funny look in response to my inquiry, but I saw no reason not to be polite.

"I do not know *what* I am going to be *able* to do. Maybe I will just go right on out to California in September," she smiled coyly, "and live with my son-in-law and his wife." She looked at Leila, whose eyes, on hearing this maternal suggestion, went from blue to steel-gray and back again.

Then Mrs. Thurston efficiently and speedily began clearing off everyone's dishes. Joely tried to protest that he had not finished with his plate; Wolfstein clutched his cup to his chest and faltered into the living room. Everyone left but Leila, her mother, and me.

As Mrs. Thurston scrubbed down the table top with a sponge, she told us in some detail the details of her sister's death.

"Nadine," she explained, "simply refused to make an effort to be happy. She was always given to a sullen disposition, as Leila here can witness, and she just got more and more soured on life as the years went by, especially after your uncle Ethan destroyed his bodily organs, as you know he did, honey, from the constant consumption of alcohol, just sat down in that basement and drank himself into the grave. Which is not something that it is easy for a wife to watch her husband do, especially a woman like Nadine who is prone anyway to look at the dark side of the street."

I nodded. Leila was making stacks of meatballs, storing them in the freezer.

"Well, she just let herself go. Sat in that house with not enough lights on to properly see by. Lay on that bed day after day watching television programs, eating sweets and undermining her system with those nerve pills (which, it might as well be admitted, are just about as addictive as her-o-in), until she simply did not have the will left in her to make an effort.

"I begged her, Devin. I went over there every single day and pleaded with her, 'Get out more,' 'Take a drive to the shopping center some Saturday.' Why, I invited her to visit my Toastmistress Club with me. But no, she preferred to lie there and complain and take a gloomy attitude. I made every effort in my power. I invited Father McGray over to advise her to get herself some professional help from a psycho-ther-a-pist, and, I'm sorry to have to say it, but she was practically *rude* to that good man."

"Mother," Leila said, as she pried the sponge from Mrs. Thurston's energetic hand, "we aren't going to *operate* on this table!" Mrs. Thurston gave up trying to restore the kitchen table top to its natural grain, and began instead to scald the dishes clean in the sink. Meanwhile, the flow of her report was unbroken.

"It got so bad, she would just leave that television set on all night long rather than exert herself to the point of reaching over and turning it off, at least until the morning shows came on. Just left the *test-pattern* buzzing away."

She sat down for a moment and dropped her voice to a whisper, "Why, Leila, she began to neglect her personal hygiene to such an extent that it was not merely embarrassing, it was downright un*pleasant* to be around her. Now, I cannot help it, that is *true*. But *somebody* had to take care of her, and who was there to do that, honey, but your mother? But even I, close as I was and watching her every day before I went to work and every night when I came home just as soon as I possibly could, even I had not realized that your Aunt Nadine was as unwell mentally as she apparently had become over the years. And you simply cannot stand over a person every single moment of the day and night when you have to work for a living and when they are unwilling to help themselves *or* seek medical assistance."

"Yes, that's true, mother," Leila said, quietly. Was she thinking of Mittie?

"It is, isn't it? There is simply no way," Mrs. Thurston shook her head. "She had saved up an en-tire bottle of those pills, and when I reached her bedside the next morning, she was gone. That bottle was right there beside her—and not a note, not a word of explanation! Her television set was still playing. Still playing on and on, and her there dead in front of the picture."

Mrs. Thurston stared at the wall with a puzzled look, then jumped up and went back to the dishes. "The doctors said she had consumed *thirty-two* of those pills, had collected them for God knows how long—and why in His name Ethan ever let her have them in the first place—saved them up, and consumed them late that very evening. I have had many tragedies to bear in my life, Leila, sorrows I have not burdened your young heart with."

Here Leila rolled her eyes to the ceiling and lit another cigarette. She looked to me as though she might be playing an imaginary violin in her head.

"But when I saw your Aunt Nadine lying there that awful way in that dusty room"—Mrs. Thurston paused as if to let us call up the image in our minds—"why, if it hadn't been for Father McGray's comfort, I doubt I could have gotten through it."

By that point, Mrs. Thurston had finished washing and inspecting all the dishes, including those we had not used on the shelves. She had even emptied the sugar bowl into a measuring cup, washed it, returned the sugar, and then washed the measuring cup. This done, she popped off her rubber gloves and sat down. She believed, she said, in doing things right.

In order to accommodate her mother, who was visiting, it seemed, for an unspecified length of time, on leave from the dry cleaning plant, Leila had to make a few alterations in our living arrangements. Seymour and Sabby were deported to the company boarding house downtown, and their room was made over for Maisie and Davy, so that the children's grandmother, who didn't think it would be proper for her to be sleeping in the basement with two young men (Joely and myself), could have their room.

This usurpation of territory did not endear Grandma Thurston to Maisie, nor did the child receive with docility Amanda's persistent directives on her behavior, manners, language, cleanliness, and godliness, in none of which areas the child was, in Amanda's opinion, making enough of an effort. Maisie pointed out to her grandmother that she was not her mother, and that, lacking such authority, she might do better to mind her own business. Amanda had begun by saying that

Maisie certainly was a precocious little girl; she ended by observing to Leila that the four-year-old might not have been raised with the proper respect for her elders, an attitude that perhaps should be closely watched, since it often indicated underlying sociopathic tendencies, and even criminal impulses. To this, Leila repeated, in effect, that Mrs. Thurston might do better to mind her own business, and in this echoed suggestion, Amanda heard once again the battle cry of her age-old foe, a mad genetic inheritance; in this case, as with Genesis's, congenital failure to honor thy parent.

Meanwhile, to my surprise, Mittie and Mrs. Thurston seemed to get along beautifully together. Leila said one day that she had read somewhere that everyone marries his or her mother, and while she had been at first skeptical of this theory, she had subsequently admitted to herself that her mother and her husband had a lot in common.

"Now, Mittie honey," Leila would say, playfully addressing me in a brisk imitation of her mother's voice, "you have a college degree, and I myself have attended college for four years and received my diploma, and so I know you will understand what I am talking about: that it is the good Lord's blessed truth that our darling Leila is simply not a terr-i-bly neat person. Now, that is a literal fact that simply cannot be denied, darling Mittie. Our Leila is...well, honey lamb, she is a little ole pig. And the reason she is this way, darling angel, as any professional psychoanalytical therapist who has his diploma would tell you himself, is that she just *will not* exert herself to the point of making an effort."

Well, as a matter of fact, the house had been considerably cleaner since Mrs. Thurston joined us. Plastic runners extended like an artificial starfish from the front door to all other parts of the house. It served the purpose of prohibiting us from bringing the outdoors inside on the bottoms of our shoes because everything belonged in its rightful place, and earth and grass were definitely not meant to grow upon the floor.

The fireplace was vacuumed daily, the toilet bowl water was bright blue, the rooms were sprayed with aerosol pine-scented fresheners that, as little Davy remarked, smelled nothing at all like the pine trees outside the windows. In a week's time, you could eat off the floors, the counters, the beds, the window sills, and the chairs. You could eat off the table too, as long as you kept a firm grip on your plate—for Mrs. Thurston so disliked a dirty dish that she stared at your plate as Tantalus must have looked at the fruit suspended just out of his reach by the gods. She was as quick to clear as an eager busboy in an Automat.

During this sanitizing, Leila refused to allow her mother inside her bedroom, so she and Mittie enjoyed an oasis of clutter while the rest of us lived in a desert of order. Leila and I were sitting before the fire one evening, she singing to Davy on her lap, while I worked on a poem about Jardin. I asked her if she wouldn't admit that she went out of her way to be messy around her mother. "You're the one always talking about the importance of structure. Structure. Structure. Structure," I said to her. "Then what's wrong with having some order in your surroundings?"

"Nothing," she replied, leaning back in the couch, slowly smoothing Davy's hair. "But not that way. Listen, I used to be just as compulsive as my mother, just the way she brought me up. Crazy. And you know what I decided? It's doing things on the outside because you're too damned scared to look at the inside. So, when I talk about structure in life, I don't mean that crap. I mean having a meaning. I mean trying to learn how to just sit still inside yourself. Liking what you are. Peacefully, and with some kind of, well, gracefulness. And I've taught myself how to drop a lot of the outside crutches because if I let myself get started on that shit, I'd be down on my knees next to her, scrubbing out the drainpipes with a toothbrush."

Every now and then, Leila would come out with statements like this. They always surprised me. Usually, she was more diffident; slightly insecure, I imagined, about her lack of college education, she would hesitate, blush, and stumble over the pronunciation of words, sometimes even words you knew she knew.

Then, all at once, she would burst forth with a barrage of argument on politics or ethics or whatever, as if she dared you to challenge her logic. Occasionally, when we were dating, it occurred to me that she might be just pretending that I was inordinately brighter than she was and her intellectual guide.

The day that Mrs. Thurston arrived, Jennifer Thatcher had, with unprofessional irresponsibility, gone to Aspen to visit a college friend for a few days. So Mittie begged Leila's mother to take Jennifer's part in our next melodrama, A *Daughter's Ruin and a Mother's Prayer*. The part of the mother. At first, she modestly demurred; she was not a trained stage performer, she explained to him, and had never considered appearing behind the footlights before a live audience, though she appreciated Mittie's confidence, and though she certainly wished to make herself useful in any way she could. Mittie assured her that anyone who had served for two consecutive terms as Co-Chairwoman of the Toastmistress Club could not fail of theatrical success, especially someone of her intelligence and education.

Finally she accepted. She studied her part diligently and, during rehearsals, exerted herself to such a point that Mr. Wolfstein began drinking twice as heavily as he had before she joined the company.

As she delivered each speech, she would walk to the footlights, shade her eyes with her hand, and call out to Wolfstein for confirmation. "Now, was that all right, Nathan? Or would it be better if I said it this way, 'A-lasss, where *shall* I find the money to save my hapless child?' You know, accentuating it like that?"

Wolfstein would invariably reply, "Fine, Amanda, you're doing fine. But let's go on through the play and see what we've got in a broad run-through. We can work out the fine points later."

She would smile, nod, return to her speech, and be back peering out in five minutes, "Or maybe it should be, 'A-lasss, where shall I find the *money?*' Would that be better?"

Rehearsals began to run three or four hours longer than usual, as Amanda exerted herself through a line-by-line linguistic analysis of her part. Leila told me that now I ought to understand what her mother had asked of poor Father McGray: "But suppose cannibals tortured you and then you denied Christ because you were afraid you would be eaten if you didn't, now would *that* be loss of faith? What is the difference between despair and just, you know, being depressed? Am I remiss not to spend more of my time trying to convert the people at the dry cleaning plant?"

Amanda spent a great deal of time talking at Wolfstein, even apart from rehearsals. She solicited his advice on personal and philosophical issues, prepared healthful snacks to pick up his appetite, and warned him not to abuse his body, which was the temple of his sacred soul. He began leaving the house at dawn and retiring to his room immediately after dinner. Amanda did not take this behavior as a personal slight, but told him she was delighted to see he was letting his organs get the rest they needed. Wolfstein told Mittie that he felt certain Tennessee Williams and not God had created Mrs. Thurston.

On opening night, Amanda was a great success in A *Daughter's Ruin*, etc. At first she herself had thought that the play was failing miserably; no one had really explained to her that the melodramas were played completely for laughs and not for drama. The regal indignation with which she stared down the audience for their disrespectful attitude only delighted them more, and they gave her a big ovation at the curtain calls.

During this time, Leila and I had become much closer than we had been in the several weeks subsequent to that first rainy night. I think she needed an ally in her stand against the past, a past that her mother represented, and I was the one person there with the relational longevity to fill that role. My memory was to be her witness for the prosecution. Soon we began going over to the Red Lagoon Bar together and reciting over drinks the litany of our shared recollections. I liked being with her this way. She sympathized with my pain over losing Jardin to James Dexter. And so I decided I had been wrong to doubt the reliability of her feelings for me as I had done in the weeks since the night of the storm. Now things were right again.

Then one evening after I had returned from marching the streets to advertise Mrs. Thurston in *A Daughter's Ruin*, Leila confided to me that she was worried about Spurgeon Debson, that he seemed lost and confused (!), that she cared a lot about him.

"Not, I assume, for his engaging personality or political wisdom."

"No," she said, "I care about him. Like I care about you."

To be coupled with Debson dampened my spirits and made me feel like a fool sitting there in that stupid sheriff's outfit. Besides, I had a feeling it was really because she thought he was great in the sack. I excused myself and left the bar.

And having decided that, after all, new friends were more reliable than old flames, I searched out Joely Finn and invited him to come over to the arcade shooting gallery with me. Pistol in hand, I saw myself black-fur caped at dawn in a Russian forest facing Spurgeon at fifty paces. For scoring a bull's-eye, I won a plastic dish with the profiles of J.F.K., R.F.K., and Martin Luther King stamped on it. As we left, we saw Leila coming up the arcade with the three old Mexican women who hung around the streets in the summer selling weedy flowers to tourists. I ignored her.

Across the theater parking lot, Mittie was sitting over by the creek. He had a rope in his hand and was idly tying a noose in it, untying it, tying it back. Squatting down beside him nonchalantly, Joely and I threw some twigs out into the quick brown current and waited quietly to see if Mittie wanted somebody to talk to. I didn't imagine he would.

Mittie had been acting very withdrawn and distracted in the last week or so. That was why Wolfstein had taken over directing the melodrama as well as the "real" play. Mittie spent his time up in the lighting booth, or off in his room, or over by the creek, reading book after book about wars. Or he was in the bar drinking. He had hit Maisie and yelled at Davy. They avoided him. So did most everyone else. I didn't know Mittie well enough to judge how different this was from his normal behavior; I was worried that he realized Leila was reinvolved with Spur, but I didn't want to say anything about this to Joely because I wasn't sure *he* knew. He had never mentioned it.

After a long silence, Mittie looked up moodily and told us that he'd rather be by himself. So we walked on home without him. On the way, Joely said he had found a length of rubber pipe in the trunk of Mittie's bus.

"Good God," I said. "He's acting like he's going to commit suicide or something. Why doesn't somebody do something?"

"Like what? What can you do?" Joely shook his head. "He's been acting like that since I've known him. You know, Mittie really wanted to succeed as an actor. It meant everything to him. Now here he is, dependent on his father even for this. Of course, the way actors play with their emotions, you can't be sure what's going on. He was the same way about drinking."

"Which he's back to," I pointed out. "*And* so's Wolfstein. Is that performance too? With the state his liver is in?"

"I don't know Mr. Wolfstein as well as I know Mittie Stark," Joely said. He kicked a piece of gravel, and it spun down into the dirt gutter.

The next afternoon, Leila picked Fitzgerald up at the bus station in Denver and brought him back to Floren Park. He told us he had been elected president of his conference and showed us thirty-six photographs of the assembly hall. He also had two shopping bags of Salt Lake City memorabilia with him, including a quart bottle of the lake water.

Everyone in the company seemed to take to Fitzgerald immediately, and he was quickly at home in his Red Lagoon Players sweatshirt and with his cot at the boarding house. He preferred to live there rather than at the Starks', so I didn't really see that much of him, which I occasionally felt guilty about; unnecessarily, for he loved summer stock life. Exciting as politics, he exclaimed.

Mittie put Fitzgerald in charge of the concession stand for the duration of his stay, and it was the only time that part of the business ever showed a profit. Under his management, popcorn soared from a dime to a quarter; the ratio of coffee grains to cups of water shifted to the weak side. Even the company members were now required to pay for their refreshments. Before, we had simply taken Cokes and candy whenever we liked. Now the counter and the freezer were locked, and you had to sign a voucher for whatever you wanted. Fitzgerald was like a relentless Pinkerton man in tracking down apprentices who failed to record what they took or were behind in paying up their I.O.U.s.

Mittie was impressed; he offered to promote Fitzgerald to company business manager if he'd come back the next summer. Mrs. Thurston said he was a very enterprising and sensible young man; her tone implied that these were two of the innumerable qualities one would not expect to find in a Donahue. Sabby Norah lost all interest in Seymour Mink and became noticeably enamoured of Fitzgerald, who, despite his youth, looked quite prepossessing in his seersucker suit as he counted the concession stand receipts every evening.

Seymour Mink was having other troubles as well, more immediately problematic than being usurped in both theater finances and Sabby's heart by my younger brother. The boarding house apprentices, led by Marlin Owen, had not taken kindly to Seymour when he was deported to their lodging after Mrs. Thurston's arrival. Sabby was forgiven, but they decided to punish Seymour for ever having lived in the "big house" in the first place.

So a guerrilla campaign began. And barbarism chose sides.

The day after he arrived there, he found all his bedroom furniture carefully arranged in the hall, and his room sprayed with shaving cream. His bed was short-sheeted; a bucket of green paint was dropped on his head; the double-framed photographs of his father and mother disappeared and showed up in the theater lobby as WANTED posters; his shorts showed up on the branches of a tree in the front yard; two mice showed up in his top drawer; and a package of Mexican condoms was sent with his love to Mrs. Thurston.

After suffering a week of such hazing, Seymour told Joely in tears that he was going home to New Jersey. So Joely and I determined on a counteroffensive. (Fitzgerald sided with the company.) We struck directly at the leader of the opposition by sneaking into Marlin's bedroom while he was sleeping and wiping off his eyebrows and sideburns with Nair Hair Remover.

The feud escalated. Marlin's girlfriend Margery (who had taken over command since Marlin was reluctant to come out of his room until his eyebrows grew back) put a mousetrap in Joely's stack of *Ramparts* magazines and almost cost him a finger. Somebody put cayenne pepper in Fitzgerald's coffee machine, and customers asked for their money back. Sabby's old affection for Seymour reared itself, and when Pete Barney, the fat piano player, played wrong notes loudly throughout Seymour's onstage tenor solo, Sabby sneaked into the shower and snapped a photograph of Pete in naked girth, which she pinned to the theater's portrait gallery entitled "Before?" We were impressed by her unexpected flair.

Like a chain of firecrackers, the company crackled in a series of cruelties, the herd-supported raze of summer camps, fraternities, of armies.

A weekly discussion of general company business was held regularly after Saturday night dinners, and for these occasions, the home residents came over to join the rest of the company at the boarding house. This boarding house, set back off one of the the town's gaudy main streets, was a three-storied structure of Victorian gingerbread, yellow with brown latticework, and bordered on two sides by a wide porch. Apart from the Red Lagoon apprentices, there were usually a half-dozen other guests (weekly vacationers or commercial travelers), most of whom, apparently, preferred to eat elsewhere. The landlady, a Mrs. Booter, was the sister-in-law of the local sheriff and the widow of a man whose photographs, citations, and personal effects decorated her dim parlor.

In the dining room were two long wooden tables. Mittie always sat at the head of one for these business dinners; Leila sat at the other. Nathan Wolfstein ate at a small separate table, where he had lately and enthusiastically been joined each week by Mrs. Thurston. On the Saturday after "Operation Seymour" began, Mittie sat at his table morosely drinking tequila, so Leila opened the meeting. She began with an exordium regarding the feud and, with some annoyance, addressed herself to our presumed common sense and incipient maturity, and called for an end to hostilities. She acted as though she were about fifty years old, and somehow managed to pull it off, to the extent that everyone seemed to feel a little sheepish. So, after a brief parlay, the denuded Marlin shook hands with the green-haired Seymour, and a cease-fire was declared.

During this conference, an elderly, soiled waiter, assisted by the cook, an equally depressing middle-aged woman, served our food. (Mrs. Booter generally ate alone in her mausoleum to Her Departed.) Both her assistants looked on the company with suspicious hostility and frank curiosity; it was obvious that they considered us potentially dangerous. And one had to agree with Mrs. Thurston that neither the clothing, the language, nor the table manners of the apprentices were of the most refined quality.

For one thing, because the food was neither plentiful nor appetizing, the collective idea seemed to be to get down as much of it as you could before the taste hit you. We who were used to eating at home under Mrs. Thurston's eager hand, however, appreciated at least being able to finish our meals—whatever their quality—before the plates were snatched away. And so, despite the savor, we tended to proceed at a more leisurely pace than the regular boarders.

For that reason, as Marlin and Seymour were affirming their treaty by leaving the room side by side, I was still trying to soften up my stolid tapioca pudding by beating it with my spoon. A door slammed. And Spurgeon Debson appeared in the dining hall.

chapter 12

I Assist at an Explosion

There seemed to be some sort of automatic emote mechanism in Spur which went into effect whenever he was confronted with a gathering of one or more persons.

Here was a whole roomful.

"What a picture! The sons and daughters of New Rochelle and San Clemente. Stuffing our little shiny faces while kids starve in the ghettos. Groovy!"

Joely spoke for everyone, "Why not cram it, Spur?"

I looked at Mittie and at Leila. Leila looked at Spur. Mittie looked at his plate. Mrs. Thurston tapped her napkin to her mouth, then folded it and replaced it on the table, and looked around for the hospital attendants and the police. Everyone else watched the principals.

Spur pulled two handfuls of silver jewelry from his blue jeans pockets and flung them onto the table nearest him. A necklace landed in the bowl of stewed tomatoes.

"Okay," he said to the assembled young ladies of the company, "Put 'em on. I'm closing out the business. Remarkable, isn't it? Me! Hammering out trinkets to stick in the fat ears of infantile chicks! Wow!" He shook his head vigorously over this amazing situation, weaving it like a maddened bull labyrinthed with unappetizing maidens.

"What is going on?" Mrs. Thurston asked Nathan Wolfstein.

He replied in an almost dreamy tone, "The playwright's back, it seems, and he's high...it seems."

Mrs. Thurston did not seem to consider this a satisfactory explanation.

High or not, Spur was certainly not looking his best that evening. His cheeks were flushed, perspiration beaded his face, and his pupils were as large as a night cat's.

Suddenly he slammed his fist down on the table and began yelling, "Who do you people think you are? Do you think you know what the theater is all about? People like me sweating in pain writing the TRUTH about this garbagepile world; but no, you couldn't be bothered putting my plays on, you're too busy wiping your baby-pink asses on COTTON CANDY!!!"

Mrs. Thurston again asked Wolfstein for information: "Would somebody mind telling me what is hap-pening? Who is this person? Is he un-bal-anced?"

"Lady," Spur said to her, "you want to ask your palsied pal there to stuff his snot rag in your stupid mouth?"

But that was not what she wanted to do. Insanity had never frightened Mrs. Thurston any more than cows frighten people who have been raised on dairy farms. She stood up and shook her head. "I really think this has gone far enough," she told us. "Mittie, call the proprietor!"

Spur opened his mouth, then closed it. His eyes widened with a startled look, then he lurched forward, fell to the floor, and cracked his head on the edge of the dinner table as he slumped down. Someone screamed. Leila jumped up. So did Mittie, who called out her name sharply. "Leila. Don't!" She looked at him puzzledly and frowned. Then she knelt down beside Spur. He was conscious and rubbing his forehead; his eyes were blank. She helped him to his feet and stood supporting him.

"Leila!" Mittie called again. "Don't do it. I mean it, Leila. If you don't get away from him, that's it!"

He kept saying more of the same as Leila braced Spur with her arm and walked him out of the room. Then Mittie just stood there at the head of the table until Joely came over, soothed his shoulder, and sat him down.

Wolfstein said that the meeting was adjourned, and the company should be at the theater in one hour. Most shuffled out quietly. Everyone was embarrassed. At his little table, Wolfstein poured himself a drink from a pocket flask. Mrs. Thurston was too absorbed to notice, much less advise him against this misuse of alcohol. She walked over to Mittie.

"Would you please explain this situation to me?" she asked him. "I do think, as a mother, I have a right to ask. What is my daughter's involvement with that…deranged person?"

Joely answered her. "It's nothing to get upset about, Mrs. Thurston. We've had some trouble with that guy, but he isn't going to hurt anybody. Leila's just trying to smooth things over, that's all."

Mittie gave a short, high, ugly laugh. Joely motioned for me to get Mrs. Thurston away. But before I could maneuver her out of the room, Mittie began in brittle gasps. "Amanda," he wheezed, "when you raised that bitch, you raised a class-A whore."

She turned back against my lead. "Mittie! What is the *matter* with you? I never heard you talking in such a way in all the years I've known you."

Mittie didn't reply. She sat down beside him, "Mittie," she cupped his chin in her hand, "tell me honestly, is your marriage undergoing difficulties?"

Mittie jerked his head back and blew a laugh all over the table top. Amanda stood up and looked for reason in the person of Nathan Wolfstein.

But as Wolfstein swayed past us to the door, he just patted Mrs. Thurston on the shoulder. "Amanda," he said, "your Leila's a good woman even if, as the young people would say, she do like to ball."

This remark, from a Pro-fess-or, dropped Amanda back into her seat. She shook her head at each of us in turn. "Well, I never," she faltered, "I simply don't know what to think."

I believe it may have been the only time in her life she had made such an admission.

This public disclosure of marital difficulties took place on the evening of July 3rd, at a time when Floren Park was crowded with holiday tourists. A traveling carnival had set up its rides and booths in the wide dirt field we used as a parking lot. Red, yellow, and blue neon lights sputtered over the field to the whirring buzz of a huge black generator. There was an over-sweet smell of candied apples and spun sugar in the air. Children screamed with happy terror in the spinning rides.

We expected a large audience at the theater that night and again on Independence Day. Joely and I went over there from the boarding house to set up for the evening's performance of *Our American Cousin*, which Mittie had chosen in honor of the national holiday. It was the melodrama that had been playing at the Ford Theater the night Lincoln was assassinated, and it was a favorite of Mittie's, as he was a Civil War enthusiast: in fact, a person of nationalistic impulses, in general, who put a flag out in his yard on American birthdays and commemorative occasions. (To Joely's radical annoyance, there was one in front of the theater and the summer house now.) So, for this production, Mittie and I had researched the original staging of Our American Cousin and had tried to reproduce them as nearly as possible. He had thrown himself into this project with a silent, relentless energy that a little disturbed me. He was also playing the lead; Leila was not in the show.

Mrs. Thurston had come to the theater with us, and when I finished checking the set, she asked me to drive her back to the house. We borrowed Wolfstein's car, for the Red Bus was gone. Mittie had disappeared; so had Leila.

Mrs. Thurston had become very concerned about the children, whom Sabby was baby-sitting back at the house, and she talked about them on the way home. It was as though *her* knowledge that all was not in its proper place with the Starks had immediately been given to Maisie and Davy too, and had altered their perceptions of life's stability. She also seemed to fear that the unbalanced Spur would do "Leila's poor babies" some mental or physical damage before she could come to their rescue. To the children, and to Mittie, she assumed a, "I will never desert Mr. Micawber," attitude. For, as she said, until Leila could be brought to her senses, someone had to stay sane and hold things together.

Meanwhile, her tone toward me was cooler than usual. She was forced to talk to me because she had to talk, and I was the only other person in the car. But she blamed me *because* she was talking to me. It was also clear that somewhere inside her, she suspected that I was the cause of the entire situation, either directly or ultimately.

"I hope you will now begin to understand, Devin, why parents often have to take actions that may seem harsh to those who do not have to assume the responsibility for a child's upbringing. And you know that it is the truth that Leila was a good, Christian, and obedient child until you two started going around together defying me."

Either Mrs. Thurston chose, for rhetorical effect, to bestow on me undeserved credit as the first to lead Leila astray, or the significance of Link Richards, Dickey Brown, and my half-dozen other predecessors had never been brought to her attention. (As a matter of fact, though I had never admitted it to Leila, when I met her she taught me all the carnal knowledge I knew at the time. And such was her expertise, it was as much as I knew for many years afterward.) However, I accepted my crown of primrose leaves from Mrs. Thurston without disclaimer, and she continued.

"Devin, you cannot deny that you encouraged her to sneer and scoff at my values, to make fun of her own mother. I know that you took part in this because that child would come home and tell me to my face that I was an ig-nor-ant woman and had denied her op-por-tun-i-ties for culture. Now, Devin, everybody knows that you were always a bright boy, and now you have gone on to Harvard University, and I am sure your family is proud of you—but I have also attended college for four years and received my diploma, and I did not deserve to be mocked by you and by my own daughter. By my only child."

Actually I did remember having frequently remarked to Leila that her mother did not know her ass from a hole in the ground, and it may have been that Leila quoted this conjecture to Mrs. Thurston directly and cited her sources.

At this point, it seemed incumbent on me to make some sort of reply. And I was also willing to let bygones be bygones. "Mrs. Thurston," I said, "I hope you will believe me that I never encouraged Leila to say such things to you."

This at least partly mollified her. "Well, Devin, it may be that you did not in-*tend* for this to happen."

"No, ma'am, I certainly didn't," I nodded.

She came 'round a little more. "You know, honey, that when things got to the point of her not respecting her own parent, why she left me no choice. Why, I had to send her off to St. Lucy's for her own good."

I saw then that Mrs. Thurston was worried—either that the present marital difficulty stemmed from her parental decision years ago or that Leila would say it did. She wanted support for that decision to forestall either guilt or blame.

"I understand, Mrs. Thurston. That was the only thing you *could* do. We were just too young to know what we were doing, both of us." As I spoke, an image of Leila's disgusted look flickered uneasily for a second inside my head.

"That is exactly right," she agreed. "And now that you are older, you can appreciate what you put your own mother and myself through in that awful year."

This double *ad matrem* argument was a little unfair to Mama. For what Mama had mainly objected to in my youthful romance (besides the volume at which Leila and I kept the record player going with my Rachmaninoff records, which jangled in Mama's hearing aid) was not our going together, but the reverse—the sudden and, to her mind, ungentlemanly way I had broken up with Leila, of whom she had been, and continued to be, very fond.

Mrs. Thurston hadn't finished yet. "Of course, once she set herself against me, it was hard to keep any influence over her at all. Why, you remember how wild she acted when she came home from her senior year. Drinking. Being escorted to the door at insane hours of the night by total strangers to myself, and I actually sometimes believe, to her as well! Just like Esther! Just like her! Why *nobody* could talk sense to her!"

Her mother snapped open her purse, took out her hand-kerchief, and stabbed at her mouth with it. "Then *refusing* to go get a college education and just packing up and coming out to Colorado, a thousand miles from home! To be *an actress!*"

I kept nodding.

"Why, she just went wild, Devin, as you yourself will acknowledge, until it got to the point that I did not even know my own daughter. Then getting married out of nowhere. At eighteen! Now I have come to love Mittie as though he were my own, and he knows that I love him, and no one could care more about those poor babies than their grandmother. But it is transparently clear from what is happening right here and now that Leila was not ready to take on the responsibilities of motherhood, as I could have told her if she had ever bothered to ask for my advice. Which the Lord knows, she never did. And then, *and then*, the minute she turned twenty-one, giving that *entire* inheritance from her grandfather Beaumont—who was a pure fool to have left that money to her that way—giv-ing it *all* away to St. Lucy's, when, Devin, she had children of her own to raise! Well, don't ask me to explain it."

As Mrs. Thurston paused for breath, I pulled into the driveway and helped her out of the little car. We found Maisie and Davy asleep, seemingly unaffected by the disclosures at the boardinghouse dinner. I left them to the solicitude of their grandmother, and Sabby and I drove back to the theater, she in her Victorian bustle, me in my sheriff suit.

"Oh, I hope everything's going to be all right," Sabby said, glancing back at our house, where on the front porch moths crashed into the bare electric light.

Backstage, Joely was explaining to the company that the breach between Mr. and Mrs. Stark was only a minor misunderstanding. While no one really believed him, the assertion in itself was a relief. The company liked both Mittie and Leila; nobody wanted to choose sides. The villain was Spurgeon Debson, who, since his extemporaneous exhibitionism in the last act of *Hedda Gabler* and at the dinner, was pretty much *persona non grata* in the Red Lagoon Theatre.

"Was Mittie at home?" Joely asked me.

"No. Isn't he here? I thought maybe you'd found him back in his office."

"No. I saw him down by the creek a while ago. Reading *Othello*." Said he wanted to be alone. So I left him alone. I figured he'd come on inside after he cooled down. So now the curtain's supposed to go up in five minutes, and Mittie's supposed to be standing center stage when it does! And where in hell is he? Jesus!" Joely jerked his fingers through his hair 'til it stood out like a bright crimson sunset.

"What are we going to do?" I asked him.

"Well, Ashton's been understudying. He says he knows all the lines. I guess he'll be okay. Man, what a mess. You know, Mittie got a letter from his father last week telling him this was the last summer he was going to shell out for the stock company, and Mittie better resign himself to Portland and an office at the Metal Works. That's what's driven him nuts like this."

I thought it was Spur.

After the show that must go on went on without Mittie, Joely and I left Marlin in charge of closing up, and we borrowed Wolfstein's car to patrol the town. Neither Mittie, Spur, nor Leila had been seen for hours, and we weren't sure who had the Red Bus as part of an impromptu property settlement. But if Spurgeon and Leila were in Floren Park together, I thought we ought to find them before Mittie did. I felt slightly melodramatic and a little excited. Joely said that the day before, he had seen Mittie setting fires behind the theater, throwing on them papers, books, even costumes. He had hidden Mittie's sleeping pills. But there were other possibilities: he even had the *Hedda Gabler* gun.

First we stopped next door at the Red Lagoon Bar. Lady Red told us that none of the three had been there and added that she didn't want any trouble. Her husband stood behind her and nodded. Next we tried the other bars, the fairground, the dance hall, the arcade, the motels, hotels, hostels. I even called Verl. He said, "Well, if the guy was passing out, she probably took him to a doctor." So we called Dr. Ferrell's office and learned that Leila *had*, in fact, brought Spurgeon there, but they had left some time ago. We kept searching. Nothing. Finally we gave up and went back home.

There we found the children still asleep and a bathrobed Mrs. Thurston inquiring of Wolfstein's looked door whether he was certain he wouldn't have a cup of hot cocoa. He was quite certain.

We reported the failure of our mission to her, and she shook her head sorrowfully. Pulling a chair up beside the tidied fireplace, she sat down. "Why, Devin, I really do not know what to make of this situation, and no one has bothered to offer me an explanation that I can consider satisfactory at all. Just what is the matter with Leila? She was not brought up to act in this manner."

Joely and I stood in front of her looking at the absent fire.

"Well," she concluded, standing up, "I am obviously to be kept in ignorance by everyone, including my own son-in-law and my own daughter."

"Well, ma'am," Joely offered, "I think Mittie is pretty upset."

"Joely, I re-a-lize he is upset. We are all upset. But we are not all simply running off and neglecting our responsibilities to others."

We agreed. Then Joely and I left her to straighten up just a bit before she went to bed so that things wouldn't go to pieces. She envisioned order unraveling in her hands like a ball of yarn jerked on by three wildcats.

Down in the basement, we heard her plowing the vacuum cleaner in straight furrows back and forth, back and forth across the living room floor right over our heads. Slowly, like the sea, it hummed us to sleep.

I dreamed that I was running after Jardin, running across a chasm over a maze of thin strips of pointed rock with jagged spears of glass protruding. On the other side, James Dexter sat at an enormous glass desk, signing papers with a gold pen. I tore a rock loose from my path and hurled it at him. Then shale gave way, my foot slipped, and I fell for hour after hour, turning in a circle, down to the floor of the chasm. It was dark and unbearably hot; the rocks were volcanic and seared my feet and hands. Then I looked up and far above me; I saw Verl leaning over the edge, passing down a rope. I leapt to catch it; my fingers scraped down the side of the chasm wall; hard lava broke off and crashed around me. I jumped again and sat up, awake.

The scratchy, ripping noise went on. Groggy, I thought of a bear outside the window; the screen was being torn open. But as my vision cleared, I could see that the blurred shape now crawling through the window opening was definitely human. It was cursing too. It was Mittie.

"What are you doing?" I asked him.

"Go to hell," he replied.

He jerked his torn pants loose from the screen, jumped to the floor, and then headed quickly out of the room and up the stairs to the first floor. Joely had also been awakened by the noise of the break-in. He pawed for his glasses. We flung out of our beds and chased up the steps after Mittie.

Upstairs in the living room, we saw Spurgeon Debson rising barefoot, but otherwise clothed, from the couch. A towel fell from his forehead. Mittie stood across from him with Hedda Gabler's pistol in his hand. Leila was nowhere to be seen. Presumably she was (once again) in bed asleep. I took a second to note this further evidence of her egalitarianism: apparently she went to bed not with, but, so to speak, on just about everyone.

Just as this thought was taking shape, Mittie raised his arm and fired. This time, as if to make up for the embarrassment it had caused in the finale of Ibsen's play, the pistol did go off. And neatly blew away one of Aunt Nadine's pink flowered glass globes from the mantelpiece.

Spurgeon's body froze. His mouth, as I expected, opened. He didn't, however, bother to phrase his remarks with their usual periodic eloquence.

"Mother fuck! Are you crazy, man?" was all he had to say.

Mittie stared at him.

Spur stared at the gun. "What are you doing?" he asked.

"I'm going to kill you," Mittie replied.

Spur closed out the colloquy, flung the manuscript he was holding (a copy of his latest play, *Napalm U.S.A.*) at Mittie's gun arm. It hit him instead on the temple and momentarily stunned him. Spur did not pause to pursue the matter or even to retrieve his opus; he sprinted agilely to the porch, unlocked the front door, and went through the screen door without even bothering to unlock it. The broken latch hung limply off the wall.

Mittie was on his way to the bedroom.

"Hey, Mittie! Hey! Come on now, Mittie!" Joely and I both yelled as we stumbled over each other to get to the bedroom door.

But Mittie swept us aside and stepped into the bedroom, where Leila sat up in her bed, naked in the blue silk sheets like Aphrodite waist-high in sea foam, awakened by the shot. I edged past him toward the bed. "Look here, Mittie," Joely said hoarsely.

Mittie stared at Leila, his face as still as madness. "It is the cause, it is the cause, my soul," he quoted at her in a strangely horrifying deadpan whisper. Then, "Put out the light," and he shot the bedside lamp off the table. Crawling quickly, I scrambled under the bed, frozen in darkness.

A third shot was fired. Above me the mattress bounced. From my seclusion behind the bedspread, I saw Leila's feet hit the floor with a sharp pat. They walked over to Mittie's feet.

"Give me that stupid thing, and get the hell out of here, you idiot," we heard her say.

A thick silence followed, broken only by the rasp of Mittie's breathing. Pressed around my face and arms, objects grew distinct. A suitcase, a white boot, a dusty copy of *The Pearl*, a crumpled cigarette pack, a peach core, a doll without arms in a white dress. I waited for a fourth shot to send yet another of the Sluford heirs violently heavenward.

Instead, Mittie's loafers slowly turned and left the room. Leila's bare feet followed.

chapter 13

A Greater Loss

Roused by the shots, Nathan Wolfstein and Mrs. Thurston had both come out of their rooms to investigate. By 3 A.M., Wolfstein looked like Ray Milland at the end of *Lost Weekend*, while Mrs. Thurston's face recaptured the precise expression it had worn at the climax of *A Daughter's Ruin and a Mother's Prayer*. She clutched the neck of her violet quilted bathrobe with one hand and Wolfstein's thin upper arm with the other. Seeing her there, I concluded that Mrs. Thurston must sleep sitting up at her dressing table, for she was as immaculately made up at 3 A.M. as she was when she appeared to set the breakfast table at 6:30—which she always did, despite the fact that no one else ate breakfast until eleven. Her hair was lacquered into its faded blond French bun, slicked into place like Dolores del Rio's, for one of her preoccupations was applying hair spray to her coiffure. She aerosoled her head at least a dozen times a day and kept six spray cans on her bureau for that purpose. If anyone had ever lit a match in her room, the whole house would have gone up like Valhalla. Only later did I learn that she also had two wigs—each one exactly duplicating her hairdo. She slept in one of them every night, presumably for just such emergencies as the one she was now trying to assimilate.

"Leila, darling! Your clothes!" she squawked at her daughter.

Leila stood, fully naked, her hands on her hips, staring at Mittie, who, fully clothed, stood staring slightly to the right of the top of her head.

"No one would blame me for killing you," Mittie said in a slurred drunken voice. "You'd deserve it for what you've done to me!"

Leila spoke intently, "And what have I done to you, Mittie? He slept here, okay? He had no place to go. Try getting outside your own needs for once."

"YOU'VE FUCKED HIM!" Mittie screamed.

"Oh, my God" moaned Mrs. Thurston and swayed into Nathan Wolfstein.

"Oh, my God," Leila softly echoed her mother. And added slowly, "And if I had, would that really make you feel like this? Would it make you less? Oh, Mittie, what's—"

"YES," he yelled. "Yes, it DOES. You have no right! NO RIGHT."

"Crap," she said. "Rights. Do you want to talk about rights, or do you want to talk about us? Oh, Mittie, Mittie, it's not Spur. Spur is not the problem. Mittie, what's really wrong? Tell me—"

She put her hand to his cheek, and he knocked it away. "Don't touch me! Just shut up!" he screamed. Leila stepped back, but he grabbed her arm, spun her around. Twice his hand came up, then fell to his side. His face tightened, distorted, froze in a twisted grimace.

Then he hit her. Hard across the face. Long streaks of his fingers reddened over Leila's cheek. The side of her mouth began to bleed. She didn't touch it.

"You poor schmuck," she said softly. Then she walked back toward her room.

"Leila!" her mother called.

Leila shut the door behind her. For a long time, Mittie looked at the closed door, then at his hands. The finality of what had happened took shape and filled his eyes. Stepping forward quietly, Joely reached his arm out to Mittie, who was staring at the picture of Leila over the mantel.

"Hey, man," he murmured.

Mittie's eyes jerked into focus. He saw us all carefully poised around him; maybe it was the first time he noticed us there. Before Joely could touch him, he twisted around, ran out of the house, and down the walk. We heard the Red Bus rev, choke, and then accelerate with jerked coughs.

Mrs. Thurston looked at us all as though our presence implied our participation in, perhaps our instigation of, what had happened. "The children?" she asked. "And where are the children?"

"They're asleep," I assured her. "They're still downstairs asleep." Fortunately, Maisie and Davy had been bred on noise and could have slept beatifically through the Götterdämmerung.

"Well, we can be grateful at least for that mercy," she said. "We can thank the Lord that they were spared this sorrow for now. Though what explanation is to be made to those poor babies, I honestly do not know."

Wolfstein sighed and sank into the armchair. "I don't think anyone need say anything to them, Amanda. Mittie and Leila will work this out. It doesn't really involve us."

She gathered her robe around her chin. "Do not," she said, "advise me that I am not involved in the affairs" (she faltered at the word) "at the misfortunes of my own family."

And with a clean sweep, she cleared the corner and retired to her room. Wolfstein shrugged, took a cigarette from his bathrobe pocket, lit it. Heading for his bedroom, he called back, "If you want the keys to my car, they're on the mantel."

I wanted to go in to talk to Leila, but I didn't know what I could say. Instead, I helped Joely pick up the pieces of the glass globe lamp from the hearth. We talked it over, and I decided there was no point in looking for Mittie in the middle of the night. Maybe everything would be over by tomorrow.

"That's enough for today," I suggested.

And so to bed.

The next day was the Fourth of July. Mittie did not return home, but clues as to his whereabouts filtered in throughout the afternoon. He was not reconciled. Marlin found a note taped over the theater doors informing all customers that the building was quarantined because of pestilence within. We took it down. The flag on the roof had been lowered to half-mast. We raised it.

Around five, Mrs. Thurston called us in some agitation from the house. She screamed at us to return immediately, then she hung up.

When Joely and I squealed to a stop in front of the steps, she was standing outside waiting for us.

"Oh, Devin, honey," she moaned, "that poor boy has gone totally out of his mind."

"Is he here?" I asked.

"No. I couldn't hold him. He shoved me, pushed me physically aside, and went on his mad way. Reasoning had just no effect on him at all. Thank the Lord above that Leila had taken those babies off to the fair."

"What was he doing here?" Joely asked her.

She told us as we led her up the steps back toward the house. "When I returned home from a little shopping, which I had walked into town to do (she looked reproachfully down at the Austin we had arrived in) because after all, we do have to keep eating, and somebody has to provide, I found him, found him right *here*."

She had led us into the kitchen. Now she flung open the oven door and pointed inside with a dramatic forefinger.

"'Mittie,' I called out to him, 'Mittie, think of what you're doing!' That's when he pushed me, without a word, and left this house." She sat down at the table, sadly scraping off a bit of dried food with her fingernail. "It was just what I went through with Leila's Aunt Nadine. The same exact thing. Devin, what is the matter with people? What is in their minds?"

"I don't know, ma'am," I told her.

Joely pointed out the kitchen window at a coil of rope hanging from a broken branch in the backyard. The branch was very slender. We still didn't know how seriously to take Mittie's warnings, if that's what they were supposed to be.

That evening, we ate dinner in silence. No one mentioned Mittie. Or Spur. Leila said she was taking the kids back to ride the rides. On my way out of the house, Maisie called to me from Leila's room. I found her lying on the bed there, thoughtfully staring at the ceiling.

"What does this spell?" she asked. "W-H-O-R-E?"

"What?"

"See?" She pointed over her head. "'F-U-C-K. Fuck them all, you W-H-O-R-E.' What does that mean?"

I looked up. The words were painted in black letters on the ceiling right over the bed. A message from Mittie to Leila, I assumed. Mrs. Thurston had followed me into the bedroom. She grabbed Maisie off the bed and came back in a moment with a can of Ajax and a sponge. So passed the day.

The holiday performance of *Our American Cousin* went on as scheduled with Ashton again taking Mittie's part and Fitzgerald doing a record business at the concession stand, selling red, white, and blue popcorn.

Then, partway through the play, a voice came over the theater loudspeakers—Mittie's voice, interrupting the actors, who undoubtedly thought first of Spurgeon's return. They all froze. The voice was drunk and sonorous as it intoned:

"On this anniversary of our country's independence, it is fitting that we pause to commemorate the tragic instant when at this precise moment in *Our American Cousin*, a great leader was treacherously slain, and the cause of freedom mortally wounded."

The voice stopped. The players and the audience waited, in awe, or expectation. A few seconds went by. Then Mittie (who must have climbed up a ladder in the wings) jumped down on the stage. He stumbled, righted himself, and stood there dressed and made up to look like John Wilkes Booth. Then he yelled, "*Sic semper Tyrannis*," and pulled Hedda Gabler's pistol from his frock coat. The players edged off the stage; then people in the audience started to scream. Mittie drunkenly raised his arm slowly, and fired two shots at the spotlights, putting out the lights once more.

"He's going to burn the place down!" someone irrelevantly yelled. People stood up and looked around. Gun in hand, Mittie jumped off the stage and pushed his way through the crowded aisles, thus hurrying the departing guests, who, like Lady Macbeth's, stood not upon the order of their going, but shoved, jostled, and elbowed each other to the exits.

Onstage, Joely yelled, "Calm down, calm down, it's all part of the show. Take your seats, please. There's no cause for alarm. Please."

But no one paid any attention to him. He told Seymour to call the sheriff and told the actors to get back onstage. He called out her next line to Suzanne Steinitz three times before finally she delivered it; the others came back on stage; the play went on. Gradually, with pockets of nervous laughter throughout the theater slowly subsiding, what was left of the audience settled back into their seats.

Handing the prompt book to Margery Dosk, Joely told me to follow him. We went out the backstage door. Outside in the parking lot, the Fourth of July carnival was crowded with cele-brators. Boat rides, rocket trips, Ferris wheel, carousel, tilt-a-wheel, all gaudily twirling in the night. Garish signs announced the easy promise of prizes, the temptations of chance. We spotted Mittie by a chain of cars swooping up and down a circular track; a long ribbed top closed over the cars, opened again, then closed, muffling the screams of the riders. The Caterpillar, it was called.

Mittie was easy to follow; his frock coat and the look on his face left a wake of backward glances we could track by. In and out of faded canvas booths, we chased him. Guess-Your-Weight, Tell-Your-Fortune, Test-Your-Strength, See-the-Freaks-of-Nature.

I saw Leila on the carousel, serenely swaying up and down on a flowered unicorn. Davy was on her lap and Maisie in front of her on a one-eared black horse. Mrs. Thurston stood by the ticket booth holding Leila's pocketbook. We saw Mittie notice them. He stopped and watched, still removed, but interested, as though they were on film. We were afraid if we came up on him from behind, he might shoot at them; he still had the gun. We stopped too.

They hadn't noticed him. The merry-go-round kept circling in time to the bleat of its mechanical organ; the black horse and the white unicorn swung into sight, rocked past Mittie, then slowly, languidly, floated away.

We started walking quietly toward Mittie. But Mrs. Thurston, who had bent down to remove a speck of dirt from her white pump, saw us, upside down, behind her. Then she saw Mittie.

"Mittie Stark!" she announced.

Mittie flung himself around in a circle, realized he was flanked, and raced toward the creek at the far end of the parking lot.

"Maybe we should just leave him alone," I said to Joely. "We're chasing him like he was a criminal, or something."

A police car had pulled up in front of the theater. Mittie saw it, turned upstream, and ran across the bridge.

"I don't know." Joely banged his head with his fist. "I don't know what to do."

"You don't think he's going to burn the theater down, do you?" I asked.

Joely was pulling on his hair as though he could force it to think for him. "No, no," he mumbled. "But, he could do something crazy. What's he going to do, what's he going to do?"

Then he started running. I ran after him. We were halfway over the bridge that forded the creek when the explosions began. The first one threw us down. At the second, we scurried in a crawl back toward the lot.

The carnival crowd was rushing to the bank.

"Oh, look!" they exclaimed. "It's like a fairyland. Oh, it's beautiful."

"I thought the fireworks weren't supposed to start 'til later."

"I think something's wrong. It's happening awful fast. I mean, so many of them going off all at once."

The sky burned brightly as a Las Vegas postcard. Flares, comets, stars, twisters, blue streams, gold bursts, green clusters flashed and sputtered out above us. Then stripe by star the spangled banner of the American flag exploded into outline, followed by a huge explosion.

Joely clutched my arm. "Oh, Mother of God."

A policeman was hurrying to the bridge. We ran too. I saw Leila pushing her way through the crowd behind us.

On the ground where Joely was kneeling, Mittie lay twisted; his arms still bunched around his head, his hands waxy and blistered like oil burnt. One leg was bent out sideways from the knee. His foot was caught in a charred coil of electric wires.

chapter 14

I Enlarge My Circle of Acquaintances

"We're very sorry, Mrs. Stark," they told her.

She nodded.

"I am sorry as I can be," the sheriff said. "A horrible accident."

A deputy gathered, with meticulous reverence, the remains. All artifacts were now talismans, as sacrosanct as the body: a cracked watchband, a blackened key chain, a gleaming belt buckle. These they placed in a crisp manila envelope with Mittie's name on it. Mittie they took to Saul Fletcher Morticians' place of business.

And the sightseers, having seen until there were no more sights, went back to the fair satisfied. We went home and sat down in stunned silence.

There followed through the long evening a series of conferences. The sheriff, Gabe Booter, a tall, gaunt, loud-voiced man, came and interviewed us, first together, then individually. He asked if in our opinion Mittie had been an arsonist, or if he had smoked and been careless with matches, or an anarchist, or if there was a history of insanity in his family. Mrs. Thurston shone in these, to her, familiar surroundings. She summed up her anger at the sheriff's insinuations by saying that she was positive the

entire thing had been a dreadful accident and the town of Floren
Park ought to be sued for leaving wires and cables around where
someone could trip over them and drop a cigarette into an
opened box of fireworks.

I went in Leila's room and called Verl. Then I called Mama.
I thought that if I could hear myself saying it had happened, by
their believing it, I could believe it too.

Dr. Ferrell came to say he had seen the body and signed the
papers; he kissed Leila and gave her some capsules. She put them
down on the side table next to where she was sitting, leaning
back in the corduroy armchair that had been most often Mittie's.
She didn't seem to be listening, or to be listening to anything
going on. There was just the methodical motion of her arm rising to her mouth with cigarette after cigarette.

Wolfstein brought, without asking her to acknowledge him,
a glass of scotch. She would drink from the glass, hold the liquid
in her mouth a long while, remember it was there, and swallow
it. Several hours went by.

Mr. Saul Fletcher came in crepe soles along Mrs. Thurston's
plastic runners. Under his seersuckered arm, he pinched a black
catalog book. Introductively clearing his throat, he whispered
that there was the question of arrangements. Without looking
at him, Leila spoke tiredly, "Maybe you'd like to put him in the
display window and have 'The Merry Widow Waltz' piped in
over the coffin."

Her mother burst into tears, and Mr. Fletcher nodded at her
supportively out of his twenty-three-years-in-the-same-location
understanding of the irrational bereaved. Then he whispered that
perhaps it would be better if he came back later. No one disagreed.

Most of the members of the theater company were there,
clustered in the living room or on the front porch. There was
nothing to be done, but everyone wanted to be there—as if
there were a pelting storm outside and we huddled together for
warmth and safety.

Leila rose; everyone stood up and stepped aside for her. She
went to her room, closed the door, dialed the phone. I heard her

ask for Portland, Oregon. Person to person. Bruno Stark.

We sat there. Downstairs, Maisie and Davy slept. Mrs. Thurston had put them to bed long before the rest of us had returned home. They had not seen what happened at the fair, nor had they asked about Mittie, and didn't in days to come either, perhaps already knowing, perhaps not knowing how to know. I don't know when Leila told them.

I felt hungry. I felt guilty for feeling hungry, but unwilling to accept the guilt and go surreptitiously to the refrigerator. So I left and walked downtown to the Streetcar Diner, where I ate a lot of food I couldn't taste.

I wanted, if possible, to know exactly what I felt. The waiting in the living room had seemed, finally, inconclusive. Were we doing nothing because it was assumed inappropriate to do anything for some unspecified period? And were the others waiting in a way different from me? With some sureness of sorrow? I couldn't tell.

But in downtown Floren Park, I found no visible evidence that would help define the meaning of the loss. No lights dimmed, shopshutters closed; no one stopped to ask, "Didn't you know Mittie Stark?" It isn't so much that there isn't a gap in nature, I saw. There is rarely even a reference.

Walking back toward the road that leads up the climb to Leila's, I passed a signpost on which was carved, Chapel of St. Lucy's. I saw a small wooden church, hardly larger than a cabin, cloistered by trees on an incline away from the street. There was a single light on inside, white as the moon.

I began to feel a little tired and lay down on the dark slope. I looked up at the night sky. The stars had not changed either.

I had heard and discounted the noise twice before the yellow Triumph pulled to the curb. Verl got out and went up the path. The light in the church got brighter a second, then dimmed again. For some reason, I made no effort to call to Verl, even to raise my hand. That puzzled me. I had the strongest sensation of immobility. It wasn't that I was too exhausted, or in need of solitude, or grieving. I wasn't any of those things. What was strange was that I wasn't anything—except that I couldn't, didn't want to, move.

Some time later, they came out. I turned my head on the grass to watch them. Leila had a white shawl on her head, lace. I was so surprised to see her wearing something like that, I didn't wonder until afterward what she was doing in a Catholic church. I had thought she no longer believed in it. Verl was leaning down toward her talking softly, nodding his head, as they walked to his car and got in. After a while, they drove away.

Leila came back to Floren Park from Oregon six days after she left. Bruno Stark had wanted his son returned to him. So Mr. Fletcher's morticians, apart from some long-distance phone calls, didn't get to make any arrangements other than transportational, after all.

While she was away in Portland and then in Los Angeles, where she flew with Mr. Stark to settle matters about the house, I guess, and the insurance, we of the Red Lagoon Players carried on. That was Mrs. Thurston's advice and self-directive—that we all should get organized, be productive, and carry on.

And so, under her counsel and exemplum, we did. It was by her motion, for example, that at our first emergency assemblage we changed the name of our company to "The Mittie Stark Memorial Players." Joely voted against it; the Red Lagoon Players already was Mittie Stark, he said.

New posters were printed with a black border and with a brief threnody Mrs. Thurston had composed on Mittie's tragic accident and his (prior to that) love of the Floren Park community, his work (which brought happiness to old and young alike), his family, and his friends.

"Devin," she told me as I helped her fold sheets at the Laundromat, "we must realize that if we who are so intimately concerned appear to be close-mouthed or secretive regarding what happened to poor Mittie, others will think the Worst."

"Ma'am?"

"Now, that is the way of the world. Yes, it is. People Will Talk. And what they will say will not be very nice for my Leila or her babies. I can just imagine what those young people down at the boarding house have already been conjecturing, after that strange and peculiar incident we were all subjected to at the dinner table the very night before Mittie passed away."

"I don't think anybody's going around talking about Mittie," I reassured her.

"Of course they are! Of course they are! And I'm sorry to be the one to have to say so, but you are a fool, Devin, if you think otherwise."

Her annoyance with my innocence was such that she snapped my end of the sheet we were folding out of my hands. It fell to the floor, and she scooped it up into a washer, took a quarter from her clear plastic coin purse, and started it on a new cycle. We went back to our work. The dance of folding sheets with Mrs. Thurston was as brisk as a mazurka. Her partner had to memorize intricate forward and backward patterns synchronized in fixed sequence, through which even stubborn contour sheets were popped, snapped, and creased into a surface fit for a frictionless puck.

After another sheet, she decided to forgive me and go on. "Oh, I know by sad fortune that persons about whom you would never think such a thing are perfectly capable of destroying the gift of life. And I am the kind of individual, Devin, who is prepared to accept a truth that is flatly staring you in the face." She looked down as if she saw her disgruntled sister, Nadine, on the linoleum floor. "But," she continued, dismissing that image, "those are not the clear facts of this situation. Are they?"

"No, ma'am."

"Should I have *insisted* that my papa did not fall, but deliberately propelled himself into the attachments of his tobacco machine?"

"No, ma'am," I mumbled from behind the stack of laundry she had doweled up my arms.

"And, Devin, I am as sure as my own name that in their secret hearts, Bruno and Emily Stark are placing the entire blame for their loss on my Leila. That man has always disesteemed me. Though, naturally, there is only his own defensiveness behind it.

However"—she resealed her box of Tide with a strip of masking tape—"we may as well acknowledge that Leila has left herself liable to all sorts, yes, all sorts, of conjectures. And my only prayer"—she emptied the lint tray into a waste basket—"my only prayer is that from now on she will understand the importance of watching your step."

With that hope, she led me by the elbow out the door of the Laundromat. Sightless, my nose nestled in soft sheets, I followed her to the Red Bus.

Joely drove the old red schoolbus to the airport and returned with Leila. She stood, that hot, sluggish Saturday morning, on the top step of the porch, stood quietly, laden with presents, with recipes from Grandmother Strovokov, with appropriate clothes from Mrs. Stark, with appropriate toys for Maisie and Davy, who tugged at her appropriate dark brown suit and pulled her into the house.

I walked down to help Joely with the luggage. "How is she?" I asked him.

"She seems okay. I gather it was pretty rough. The mother sounds catatonic; I doubt she's been much help. And Bruno seems to be laying a heavy trip on Leila. Jerk. She's already blamed herself enough as it is. You know, she didn't even know Bruno had written Mittie he was pulling the money out; I guess he was too scared to tell her, finally admit he'd failed—he'd see it that way. I would have told her if I'd thought he was keeping it from her." He handed me her suitcase. "Poor kid."

"What's she going to do?"

"All she said was she wasn't going to let Stark close Mittie's place down. At least not this summer. She said she had a plan."

Part of Leila's plan was another present, one that led her mother to conclude that she was so far from grasping the principle of watching your step as to be liable to all sorts of conjectures. The present arrived that afternoon; it was a gift for Nathan Wolfstein, and the gift was Calhoun Grange. It took me a second to recall that Grange was the cowboy star whom Wolfstein had once identified from the magazines as his unknown son.

Leila had taken home a son that had been lost. Now she had brought home a son that had been found.

"I had a friend who worked with him in L.A. That's how I found him. And so here he is, Nate."

The new father was standing by the kitchen table and looking as the mornings always left him—his high thin sheath of bathrobe pulled almost twice around, his hair lank wisps, his feet long and yellow, the toenails curved in. He sat down and frowned at his hand shaking ashes loose from his cigarette.

Grange stepped into the room like the sun coming up. He looked down at Wolfstein and grinned. Behind all his fringe of eyelashes and leather, I sought out Wolfsteinian similitudes, that irrefutable idiosyncracy, the shared strawberry mark on the left shoulder. I found none. They shared angularity; that was all. For the rest, Grange had a clean, bright glisten; Wolfstein was gray, opaque. Wolfstein was reserved, distant, unapproachable. Grange came straight at you with an amble, then hosed you down in affability while you were still trying to figure out the secret of his shuffle. He talked the way they taught him to talk in *Over to Amarillo*, and he seemed in general to have lost, if he had ever owned, any distinction between private and public "Grangedom." Knowing that, you didn't want to like him, but all of a sudden you did anyhow, the way you may not want to like John Philip Sousa, but your heart thumps when you stand close to a live band.

"Well, hi, Mr. Wolfstein. Leila tells me you and me should of met," he beamed.

Wolfstein, however, was waterproofed against Calhoun's hose of charm. He had faded since Leila left, browned out, as though a source of current had been cut in two, and the other half been transferred elsewhere by the power company. Now, presented with an old dramatic sawhorse, an Act V Recognition and Reconciliation Scene of the sort he had directed easily for twenty years, he couldn't stage it, couldn't see it. Even an impulse of embarrassment over his collapse gave up the struggle toward his brain and oozed back into the daze.

When Grange stuck out his brown-gold hand, Wolfstein shook it indifferently, then turned and poured himself out a drink of bourbon from the near-empty pint beside him. Grange looked quizzically at Leila for direction. Then, at her nod, he swung a chair around to Wolfstein's side and saddled it.

"Well, you see, I got these couple of weeks off, and then I'll be doing *Cat*, Brick's part, you know, *Cat on a Hot Tin Roof*—my first chance at doing something like that. On the road. And so Leila here"—he gave her his grin—"Leila runs into me and she says, Why don't you just fly on out with me? It's real pretty country, she says, and you can try *Cat* out on us, and meet, meet… folks, and all. And…"

He realized that Wolfstein was not listening, or at least not acknowledging him, so he leaned the chair back and gave us his grin instead. We soon were mesmerized by that rhythmic beacon of perfect teeth. All of us made fans of the flicker, we who were presumably theater people ourselves, but who had never met a star.

"And hell, Lord," the star went on, "I don't know why I do any of the fool things I end up doing, but if it feels good, why then I just take off with it. And here I am! Oh, man, is my agent gonna fry my ass." He rolled a laugh like a cigarette, smoothly, and we all found ourselves laughing too, without knowing why, or at what.

"Well, if y'all ul excuse me, I guess maybe I oughtta clean up a little bit." He stretched up, and up, and up, and swung a perfect leg over the chair back. "And just call me Cal," he added. Fitzgerald and Maisie and Sabby Norah led his processional to the bathroom.

Yep, evuhbody sure did like Calhoun Grange. His brightness blew into our house, throwing up the black shades of mourning and luring us all outside. Eventually, even Mrs. Thurston had to lash herself to her principles and stuff reputation in her ears to resist him. She would not deny that he was quite engaging, she said, but, of course, that was all the more reason why he was liable to be connected with any tripping and falling Leila was conjectured to have done.

And everyone was quite happy to have Grange practice his play on us, and so we did *Cat on a Hot Tin Roof*. No one had known whether, with Mittie gone, there would be any more plays. Sabby had told us Leila would think of something, but not even Sabby had predicted a movie star. Sabby was to be Little Mama, Leila was Maggie the Cat, and Mrs. Thurston agreed to portray Big Mama. Wolfstein had been right about her affinity with Tennessee Williams. She really got into the part.

"Nathan, according to my understanding, this woman has borne the burden of her sorrow with what I believe I would call dig-ni-ty. For she has to face the fact that it is not at all a spastic colon, as she and Big Daddy supposed, but cancer, which is going to kill him. And yet others are attempting to make a fool of her. Now, Nathan, is that your understanding also?"

"Yes, Amanda," he would nod, "I think that's a way of getting into it…"

And Wolfstein himself had gotten into the play, had charged what little current was left to him so that it could throw a focused beam on the stage, had generated the energy from some inexplicable storage cell in his frame of bones. Maybe it was because Grange was there; maybe he wanted to do it for him. Though if he had embraced Calhoun as his son in some private Ithaca, none of us knew it. They didn't say. At rehearsals, they called each other "Nate" and "Cal" and were polite. I had pretty much decided that Wolfstein had made up the story just to be telling it, or that maybe he had always wanted a son and dreamed it, or that maybe there really was a script girl in his life and *she* made up the Calhoun Grange part out of *her* dreams. Leila believed it, but Grange seemed a lot more interested in her than in Nathan Wolfstein.

Through those weeks, our lives orbited around this visit from a star. And for his part, Calhoun apparently thought Floren Park "felt good"; at any rate, he took off with it. He appeared at a local rodeo and an Elks-for-Nixon barbeque picnic, had himself pasteled in the Plaza, signed autographs at the dance ball, allowed himself with perfect affability to be endlessly photographed and

interviewed, ran up the biggest bill in memory at the biggest
hotel, received with grace the grateful offerings of merchants—a
fishing rod, a blue suede overcoat, a Tyrol hat, an authenticated
totem pole, the memory of pleasures received, the tributes of flut-
tered hearts.

So after we sprayed the afternoon streets with posters
announcing his coming, the Mittie Stark Memorial Players
played to full houses each night of our run. As for *Cat on a Hot
Tin Roof*, no one seemed to pay much attention to it, except
one night standing in the back of the theater, I watched Leila
prowling the cave of Maggie's bedroom for a while, and I felt a
terror, like a shame, from a source I couldn't define. She seemed
to burn with an energy that could be either desire or grief. How
did she really feel about Mittie's death? She had never talked to
me about it. And so I didn't ask.

"That girl is one fine little actress," Grange told us. "Let me
tell you, she *is something.*"

But I had been Mrs. Thurston's fool after all, for people
were talking about Leila and Calhoun Grange. Lady Red made
a "remark" to Marlin. Ashton, who had been rubbing around
Grange like a black cat all week, made insipid jokes in the dressing room about cowboys easing into oiled saddles.

On Friday afternoon, I had to march in the street pantomime
with Suzanne Steinitz, whom I rarely saw now that my desultory
slide toward seduction by sneering with her at Broadway and
Hollywood had languished. After I shot her with a cap pistol and
she shot me and we passed out our last handbill, she said coyly,
"Funeral meats and wedding feasts."

"What?"

"*Hamlet*, stupid." She smiled by arching her eyebrows.
"Guess who I saw at the Valley Druggists yesterday. Our
much-loved Mrs. Stark. She evoked quite a study from the
pharmacist by handing him a prescription for enough birth-
control pills to immunize the Rockettes for a year. Right after he
offered her his condolences about her husband. There's an
Antigone for you."

"Antigone?"

"Oh, forget it."

But perhaps it was all a matter of envy with Suzanne, for she did not deceive me by pretending to be contemptuous of Calhoun Grange, even if his "Method" was wrong. Of course, she wasn't as infatuated as Sabby Norah, who followed Calhoun around looking like Judy Garland mooning, "You Made Me Love You" to Clark Gable. Grange was as close as Sabby had come yet to the world she worshiped, and she was memorizing him like a poem.

The next day I tried to tell Verl what Suzanne had said about Leila, but he just grimaced in an annoyed way and muttered, "Oh, for Christ's sake, Devin, Leila hasn't got the *time* to do all the stupid things you keep fantasizing about her in that pulp-fiction brain of yours."

"Well, who are you supposed to believe?" I asked him, annoyed myself. "I mean, do you think people just make things up? Because if it's true, then Leila's making a fool of Mittie. Of his memory."

"So now you're worried about poor Mittie's memory? If I were you, I'd worry a little more about making a fool of yourself and a little less about Leila. You're so obsessed with this imaginary sex life of Leila's, I'm beginning to think you must be in love with her."

"You're the one with the pulp-fiction brain. Pop psychology too."

"And lo, in conclusion, the Preacher sayeth unto you, t'aint nothing more foolish than faith. Walk me over to the bookstore. I want to buy you a copy of *Emma*; she thought she knew everything that was going on too."

After that night's performance, I sat in the Red Lagoon Bar to read the book, but when Marlin and Joely came in, I put it away and ordered a drink with them. Soon we heared a murmur wave through the room; it was followed by Calhoun Grange, who swung smoothly into our booth.

"Lord God," he smiled. "I am really awful. I am really one rotten actor. Did you *see that*, when I just popped up and headed over to the window, cool as a bluejay, just clean forgot that Brick's crippled and can't move without those damn crutches!" He laughed, slapping the table. "Well, they can wire Paul Newman not to worry. Hey, now, come on," he pulled Joely's hand away from his pocket. "Let me get this round."

Tourists stared at Grange (and therefore at us, who were incidentally in the frame) with a frank sense of possession. He was *theirs*, and they watched to see what he would do next, as openly as they might watch a bear or a baby, presuming he was as little bothered by self-consciousness as either of those. And, as a matter of fact, he appeared, by habit, artistry, or nature, really to be effortlessly unaware of his audience. Perhaps all the eyes had finally come to be just the camera's, and the only shyness left was of solitude.

I watched the tourists watch him eating peanuts until finally I too saw it framed by a proscenium, the act taking on for me as well a kind of primitive magic and mystery. If you say an ordinary word over and over, sometimes it will lose its ordinary meaning and take on that kind of incantational significance.

"When are you going to have to leave us?" Marlin Owen asked him unselfishlessly, for his girlfriend, Margery, was one of the few nonsmitten women around.

"Oh, I guess I'll head on down to Vegas Monday A.M. Did I tell you? My agent caught up with me yesterday, and you can just believe it that guy sure did rake my tail over the coals."

He rolled one of his laughs, and it rippled into tourists' smiles throughout the bar. "If he can't get hold of me, sooner or later he just starts to piss in his pants. Well, you know, I was supposed to be seen putting in an appearance at this particular club with some contract broad a couple of days ago. That's what this game's about, being seen putting in an appearance. That's what my agent keeps trying to impress on my head, he tells me. And so now she's P.O.d, and so he hopped on the studio's back about it and rode them around a while, and then they hopped on my agent's back and rode *him* around. So naturally he spins on around and climbs up on *me*. Well, you know how it goes in that world."

We didn't, but we nodded anyhow. I was wondering how I could ask him about Wolfstein.

"Well," Joely summed up for Floren Park, "it won't be the same here without you."

"Well, thank you. Hell, I think this is a *nice* little place. People are real friendly. And natural. I've been kind of enjoying myself and feeling pretty free. 'Course it *was* a crazy-ass thing to do, taking off like my agent says. I'm one dumb bastard. Lord knows what gets into me."

He invited us to grin with him at the puzzling mystery of his own motivations. We did.

From a lingering waitress who took his smile like an unexpectedly large tip, Grange ordered another beer. She gave his empty can to a teenage girl standing beside the jukebox. The girl wrapped it in a napkin and put it in her cloth handbag. I noticed she had one of the handbills with, "Yours, Calhoun Grange," sprawled across the front that Fitzgerald was selling in the lobby for five dollars.

He popped the can open and smoothly brimmed his glass. "But I tell you," he said, "I really took to that Leila of yours."

We did not know what he meant by "ours," or more to the immediate point, "took to." Sitting a bit more stiffly, I tried to look at once both comprehending and nonchalant.

"You know, she's a pretty weird broad in a lot of ways. I mean, she's not what you'd exactly call easy to figure. But pals, you can believe it, she is one fine woman. After losing her husband that way! Listen, she has got guts! Keeping the show going! 'Course I'm not telling you something you don't already know. Yes, sir, I liked her right off the bat. So when she busts her way onto the set like that, good Lord, just right past the bosses, and tells me this guy working with her out in Colorado is *my old man* and I oughtta go meet him, I say, why hell, why not? See what I mean?"

We said yes and waited.

He noticed what we were waiting for, so maybe Suzanne Steinitz had underestimated his Method.

"'Course I never really figured I was going to actually run into my old man out here. Lord, that's just a little too much to believe.

"Besides, my mom's told me for fifteen years how he died from his liver in the V.A. hospital in San Diego. But, still, who knows, you know?"

We waited.

"Hell, Nate's okay. But I could see that first morning there wasn't anything between us. Tell you the truth, I can't see much resemblance, can you?"

"But," I asked, "is your mother the woman Wolfstein knew?"

"Well, yeah. I guess he knew her. I asked him and he said he did. Far as I could tell, he didn't act like he 'specially wanted to go into it. And so what's the point anyhow? Lots of people know lots of people."

He finished his beer and we left. In front of the bar, he signed his name across the cast on a young boy's arm and rumpled his hair. The parents beamed.

Outside in the parking lot, an old familiar strain slapped at us across the summer night. "Pile of dung! Sarcophagus! Junkshit! Junkshit! Junkshit! JUNKSHIT! JUNKSHIT!"

"Oh, no," Joely said.

And indeed it was Spurgeon Debson howling in the moon-light as he rhythmically kicked in the headlights of an old black Chrysler. For whatever rolled from the assembly lines of Detroit violated and terrorized Debson's soul as the unstoppable breed-ing of the Chinese does the John Birch Society.

"Hello, Spur, what's going on?" Joely asked. You had to ask the regular questions, though the regular answers were never forthcoming.

Spur looked around, perhaps placed us as figures dim in some insignificant slot of his memory. He flipped the car's hood open with a right uppercut that split the skin on his knuckles.

"There!" he slammed his bleeding hand into the engine. "THERE is the heart of America. That worthless package, metal DUNG! That WOMB of mediocrity!" He stared, infuriated, at the engine. "FASCIST!" he screamed at the carburetor.

"What's eating that guy?" Calhoun wondered.

"The war in Vietnam," I chose at random.

"Yeah, I guess I know what you mean," Calhoun nodded. "It's pretty hard for some folks to figure what's right. Was he drafted?"

"No, I don't think so," I said. "But if he were, I don't much think he'd serve."

That, in fact, I knew absolutely. No number of U.S. eagles chewing away at his entrails would ever make Spurgeon say yes to President Johnson.

"Where'd you get that car, Spur?" Marlin asked.

From the monologue that followed, whirred around us like chips of cuneiform scattered in the sands of Mesopotamia by a crazed archaeologist, we glued this story together. Spur had left the Starks' home on the evening of July 3rd. After that useless scene with that cretinous madman living with Leila, he had advised himself to get the fuck out of this plastic-fucking middle-class pig hole in order to preserve his goddamn integrity. He had, therefore, split. The Chrysler, which he was now disemboweling with the jack, he had purchased for his last $120 (earned by the prostitution of bauble-vending to plastic cunts). He had bought it from a baboon whose baboonery consisted for one thing in his ever having owned the vehicle, and for another, in his selling such a metal coffin to a human being.

Spur then headed west to the desert, where he could fill his lungs with something clean for a change. Besides, he had a mission to perform in the City of Syphilis and Gonorrhea summed up as Los Angeles. With the help of certain cats and chicks who comprised the Anti-All Living Theatre of Topanga Canyon, he would produce his masterpiece, *Napalm U.S.A.*, there on the steps of the Wilshire Boulevard branch of the Bank of America.

But like modern Eumenides, the locusts of General Motors had pursued him even down the pure flat stretches of the Mojave Desert. They gnawed holes in the radiator, they gobbled the rear axle off, threw a rod, sucked out the pistons. So in the dry noon dust, Spurgeon stood, his vision in overdrive, his Chrysler driven over into a sand rut. Elijah in a chariot with the wheels gone.

Did a single lousy church-going Babbittrabbit stop to help a poor one-armed son of a bitch?

NO.

And so alone, he himself pushed that Symbol of America, that iron heap of shit, 250 miles to the Half-Ass Garage, where they charged him the other arm and a half to half-ass fix it. Collect, he called the Living Theatre of Topanga Canyon and learned that it was dead, for certain of the cats and chicks no longer comprised it. Two had been busted for not sucking up. Two had damned themselves by going back to college.

So the apocalypse was postponed.

And why had he returned to Floren Park carrying that car strapped on his blistered back? Only to shove every jagged piece of Chrysler Inc. up the fat pink ass of the baboon who had sold it to him.

"Hell, that's hard luck," Grange said when, after what felt like forty-five minutes, Spur paused in his outburst. We were all still standing around the Chrysler watching him break off the windshield wipers.

"Hard luck? LUCK?" Spur rolled his prophet eyes over Calhoun. "There's no luck, you dumb shitkicker. There's EVIL. THERE IS TOTAL EVIL. Cheap, dirty, hairy evil, and it's sitting with its white ass in big leather chairs, and it's punching metal buttons with its big hairy fingers, and it's running this fucking country. And if there's a God, he's the Chairman of the Board of Dow Chemical. He's a S.S. fucking Pentagon Nazi five stars in his rear Admiral cocksucking Commander in Chief. I HATE GOD, and if I ever get my hands around his fat oily neck, I'll pull out his jugular vein and choke the pig with it. I hate him now, and when I'm dead I'll keep on hating him!"

"Hey, hold on there, buster," Calhoun stretched his mouth to show just a flicker of perfect teeth. Perhaps a personal, a patriotic, or a religious affront that stirred him.

I imagined the movie, as Cal would push his chair slowly back from his table in the saloon, slowly stand and walk to the bar, place one boot on the rail, never taking his eyes off Spurgeon, never blinking, his gaze steady with the serenity of knowing that in his personhood resided perfect rightness.

"He's nuts, Cal. He ought to be in an institution," Joely told him.

"Oh," Grange nodded slowly, kindly. It was a different movie if the man were crazy.

Uninterested in the world's diagnosis, Spurgeon had reached that pitch in his panegyric when words are puny. Unzipping, he urinated on the hood of the Chrysler. The high, steaming arch of his contempt spewed out splashing the headlights.

We left him there. I walked back to the bar.

chapter 15

I Am Involved in Mystery

In a back room of the Red Lagoon, couples danced now. They jerked in a sputter of strobe light, bodies projected at the wrong speed, screened in awkward tableaux by the red, white, red, white flicker.

Recently Lady Red Menelade had built a discotheque, and some thought a brothel, behind the original barroom. Her husband, the manager, had not objected as she proceeded to take possession of the property. Had he not predicted her victory, down to the saltshaker, even before her arrival? Now validated in his fatalism, he gave his time to summer reruns of daytime quiz shows, watching them from his stool by the cash register on a small gray television, games played months earlier so that the deal had long since been made, the password guessed, the final jeopardy wagered. Yet each chance won or lost was here again on the screen, capable of endless repetition. It pleased him to watch the working out of destinies already foreknown and resolved, months, years earlier, as he knew his own had been. He almost never talked with the customers any more the way he used to.

The discotheque was large, dark, and hot. Lady Red had crowded a wide four-sided balcony with cheap tables from which drinkers could look down at dancers. Below were more tables ringing the dance floor, and at either end, a dais—one for the band, one for the two girls, the "go-go" girls, instructresses in gyring: illusions of a partner for those without one. They wore red bikinis splotched with sweat stains, spangled with fringe that had been carelessly, unevenly sewn on, or maybe it had frayed, or maybe night after night, anonymous hands had reached up and stolen a memento of the illusion.

I found an empty table next to the balcony rail, where I could look down on the girls and the customers. I saw Leila and Jennifer Thatcher sitting together. Jennifer was crying and shaking her head. Leila pulled her chair over, put her arm around Jennifer, stroked her hair, stroked her hand, kept nodding as Jennifer talked.

I watched the performers. One was a soiled blonde with too much flesh that was too soft now, even for her big frame, flesh that shook loosely without effort or interest as she moved bored muscles through the jerk, the pony, the monkey, the slide. Her muscles had memorized how to give the semblance, if not of energy, at least of life. When the red filter blinked off, her skin was that chalk white of someone who for years wakes up only when the sun is setting, whose shades may be taped to their runners and are never pulled up. Her eyes stared just above the heads of her customers. They were eyes an indifferent maker of mannequins might have painted on, and nobody was in them. I saw stretch marks on her stomach, and a long green bruise on the inside of her thigh. Joely told me later that she called herself Kim, that she was from somewhere in Arkansas, was thirty-two and divorced twice, and had a seven-year-old boy named Cary. He said she wanted to get to California like Marilyn Monroe in Bus Stop, but after watching her a while, I didn't think she was going to make it.

The other girl was younger, black-haired and thin, and her eyes deliberately did not look at anyone in the room, but instead studied some self-realization that her dancing there either confirmed or demeaned, I wasn't sure which. She reminded me of someone. Suzanne Steinitz?

No. Jardin. She looked in the strobe light like slides of Jardin

changed too quickly. Jardin superimposed over the dancer. I
pressed my drink glass against my forehead, stared through it.
The dancer blurred, dissolved, merged with Jardin. A black
moth with white and silver eyes, Jardin in jagged webs of black
silk floated at me in a forest twisted full of black branches and
black sky. Small white stars cut into the sky. The moon made
a narrow strip of light, and she moved down it. I made a white
stone god with a statue's sightless eyes step out of shadows. He
gathered her into him, her black moth wings folded in his white
arms. They floated backward silently into the shadows.

"Devin! Hey, Devin! Look who I've got here."

The thin girl snapped her head back and forth. Her hair
twisted around her neck, uncoiled like a black lace fan. I jerked
away, shaded my eyes, squinted down into shafts of smoke to
locate the voice. At a table just beneath me, Ashton Krinkle in
his black turtleneck sat with two other men—one of them young
and languidly postured, the other much older. I stood up to lean
over the balcony and saw the familiar linen suit, the gray hair
that needed a cut. He twisted a strand of it against the back of
his neck with his forefinger.

"Professor Aubrey!" I called. "Is that you? What are *you*
doing here?"

He waved his hand at me, but with a funny motion, as if
he were trying to push me away. He raised himself in his chair.
"Hello, Devin, hello. It's good to see you again. Like all the best
literature, the similitudes of life, don't you think? How have you
been?" The voice had its old sure warmth; it floated over the
noise of the room and over the embarrassment that pulled at the
corners of his mouth.

Ashton smiled at me, "When he said he taught English
at Harvard, I told him you were here. And he verified you,
Donahue, so I guess you really did go there."

And I guessed so, really, for the same reason. After I had
decided to write poetry, I had become one of a group of students
who, in new collections every fall, drew up beside his fire and
grew in love with learning what he knew. He wrote thick books

of criticism and thin books of poems, and we all had copies of both. In his gold-brown rooms at Pinckney House, we listened to music by men with Italian names, and the fire shine gleamed on rows and rows of books. He had saved me from suspension, too, and warned me against political involvements. Now I wished Verl were there so I could introduce them. How incredible that my past should come to me out here in this citadel of mountains to which I had escaped.

The young man with him crossed, recrossed his legs, smoothed the fold of his trousers. His face was carefully set in petulant ennui. Then I recognized him. Randolph something or other, who was never called that at Harvard anyhow, but referred to as Oscar's Folly, and at the English Club as Belphoebe, and at the dining hall as the Queen of the Yard. We had never liked each other. And now he was sitting here, incomprehensibly, with my teacher. Why? I didn't remember that he had been in any of Mr. Aubrey's classes.

"How are you enjoying your summer in the theater?" Aubrey asked me.

"Very well, sir. It's a new experience. And you? Are you vacationing? With Randolph Wheeling?"

"Ah," he smiled in that voice that held for us in each slow syllable all the wise humor we hoped for our own maturities, "a long car trip across my native land. Something I'm ashamed to say I've never done before. We New Englanders tend to a defensive insularity, don't we? So proudly attached to our discomforts." He tapped the tight noose of his tie. "And then down into Mexico to research some folklore. Perhaps I can rifle a bit of poetry from their past. Plumed serpents in my infirmity instead of one more birch tree sagging with tradition. Rather late in life to be developing a Lawrencian streak, wouldn't you say?"

I smiled.

"I think," he had to say, "you might have met Randolph Wheeling in Cambridge?" Randolph acknowledged me with one eyebrow. "He speaks Spanish quite well and kindly offered to help me bargain with the natives for a week or so."

"I hope it goes well," I said. "I've got a copy of your new book, *Fortune and Men's Eyes*. It's...it's very fine, sir."

"Oh, thank you. Thank you very much. And you? Have you made plans yet for next year? Ah, well, let me know when you do. Please remember I'd be happy to write a letter for you if you wish." Then all at once he said they had to be leaving. They planned to travel all the next day, and now it was long past midnight. He doubted they would be back through.

"Good-bye, Devin. Take care."

"Yes, sir. And you."

Ashton stopped them at Leila's table, introduced them. Professor Aubrey bowed and took her hand. They went on, passing Dennis Reed, who was entering the bar. He took a seat next to Leila and pressed her hands in his. I didn't realize he and Leila had met. Maybe Verl had introduced them. Maybe me. I had forgotten.

"I'm trying to attract your attention," a voice murmured. I looked up. It was the black-haired dancer. "You were watching me," she said, brushing a strand of hair behind her ear. The strobe light flashed red on the loop of a silver earring.

"I'm sorry," I said standing up. Now I couldn't decide whether she looked like Jardin or not.

"Why?" she asked. "Sit down." And she sat down too.

"Devin Donahue," I told her.

"My name's Tanya."

Tanya told me that she would like a scotch and water, and that she would like me to tell her all about myself.

An hour later, Joely came to offer me a ride home; Leila and Jennifer had already left. "I hope I'll see you again," Tanya smiled.

"I'm sure you will," I smiled back.

"Smooth," Joely lisped through puckered lips. Then thumping me on the back, he aped a sick look. "What a pity you're already in mourning for another maid, Donahue. That's right, isn't it? Aren't you already bespoken to your brother's wife? What a pity."

Why had I ever shared my secret feelings with such a clod? I didn't bother to answer him.

chapter 16

A Dissolution of Partnership

Not everyone wanted to wait around to see what Bruno Stark was going to do with his son's company. The next morning, Ashton, leaving a note that forfeited Mittie's tuition deposit, drove off to Mexico with Professor Aubrey and Randolph Wheeling. Word of his break-out buzzed through the company, but only as a minor accompaniment to the noisier departure of Calhoun Grange that afternoon. Mr. Ed Hade, owner of the largest car dealership in the state, had offered a car and driver to carry the star to the airport; he reminded us all that he had had the honor of introducing Cal at the Nixon picnic and that he was proud to be of help.

And so that evening at sunset, a white Cadillac convertible brought Grange from his hotel to the theater, where his crowded leave-taking left Sabby Norah tearful, many of us drunk, and Floren Park eclipsed. Having invited evuhbody to be sure and come on out to live with him in Hollywood, he left us in order to put in an appearance being seen with a starlet at a table in Las Vegas before his agent fried his ass. Wolfstein stayed at home.

And bright as sunlight on ski snow in his pure white perfect suit, white boots, white belt with golden buckle, white teeth, he kissed Leila good-bye, looping the treasure of his gold scarf with easy grace around her neck. Leila looked upset—whether because of Wolfstein and Cal or *her* and Cal, I didn't know.

Sliding into the car with a last grin, a last wave, Grange drove off. Through an amber spin of dust, we saw his long legs swing up, cross; his immaculate boots come to rest on the front seat, just beside the driver's head. We saw his long arm drape over his authentic totem pole, gift of a grateful town. Silent under a starless sky, we carried on without him. That night Leila took Wolfstein all the way to Central City for dinner; no one else was invited.

The next day she revived *The Fantastiks* for our dwindled audience. Wolfstein wanted no further new productions; there was no word from Mr. Stark, and we couldn't survive forever on our Calhoun Grange profits. In the next weeks, Wolfstein began more and more to sit in his gloom and drink. And so Leila began more and more to assume full management of the Red Lagoon Theatre, calling rehearsals, casting, supervising set construction, soliciting advertisements to pay the bills. And she assumed an authoritative tone that startled the cast into obedience She made Ronny Tiorino recite his lines to her at dinner until he had successfully memorized them, rather than continuing to rely on the inspiration of improvisation as he used to; she made Marlin help Pete Barney sweep the stage, even though Marlin was second year; she made Suzanne help Sabby wash the costumes; she made Jennifer Thatcher work on stage crew duties; she made me rebuild three flats and work the box office, so there was no time to hang around the Red Lagoon Bar where I might run into the girl who called herself Tanya. Leila called meetings after performances so we could "analyze our mistakes," a privilege nobody particularly wanted. Rebellion began to mumble.

And a week after Ashton, Jennifer left. She left because she was homesick for Alabama, and because the food at the boarding house was ruining her complexion, and because she didn't like being a stagehand, and because she thought she would after all marry the guy who hadn't wanted her to be an actress in the first place. Mrs. Thurston told us that she herself should leave, but added immediately that she was staying, as she was needed. Needed to pull the shades of her respectable motherhood over the windows of our home. For otherwise, it appeared that what she had been obliged to define as the lunacy of Leila's actions would be horrifically silhouetted for every stranger in town to see.

For, without bothering to consult the household, Leila had moved Spurgeon Debson in. And now, to our amazement, his cot was set up on the front porch. His careful rags of clothes hung on the chain in Leila's bedroom. And Spur hung on the kitchen table, pounding vengefully throughout the day at an ancient typewriter that rumbled and shook the walls so that cups trembled in their saucers and lampshades quivered.

Spurgeon's endurance was remorseless. Pausing only to relieve himself, he beat out hour after hour of *Dachau, District of Columbia* on his faded keys. Occasionally he broke off to slam out a letter of blunt outrage to the F.B.I., the C.I.A., the IRS, the Santa Fe, to the Writers' Guild, the Chrysler Corporation, the Mormon Tabernacle Choir, to William Buckley, and to Sara Lee. Each he threatened to line up against a wall, to burn, blast, bludgeon, belch on.

At home, we grew tense and silent. We woke to the rage of a misanthropic Chanticleer who screamed excerpts of the morning newspaper at us. Maddened by the new evil each new day proclaimed, he lashed a piece of paper through his machine and clanged us to breakfast with its bell. Hidden behind chairs, Maisie and Davy stared at him. Mrs. Thurston stared at him face to forehead as she scrubbed the table around his jumping type-writer, emptied the wastebasket of his balled and ripped sheets, futilely struck him with her looks of indignation. Whenever Spur went to the post office to mail his missiles, she boxed up his typewriter, folded up his cot, tied up his manuscripts, and stacked it all next to the porch door. It had no effect.

Having packed Spur up one evening after dinner, she joined Wolfenstein and me in the front yard. Our director was hunched on the steps watching his shoes. I was watching Davy tirelessly pull Aunt Esther's old bear by a string around and around in a small dusty circle. It seemed a fitting symbol of the way things were going.

Folding ironed napkins into tight square packets as she talked, Mrs. Thurston expressed her dissatisfaction with our present circumstances. "Nathan, Nathan," she sighed. "The situation in this house."

Wolfstein said nothing.

"The situation in this house," she repeated, "has simply gone beyond the pale. My dear God, is Leila running a lunatic asylum in her own home? Are we to be made the servants and custodians of a mad fool? Are our ears to be ravaged by such perpetual pandemonium that a person simply cannot hear himself think? Nathan, why hasn't that man been committed?"

Wolfstein pressed his fingertips into his eyes. "Why indeed?" he coughed. "I myself am already committed." He tried to stretch his lips into a grin. Then spitting a cough into his handkerchief, he stood and struggled back up the steps to the house. We watched him go. Jumping up quickly, Mrs. Thurston caught Davy in his circle and slapped the dirt from his pants. "I should just take these babies back with me to Earlsford. That's the truth, Devin," she nodded at me.

Inside the house, the phone began ringing. "I hope," she said, "I deeply hope that the Federal Bureau of Investigation is telephoning us about that man. The government is just not going to tolerate being addressed that way, in that violent manner, through the United States mail."

But the phone call was from Mama, the distance crackling around her voice. "Well, Pooh," she embarrassed me by saying, when I'd asked her for years not to call me that any more, "I guess you just can't afford the postage, so I'm sending you some stamped envelopes."

"Oh, Mama."

"Because we're funny that way, and we would enjoy hearing from you every year or so."

"How—"

"But I'm not calling to stir up old memories of your happy childhood."

"Is everybody okay?"

"What? Good. I'm glad things are fine."

"No. Are YOU O-KAY?"

"Devin, there's no sense in trying to talk to me on this damn thing."

"Yes, ma'am."

"So just listen, and then I'll put Colum on—he's right here—and you two can talk."

"IS EVERY THING O-KAY?"

"Yes. We're all getting along here. Harnley's finished up marching around in a bog for the army, and Maeve's gone back to Richmond with the baby. He's walking again. Of course, Colum's not, but one recovery a month may be all you get. Now, the reason I'm calling is Fitzgerald. I'm sending a money order and—is he there?"

"No, ma'am."

"Put him on for a minute."

"NO, MA'AM. He's not here."

"No? Well, you two cash the money order and put him on the bus the 31st at the latest, the 31st, send him home. With everything else that poor child is trying to deal with, she doesn't need an extra person to feed and take care of."

"Leila? Fitzgerald's working for Leila," I said. "She's not taking care of him."

"And, Devin, I hope you're being as helpful and supportive as possible. Of course, I know you are. My heart just aches for her. Well, God bless her, she's had more than her share to bear in her short years. You write to me, and take care of yourself. I love you, Pooh. Give my love to Fitzgerald. And to Leila. Now here's Colum."

"Mama—"

"She's off," Colum said.

"How's it going?"

"Soft life. Sore butt," he answered. "How're you?"

"Hell, I've been better. Look, is the wedding still on? What's happening?"

"Sorry, kid. The invitations are in the mail. I don't think they sent you one, but I'll save you a copy." I heard a sharp rap, then Colum muttered, "Come on, Mama, he asked me! Devin, she wants to know what your plans are." I told him to tell her I didn't know. I might go to graduate school, but I wasn't sure. She told him to tell me not to get drafted.

"How is the Rock of Gibraltar?" I asked him.

"Oh, she's okay. But, I tell you, ole Eleanor Roosevelt here is going to get us booted out of this apartment too. She's got a big placard, Mothers Against the War, stuck up in the front yard, and the neighbors don't like it at all. I give us a month at the most."

He passed on some more questions from Mama about my health and diet. Then after we hung up, I walked over to the theater to tell Fitzgerald that he'd been recalled. He was disappointed. When I got there, Leila was going over his candy orders with him. She had on a white linen Mexican shirt embroidered with green leaves that was too short to wear without a skirt. Her legs were bare. Seeing her, a knot of anger tightened my stomach. Since Calhoun Grange, since Spur's settlement, since her criticism of my sets, I had little desire to be around Leila, but I went ahead and delivered my message. "Mama said to send you her love."

"Oh," she bit her mouth, "I'm sorry I wasn't there. I wish I could have talked to her. I wish…" She frowned, tore off her list of supplies, and put it in her huge pocketbook. "See you later," she said.

"Leila," Fitzgerald came around to the front of the counter, "hey, listen, Leila, I don't want to go. Really, I like it here, and there's not any reason I have to be back there. So couldn't you call her up and say how I'm not really any trouble and all and ask her to let me stay? Could you?"

She smiled at Fitzgerald, touched his hand. "Sure. We'll call her and ask. We can try, can't we?" Then she put on her sunglasses, called Maisie away from the box office where Margery Dosk was putting makeup on her, and took her out to the Red Bus. She drove away.

I took a Coke from the freezer. Noting it in his account book, Fitzgerald asked me, "Are you going to leave too?"

I sat up on the counter, looked at the pictures of the company lining the wall—Mittie's bordered in black: 1940–1968. "Maybe. Maybe we all should. The whole thing's going to hell anyhow."

"What do you mean?"

"I'm going over to the bar. See you later."

When they called, Mama told Leila that she felt Fitzgerald should get back home, and so he began packing up all his new possessions. There were always new arenas. Maybe, he said, he could put the Earlsford High School Drama Club on a paying basis.

Before he left, he took a series of souvenir photographs. Me sitting under a tree looking at the creek. Me in my sheriff's outfit. Sabby Norah frowning at the bobbin of her sewing machine. Pete Barney eating a pizza. Seymour Mink brushing his teeth. Shirtless Ronny and Marlin crushing beer cans. Nathan Wolfstein pouring a drink over his hand. Suzanne Steinitz reading *The Rich and the SuperRich* with her fist between her legs. Joely and me with Margery Dosk standing on our shoulders. Mrs. Thurston's finger on the nozzle of her hair-spray can, half her face looking surprised. Davy peeing in the bathtub. Maisie staring at Spur's leg under the kitchen table. The entire company strung in a row across the concession stand, everyone holding up money. The concession stand itself. The main curtain. The front of the theater. The front of the house. The front of the boarding house. The parking lot. The portrait of Leila on the lobby floor.

On July 31st, a day sullen with humidity after weeks of dry heat that seared the grass brown, a farewell luncheon was given. Verl appeared with gifts for Fitzgerald of indigenous rocks, leaves, newspapers, match covers, ore samples, a Coors beer can. Fitzgerald made a speech. Leila presented him with a special bonus of fifty one-dollar bills for his success in selling refreshments. Everyone cheered her. Fitzgerald made a thank-you speech. Everyone cheered him. Mrs. Thurston offered a smile. Sabby and Margery kissed him. Verl, Joely, Marlin, Seymour, and I carried his baggage to the Red Bus, and Leila drove him away.

Then Verl walked with me out to the edge of the empty parking lot, where we watched the brown swirl of creek water swell past us. The sky was brown too, full of thick, sluggish clouds. "Where's your car?" I asked him.

"Dennis Reed borrowed it. He said he wanted to take a girl to Aspen in a sports car. To impress her. I've got his truck over there by the bar…So you're staying. Kind of thought you'd take off with Fitzgerald. You going to hang in there and show you can take the pace? All the way to the finish line. Sign your name: 'I, Devin, did not desert.'"

We sat down on the dry spikes of grass banking the creek. "Desert? What's deserting got to do with it?" I asked. "That's not the point. I mean, come on, what is the finish line? Wolfstein's mildewing in his room. Mittie's in a damn box. She's got that jackass Spurgeon machine-gunning the universe at the kitchen table. She's ordering everybody around. Everybody that's *left*. Working them to death. The whole damn place is going to pieces."

"You're free to go, you know."

"Yeah, I know. I guess I'll stay. I don't know. You think I should?"

"Stay? Yeah, I think you should." He stood up, brushing dust from his long thin legs.

We headed toward Reed's truck. There was a weird sort of silence in the air. The clouds hung in murky stillness over the roof of the theater; they pressed down from the sky onto the tops of motionless trees. "Jesus, what's it going to do?" I said.

Verl reached into the cab of the truck. "Brought your poems back," he told me, holding out a package. The poems were about Jardin, about the situation. I'd been working on them since I'd been in Floren Park, and each one was in a different verse form.

"Well, what did you think?" I asked him.

"I thought they showed a lot of technique," he said. "Well, you can read my comments. What's that tie for?" A brightly colored necktie splashed with flowers was wrapped around the notebooks and knotted on top.

"Oh, I was wearing it the day I introduced Jardin to J.D. You know, a kind of reminder. But listen, I'm not working on the poems now. I'm thinking about writing down all the stuff that's been happening this summer. Something Gothic. All the funny stuff."

"*Funny* stuff? Like what do you mean?"

"Oh, you know, like stuff about Wolfstein and—"

"Wolfstein? What's funny about Wolfstein?"

"You know what I mean, Verl—the bugs and drinking and all. And Spurgeon."

"Don't forget Mittie now. Lot of funny stuff there too." He gave me one of those looks of his.

Suddenly the tie began to flutter, then to flap against Verl's hands. Dirt flew up from the lot and stung our eyes. "Hey," I said, "feel that wind. It's going to let loose."

"No," Verl said. "Look!" He pointed up into the molasses sky. An amorphous shape like some monstrous bird came down at us, sinking with a shrill piercing noise through the bottom of a yellowish cloud.

"My God, what is it?"

"A helicopter," Verl said. He reached into his shirt pocket, pulled out sunglasses, and put them on.

As the thing circled down, the huge propellers lashed a whirlpool of wind at us, flattening our clothes against our skins. The wind whipped dust into pellets that burned my eyes shut, and I fell blinded against Verl's shoulder.

Slowly, as if weightless, the helicopter touched ground, squatted like a black condor in the middle of the parking lot, its long, thin tail still quivering in the air, dust still storming around it. I held to Verl's shoulder and followed him forward. The awful noise of the motor died away, the thrashing circle of propellers decelerated into distinct silver blades. The door creaked open, and a ladder descended. We waited. Finally, two thin men came hurrying down the ladder, each wearing a thin gray business suit, a thin blue business shirt, a dark tie. Each with a thin gray briefcase. On either side, they stood at the bottom, turned, ties

waving, hair gusting about, and looked up into the hole of the
helicopter. A large, thick man emerged, black-suited with a gray
silk tie, with white wiry hair crisped close to his head, a straight
white mustache, and straight lines of black eyebrows. He stood
at the top looking, then put on the dark glasses he carried in his
hand, and walked down to where the other two waited.

I said to Verl. "It's like in the movies, you know, where
Murder Incorporated flies in to wipe out the opposition."

The older man strode toward the theater, stared at it sternly,
stared at the creek, the bar. Finally he noticed us by the truck.
We walked over.

"Can we help you?" Verl asked.

"Are you connected with the Red Lagoon Theatre?" he
asked in a deep voice used to authority. I thought then it must
be the government come to arrest Spurgeon Debson for threats
of violence.

"I am, sir. Are you looking for someone?"

"Yes. My daughter-in-law. My name is Bruno Stark."

chapter 17

I Am Sent Away from Home

"These are two of my employees—Mr. Edgars, Mr. Edmunds," Mr. Stark added summarily as he swung open the theater door with a steely hand, white wires of hair bristling on his fingers. He didn't ask who we were. Learning that Leila was then on her way to the Denver bus terminal, Stark told us that he would first inspect the theater, after which he would like to visit with his grandchildren until their mother returned. Everyone nodded. Then Verl, who was going over to the library, said good-bye, while I followed Stark and his employees into the Red Lagoon lobby.

He stepped across the portrait of Leila and stood quietly in the middle of the room, unwrapping a long black cigar and slowly turning it in his fingers before inserting it between his teeth. Mr. Edgars or Edmunds quickly produced a lighter, which he jerkily snapped on beneath Stark's cigar. Stark nodded and the lighter disappeared.

Slowly, he looked around the lobby; it was, I realized with a sharp surge of adrenalin, still littered with the aftermath of Fitzgerald's farewell picnic. On the concession stand counter, on the floor, on the chairs lay the clutter of crumpled napkins, paper plates soggy with chicken bones and half-chewed biscuits, with Coke bottles, beer bottles, wine bottles—some with cigarette butts floating in the remains. The air smelled of old smoke and stale beer and souring food, all worsened by heat and humidity that sat in the room like crowds of people. Helpless, I watched Stark take it in. Then he walked over to the wall of photographs, studied them sequentially, pausing no longer over the black-bordered picture of his son in the center than over the others.

Behind his cigar smoke, Stark's face appeared bland, the dry, smoothly shaven skin sleek, untroubled by the heat, the lips calm beneath his white mustache. He seemed impenetrable, a closed circuit. Mittie had been his only son. But watching him, there was no way to know what he was thinking, why he had come, what he wished to discover.

In back of him patiently stood Mr. Edgars and Mr. Edmunds, each with both hands clutching his briefcase across his chest. Their hair and collars had wilted, bubbles of sweat popped silently over their noses, but neither moved to wipe them away. After a few minutes, Stark stepped toward the rear door of the box office. The two men filed noiselessly after him. He opened the door onto more disorder. Tickets, posters, candy wrappers, a Eugene McCarthy poster, bills, letters, a roll of toilet paper, a yellow truck, a pipe, a T-shirt all jumbled into open drawers; a chair had fallen over onto the desk as if shot from behind. From the wall one of Ronny's *Playboy* playmates simpered at her ballooning breasts, her legs curled up by the humidity. Righting the chair, Mr. Stark dusted it with the T-shirt and sat down.

Suddenly, from inside the theater itself, shrieks of laughter blew out. Staccato chords clapped up and down the piano as a loud falsetto voice began to sing: "Whatever Lola wants, Loollllaaaa gets, and, little man, little Lola wants *you*."

Horrified, I edged my way past Edgars and Edmunds, crossed the lobby, and squeezed through the doors to the theater, shutting them immediately behind me. Fitzgerald's party was still going on. On the stage, Seymour Mink was drunk. And drunkenness had crushed his usual reticence, for, nude to the waist, with a woman's blond wig on his head, strings of beads around his neck, a spangled skirt hanging around his hips over his pants, Seymour danced the hula before Ronny Tiorino, who sat bare-chested on the stage floor, vodka from a bottle down his upturned throat. At the piano, Pete Barney was drunk. Seated on the steps of the stage, Marlin Owen and Margery Dosk were drunk.

Pete slammed out another round of chords as Seymour swerved back into song. Wriggling his hips, he beat Ronny back and forth across the stomach with a huge fan of pink ostrich plumes. "I always get what I aaiiiim for, and your heart and soul is what I caaaammme for."

"Kiss me, sugarpants," Ronny leered at him.

"Take that, you tewwible, tewwible old monster," Seymour lisped, with a swipe of the fan at Ronny's crotch. They all twisted with laughter.

Rushing to the stage, I tried to beat their noise down with my hands. "Shut up. Shut up," I whispered. They doubled over with giggles. "Mittie's father is in the lobby," I grimaced, pointing in pantomime.

Pete Barney played the opening notes of *Dragnet*. "Dum De DUM dum," he sang.

Furious, I grabbed his arm. "Damn it, I mean it!"

"Sure," Ronny guffawed, holding his stomach.

Seymour peered down the dark theater aisle. Then jerking up, he dropped the fan as if it were on fire, ripped the wig from his hair, snatched his shirt from the floor and held it in front of his chest. "Oh, no," he moaned under his breath. Light from the open door caught the swirling rings of white cigar smoke.

"I'd like to speak to Joely Finn, if he's back there. Is he?" Stark's voice echoed down the huge empty room.

Margery stood up, her beer bottle behind her back. "He's in the scene shop."

"Hello, Margery. Send him out here, please," Stark said. The door swung shut.

Seymour, his face pasty with quick sobriety, pulled on his shirt and stepped out of the spangled gown. Then he sank to the floor beside Ronny. "Holy shit," he shook his head. "This is it."

"I'll get Joely," Marlin said sadly. He went backstage.

"You know Stark?" I asked Margery, who was picking up beer bottles and paper plates, dropping them into a waste can.

"Sure, we all met him last summer. He flew down for a day so he could point out to Mittie that he didn't know how to run a business. Scared the shit out of everybody."

"Why?" I asked. Did he think we had murdered his son?

"Boy, we've blown it now." Seymour kept shaking his head. He kicked out at the ostrich plumes.

Followed by Marlin and by Sabby, who was biting her fingernails, Joely hurried from the wings down the stage steps. "Donahue," he called, and I went over. Pulling me along with him by the arm, he spoke rapidly, "Go next door to the bar; call home. If Leila's not back…"

"How could she have even gotten…"

"Tell her mother that Bruno Stark is here. Tell her, well, she'll know."

"Know what?"

"Where are the kids?" he snapped.

"Leila took them with her," Sabby whispered.

"Okay. Then, Devin, you get over there and see what you can do about Spurgeon."

"And what would that be?" I asked, jerking my arm away.

"Think of something," he growled, throwing open the door to the lobby where Stark stood giving instructions to Mr. Edmunds or Edgars: "Tell Gurley to stay with the copter 'til I get back. And get me a car. Then get us three rooms, wherever looks best."

The employee jerked his head down in acknowledgment of each command, then, dismissed, slid noiselessly away.

"Mr. Stark. Hello," Joely offered his hand. "This is a surprise."

Stark shook the hand perfunctorily. "So it appears," he replied.

Slumped in a dark corner booth of the Red Lagoon Bar, Wolfstein gazed dreamily at a glass of bourbon. His short-sleeved shirt was sweated flat against his breast, his bony arms dangled loosely out of the wide openings of the sleeves. "Nate," I nudged him. "Nate. Are you going to be here long?"

"World without end," he slurred softly, not looking up.

"What I was wondering was, could I take the Austin back to the house for a little while? Bruno Stark's here. Mittie's father. He just showed up. Everybody seems to be kind of panicked. Leila's not here."

Wolfstein appeared totally uninterested in my news. After a pause, he said, "Herr Vater. The Boss, huh? Pay up the mortgage. Out onto the ice." He twirled the ice cubes in his glass. "Devin," he asked, staring into the spinning bourbon, "you think the truth is in here?"

I hesitated, then decided to say it, "Well, I think one truth is…you're hurting yourself."

"Hah." He glanced up at me with blurred eyes. "What do you know about truth anyway? Punk kid."

I looked down at the floor.

Then he slid the car keys across the spilt liquor on the table.

"Thank you," I mumbled, embarrassed. "I'll bring the car back here."

"All the time in eternity," he whispered to his drink.

At the bar's pay phone, I called our house. It rang eleven times before she answered. "Stark residence, Mrs. Amanda Thurston speaking."

"Mrs. Thurston?"

"Yes, this is she."

"This is Devin." I could hear the rumble of a motor and the clack of a typewriter.

"What? Devin? Just a moment. It's simply impossible to speak under these conditions."

"Mrs. Thurston…" But she put the receiver down. I heard footsteps receding. A click. More footsteps. Another click. The noise was silenced.

"I'm sorry, Devin, but I had to come in here to Leila's bedroom in order to hear you. I was vacuuming and that is why I didn't hear the phone ringing at first. Of course, that man was sitting right beside it in the kitchen typing at his fool machine, but naturally one can't expect miracles, like Spurgeon's pausing one simple moment to pick up a receiver four inches from his elbow."

"Mrs. Thurston, Leila's not back, is she?"

"Why no, she left only an hour or so ago."

"Mrs. Thurston, Mr. Stark is here."

"What do you mean, Mr. Stark?"

"Bruno Stark."

"Devin! How can that be?"

"I don't know, but he's here at the theater, and he wants to see Leila."

"My Lord above! Where is Leila's head? She did not give me a single word of warning about this. Bruno Stark! And Emily?"

"No, ma'am. He landed in a helicopter in the parking lot with two of his employees. They're inspecting the whole theater now. I don't think Leila knew they were coming."

"Well, good heavens, I shouldn't imagine she did! Oh, dear Lord, and she is going to walk into this house wearing that skimpy little foreign shirt and nothing else, and half of her entire body fully exposed to every wind that blows. Devin, I am going to try to have that child paged at the bus terminal."

"Wait, Mrs. Thurston. Mr. Stark is coming over there."

"Here? Now?" she inhaled.

"Yes, ma'am, pretty soon, I think. So is Spurgeon there?"

She groaned.

"Is there anything you can do? Joely doesn't think it's such a good idea for Mr. Stark to run into him."

"Well, I don't need Joely Finn to tell me that. Of course, you don't suppose I can physically pry that man loose from his typewriter, which is what it will probably require, do you?"

"No, ma'am, I'll be there in a minute."

"And Devin, honey, bring the floor-buffer with you." She hung up.

Someone was tapping at the glass of the phone booth. Tanya. She ran a red fingernail slowly down the pane. Replacing the receiver, I tugged the door open and sidled out. Damn it. Why now, when I had to go?

"Hello, Devin Donahue," she said, shaking her hair back from her face, brandishing the curve of her neck at me. "Where have you been?" She pushed two fingers through openings in my shirt; squeezing them together, she undid a button. "I thought we were going to get together."

"We are," I said, sucking in my stomach as I stepped back. "Can we have a drink tonight? Around ten? Here? I gotta go."

"You scared of me?" she smiled.

"Nope," I smiled too. "I just have to go."

She flicked my chin with her forefinger. "Okay," she said.

Outside the bar, I noticed that Sheriff Booter was standing with his deputy across from the shooting gallery in the arcade talking to those three old Mexican women of Leila's who sold flowers in the streets during the summer. The old ladies were chattering and gesturing frenetically at the stolid Booter while his gum-chewing assistant packed their tin cans of flowers into cardboard boxes and shoved them into an open patrol car parked at the curb.

I drove home to find Mrs. Thurston, who had conceded neither stockings nor dress to the heat, spraying the house with an aerosol can. "Don't walk on the floor," she warned. "Where's the buffer?"

"I couldn't get it," I apologized.

Patting her forehead with the handkerchief she kept stuffed in her sleeve, she pursed her lips; her nostrils tightened. "You know, there is a peculiar odor in this house, Devin. I am not familiar with it, but I was not born yesterday, and I am practically convinced that that Spurgeon is smoking marijuana cigarettes here on these premises."

Somebody was, at any rate. She released another gust of pine scent at the ceiling. Then thrusting a bucket of ammonia at me, she proposed, "Now, honey, you could be a real help in this situation if you wouldn't mind washing down these few front windows."

The fumes made me gag, teared my eyes, but I splashed a clearing through the glass mist as Mrs. Thurston, beside me, began waxing the woodwork. Already, a bright veneer of order glistened throughout the house. On the tables, vases of roses and marigolds. On the mantel, portraits of Mittie and Leila, Mittie and the children. Between them the remaining pink glass globe, the one Mittie hadn't shot.

Ten minutes later, Spur came out of the bathroom, zipping up his fly. He wore a tank top stamped with the Vietcong flag. His hair was pulled back in a red rubber band. At the sight, Mrs. Thurston's face tensed. She held him at arm's length with her aerosol can. "Spurgeon, I am going to be mopping the kitchen floor, and I hope you will take this opportunity to get outside and get yourself a breath of fresh air. Sitting around like this all day is not good for your health."

He lifted his shirt, scratched the hair on his stomach. "Lady," he said, "would you say Nietzsche was sitting around all day? Was John Brown sitting around at Harper's Ferry? Do you think I'm sitting around all day? Wow, man! I'm starting a *revolution*! Do you think I care about my *health?*"

"Well, I'm sure that's very nice, Spurgeon, but the floor has to be mopped."

"FAR OUT! She thinks you can wash away BLOOD with a MOP! Listen, chick," he stabbed her with his finger, "your values are screwed, I mean, fucked up! Look at this can!" He grabbed it from her, threw it in the fireplace. "Junk! Plastic poison! Plastic food! Coffee! Cleaning! WOW! You need to get your ass loosened, lady."

Mrs. Thurston's cheeks flushed, she drew herself together, adding three inches to her dignity. "Young man," she replied with slow precision, "I will, not, honor, that vile, remark with a reply, except to say, that you belong, in an insane asylum, where you could receive some professional, help. Or, in a, prison, for the protection, of others." Having retrieved her can, she marched to the kitchen.

"Hey, Spur. Hey, Spur," I dangled my voice before him. It

caught his attention. "Hey, look, I wanted to ask you if you wanted to come down and take a look at something with me. It really sort of sums up the whole military industrial complex of this, you know, this stupid junkpile country." He was listening. "The cops—uh, the pigs—are busting some old elderly Mexican ladies down at the arcade. Busting them! And why? Why? Can you believe this? *For selling flowers!"*

I had him. His eyes whitened; he was visibly salivating. "Rich. Rich. Heavy. WOW!" He threw his hands up in laughter. "Oh, wow. I can use it, man, I can USE it. It's perfect."

"I'm going back now," I urged.

"Yeah," he crooned. "Wheels?"

"Sure," I reeled him in. "I've got Wolfstein's sports car."

"That Nazi death trap?" he balked. For a minute I thought I'd lost him, but he stopped only to stuff a spice jar and a red packet of cigarette papers in his blue-jeans pocket, then grabbed up a legal pad and ran past me out the door.

Quickly I sprinted to the kitchen. "We're going," I told Mrs. Thurston, who was on the floor sudsing with two scrub brushes. She jumped to her feet and crammed Spur's typewriter into its case. "Thank the Good Lord, and thank you, honey. Now, I could not reach Leila at the terminal, where the switchboard girl was, frankly, rude to me over the telephone. So we will just have to Hope for the Best." Handing me the case, she pushed me out to the porch, where she fell to her knees and ripped the blanket from Spur's cot.

While I drove him down to the arcade, Spurgeon excommunicated Wolfstein's car in his grandest style. Of course, he was just revving up his larynx. Noticing the helicopter in the parking lot as we pulled in, he screamed at it, shaking the dashboard with both hands like a hysterical chimpanzee, "Will you LOOK at that? Bastards! *The pigs have brought in the fucking National Guard!* They're going to BAZOOKA those downtrodden women! THE WHOLE WORLD IS WATCHING YOU!" he yelled out the window at a man who was leaning up against the side of the helicopter, flipping through a magazine.

Jumping out before I could stop the car, Spur raced past the bar, up the arcade lane, where three of the elderly flower-sellers still stood. The police were gone, so were the flowers. As he flew toward them yelling, "Fascists! Murderers!" the women shrieked, threw up their arms, threw off their shawls, and scampered up the lane in the opposite direction. They flapped around a corner, and Spur sped after them.

I parked the car. "What's going on?" the man, who I figured must be the copter pilot, called over to me.

"He's writing a play," I yelled.

"Oh," he shrugged, and went back to his magazine.

• • •

I stood at the door and squinted down into the dark theater. Around a table set up on the stage, Joely handed ledger books to Mr. Stark. Mr. Edgars and Mr. Edmunds were bent over other books, their ties loosened, flicking their hands across their noses at the flies that were buzzing around them in the sticky air. Their tongues twitched from side to side to catch the sweat gathering at the corners of their mouths. I started to close the door again when Stark looked up.

"What's his name?" he asked Joely.

"Devin Donahue."

"Ah, Devin," he called out. My hand started to sweat, slid on the doorknob. "I wonder if you would mind doing me a favor."

"Glad to."

"I'd like you to go next door and tell Mr. Menelade that I want to speak with him for a moment."

"Sure." The Menelades, I had learned, owned the Red Lagoon Theatre as well as the bar, and so it was from Tony (or Lady Red, rather) that Mittie had leased the property. The lease was in his and Leila's names, but of course Bruno Stark was paying the rent.

"And Devin, I'd like to speak with you as well, sometime this evening. I hope that will be agreeable." Assuming it would be, he lowered his head back to the books, and so Edmunds and Edgars, who had been staring at me while he spoke, their mouths open like dogs breathing in hot air, lowered their heads with him.

I didn't want to do it. Why should I have to explain myself to him? I wanted to go home, but I couldn't go home because that home was making itself ready for Stark. And it wasn't my home anyhow. Fitzgerald was going to my home.

"Okay, fine," I said, pulling the door closed behind me.

Back at the bar, I found Tony Menelade in front of his little television set, crouched in his shirt-sleeves, wiping the back of his neck with a dishtowel. Near him, at the cash register, his wife pushed nickels into paper rolls. I leaned across the counter to tap him. "Excuse me, Tony, Bruno Stark is next door—Mittie's father. He'd like to speak with you—something about the theater—if you have a minute."

"Shit," Tony said without moving; he was watching *Truth or Consequences*.

"Put your jacket on." Mrs. Menelade tossed it at him.

"Aw, come on, Red, it's sweltering," he grimaced.

"You want him to think you're a slob?" Annoyance snarled out of her face.

"What do I care?" Tony sulked, pulling on the jacket.

She packed the rolls of change into drawers, closed and locked them. "What do you care? Let me get this through your head: I'd like to sell this dump. I'd like to go someplace for once in my life. And this guy may want to buy it. You see that? So we're both going over there now, and we're going to make a good impression on this Mr. Stark." The words were like twists of his arm behind his back.

"Kim," she called to the big, dough-white dancer who sat near the jukebox, frowning as she read some kind of movie magazine. "Watch the register for a few minutes." Kim slowly pulled herself up out of her chair, dragged herself over to the bar. Lady Red took her purse from under the counter and left with it for the bathroom.

"Stark's up on the stage," I told Tony. I looked around for Tanya, but she wasn't there.

Passing Wolfstein fogged in vapors of smoke, I raised my hand to him, gesturing greetings; he didn't notice me. Once outside again, I stood, irresolutely, in front of the door. To go back to the theater now was awful. Stark's capacity to intimidate was awful. What right had he to such assurance, what right to frighten us by his authority? But then he must have loved his only son. So that excused it. But Verl said that while not loving enough is always wrong, loving too much is not always right. He said this was true because we can warp love to fit us. I thought about this. Stark must find it inexplicable that his plans could be so violated, so carelessly set aside, when he had all that money and all that power to make them work. He should have been able to stop Mittie from dying, from drinking, from failure, from unhappiness. So he had come to learn why. Maybe he would interrogate us all, one by one, until he had found out the reason, had identified and punished the saboteur was Mittie himself, and he had wrenched the shape of his plan. But the saboteur had already slipped through his grasp. And I didn't want to be questioned about it.

Lady Red pushed Tony past me; she brushed at the back of his jacket, straightening it as they went into the theater. Crossing the lot finally, I stood at the point on the little bridge where Mittie had jumped into the shallow water, warning us with a burlesque joke. Afternoon was over, the rain had never come, and now the sun, undefeated, began with a grin to set. I strained my eyes open to watch. When it sets, I said, I'll go in and ask him, "What did you want to talk to me about, Mr. Stark?" When it sets.

Since childhood, I had called up a special vision as my tranquilizer against fear, anxiety, humiliation, hurt feeling. I ran it over and over through my head until I escaped the missed catch, lost election, broken heirloom, broken date. The image was that I swim up, up from the suffocating bottom of a dark pool, up to lighter water, my lungs bursting; then I shoot out, breaking the surface, keep going; I fly past the tops of buildings, past planes, past clouds. My problems clutch at my feet—the school principal, the coach of the baseball team, the draft official, James Dexter—but I kick them off, soar higher.

So now, to exorcise Stark, I resurrected the image and flew. His hairy steel hand grabbed again and again at my ankle, held fast, so I couldn't kick. And so my arched wings dropped wax to burn his face. Screaming, he let go, and I climbed to the sun.

The sun flared as it sank, striking my face with light, the shaft burst my image, and I opened my eyes to see Leila standing framed in the gold, her hand opening in hello. Beside her in the lot, Maisie and Davy ran laughing around the helicopter.

"Who's come to call?" she smiled.

"Your father-in-law's inside," I yelled.

She nodded several times, started toward the theater.

"Leila," I ran toward her. "Leila, listen, your mother tried to get you at the terminal. She thought, you know"—I pointed at her Mexican shirt and bare thighs—"she thought maybe you'd want to change your clothes first."

Leila looked at the pattern of green leaves growing on her arm. "No," she smiled, "I don't think so. Why should I? Everybody having fits about Bruno?" She'd expected him, I suppose, sooner or later.

"Boy, you said it." I smiled.

She called Maisie and Davy to her. "Oh, Devin," she turned back to say, "Fitzgerald got off fine." She picked Davy up, gave Maisie her large pocketbook to carry. The three of them went inside the theater.

I stayed on the bridge, my legs nearly numb with tiredness, the ache to go to sleep. Five minutes went by. Then Mr. Edmunds or Edgars hurried out and called over to Gurley, the pilot, who was now sitting on the ground near his helicopter, smoking. Beside him, a row of white butts stuck in the dirt like anonymous grave markers. The two men spoke briefly, then Gurley stretched his legs, stamped down the cigarettes, buttoned up his jacket, climbed up into the machine, and pulled the door closed after him. Stark's employee waved a brisk good-bye as he rushed back to the theater, where he bobbed his head at the Menelades, who were then coming out the door.

Slowly the motor wound to a hideous roar, spinning the blades faster and faster into a blur. Dust whirled again, and weightless, the black machine slowly lifted, sucked upward toward the sun. The sky was on fire.

part three

The Land of the Wolf

chapter 18

I Become Neglected and Am Provided For

There is an eyesore in downtown Floren Park, a village other-wise glossy, called Slough Lane. A dim, dirty street, little more really than a dirt ditch, Slough Lane runs a short way at a right turn off the Arcade and ends in a mud field that is littered with communal rubbish, with rusted parts of indefinable machinery, with a rotted mattress, rotting tires, toppled pyramids of rusted cans and broken bottles. It was all incompatible with the Alpine chalets and Victorian gingerbread, and the residents preferred it hidden from the tourists in Arcadia.

Along either side of the lane slump a dozen tin cabins, one-room square ruins, whose orange or pink rouge is peeling down their faces. There are rusted cars decaying beside a few of these cabins; rusted T.V. antennae lay crippled on the roofs; there is broken glass in the yards.

I walked down Slough Lane waiting for the sun to set and stopped in front of a grimy store that crouched in the middle of the row, shoved between two cabins, the only two rejuvenated with fresh rose fronts. By squinting through the window soot, I read that it called itself a store for adults. Peering further in, I could see its offerings: cigarettes, beer, fishing tackle, aged potato chips clipped to a stand, movie magazines, newspapers, and three dusty shelves of dusty books for adult reading. Calhoun Grange was on a magazine cover in the window telling his fans that draft dodgers ought to be jailed. I went inside where a dusty sign, in front of a row of bared breasts and bared buttocks, told me I would not be allowed to loiter. Opening a magazine anyhow, I turned the pages quickly until a dwarfish man with dirty hair, his eyes horrifically magnified by opaque glasses, came at me from somewhere in a dark corner, and I retreated back outside.

On the other side of the ditch, a plainly dressed man was talking to a colorfully dressed one. The latter frowned, shook his head impatiently and walked off; his black patent boots stepped with distaste in the dirt. His hair was black patent too, and his modish suit a brilliant blue with black trimming. The plainly dressed man watched him saunter to the last cabin, kick dirt from his boots against the step, then unlock the door and go in. He stood watching even then, until he noticed me standing there, at which point be stuck a small notebook back in his coat pocket and unhurriedly retraced his steps up Slough Lane to the Arcade. I followed him out.

By now the sky had blotted out all color left by the sun, but had not lightened the day's heat or its humidity. Pulling my shirttail from my pants, I flapped it against my skin to cool myself. The man with the notebook had disappeared. In the Arcade, tourists were firing rifles at tin animals that sprang jerkily out of tin bushes. They were waiting for fat trout to hook themselves onto lines dropped among bread lumps in plastic bins. They were buying Navajo jewelry made in Japan and mountain landscapes painted in Manhattan. They were strolling out of the grand promenade of Main Street into this little promenade, dripping slices of pizza, ears of hot corn, frankfurters blobbed with mustard. Sluggish with heat, I leaned against the side of the shooting gallery and watched them.

The moon rose up, red as the sun. And I walked back to the theater. In front of the doors sat a long, gray Oldsmobile; in front of the car stood Bruno Stark talking to Leila, who held Davy in her arm and Maise by the hand. Behind Stark waited Edgars and Edmunds, briefcases against their chests. I came to the edge of their circle.

"Well, Bruno," Leila said, "you'll do whatever you decide to do."

He smiled at her wryly; it was by no means an affectionate look, but hate was curiously tinged with respect. "True enough. So. All right. We'll go over it all tomorrow. And I'll look over the papers tonight. So. You're a smart cookie, Leila. But all in all, I think this is going to be the best solution. Tomorrow." He took Davy from her and squeezed him appraisingly between his hands. "What do you say, boy?"

Davy said nothing.

"You're a rich man, David Stark. You don't know it, but you're a rich man someday. When you finish up college, you and I will go to work. See things. So. Eat. Grow big. Strong. You're going to have it all." He tightened his fingers, frightening Davy, whose eyes widened and whose mouth began to quiver. Stark set him down on the ground beside Maisie, then sharply rubbed her head with his knuckles. "And how about you, young lady? What do you say to one of those talking dolls, maybe a carriage too. How about that?"

Maisie ducked her head from beneath his hand. She kept staring at Stark as she pressed the end of her red bead necklace to her mouth.

"A choosy buyer, no less." Stark asked his employees to observe Maisie's sagacity. Grinning, they bobbed their heads, "Maybe a bicycle, then," he bid. "What do you say to a bicycle, princess? Maybe with a horn. A light. A basket. How would that be?"

Slowly, after deliberation, Maisie nodded her head yes.

"Good, good." Stark nodded too. "Smart girl. Don't settle. Hold out for what you want."

Leila spoke. "Listen, Bruno, you're welcome to come stay at my house. We can make room. Why should you stay at a hotel?"

"No, no, no, I already made arrangements."

Leila shrugged. "Okay, if you're sure. Mother will be disappointed."

"Tomorrow," Stark told her. "Edgars, I'd like to make arrangements to talk to this sheriff, what's his name—Booter. And this Dr. Ferrell guy. Okay, let's go."

Edgars got in the Oldsmobile, started the motor. Edmunds opened the back door.

"Excuse me. Mr. Stark?" I stepped forward.

He ran me through his memory bank. "Devin. Yes. Tomorrow. All right?"

I stepped back.

"So. Nine o'clock," he said to Leila, and in silence she agreed.

The lights of the Oldsmobile swung past the creek, past the bridge, and scanned the woods across from them, then swinging around, light jabbed through the lot and was gone. Leila got in the Red Bus with the children.

"Mind if I ride back with you?"

"No. Let's go." She turned off the blaring radio that told us the North Vietnamese said they really didn't see how they could talk to us unless we stopped bombing them. Leila drove quietly, one hand at the base of the wheel, one on Davy, asleep in her lap. Maisie had her head stuck out the window, her eyes shut, her mouth opened happily to the wind.

"Are you okay, Leila?"

"I'm fine." She pulled Davy closer to her.

"Can I ask you what this new 'best solution' is?"

"Well, let's see. First of all, Bruno wants to close down the theater. I show," she smiled, "a low margin of profit. And so I'm a bad investment. Meanwhile, Lady Red's trying to sell him the two buildings and the lot, and if they show an even lower margin of profit, then he'll buy them. And that will be a good investment."

"Yeah. Taxes, I guess. What will he do with them?"

"Tear them down and build something with a high margin of profit. Oh, who knows what Bruno's up to. I don't think he's decided yet."

"What does he want you to do?"

"Well, he thinks it would be appropriate for Mittie's children to be moved to Portland and be given allowances. Well, it's okay if I don't want to come along, as long as they are there by the end of the month."

"Oh."

She added nothing further until we reached the house, when she asked me to carry Davy in for her.

Dressed in a pink chiffon garden dress in the polished perfection of our living room, Mrs. Thurston was seated, handsomely arranged beside the vacuumed fireplace, doing needlepoint. She swanned her neck past us expectantly as we entered. When no one followed, she stood to peep around the lace curtain freshly stapled to the front door.

"And Bruno?" she chirped to the crickets outside. "And Bruno?" She cricked her head to one side. I shook my head. "Why Leila, honey, where is your father-in-law? Where are ou-er guests?"

"He's staying at a hotel, Mother."

"At a *ho*-tel? Why surely that can't be, Leila. What in the world do you mean, a *ho*-tel? What about his dinner? What about his business associates? Leila Stark, surely you did not fail in your manners, you did not neglect to invite your own relative to share your hospitality? Did you hear me?"

Leila had taken Davy into her bedroom. Coming out, she touched her mother's arm. "No, I asked him, Mother, but he'd already made other arrangements. Probably he didn't want to impose on us at such short notice."

Mrs. Thurston's mouth pursed in and out; she stabbed her needle through a pensive shepherdess in her embroidery. "*Impose?* I never! Oh, Leila, Leila child, you are deceived. But I believe I can understand reality when it is staring me in the eyes. That man, Bruno Stark, has deliberately chosen this opportunity to make a statement. And what he is saying is, he has *never* considered us good enough for His Royal Highness. He has always disesteemed us and begrudged us Mittie's love, and now he is announcing, just as big as your life, 'It is all YOUR FAULT.' Saying it just as loud and clear by his actions in checking into a public hotel as if he had stood right here in this very yard and painted those words across the front of the house a mile high."

"Mother..." Leila undid her sandals, stretched out on the couch, and put her feet up on the armrest. With a wince, Mrs. Thurston restrained herself from removing them.

The kitchen door swung open. Stuck all over with white pasty patches, as though she planned to glue herself to the wall, Sabby Norah walked disconsolately out of the kitchen.

"Oh, Mrs. Thurston," she sniffed, wiping more paste across her cheek, "the dough won't come off the rolling pin."

"Darling, darling," Mrs. Thurston tapped Sabby toward the kitchen again. "Go back and flour. Evenly. A steady motion, keeping the wrists firm. Roll and lift. Roll and lift. And flour, Sabby. *Flour.*"

Already floured, Sabby left.

"That child," the home economist sighed, "is a good child, an industrious child, but she is simply not a...talented child."

I took a radish from a plate of concentric hors d'oeuvres on the coffee table.

"Devin, don't eat that!" Mrs. Thurston called.

I spat the radish into my hand.

"You're going to ruin your supper," she explained. "And, Leila, I want you to know that I had made the effort, in addition to everything else I had to do"—she panned the house with her eyes—"to prepare a native dish for that man. Went to the trouble of preparing Hungarian goulash, as well as a cherry soup from Budapest."

"Bruno's family is Russian, Mother," Leila murmured from the couch.

Mrs. Thurston's rejoinder was taken from the political sciences. "Well, it is a known fact that both those nations are members of the same Iron Block. And even you, Leila, who persist in establishing your own identity in defiance of your elders, in defying your training by glorifying communism as if it were the

Promised Land, even you cannot deny that the result of their policies has been to completely wipe away our right to be an individual. And I'm certain that if they require everybody, regardless of their education, to toil in the field and work in the subway booths, then they also require everybody to eat the same food. And all I can say is, it is curious to me to be disesteemed by a Man from Russia, when your family has been living in America ever since...why ever since there was an America for civilized people to live in!"

As no one appeared to be ready with a rebuttal, Mrs. Thurston retired to steady Sabby's wrists, noting only in departure that it was remarkable how some people could lie there with their eyes shut while other people were going around publicly insulting them.

The phone rang, and I answered it in the kitchen, "Hello."

"Yeah. Who is this?"

"This is Devin Donahue."

"Listen, man, the pigs have got me. Pulled me in. Chained me. Wow! Gestapo City!"

"Spurgeon?"

"This is it, man. They got Kafka. Dreyfus. Leary. Now they got me."

I thought of his threats against the F.B.I., the C.I.A., Sara Lee. "Where are you, Spur?"

"*Where am I?* I'm in a slimy sink of Stalag blood. I'm in Auschwitz, jerk. I'm in Wounded Knee. They can't hide from me now. I'm seeing through their glasses face to face. I'm sitting in the silent secret closet of the U.S.A. The *water* closet, man. The *slop hole*, where the shit's packed down three hundred years thick. The turds on the top are floating in piss!"

"Spur? Are you down at the station?"

"Can you believe it?"

I thought of the spice jar, the cigarette papers in his pocket. "Was it"—I tried to whisper, for Mrs. Thurston was in the kitchen too, helping Sabby pry dough from a rolling pin— "possession of...um, Mary Janes?"

"Possessed? They're the ones that are possessed, jack. The whole militaryindustrialcomplex is possessed! Repressed, regressed, obsessed, and abscessed!"

I translated. "Did they bust you for pot, Spur?"

"You think I'm a shit-kicking fluff-of-cotton-candy-in-my-pants MORON? You think I'd let those mule-eunuchs grass my ass?"

"What did you do with the stuff?"

"Dropped it in a can of flowers. They were taking them in too, man!"

"The women?"

"The flowers! The S.S. is confiscating hydrangeas! Can you dig it? A dragnet for lilacs! Oh, shit, this would blow Shelley's mind!"

"What was the charge, Spur?"

"Put the chick on."

"Leila?"

"Yeah. Put her on. I gotta be sprung, man. This is Gas Chamber, U.S.A."

Mrs. Thurston was sledge-hammering a ball of dough with anthropomorphizing fervor. I called Leila to the phone. "A poor one-armed son of a bitch would like to speak to you, Leila."

"Devin!" her mother clucked, disapproving of profanity even against the profane.

"Hurry up, Leila. You're his one phone call; he's in jail."

"Oh, Good Lord," Mrs. Thurston said, and raised her eyes, I thought perhaps in thanksgiving for an answered prayer.

"Hello, Spur, what's the matter?" Leila said. Ten minutes later, she spoke again. "Okay, I'll be there as soon as I can."

"Leila Stark," her mother followed her to the door. "Now, don't you start interfering with the police in the performance of their duties. If they have arrested Spurgeon, I am sure they had a perfectly good reason why."

"What did he do?" I asked Leila.

"It's hard to tell," she said, binding on her sandals. "But it sounds like he tried to talk some of the flower ladies into attacking Gabe Booter, and he got carried away and scared one of them yelling at her, so she started hitting Spur over the head with a can of flowers," Leila began laughing, "and when Booter went over to stop her, Spur bit him on the thigh, and then peed on his patrol car."

Mrs. Thurston vigorously nodded. "I am not surprised, not surprised at hearing even this. That man is right where he belongs, unless they decide to commit him to an insane asylum. It may not be his fault, but the truth is that Spurgeon Debson is a pure and simple maniac."

"What's the charge?" I asked.

"Obscenity. Indecent exposure. Assault. Resisting arrest. I'm going to go talk to Gabe. He's probably completely baffled."

"*Baffled?*" Mrs. Thurston's incredulity sank her to the couch, "Is that the word to use for a law officer who has just witnessed a deranged man *urinating* on state property in broad daylight in the middle of the public streets? Why, this is the worst possible time for this to happen! Here you are traipsing off, scarcely clothed, a widow of less than a month's time, to assist an unmarried madman who *bites* public officials, at the very moment that your husband's father can have the news broadcast in his face. Now, you can get on your high horse, Leila, and say 'What do I care?' but, honey, the reality of this situation is that you are dependent on Bruno Stark, if only for the future of your babies. So please, Leila, this careless disregard of watching your step, please make an effort to overcome it. Spurgeon made his bed, and if he chooses to place himself on a prison cot, why, honey, let him lie in it alone."

Leila picked up her pocketbook. "Mother, I understand what you're saying, and I know you're just thinking of me, but it isn't going to hurt me to try to help somebody that's mixed up."

"Leila, you are a fool. I don't know where you received your genes, but you certainly did not receive them from me."

Leila left.

Our diminished family quietly ate the Hungarian goulash, after which, I asked Sabby if she'd like to walk downtown with me to the Red Lagoon Bar. She said no, she was going to try to get Mr. Wolfstein to play gin rummy with her and Mrs. Thurston, so I went alone.

The man with the notebook was coming out of the bar. Inside, Lady Red called me over to the cash register.

"Hey, kid. Who's that friend of yours in the dance room?"

"Who?"

"Tall, good-looking blond guy. You know him, don't you?"

"Dennis Reed? Wears a suede coat?"

"Yeah, what a nice guy. Friendly. Always a nice word, you know, never too busy to gab a minute."

Kim, the big dancer, pulled herself up on a stool beside me and asked for a drink.

But Lady Red came over and shook her head at Tony. She spoke flatly. "You know what, Kim? You keep boozing your salary away like this, you're gonna end up owing me at the end of the month. Much less getting to California. It ain't exactly working wonders on your figure either."

"Yeah, yeah, I know. But it's this goddamn heat. Come on, give me the drink. Gin and tonic, Tony?" She glanced down at her arms, hanging flabby from a sleeveless sweater, her large breasts spread out against the counter. From behind his wife, Tony handed her the drink; nursing it, she said, "Oh listen, Red, the fellow I was talking about—Rings told me somebody acting like a dick was asking him a bunch of questions outside earlier on. He told him to get lost. Wonder if it's the same one."

Lady Red stuck the key in her cash register. "Just let me tell you something. If that guy comes nosing around again, you just send him to me, hear? Just tell him to come see me. I don't want snoops in my bar."

"Okay, sure, Red, sure," Kim drawled. A limp, heat-wet strand of lemon hair drooped across her face; she left it there.

I excused myself and went toward the back room. A blast of noise and heat swarmed around me when I pulled the door open. Tanya wasn't there. The discotheque was jammed with dancing couples, half hopping in one direction, half jerking in the other, while Tony Menelade and two new waitresses shoved their way through them, poking backs, pushing arms aside as they steered drinks to sweaty customers. Business was good.

T-shirted, Ronny Tiorino straddled a chair near the dance floor; beside him a tanned teenaged girl applauded with giggles as he pulled off the cap of a beer bottle with his teeth. Spitting the cap at me, he yelled, "Donahue, c'mere!" I went over. "What's going on next door?" I shrugged. "Has Mittie's old man slapped a lock on the place yet?" I told him I didn't know and didn't want to talk about it.

"Be fine with me," he said. "I'd just as soon hang around here the rest of the summer. Sure staying away from my draft board 'til the smoke clears. Joely's looking for you to help him backstage." He handed the girl the opened beer and stuck another bottle in his mouth. Seated on the edge of a chair, I theorized, "You're going to pull your teeth out like that, Ronny."

"Nnnn," he shook his head vigorously.

"Can I ask you something?"

"Mminni," he mumbled around the bottle.

"You heard of somebody named Rings?"

His face contorted, Ronny bit the cap off and spit it out; there was a cut on his lip. "Shit!" he licked his mouth. "Yeah," he nodded knowingly, "Rings Morelli. Friend of Lady Red's. I think they're partners. He owns the little porno store. Runs a poker game. But the real cash comes from pimping, that'ud be my guess." He grinned.

"Awh, come on, how do you know that?"

He flexed his arms, Brandoesque, rippled his fingers. "Whaddayah think, I'm sitting around playing Chopsticks with Pete Barney? I get around."

The teenager sucked at her beer bottle, looked from Ronny to me to Ronny with huge-pupiled eyes.

"Sure," he went on, "what do you think they call Slough Lane? Twenty-twenty Street."

"What does that mean?"

Impatient, he snorted, "Harvard! Twenty bucks for twenty minutes. Wanna know what that means?"

"Aw, shut up. This guy Morelli. What does he look like?"

"Mid thirties. Good body. Sharp dresser. Black hair, slicks it back. Mafioso looks."

"Wears patent leather boots?"

"You wanna make a date with him? How the fuck should I know!"

"I got to go. See you."

"What for? Maybe Bonnie's got a friend?" He pulled the beer bottle from his companion's mouth. "You gotta friend, kid?" She shook her head, and he put the bottle back. "What are you looking at?" he snapped at me.

I had been staring at his eyes; Maisie had told me one of them was glass. I couldn't tell which one.

A few feet away, a strobe light caught Dennis Reed's hair, the "Golden Fleece," Verl called it. Across a table from Suzanne Steinitz, he shook the gold in her eyes. As I neared them, he was saying, "You're right. *Medea* would be great for you. A part like that—'fire, passion, darkness'." He took in her face and hair, then chanted, "Ah, my father! My fatherland! To my endless shame I left you, left you after murdering my own brother." Well, I guess Dennis really was a Greek drama enthusiast, after all.

Suzanne breathed, "Oh, you know the play?"

"Well, I know a little Greek. Euripides has...always...fascinated me."

"Hello. Suzanne. Dennis," I said passing by. They ignored me.

Drinking alone away from the dance floor, I pondered the identity of the man with the notebook. Was he a detective, the Vice Squad after Rings Morelli? An F.B.I. agent checking out Spurgeon's threatening letters? Maybe Bruno Stark had hired him to spy on Leila. Suppose he found out where Leila was right now. Or Tanya—perhaps she had committed a crime and escaped, or more likely, was a runaway heiress, whose real name was something like Babs. Or maybe he was a journalist doing research on Floren Park. I had to hurry, write my own material down before this guy with the notebook stole it. But that didn't make any sense. I calmed myself; how could a stranger be writing things that were happening to me? I must be drunk.

Dennis Reed suddenly swooped over me and became confidential, "Look, have you seen Leila around? She's kind of hard to locate. Thought I'd run into her here, maybe, see how things were going. Really, I mean, what a nightmare she's been through. Somebody ought to help her have a little fun. Have you seen her around?"

"She's in jail."

"What?"

"She had to go see a guy at the police station about some flowers."

"Oh." Reed decided not to pursue it. "Well, give her a message for me. Tell her I dropped by to see her; ask her to give me a call sometime."

"Sure...I didn't know you knew Suzanne."

"Just met her. She's a nice kid."

"Yeah. Fire and passion."

"You and her?..." He spun a spiral with his forefinger.

I shrugged. "I'm talking about her acting."

"Oh, so am I, pal, so am I." He grinned at me. I thought I probably wouldn't give Leila his message.

I had to get a pencil and some paper. Making my way back to the front room, I saw Lady Red and Kim still talking at the bar. With a bovine lowing, Kim was swaying her head back and forth; the tips of her hair were stiff with dried drink from the counter. "Fred was a no-good creep. That's what Fred was. Always with a fresh flower in his suit, Red. Everyday fresh. And nice to Cary, good to the kid. And he could talk your ear off with sweetness. So, how do you figure a guy like that's gonna send you out with a bad check and rip you off while you're gone? You know?"

"Most women are saps. Kick 'em down, and they lick the foot. Not me," Lady Red told her.

Kim plopped her hand heavily on my shoulder. "See if they got 'Sleepless Nights' by the Everly Brothers, kid. That's what I listened to after Fred left me. Here's a dime." She fell toward her purse.

"That's okay," I said. "Let me get it."

At the jukebox, a fingernail slid down my spine. "You don't like your music live?" Tanya asked.

"It's too hot back there."

"Heat's good for you; it opens your pores. That's one reason dancing's so healthy. All sorts of exercises are good for you." Her arms and legs, the color of caramel, glistened against the red fringed costume. "So, Devin. You finally showed up. I'm flattered."

"I'm flattered you're flattered." But nothing further coming to mind, I turned to look at the selections on the jukebox. She leaned over beside me, fanning her hair against my hand. I could feel the cold weight of her earring.

I plunged in. "Can I ask you something? What's going on here?"

She swiveled around, rested her elbows on the jukebox, lowered her chin, and looked up at me. "Why do you ask?" she smiled.

I shrugged. "I don't know."

"Well, what kind of question is that?"

"Never mind."

Her grin widened. "Hey, how old are you?"

"I'm older than you."

"Yeah?"

"Sure, a lot older," I figured she was around twenty-one or two.

She lit a cigarette. "Well, let's see. 'What's going on...?' I like the way you look...."

"And."

"That's it. Does there have to be more?"

"Thank you. I like the way you look."

She smiled. "Thank you."

"Have you run away from home?"

She burst out laughing.

"I mean, does your family know you're in Floren Park?"

There were a lot of runaways in Floren Park that summer.

"No, they don't."

"I didn't think so."

Ronny and his new girl, Bonnie, walked out past us. Ronny gave me a nudge and a wink.

"Awwhh," she crooned. "What's the matter?"

I shrugged.

"Waiting for me to unzip your pants?"

I shook my head. "No...this is kind of confusing."

I sensed she was losing patience. "Okay, let me know when you figure it out."

"It's too noisy in here." I turned to face her. She could keep her eyes from blinking an incredibly long time. "Are you through?" I said. "I mean, do you have to work any more tonight?"

"Until one."

"Oh, okay."

But she shook out a key she had stuck beneath the cellophane of her cigarette pack. Pressing it wetly into my palm, she said, "Why don't you go over to my place and get it all figured out where it's nice and quiet. How's that? Cabin 6, in the lane. Don't lose it now," she squeezed my fist around the key.

"*Slough* Lane?"

"That's right. Just around the corner."

"You live on Slough Lane?"

"Why not! It was the first place I could find; it's cheap. Lady Red got it for me. If I decide to stay here, I'll probably get a bigger place. Okay?"

"Are you sure you ought to be living in a place like that?"

She looked me over. "You know, you're pretty weird."

"I guess so," I allowed. "I'll see you later, then."

"Make yourself at home."

"Thanks. Look, do you have a typewriter I could borrow?"

"See what I mean," she laughed, "really weird! No, sorry, I don't. What do you want to do, write a letter home? Does *your* family know *you're* in Floren Park?"

"Got any paper, then?" I asked.

"Jesus! Sure, look in the drawer beside the bed. You'll be able to find the bed, won't you? Big square thing in the middle of the room." With a wave of fingernails and fringe, she went back to dance.

Outside was barely cooler than in the bar. Starless, muggy, hot smog. Slough Lane was not lit, so I worked my way slowly down the ditch, peering for numbers. Cabin 6 was one of the fresh rose fronts next to the store for adults. Rings Morelli's store, I decided.

Expecting a stiletto in my back, I put the key in the lock. Surprisingly, it fit. I tripped over the bed, stumbling for a light switch. Her bed was a large, firm mattress on the floor. Above it hung a chain of copper bells. I pulled, and a dimmed light came on over my head, shadowing a giant poster of a rock star on the wall. Beneath me was a big white sheepskin flung over the bedspread. In one corner, a tiny refrigerator-stove beside a dish-filled sink. In another, an open closet spilling out clothes. Two full mirrors. A dresser chaotic with the tools of makeup. On the rug, a little record player, a little television, and a suitcase. On the bed table, an antique pistol that appeared to be made of mother-of-pearl and silver. What was Tanya doing with a gun? Was it a loan from Rings Morelli? A No Trespassing sign planted near the bed? It seemed a false note in the room—a gold goblet on a table with plastic plates and catsup bottles. Perhaps I should find out what I was getting into. Still, wherever I am, I thought, I came by myself. Not like the Cub Scouts that Mama took me to (canceling my enlistment after the Den Father told us to grow up as quickly as we could and destroy Red China). Not like the State Science Fair, the Harvard Dining Hall. I am free to be here, I thought, and no one who knows me knows where I am. As disconnected as if I were riding on a long-distance bus. More, for on a bus Fitzgerald is pointed home right now. But me, I could at this moment choose to be *anything,* at this moment somewhere in Floren Park. And somewhere now Bruno Stark was looking over Mittie's accounts, while Sabby and Mrs. Thurston lured

Wolfstein to the alertness of gin rummy, while the man with the notebook looked for clues, while Leila rescued Spurgeon from the law.

And I stretched out on Tanya's bed. But not yet comfortable. My clothes were pasted to my skin by sweat, and my body itched. No doubt I was allergic to the sheepskin. I threw it off. But the itching worsened. Heat, then. A rash. Scratching soothed me only while it lasted. I'm dirty, I discovered. My fingernails aren't clean, my hair feels like bugs are nesting in it. Probably I smell. Even though I had showered yesterday, maybe it would be better if I did it again.

Tanya had a small yellowed bathtub. Sticking a cloth in the drain, I filled it and floated down in coolness. Dunked my head, soaped, and lay there until film gathered on the top of lukewarm water.

I felt constricted, restless, studied the hair beneath my navel floating aimlessly.

Then a desire startled me upright. Rubbing myself dry, I ran to the table, jerked out a pad of paper, the cover doodled with flowers, and on it wrote down: "When summer started..."

Time lost, sometime the paper ran out. Shaking loose my clinched fingers, I rolled onto the bed and sank smiling to sleep.

chapter 19

I Begin Life on My Own Account and Don't Like It

The smell of something richly sweet fumed into my dream and half-awakened me with a confused impression of flowers, of Mrs. Thurston's marigolds, the sheriff's lilacs, honeysuckle at home. Then a sharp tingle of wet cold stung my skin and opened my eyes on Tanya. She sat pressed against me, slowly sprinkling down my chest, like wax from an ice candle, drops of an amber cologne. I sat up, the rivulet of scent ran shivering down my belly toward my crotch. Tanya didn't move as, grabbing the sheepskin from the floor, I covered myself.

"Finished your letter?" she asked, looking down at the written pages scattered across the floor.

The pages looked to me like money found unexpectedly in the pockets of a forgotten pair of pants. "Yes. Thanks a lot," I said. We gazed at the pages politely. Then, having rubbed my eyes and hair awake, I asked her, "What time is it? Is it late?"

"One-thirty."

"You must be tired."

"No. I'm a night person."

Reaching forward, I moved my hand along her arm over her neck and down her back, pulled her to me and kissed her, laced my fingers through her hair. She still held the bottle of cologne, and its odor merged with the warmth of her mouth opening with mine, her tongue sliding slowly down the side of my neck toward my heart.

In a while, sitting back, she handed me the cologne. "Put it on me," she said, and reaching behind her, unfastened, let fall the red-fringed and spangled bra. Her breasts were moonwhite, raised in the shadows of tanned skin. She shook back her hair, then stood and pulled down the spangled pants past more white, set with a shadow of crisp black hair. A taut wire that stretched between my neck and groin tightened, as if to jackknife me.

"Put it here," she said, and cupping my hands, poured perfume in them, pressed them against her breasts, skin strangely cooler, strangely softer than other skin. The nipples stiffened and pushed into my palms.

"Hey, breathe," she said.

I stroked her body with the flowered water until she lay beside me. "This feels good," she said, fluttering her nails across my chest and down under the sheepskin. She closed her hand around my prick. Cupped it in the dark heat of her palm. Then turning around, she took it in her mouth. Her breasts floated over my stomach.

"Don't come," she said.

"No," I promised. Then I lowered her over me until I was hidden in shadows of legs and hair and darkness. The wire tensed tight as far as my feet and my head; my hips jerked upward as I pushed into her mouth, but she moved away. Her hair swayed, brushed my skin. She knelt above my groin and sinking slowly down, she encircled me, and like a flower as sun sets, folded close around me. The wire wound fast, sprang, snapped apart, scattering my seed inside the petals.

My sleep was troubled by Tanya's unfamiliar presence, by the unfamiliar noise and feel of breath close to my ear, the unfamiliar sticky pleasure of a leg brushed against mine, the weight of an arm across me. A small rotating fan blew on and off me disconcertingly. It was 3:45 A.M. I remembered I had told no one I wouldn't be home. They must be worried. Four o'clock; I thought, is Bruno

Stark going to ask me to tell him everything Mittie ever said to me that might explain it? Should I say what Mittie had said about Spurgeon? I thought I shouldn't. I rehearsed Stark's questions, my answers. Four-thirty; I heard Verl saying, "I hate waste. Love is not a waste." I hate waste. Love is not a waste. Over and over, until finally I fell into a sleep uneasy with dreams.

The last one waked me. I was walking toward a bright clearing far in the distance of thick woods. A crazed old woman stood there, gaping at me with straggled teeth. She bent over cackling, slapping her hands against her scrawny thighs. Fog whirled around her as I approached.

"Come over here. Come over here," I heard her squeal.

I climbed to the clearing. Tanya stood there. In silence we began to kiss. She unzipped me, put her hands inside my pants, drew out my prick, and squeezed it in her fist so that at first it hurt.

"Are you happy?" she asked. 'Why don't you stay? I know what you like, don't I? Don't I. Don't I. Don't I."

On a hill above us, Leila was standing with Verl beside his yellow Triumph. "Who is that with Devin?" I could hear her asking him. Embarrassed at being seen by them, I tried to pull away, but Tanya wouldn't let go. She tightened her fist.

Verl came running down the hill at us and started tearing off Tanya's clothes. As he ripped them from her body, she laughed hysterically. I pulled at his arms.

"It's Jardin, Verl. It's Jardin!" I screamed. "Leave her alone. Are you crazy? Stop it." He threw my arms off and went on like someone possessed until she was naked. Then he grabbed me by the back of the neck, shoved me to my knees, and stuck my face in Tanya's stomach. The skin bubbled and spat out big running sores like a pot of boiling fat. Large bubbles of burning flesh burst, scorching my face. I gagged at the stench, but Verl held me there against my struggles as he rubbed my face back and forth in the sores.

I woke up sick and startled. Tanya, smooth and perfumed next to me, posed like a dancer, was sleeping. I stared at her, horrified, then heat sunk me back to the mattress. The little fan churned the same worn air back and forth. I turned it off. My dream faded. It was 9:15. Somewhere now, Leila was talking to Bruno Stark about her future. I should get up, but I felt queasy with lack of sleep, and thought, anyway, I shouldn't just leave without saying something.

At noon, I woke with an erection. Pressing next to Tanya, I rubbed it against her thigh, then nudged under her arm to take her nipple in my mouth. Sleepily she groaned and moved beneath me.

"Are you awake, Tanya?"

She made a mumbled sound, pulled me over her, and led me inside. I came almost at once, then fell back asleep,

When I woke again at 1:15, she was gone. A note had been scrawled on the back of a page of my writing. "Had a lunch date. Hope you don't mind. Took a loan from your wallet. All you had was a twenty. Pay you on pay day. See you. Leave the door on 'lock.'"

I gathered my papers and collected my clothes, I dressed and left the door on lock. My wallet was in fact empty.

At the theater no one had returned from lunch except Joely, who was splicing wires in the lighting booth. "Where the hell have you been?" he snapped. "Great time to wander off!"

"I'm sorry," I told him. "I feel like shit."

"You look it," he agreed.

"What's going on?"

"You're supposed to be on box office today. You're a half-hour late."

"Oh, Christ, I forgot. I'm sorry, Joely. Really. Just let me use the bathroom. Is there some coffee behind the counter?"

"Yeah. And Mrs. Thurston made doughnuts."

"The Good Lord bless her."

"Are you hung over?"

"Naw."

"Well, come on, don't be coy. Why didn't you show up last night?"

"You didn't call the cops, did you?"

"Boy, are you paranoid! No, the cops already had their hands full with our friend Spurgeon. You know, Leila got him out; how do you like that? Of course, she's had practice. She's talked Mittie's way out of the can enough times to know how."

"Did you talk to her?"

"No, I didn't finish up here until two. By then everybody at home was asleep. Ronny told me he saw you over at the Red Lagoon, so I figured you were probably passed out under a table or off humphopping with that Dennis Reed guy."

"Are you kidding? Anyhow, I don't like him."

"No? I thought you said he was a soulmate. Didn't you tell me Reed was a real soulmate? A poet, a prince?"

"Get off my back. So I made a mistake."

"You made a mistake? Oh, boy, boy, boy. Let me be the first to congratulate you. Go wash your face."

Cleansed in the dressing room sink, I took a cup of coffee and four doughnuts to the box office, where in the next two hours I sold twelve dollars' worth of tickets to *The Belle of Black Bottom Gulch*, reread my newly written pages, and fought back against a headache, hunger, sweat, heat, and an itching crotch. Finally, Sabby Norah brought me a cheeseburger from the streetcar diner.

Seated in wide plaid overalls on the stool beside me, Sabby told me what had happened with Leila and Mr. Stark, punctuating her sentences with that unrelieved series of sniffles that had led Mrs. Thurston to advise her to make blowing her nose a regular habit.

"Oh, you should have been there this morning, Devin, when Mr. Stark came to get Leila and the babies. Mrs. Thurston made him come sit down and eat breakfast. She was all dressed up and had the table all set. And Eggs Benedict. Grapefruits with kinds of designs, you know the kind I mean? Cut right into them. I thought it was really nice of her, but I don't think Mr. Stark wanted to stay there for breakfast. Then Mrs. Thurston told him she just couldn't allow him to leave that way. At least, if he was going to *sleep* in a public hotel, he could eat one simple meal with his relatives."

I laughed; her imitation of Mrs. Thurston was better than Leila's. "Well, how did it go? WATCH OUT!" Sabby had knocked over her careful stack of interleafings; they floated to the floor. She blushed and bit off a fingernail.

"It went okay," she said, as we crawled about collecting the pages, "but I don't think anything's been settled yet. Mr. Wolfstein stayed in his room. Mrs. Thurston talked the whole time. You know how she sort of gets going. About how she had been through so much herself, and could certainly understand how Mr. Stark must be feeling. And it's true, Devin, she has been through a lot; so many deaths she's had to deal with. But anyhow, how he was holding up wonderfully, which was what people had to do. Then she said how she had been to college, and that if Leila went to live in Oregon, maybe she could go to college too, because she had already been practically on her way when Mittie talked her into marrying him. You know, I thought Leila *had* been to college. She's really smart."

"Sabby, you suffer from hero worship."

"I don't either," she flushed. "I just happen to admire Leila a lot. And I don't think there's anything wrong with that. She's beautiful. And talented. And nice. I wish I could be like her."

"You *are* nice, Sabby; you're very nice."

She pointed at her face, glasses, body, tapped her head despondently. "Well, that leaves a lot behind. Leila got the sheriff to release Spurgeon. Last night on bail or bond or something. I forget. Isn't that amazing about him getting arrested? Somebody you actually know. I never knew anybody who went to jail, except the husband of the lady who worked for my mother. He beat her up. Did you know anybody?"

I thought of university sit-ins, the cacophony, the smell of sweat and adrenalin, the surge of group outrage, and the set faces of nervous policemen. Then the yells of indignation at physical hurt, and the protest of limp bodies. "Yes," I said. "Some students."

"Oh, that. I mean real jail. Spurgeon went to Denver in the middle of the night in that beat-up old car of his to buy some supplies. He went off in a rage because Leila said she'd never told him she was going to put his play on—you know that one, *Napalm*, the one he took to California because Mittie wouldn't do it either. You should have seen him. Well, you know how he gets. And after she'd just gotten him out of jail! He borrowed ten dollars from me for gas."

"Jesus, Sabby, why did you give it to him?"

"I don't know. He didn't have any money. Do you think I shouldn't have?"

Someone in a straw hat with pointed sunglasses sewn into the brim tapped on the booth and bought six tickets for the evening performance. Sabby was elated and took it as a sign that things were going to get better.

At 4:00 the Oldsmobile braked to a stop in front of the theater. Mr. Edmunds and Mr. Edgars hurried out with one orange bicycle, one blue tricycle, one push-pedal sports car, one doll that looked like a midget in a Broadway musical, two shopping bags from the delicatessen, and Mrs. Thurston, Davy, and Maisie.

"This day has absolutely worn me out," Mrs. Thurston announced. "Go with your Aunt Sabby," she pushed the children in our direction, "Sabby, honey, take them straight to the ladies' room. They are simply covered with food, and the Lord knows what else. And try not to let them get soaking wet and catch their deaths. Mr. Edgars, it is impossible, no matter how much effort you put into it, to keep children satisfactorily clean." Both Stark's employees nodded yes. "Are you parents yourselves?" she asked. They bobbed no.

The theater door was jerked open. Bruno Stark, gray with anger, followed Leila inside; he spoke with an almost choked calmness. "I can't force you to use your head, but you listen to me, young lady. Don't think for a minute you're going to keep up this horse-assery at my expense!"

"I told you, Bruno, I don't expect you to keep paying the rent. The lease is in my name. I can manage myself."

"Bull. You and Mitchell were out here playing GAMES, that's all, GAMES. And now this is the real world, and this theater is coming down just as soon as all the business is taken care of. In four weeks it's coming down! Understand me? And this caravan of crap is going to be sold!"

"So I have until then," Leila said calmly. The rest of us were frozen silent.

"And as for Mitchell's children and the rest of the legal situation, I'll be talking to my lawyers. I won't have David mixed up in this craziness. You'll do something to close it. Or *I'll* do something. And, Miss, you had better believe I mean that. EDMUNDS!"

Edmunds and Edgars scurried over. "Get in the car!" Stark ordered. "We're going to the airport."

I realized it might not be the best time, but I had promised, so I went ahead. Stepping from behind the booth and clearing my throat, "Mr. Stark," I said.

"Yeah?" It wasn't encouraging.

"You said you wanted to talk to me?"

He stared with what I couldn't help but regard as disgust.

"You went to Harvard?"

"Yes, sir."

"Mitchell went to Stanford. I sent him four years. He graduated."

"Yes, sir."

"It was a waste of time and money."

I didn't know what to say to this.

"What the hell are you doing here?" he suddenly rasped at me, jabbing the air with his cigar. "Why don't you grow up? Why don't you all grow up? Do something with yourselves! Nothing's good enough for you. Nothing real's *clean* enough for your lousy hands to touch. Well, let me tell you something, boy, if you don't grab it, somebody whose hands ain't quite so clean is sure as hell gonna pick it up. And all you spoiled brats are gonna be left sitting in the dirt, bawling."

I could feel my face flushing as Mrs. Thurston interrupted Stark's outburst, "Bruno, whatever is..."

218 • michael malone

He didn't wait for her to finish, but spoke as he threw open the theater door, "Amanda, if I was you, I'd have a little talk with your girl about who's holding the keys to the bread box!" He went through the door.

Edmunds and Edgars left with him, and the door slammed shut on Mrs. Thurston's open mouth.

"Lord God Almighty! What is the matter with that man? What's been the matter with *everybody* since we've been in this fool town? Leila, what in the world did you say to him to cause him to carry on like that?"

"Can we talk about it later, Mother? I'd like to go home. Would you mind putting the kids in the bus? Where's Joely?"

"Backstage," I mumbled, still shaken by Stark's attack.

Leila went to find him. Her mother took a seat under Mittie's picture. "I don't mind telling you, Devin. This entire population is closer than some people may realize to downright insanity. Maybe it's the lack of oxygen in this mountain air," she mused, "but it wouldn't surprise me one little bit if before the summer's out, every single one of us wasn't committed, lock, stock, and barrel, to a mental institution."

I smiled as much as I could manage, and she bustled the children out to the Red Bus. Soon Leila went through the lobby without speaking to me and left too.

I went back to the booth, where, in a few minutes, Joely tapped on the window. "The plot thickens," he grimaced.

"What is it now?" I asked. "Termites ate up the stage?"

"Close," he grinned. "We've all got crabs."

"What are you talking about?" I said, but I already knew. The itching I'd blamed on the weather. But how did we all get them?

"Apparently we have Spurgeon to thank; that's what we get for befriending a poor artist in a military-industrial society. Leila saw Dr. Ferrell today. He told her. Maisie and Davy have got them too. And, man, if Mrs. T's got crabs in her privies, I'd sure hate to be in Debson's boots!"

"The *kids?* I thought you had to sleep with somebody that had them."

"Listen," he laughed, "once those little buggers get going, they breed like the lower classes. Sheets, towels, combs! So if you're itching, it ain't lust. You know, maybe that was what was wrong with Wolfstein the night we thought he'd gone nuts over the bugs."

"Boy, this is it," I slammed the box office shut. "She's really doing a number on everybody ever since we got out here. One damn thing after another."

"Who?"

"*Leila*. Who else is responsible? Who dragged Spur off the streets to infect everybody? Goddammit! Oh, Jesus, this is really perfect. Jardin's getting married tomorrow, you realize that. Tomorrow. My *brother* is marrying her tomorrow!"

"So?"

"She's getting married, and I'm getting shaved for V.D.!" I felt like kicking in the floor with Leila's face on it. "And now I've got to go tell Tanya, and that's really going to be embarrassing. Jesus!"

"Well, you always said August 2nd would be about the most painful day in your whole life."

"Go to hell."

•   •   •

Tanya's cabin was locked, and no one answered. I was turning to leave when the man in the raincoat I had seen in Slough Lane the previous evening startled me by tapping my shoulder.

"Sorry," he said with a smile. "I didn't mean to frighten you."

"You didn't," I told him.

"Can I ask you something?" he said nonchalantly, pulling the same notebook I'd seen before out of his coat.

My pulse throbbed once in my neck. What now? If he was here about Spur Debson, I was ready to tell him anything he wanted to know. "Sure," I nodded. "What is it?"

He offered me a cigarette, but I shook my head. He put the pack back in his pocket. "Do you know a Carlotta Sirenos?"

I felt puzzled and a little disappointed. "No, sorry, no, I don't."

"Are you sure?"

"Yes. Why?" I was beginning to get alarmed again.

He took a photograph from the notebook. "Have you ever seen this woman?" He held it in front of me. It was a studio portrait of a woman with her hair up in an elaborate way, wearing expensive looking clothes, a necklace and earrings. I held it up to the cabin door light. It was Tanya.

"I don't understand," I said. "This person lives right here. Her name's Tanya."

"Tanya? Tanya who?"

"I don't know," I realized.

"Okay. Thanks a lot," he said, taking back the photograph.

"She's not home."

"Okay."

"What do you want her for?"

"Thanks," he repeated, and walked away down the alley.

chapter 20

I Am a New Boy in More Senses Than One

Disturbed by this news on the eve of Jardin's wedding, I called Verl. He said lice and ticks were worse than crabs and asked me if Bruno Stark had upset Leila. I told him, too, about the mysterious pronouncement of the man in the overcoat, which had convinced me that Tanya was being pursued by her father or the police and was hiding under the alias of Carlotta Sirenos. Verl thought it more likely that "Tanya" was the alias.

"A lot of people stay places under a different name for less sinister reasons, Devin. Maybe she had a fight with her husband."

"She's got a gun sitting right out on the table."

"A lot of people have got guns; it's in the Bill of Rights." And then he was more interested in criticizing the National Riflemen's Association than listening to me, so I hung up.

Joely Finn kept me up all night with stupid jokes about venereal disease. "Of course, if this had happened a lot sooner, at least Margery and Marlin might not be in such a fix. The itch might have cooled them off."

"What are you talking about?" I asked him.

"Margery told me she's pregnant. Leila offered to get her some birth-control pills, but I guess they'd already got the jump on them."

"Jesus, Bruno Stark is right. This place is a caravan of crap!"
"Such loyalty!" He threw a pillow at me.

• • •

Fittingly, the next morning, Friday, August 2nd, was soaked in gray rain that slapped at the window with its tacked-on screen, the one Mittie had ripped open the night he came with the gun.

I awoke with a sense of anticipatory purpose as if on Christmas morning or the day of a funeral. From the foot of my bed, I took the blue jeans and sweatshirt that a month ago I had begun wearing every day, washing them twice a week at the Laundromat until now they were that worn, soft comforting pale blue the others wore. (When I had first come to Floren Park, I had dressed up each morning to go to the theater. Now my jackets, slacks, ties, sweaters—all the remnants of Harvard—slowly grew mossy in a dank basement corner.)

Then standing erect at the bureau, I set my watch to start making allowance for the different time zones, my countdown to the snort of the organ in whatever Charleston chapel James Dexter was to acquire Jardin. Next, I took her framed photograph, turned it face down beneath the superfluous ties in that dark suitcase.

In the after-image of her gaze, I walked upstairs. There was a peculiar difference to the living room where everyone crumbled coffee cake and struggled into raingear. Nathan Wolfstein leaned with a lank, slickered elbow on the mantel, slowly shaking his crane's face with its mournful smile. Leila was talking to her mother. And *there* was the strangeness. Mrs. Thurston was not speaking or cleaning or cooking or even standing or even moving a muscle—and to be able to lie around without moving a muscle was one of her most contemptuous charges against the indigent. More startlingly, it was 9:30, and she wasn't even dressed, but instead sat fixedly upon her chair in her quilted bathrobe and pointed felt slippers, as still as an Egyptian pharaoh.

"I'm sorry, Mother," said Leila soothingly. "I know this is unpleasant. It's a pain in the ass for everyone."

Here, Joely, slurping coffee, stifled a comic wince.

"But everybody has to get checked," Leila continued. "Because I'm afraid it doesn't matter if you always used your own towels and washcloths." (For these Mrs. Thurston kept guarded in her locked bedroom, not trusting to the warning of their woven initials, ABT, so they were in the bathroom only on these frequent, private occasions when she was.) "Crabs spread. They breed, you see, and they can get into *everything*. Of course, probably you don't, but we ought to just check it out, don't you think?"

As white and still as stone on her slab of chair, Leila's mother sat.

"All Ferrell wants to do is just examine us. Oh, Mother," Leila sighed, "I feel awful…Okay. You stay here. Lie back down. I'll bring back some medication, and then…Come on"—this to the rest of us with impatience—"get in the car."

Sheepish in the presence of that straight catatonic back, those eyes that stared blinkless as Ozymandias into eternity, we slunk past Mrs. Thurston. We left her there. Amanda Sluford, whom fraternal incest, maternal murder, paternal decapitation, sororal suicide, could not bow. Mrs. Beaumont Thurston, whom double bigamy, multiple treachery, a daughter's ruin could not break, Mrs. T felled, struck into imbecility by the thought, the image, the possible fact of Spurgeon Debson's hatched brood of insects nestled in her pubic hair.

No one spoke on the trip to Dr. Ferrell's. The outraged anguish in those staring eyes froze us, like the Gorgon's head, into silence.

We all stood in the doctor's office—as inconspicuous, Joely said, as a dozen California grape pickers in Ronald Reagan's bathroom—and were duly inspected while Ronny tore a phonebook in half to impress Ferrell's daughter, Bonnie. And indeed, crab hoards *were* leaping like grunion in the sea of our hair. Jovially, Dr. Ferrell distributed ointment and fine-toothed combs.

Then it was noon. In Charleston, 2:00. The wedding was at 5:00 there.

Having unloaded us, her small infected company, with a crate of ham sandwiches in the parking lot, Leila drove off in the rain to beg her mother to accept the salve.

"I'll be back," I told the rest. "I'm not hungry."

No one protested.

•   •   •

Slough Lane was a sewer of running mud. Under a tin awning, against the front of his dirty book store, Rings Morelli leaned in his yellow suit and stroked his black patent hair. He surveyed me indifferently as I trespassed on his domain.

Next door, Tanya was home, like a sorceress in a black kimono.

"Look who's here," she greeted me without much eagerness. "You're wet."

"Could I talk to you for a second?"

"Sure, have a beer," she dispiritedly offered, and returned to her sheepskin on the floor beside a game of Solitaire or Tarot.

I shook my head.

"Oh, he doesn't drink, he doesn't smoke. Well, have a seat. Word gets around. I heard your boss is burning her bridges right and left." She looked up with a smile.

"What do you mean, my 'boss'?"

"The girl who runs your theater."

"Oh, Leila. She's not my boss. I'm just doing this to help her out."

Tanya's eyes were so bright and vague, I decided she must be on drugs. She sucked somnolently at her cigarette. "Well, whatever, Lady Red was telling me about her. How her husband went crazy and blew himself up."

"It was an accident."

"I hear he tried to kill her over some left-wing nut she was messing around with."

"That's not true." At least I didn't think it was true, or didn't want to think it was, or didn't want to discuss it with Tanya. "What do you mean, burning her bridges?" I asked.

Tanya shuffled, fanned, folded her cards; they clicked and rippled like castanets, "Well, according to Lady Red, your friend's father-in-law is loaded, really loaded, and he was going to fix her up for life, her and her kids. But she turned him down, told him off in the bar. Red said he was pissed as *hell!*"

"Told him off how?"

"Oh, I don't know. I think the general idea was she said he was always trying to buy people, and he'd fucked up his son's head, and she wasn't going to let him do that to her kids, and she'd rather be poor. Red said it was quite a speech."

She flipped over red and black blurs in a rapid pile of secret significations. Her tone bothered me. It seemed best to say what I had to say, embarrassing as it was, and leave.

"Look, Tanya. I'm afraid I've got some sort of bad news maybe." I leaned forward with warm earnestness, mingled of guilt and placation. "I was at the doctor's this morning, and I tried to get you earlier when I first heard about it, but, anyhow, it kind of looks like I may have crabs, so you should use this." I produced the ointment and comb. "Or, you know, perhaps you'd like to see Dr. Ferrell too."

"Shit," she said, and splayed the cards across the rug.

"Of course," I hurried on, "maybe there's no need. It's not my fault. We all got them."

She looked at me with annoyed skepticism.

"What I mean is, everybody in the house got them. From the towels and sheets. Somebody brought them in from outside."

She twitched an ironic eyebrow. "And I thought you were a virgin."

"This has nothing to do with sex. Look, Tanya," I came to the edge of my chair, "I know this is awful, and I know you must be annoyed. It's my responsibility, and I'll be happy to reimburse you for the doctor's cost, if you want to—"

She laughed. *Laughed?* "We're not talking about an abortion, Devin. It's crabs, right, not the clap?"

I shook my head vigorously.

"So, it's a nuisance, but I've had crabs before."

"You have?" She laughed again. What kind of person was she? I was reminded of the plainclothesman. I looked at the pearl revolver still beside the mattress, went over, picked it up; the weight surprised me. "Why do you have this?"

She didn't turn to look. "It was a gift." I squinted down the sights at her picture of Mick Jagger on the wall, then at her back. "Is Tanya your real name?" Her shoulder blades tensed together beneath the black kimono.

"What do you think?"

Somehow, I was beginning to feel tricked. The puzzle pieces didn't fit at all, never had fit, but I hadn't stopped to notice.

"Just wondered," I shrugged stupidly.

"Did someone say it wasn't?"

I looked at her, then studiedly at the gun. "Where'd you get this?"

"Christ," she turned and snapped at me with impatience.

The rain had stopped, and a strong shaft of afternoon sun wriggled through her angled blinds. It struck Tanya full in the face. Something was funny, wrong. She looked wrong. It's the light, I suddenly realized. I have never seen her in the light. Then, with a jerk of gulled embarrassment, I saw that she was older, older, than she had said (or had she said?), much older than I was; and then my sense of our experience together slipped spinning from beneath me, disorienting me, for what had happened between us had happened for different reasons than I had assumed. It could mean anything now.

Dropping the gun on her mattress, I moved further from the glare of her face. "A guy was here when I came over earlier," I said.

"Here?"

"On the steps. He showed me a picture of you and said your name was Carlotta Sirenos. He was looking for you. I've seen him around before."

She tensed to a perfectly still alertness, like an animal at point. "What did he look like?" I watched her eyes as I described the plainclothesman; puzzlement, then decision flecked across them as she stared back at me. She was thinking so quickly and strenuously it was like watching someone do a physical exercise.

"When did you see him?"

I told her; I told her what Kim had said that night in the bar, too, about someone snooping around. "What's going on, Tanya? Is your name Carlotta? Are you in some kind of trouble with the cops? Is it Morelli?"

"Who?"

"Rings Morelli?"

She answered me absently, thinking of something else, deciding something else.

"Why should I be in trouble with him?"

"Then you do know him?"

"Sure, I rent this place from him, and I see him around with Kim."

"But is he—"

"Look, honey," she interrupted me, not listening anyhow. There was a click inside her I could almost hear, and she stood suddenly as if a phone had begun ringing. "I may be in a sort of a jam. You could do me a big favor."

"Okay." I waited for her to explain what sort of a jam while she took off her kimono, kicking it away from her feet, and walked to her closet naked. She dressed in front of me as if I were the irrelevant matron of a locker room. "That bastard," she snarled. "He's put a private investigator on me."

"Who?" I asked. "Why?"

"Stay here," she said. "I'll be back in a second." She hid her hair beneath a cloth turban, her eyes beneath sunglasses, swooped up a purse, raked cigarettes into it, and hurried out the door, as if she were late for a luncheon appointment.

"Tanya! How long—" I said too late. So I was caught there. I give her ten minutes, I told myself. It's the least I can do. Twenty went by. Probably she went to talk to Kim. Maybe she really was in trouble; her father must have put a detective on her.

It was after one, the room was muggy and hot, and I remembered with nausea that I was infested with crabs, that at that instant the bloated eggs of vile insects were stuck with ooze to my skin and hair. I ripped off my shirt and pants and followed a memory of the bug-mad Wolfstein to Tanya's tub, spun the faucets, funneled spurts of purification over my head, and aimed a steady stream onto my crotch as the bath filled.

It was not enough. I jumped out dripping, got the ointment, found in her caked soap dish a razor with a rusting, hair-clotted blade. Pawing through her medicine chest, I found a new blade, scalded the razor clean. Then, with the willed effort of a cliff diver about to plunge, I sat on the tub edge, stared carefully at the puffs of lather rising from my groin, then stroked down for the shave.

My focus had been too absolute. Someone had come in. I didn't hear the door open, but he couldn't have knocked. The open bathroom door was lined up in his sights, and he saw me before I saw him, because it was my sense of his shock that turned my head, just as his mind assimilated the shock and then roared ahead to fury. He was dark with a muscular, half-bald head; he was tan in a suit made exactly right; he was big. Even then I could think clearly enough to realize, this is the piece that connects the puzzle. Detective. Runaway. Mann Act—how did the Mann Act go? I stared back at him.

The man filled his lungs: "Who the hell are you?" Tanya ran into the cabin. He was coming at me. "Look here, Al!" she pulled at him from behind.

Instantaneous thoughts: I've got to get out of here. He's going to kill me. Wait a minute! She calls her father "Al"? Instantaneous actions: He came in the bathroom. I stood. He swung. The razor stabbed a long sting up from my groin. Vomit thick blackness flooded me, took me to the edge, and pushed my brain over.

I woke up because someone was trying to shove his fist down my throat. No one was. I felt the eye and winced, then became aware of a constant burn at my crotch and knew absolute terror. I reached down to feel, and someone took my hand.

"A close shave," Leila said.

I couldn't open my eyes. "But not that close," I managed wanly.

"No," she laughed. Then I could see her with my right eye. "Some shiner!" she added, leaning over from a chair close by. From the wall, Mick Jagger was leering at me. So I was on Tanya's mattress. Forcing my hand against the awfulness of movement, I inched slowly down my stomach until I felt gauze and tape.

"What happened? What are you doing here?"

"I saw Ferrell getting in his car, and he told me he'd just fixed you up in here. They had called him. He said you cut yourself and then cracked your head on the side of the tub. *Looks* to me like somebody slugged you. Anyhow, you were out cold."

"'They'?"

"Your friend, the mysterious dancer," she laughed. "Some friend!"

"Who slugged me?"

"That guy? Al Sirenos?"

"Yeah, who was he?"

"He said, her husband."

"Oh, Christ." A married woman! What was Spur always saying—rich, perfect! Why hadn't I known? What was Leila thinking? "Yeah, okay," I said.

She held up twenty-five dollars on the bed table. "Apparently his wife borrowed this from you?"

She'd left me a five-dollar tip.

chapter 21

Mischief

It would all make sense if I could think it through, but I didn't want to think it through just then—not while I was lying naked and queasy on her mattress. Above my head, the chain of copper bells stirred in a single spasm.

"So," was all I said.

Leila lit a cigarette, blew the smoke carefully away from me. We were quiet. Leila asked me nothing more, and for once her lack of curiosity seemed...not indifference, but just easiness, and her sitting there was pleasant, as though for us to stay that way was the right order of things, the order of long custom.

Finally she spoke, "How do you feel?"

"Kind of thirsty."

She brought me a glass of water. As I drank it, the sun fell like gold dust on Leila's sandaled foot. It was coming through the very bottom blinds, and the slant of light brought back a memory, throbbing my two new wounds.

"What time is it?" I asked. "Where's my watch? Look at my watch." Someone had stacked it neatly on top of my clothes at the foot of the mattress.

"It's a little after four, why?"

So I had missed it. They were already married. There, at 6:00 now, in some catered Charleston home that I had never seen, Jardin was pushing ceremonial cake into James Dexter's open mouth as Mama and Colum and Fitzgerald and Maeve agreed to look on. It was all over, and I had missed it. That moment when I was to feel the anguish of loss psychically, instantaneously vibrated to me across two thousand neutral miles, I had passed that moment passed out, and if the psychic sound wave *had* telegraphed my passive prostrate brain, its message was lost forever. "Jardin's married. They got married this afternoon," I said.

"What? Oh, yes…I'm sorry, Devin. Are you upset about it?"

An automatic "yes" was bubbling up, when, inexplicably, it just burst, evanescent as empty air, and I slowly allowed myself to acknowledge that incapacity of the comfort-seeking spirit to sustain its griefs. And finally I answered Leila, "No, I guess really I'm not as much as I thought I'd be." For it didn't matter as much as the sting in my groin or the peacefulness of lying there hazy in the filtered sun with her. Slowly I began to admit that Verl had been right all along about Jardin and me. Maybe about James Dexter and all those other theories of his that used to irritate me so much. Perhaps it had taken Tanya to teach me. Mrs. Sirenos and a good right hook. It shocked me to lose grief so abruptly, like a tire blown out. I was already missing the grief as much as I had missed Jardin.

Finally Leila smiled. "I'm glad," she said. She gave me the rest of my clothes to pull on over my bruises. "Can you get up?"

I left Tanya's cabin braced on Leila's arm.

"Devin, if you feel up to it, how'd you like to do me a favor?"

"Sure," I said, my head swimming like a drunk in a wool suit trying to climb out of a pool.

"I'm worried about Nate. I'm being realistic, and I don't think he has…I have a feeling he doesn't have a lot of years left. And the worst thing is that he's already just given up. *Nothing* matters to him. I think if we could get him involved in something, maybe it would help. I don't mean just being nice to him. Sabby's really helped there already, and you and Joely, and Mother. But something outside of *himself*, something he can like himself for again."

"Okay. Like what do you mean?"

"There's a play he's mentioned several times, a production he was involved in a long time ago. It seemed like it had some special importance to him. Arthur Miller's *All My Sons*. I'd like to do it for him, to get him to do it. He needs *something*. We all do."

"I don't know, Leila. People have pretty much had it."

"Look at us all," she said. "What's happened to us? We're just waiting it out here, no different from Nate, passing the time, dropping away, and we're getting bored and ugly. Waiting until Bruno tears the place down and puts up a damn supermarket. Or somebody gets drafted or gets married or the world blows up. We were supposed to be a *company*, people who felt the same way, who wanted to make something come alive. That's what I thought Mittie wanted. That was the plan." Slowly, ceremoniously, we walked out of Slough Lane and into the parking lot. "The theater," she pointed, "even a silly place like this—even an old rollerdrome in the middle of a stupid tourist park—it can be a part of the fight, you know."

She opened the van door, then suddenly just slid down into the dirt beside it, clutching her huge pocketbook in her arms like a baby and crying. I knelt beside her, holding her until she stopped. "What can I do?" I asked her.

"Help me," she said. "Help me get the others to try. They probably aren't going to want to take on anything new. But we should! Not just for Nate, or Mittie, but for all of us." She pulled herself up. "I won't let Bruno win!"

I promised her I would try.

She wanted to go home, so I helped her into the van. "Just go home and try to get some rest. It'll be okay. Thanks for coming to my rescue."

•   •   •

In a corner booth of the Red Lagoon Bar, I sat for a long while thinking. If it was all true, then why did I want whatever James Dexter wanted when I believed James Dexter wanted all the wrong things? What did I want?

Sauntering to the bathroom, Spurgeon Debson saw me. He squatted down next to the booth, peered at my blackened, puffy eye. It was the first direct interest he'd ever shown in me. "Pigs?" he asked. "Narcs?"

"Maturation," I told him.

"Yeah," he nodded, with all the sad cost of revolutions in his gaze.

"You think you got problems?" Marlin scoffed at my shiner. "Shit! You spent four years behind an ivy wall, Donahue! I got the draft on my ass, *and* the crabs, *and* a pregnant girlfriend!"

"Don't mind him," Joely said. "He's been buzzed out on bennies all night."

"He went around and switched all the nameposts on all the summer houses near Mrs. Booter's," sighed Pete Barney wistfully.

"Let no one know who they are! Let nothing in life be certain!" Marlin *was* high, and spooking me with his wild eyes.

"Listen, you guys," I told them. "Leila's had a good idea. She wants us to put on a new play. Cheer us all up. *All My Sons.*"

"Forget it," Marlin said. He was watching Hubert Humphrey at the Democratic convention in Chicago on Tony Menelade's little television set behind the bar.

"Isn't there any more Calhoun money left?" Pete asked.

Marlin gasped out loud. "*I got to get some air!*" Tugging itchily at his Levis, he rushed away.

"How 'bout sticking with him, Pete? He's totally gone." Pete obligingly chased after Marlin as Joely stood up. He too was walking as bowlegged as Calhoun Grange; everyone had "shaved." "I have to get back to the theater," he said. I stayed where I was.

"Serves you right, you little twerp." Lady Red leaned into my booth and pointed at my eye.

"I beg your pardon?"

She emptied an ashtray into a plate left in front of me and took away my glass. Obviously, it was time for me to leave. As she rang up my check, she told me, "I knew that name was as phony as a grade-B movie. 'Tanya'! And that story! Ring mark on her wedding finger. You didn't notice, of course!"

"Slumming it for kicks, that's what she was doing," Tony suggested from his stool behind the bar.

Lady Red whirled on him now. "Slumming it! Here? Are you kidding? Those two work a cheap bar in Denver, that's all. Bullshit, she was *running* from slums! And that bastard put a lousy dick on her! A lousy dick nosing around in my bar, bothering my girls!"

Tony was being reckless. "Well, she went back with him, didn't she?"

Red charged him with her raised voice. "You think you know so much? Well, listen, maybe she was a sap, but if I ever go, I go, got it? I don't get pushed around, you can sure count on that!" She slammed the cash register shut. "We're closing," she said coldly.

I left.

Out in the moonlit parking lot, Ronny and Marlin were pissing at one another from a distance of twelve paces.

"Yeah. I'll piss! I'll piss right in your eye!" Marlin yelled.

"TRY IT!" challenged Ronny back, gesturing at his open mouth. "Get it in here and I'll drink it!"

"Jesus, Pete, what's going on out here?" I asked.

"Marlin insulted Ronny. His…his virility, I guess, and then they started fighting, and then this," he said remorsefully.

"For God's sake, couldn't you stop them?"

"Are you kidding, what could I do?"

Across the creek a dog was barking. Spurgeon's Great Dane. Maybe we were on his pissing ground. Mad as his master, he charged the bridge and flew at the now-urinating duelists. Marlin, Pete, and I sprinted away, but Ronny stood like a Spartan.

"I hope that bastard gets his balls bitten off!" Marlin called back to us as he fled around the side of the theater. But Ronny raised the Dane, spun him, and hurled him into the creek. Then he crouched, waiting, his arms like prongs, to plunge the dog down when he came back at him again.

"In the name of our fathers and all our sons," Ronny shouted, while the terrified dog yelped and paddled until he could scramble away and up the other bank. Suddenly, bright headlights shot out from near the bar. A police car had pulled up. Standing, Ronny raised his head into the glare. The sight we then saw was ghastly. Behind us, Gabe Booter, the sheriff, was approaching. Before us, Ronny stared with one rage-mad eye and one empty socket.

"For God's sake, Ronny!" I cried. "Your eye fell out!"

Oedipus, the Cyclops, King Philip of Macedon, Long John Silver—I glimpsed them all like a nightmare in his very young stonewhite face as he fell frantically to his knees, spinning in a circle of dark dust, looking with his moving hands.

I Fall into Captivity

"Who threw that dog in the creek?" Booter boomed, seesawing toward us on his tall, gaunt legs. "What's going on here?" He hit us with a big-beam flashlight.

"That dog's mad," I explained, while Ronny, at my feet, kept twirling in the dirt for his eye.

"Mad?" Booter put on an official look. "Was he drooling foam? Anybody git bit?"

"No," I said, "but I think his owner let him run wild." I figured my next news would gain his support. "Spurgeon Debson, guy with a beard, used to sell jewelry on the street—it's his dog."

I was right. The sheriff's face puffed out like a goiter as a hiss steamed out the sides of his mouth. He pulled a walkie-talkie from his belt and began to bark numbers into it. From across the creek, Spur's dog barked back. "Six-four. Six-four...MADDOX! *Get off your goddamn ass!*"

Over in front of the bar, someone threw open the door of the police car and yelled, "Yeah, Sheriff?"

"MADDOX," the sheriff bellowed into his machine. "Get the pound over here. We got a mad dog."

"We don't know for sure if the dog's got rabies," Pete modified my accusation.

"Humph," said Booter, who was recalling, I knew, that the dog's owner had recently tried to bite him on the thigh.

Suddenly, Ronny's head hit the knee of the sheriff who flashed the light down to see someone crawling frenetically in the dark. Jerking away his boot, he asked, "What's the matter with him? Did he git bit?"

"He lost his eye," Pete explained.

"MY GOD?" Booter gasped as Ronny reached up, grabbed his flashlight, and ran it in short arcs across the dirt.

"Help me look for it," he groaned.

"MY GOD!" repeated the sheriff. Then the light caught a glint of green glass, which Ronny snatched up. "Boy! You need help, boy?" Booter sputtered.

"It's a glass eye," I thought I should point out. Mr. Booter just gawked at me while Ronny turned his back to us and, however one does such things, fit his eye back into its socket. Over the creek bank, the Great Dane kept barking, as out from the black, humid pitch behind us the deputy appeared, wearing a gun that reached almost to his knee.

"Pound's coming," he promised, effervescent with duty. "That the dog over there? Anybody hurt?" Nobody was. "Look here, Sheriff," he took Booter purposefully aside, but didn't lower his voice. "Lucky we happened by. Lady over there on Sloan Street just calls in and says these boys here was, well, says they was indecently ex-posing themselves, right here in the middle of the parking lot. Says she seen them out her window, and it oughtn't to be allowed. Says she's lived here twenty-two years. Says we ought to do something about it, and she will if we won't." He put his hand protectively over his gun and studied us carefully.

That lady must have had the eyes of a hawk, I thought.

Booter's eyes squinted to dots of suspicion. "Indecent expo-sure?"

"Yes, sir, Sheriff, according to the call, they was urinating all over each other. That's what she told the desk."

Memory soared into outrage. Had not Debson pissed on Booter's tires? And here we were, with Debson's dog, performing barbaric rituals in the parking lot. I could see it all on Booter's face. We were obviously all in it together with Spur, no doubt members of his cult, devil worshipers, anarchists, yippies, pissers on America, who had tricked him into sympathy. The silence grew. In it, Ronny came down from whatever rage had led him on. He slumped to the dirt, and Pete and I huddled around him. His fly was still open.

"Okay," Booter snapped. "You fairies been shining your dicks in the moon?"

"Just answering the call of nature," Ronny threw out.

The sheriff dismissed it. "Decent people use the proper facilities. All right, boys, let's go." It was a famous line. We all knew the two conventional responses: to go quietly, or to refuse to go at all. Having been taught to obey our elders, we went quietly.

"Maddox, where's that g.d. dog catcher?"

"Don't know," the deputy admitted, adding with a throw of his search beam, "Dog's gone anyhow." The Great Dane had lost interest in us and wandered off.

"Well, call in a description, have him picked up." Knowledge of his master condemned the animal to the charge of madness.

And so, prickly with fear, we were led into the car and driven off in ignominy by the proud Maddox, who drove slowly up Main Street as if he led a parade. Booter sat beside him and gassed us first with the thick fumes of his pipe, then with a trumpeting fart that announced our arrival at the Floren Park City Hall Police Station Dog Pound Seat of Government.

chapter 23

A Visitor

In the receiving room, despite all we had been taught of police methods, we were neither beaten with rubber hoses, grilled under hot lights, forced to strip, buggered, nor celled with cockroaches. Nor were we told that anything we said would be held against us. We were not advised of our right to make a phone call. We were neither fingerprinted nor photographed. We simply sat on a wooden bench in a small room that looked just the way it was supposed to, with an old desk and swivel chairs, the posters and water cooler, and file cabinet, while Maddox slowly typed out our biographies.

"Do you think we're going to have to go to court?" asked Pete mournfully. "It'll be on our records. You and I weren't even...even peeing!"

My crotch ached, so I asked permission to go to the bathroom, where I found that I had, in fact, opened the cut from the razor again. My new shorts were sticky with blood. How could I, given the schedule of my life, be washing blood from a self-inflicted groin wound in a police-station john? But, as though too aberrant to sustain significance, the fact almost didn't even interest me. Like so much else this summer, it simply didn't fit, so it faded, ephemeral and transitory as faces glimpsed from a train window.

When I went back into the room, a party had gathered. Margery and Joely were talking to Pete and Ronny. In the office doorway, Sheriff Booter was talking to Leila.

"But you know and I know, Miz Stark, that the people of this town just ain't gonna stand for this kind of disturbance and creating a public nuisance of yourself and the sort of indecent obscenity I'm getting reports on from everywhere." He paused to pull a huge lighter, a plastic trout caught in a clear rectangle of green water, from his pants' pocket and light her cigarette with it. "Because I'm gonna have to do something about it, and you understand that. And I can come down hard."

Leila nodded gravely. Booter nodded back. He said nothing to us, the indecent disturbers. "Yes, I understand," Leila said. "Thanks for calling me."

It was almost 2 A.M. now, yet in the grimy hallway, stale with the sweat of a long day's heat, she looked like morning. She was wearing a white cotton robe like a shepherd in a Bible illustration. It was stitched at the collar with gold the color of her hair. Ronny, Pete, and I, clearly, were cast as the bad sheep. I had certainly got off to a bad start in my promise to Leila to help her pull everybody together.

"So, okay, then, I'm gonna release them on your recognizance, Miz Stark, and you see if you can't keep 'em in line. Otherwise…"

Leila nodded away the alternative.

"I don't want to have to bring you boys down here again, you hear?" We heard. "If I do, I ain't gonna be quite so friendly." We assured him enthusiastically that he would never see us again as long as we lived.

And so we were given into Leila's charge, and she led us solemnly out of the valley of the shadow of detention and into the night. So passed, in my twenty-second year, the day of my brother's wedding.

Breakfast gave us Mrs. Thurston back, her face seared into heightened dignity by a day's solitary confinement in the bathroom wrestling with the demon of Spur's crabs. She did not come upon us with whitened hair like Moses returning from the burning bush, but her eyes had looked on horror and showed it.

We couldn't help but study her walk; it was, to our remorse, a little straddled.

"Are you mad, Grandma?" Maisie asked her.

Mrs. Thurston put down her coffee cup and carefully considered the question. "No, darling," she finally answered. "Grandma's not mad. The twists and turns of life," she glanced reproachfully at Leila, "have attempted to *drive* your poor grandma mad. But, honey, they have not succeeded."

The door to Wolfstein's bedroom inched slowly open. "Nathan, good morning, Nathan," Amanda greeted with concern the gray, hollowed shape lost in the fraying bathrobe. "Why, you're up bright and early today, and looking just wonderful too. Now what you need is some breakfast. Leila, angel, reach me down that pan so I can scramble Nathan here some eggs to get him off to a good start."

A queasy shudder contorted Wolfstein's face. "Thank you, Amanda, but I think coffee, just coffee will be...fine."

"Nonsense," she replied, and our spirits rose. Mrs. Thurston was definitely on the mend.

"We got a postcard from Cal," Leila announced, frowning in a funny way. Maybe she *hadn't* liked him. "He asked to be remembered to you, Nate."

"From Mr. Grange?" Sabby breathed. "Could I see it?" So Leila went to the mantel and returned with a handful of opened mail. Grange's card was a picture of a Hollywood studio—where he worked perhaps. It was addressed to "Leila Beaumont and Co." "Hi. Just so you won't forget me. Had a great time in your place. Hello to Nate and everybody. They're working my you-know-what off here. That's the way it goes. Come on out anytime. Yours, Cal."

After we handed the relic around, Sabby passed it reluctantly back to Leila, who returned it, saying, "Why don't you keep it, Sabby?" Sabby pressed the card like an orchid in her copy of *Bonjour Tristesse*.

Uninterested, his head slumped toward his cup, Wolfstein breathed in coffee fumes like ether. "Nate," Leila said, "I want to call a meeting. We'll all eat over at the boarding house. Can you be there at six?"

Space and time were of no consequence to Wolfstein. The internal wait was all. He said he would be there. He didn't much look to me like he'd be eager to direct another play.

I saw him that afternoon out in the rear of the theater, huddled, despite the heat, in a costume shawl talking to Sabby Norah. Over the past month, they had found themselves in a kind of friendship, she nursing him with her awkward but unflagging solicitude, he sharing with her the memories of a life in the theater, that golden, magical world of which she was an adoring acolyte. I would see them often together now on the wicker porch chairs in the early evening or in his room bent over a scrapbook of memorabilia, Sabby's pale, plain face flushed into beauty with wonder at his tales of triumphs, mishaps, intrigues, glory. He talked of everything but those years in Hollywood. About that, he kept silence. But the stage! He had known Them, or known those who knew Them, or at least had seen Them perform. Helen Hayes. Lunt and Fontanne. Cornell. Olivier. The Barrymores.

"Finally the prompter just yelled the line out, for the third time: 'I LOVE YOU!' And Coward—you know that look he gives." Sabby nodded eagerly, as if Noel Coward were an intimate friend. "He looked right down at the prompt box and said, 'My good man, *we know* the line, but *who says it?*'" Sabby shivered with giggles, and Wolfstein's thin, tired voice went on, "The worst instance of scene stealing I ever saw? Let me see..."

Encouraged by her Boswellian enthrallment, he offered up, in place of a future, or even a present, the cynosure of his past. Eventually, telling the stories began to absorb him too, as if by a long review, some specific meaning, summation, one he did not know yet, would ultimately evolve. More of us began to sit beside Sabby, for she was generous with her Johnson. So we too could listen to a life that, unlike our own, had already been so fully shaped, so cut to a pattern that was now pinned, experience by experience, to the inalterable past. And after we cleaned the theater aisles of what scant debris our small audience had left the night before, Pete and I brought coffee over to hear about how General MacArthur had dropped in on a musical review Wolfstein and his pals put on for their squadron in the Philippines. That the gray, palsied Wolfstein had fought in a war astonished us. And in a war we'd been taught to think of as a good one, as opposed to the bad one in Vietnam we were trying hard to avoid. To think of Wolfstein grinning into the sun under palm trees, tanned and healthy, able to squeeze a trigger with those shaking fingers that now couldn't hold a glass steady, was impossible. The young Nate Wolfstein was a completely separate person to me, and as I envisioned him card-playing in a crowded barracks, I wondered whether, in fact, Leila's instinct had been right and Calhoun Grange really was Nate's son. And maybe Nate had known it, too, but had just let it drop when he saw Grange could not care if it were true or not.

At 5:30, Joely and I started over to Mrs. Booter's together. I was talking to him about Wolfstein when he suddenly grabbed my arm. "Hey, look who's back!"

Right in front of the new Nixon campaign headquarters on Main Street, that was next to Hade's Buick that was next to Western Outfits, Spurgeon Debson was peddling his wares. Wearing his Vietcong flag tank-top, he sat cross-legged upon a carpet like a Turkish merchant. And scrawled on, as it turned out, the backs of our play posters, and leaned against the sidewalk curb were his advertisements, his sales pitch: "The Whole World Eats Shit." "You Don't Have to Take *Their* Shit." "Shit on the Shit-Eaters." "SHIT POWER."

In the past few days, Spur had obviously been diligent in whatever workshop Leila must have provided him. There was a lot of merchandise. There were SHIT POWER buttons, T-shirts, both stamped with a ring of dung. There were American flags, each with a slab of plastic poop, the sort you can get in party joke kits, glued right in the middle of its stripes. There were clear plastic toy rockets, packed in six- and twelve-inch increments of guaranteed 100 percent human product excrement. There were rope coils of rubber feces that looked like Indian dancing snakes.

From the window of the Nixon headquarters, two fresh-scrubbed teenage girls in straw campaign hats gaped and giggled at this display, ducking beneath the ledge whenever Spur wheeled to catch them peekabooing.

Apparently, the Muse nonremunerative, Spur had turned to telling by selling; he would save the American people in the American way, by building a better mousetrap and catching them in it. Spur had become a small businessman. Not that he was doing any business that we could see. The Nixonettes were only window shopping. Their mad money was not for this variety of madness. Around Spur, tourists passed down the sidewalk like painted people on a slow-moving backdrop. Their faces pursed, or pruned, or gawked, or looked politely away as if they had stumbled inadvertently into the wrong bathroom and were pretending to be elsewhere. Two of the Mexican flower ladies hurried by. Recognizing their old fellow vendor, they side-stepped him and scurried like hens to a safe intersection.

"Looks like Spur's overriding the sheriff's edict against street peddling," Joely noted, "but just wait until Booter gets a sniff of what's being peddled." He called to the merchant, "What's going on, Spur?"

Unpressed by customers, Spur was willing to talk to us. *Nothing* was going on. The truth was going down. He, the truth-teller, was going down on America, ass first. From now on, he would reason with his rectum. Once he had put his faith in the power of language—but language had failed him. The word was dead. Dead and rotten. Dead and rotten and slimy with dead, rotten maggots of no meaning. The written word was invisible: the spoken word was inaudible. The paragraph was the cocksucking queen doxy stooge of the military industrial complex, and every time we opened our mouths to let language out, we played right into Their hairy hands. All his products were alternatives to language, a kind of conceptual art in which the texts (the plastic) were accompanied by the artist's commentary (the excrement). Thus, the rockets were books of political poetry; the verse had come from his bowels.

"This whorehouse of a world," he summed up sometime later, "was built out of Those Bastards' words. Built up and up and up with all their bawdy house bricks of filthy, lying nouns and verbs. See Dick run. See Dick run for president. See Dick run and catch his fat ass on a rocket nose and shoot his wad in an astronaut's eye right on the ass-licking BUTTON OF THE NAZI COUNTDOWN..." Spur had turned toward the window and was yelling with rabid gestures at the two Nixon girls inside stuffing envelopes with promises. One of them reached for her phone.

"I saw that!" Spur let her know. "She's trying to get me busted. I don't have time for that shit." We suggested, in that case, that he move his own off the street. He said that he was waiting there for his dog, and so I told him that Booter was after his dog too, news that Spur found both "rich" and "perfect."

Out of motives he never explained, Joely actually bought one of the laminated flags. For four dollars! The rockets were even more expensive. As we were leaving, two flower children stopped. "What's SHIT stand for?" one asked.

"SHIT doesn't stand for. SHIT is!" Spur explained.

The guy bought a button. "Love, brother," he said in parting.

"Love's a word," Spur told him. "Turds are better than words."

• • •

After dinner at Mrs. Booter's, Leila brought up *All My Sons* again. When she finished, she turned to Wolfstein. "Nate, what do you think? We can't do it without you."

Nate wasn't sure. Neither was Joely. "For God's sake, why do you want to take on something else, Leila?"

She sat at the head table, where Mittie used to preside over our meetings, vacillating between dictatorial brusqueness one day and apologetic abnegation the next. Her skin was still as pale as her hair, as if she had been too busy to notice that summer might have tanned it. Her eyes, I realized, were shadowed with fatigue. "You're supposed to *try*. Maybe most of the time you don't know what you're doing, and maybe you don't do it very well. But the purpose is, the point is, we're supposed to be out here trying…" I thought maybe she was going to cry again. "And instead…and instead we're just dying."

"Leila, honey, are you okay? Why, darling, it's all going to work out," her mother promised.

No one else felt like saying anything. And in that silence, Mrs. Booter entered the dining room wearing her black widow dress.

Her face was long and thin like her brother-in-law's, but instead of the sheriff's jovial brutishness, Mrs. Booter kept her features carefully pinched in a parsimonious way, edging her words out like pennies from a snap-purse. "Mrs. Stark," she snipped off, "may I see you for a minute? In my parlor?" Her parlor was that musty relic room where memories of her escaped husband were still held prisoner.

"All right," Leila agreed, and followed the widow out, leaving us to deal however we wished with all she had said.

"I feel like a creep," Seymour began.

"Well, it hasn't exactly been the sort of summer we were promised," Suzanne told Dennis Reed, whom she'd invited to have dinner with us.

"That's not Leila's fault," Joely said.

Guilt and recriminations snuck around the room.

Then Sabby got up. "Leila's right. And I think, well, I think we all could have helped her a lot more than we have. She didn't say so, but I think she wants to do this play for Mittie; he used to talk about putting it on someday. And now Mittie's gone, and here she is, left with everything, and Mr. Stark treating her so awfully. Well, it's not for me to say, but I think we ought to do it for *her*. Mr. Wolfstein, I just know you could do a beautiful job, if…you know, if, of course, you feel like it wouldn't be too much of a strain. You could give us something to…something we really could achieve together. And…well, it's just my opinion." Sabby sat down as abruptly as she had risen. It was her first speech at a company meeting, and I think she had just realized what she was doing; she hadn't even been sniffling.

"*All My Sons*. Okay. What's it about, Joely?" Seymour asked.

"There's this guy, Joe Keller. A military contractor who made engines for bomber planes in World War II. Around 1955, he's living with his wife and his son, Chris, in good old suburbia. His other son, Tom, was a pilot killed in the war."

"But," Sabby interrupted, "his wife refuses to believe her son was killed. Even after all these years, she still thinks he's coming back,"

"That's right," Joely went on. "Chris runs the factory now. He's gotten rich, but he's still sort of an idealist. And he loves his father, even though the old man is a real yahoo."

"Okay, what's a yahoo?" Ronny asked,

"A capitalist," Marlin told him.

"You see, his father's been in jail. He sold defective engine blocks, and as a result, about a hundred G.I.s died when their planes crashed. Of course, Keller said he didn't *know* they were defective, that his partner sold them without his knowledge. It's a lie, but he gets off, and his poor partner's still in jail after fifteen years. But Chris believes him, otherwise he wouldn't be able to keep working there."

"How many parts?" Ronny asked. "And will the audience get it?"

"*The Belle of Black Bottom Gulch* was too complicated for you," Marlin told him.

"Look, Ronny," Sabby said, "the partner's daughter was engaged to Tom, the one that got killed. Now, all these years later, she and the other son, she and Chris, have fallen in love. You could play Chris."

"The main thing is," Joely finished, "the old man *did* know, and he sold those engines for the money. And that's why his wife can't let herself believe Tom is dead. Because if he is, then Keller killed him—his son was flying one of those planes with a cracked engine block. So he had murdered, you see, one of his own sons and put the blame off on his partner. When Chris finds out, his whole life is shattered, he's in love with the daughter of the man his father framed, and his own success is built on the blood money his father made in the war."

"Typical," Marlin snapped.

"Well, then the father—who's spent the whole play blustering and lying and whining, making excuses, and trying to rationalize away the immorality of what he did before (that's what business is like anyway, and you have to take a chance, and he did it for his family, and it wasn't his fault, and so on)—finally he realizes what he's done. He finally sees that they're all—*all* the boys who died in the war—they're all his sons."

"And he commits suicide," Wolfstein said, coughing into his handkerchief. Sabby brought him a glass of water.

"Yeah, okay, I say let's do it," Seymour said.

"I think we ought to change it from World War II to Vietnam," I suggested. "It's the same damn thing all over again."

"Fat chance the chairman of Dow Chemical feeling guilty enough to blow his head off," Marlin sneered. "Does the son tell the old man off?"

Wolfstein nodded.

"Then give me the part."

"And, oh, Mr. Wolfstein," Sabby beamed, "you could direct and play the father."

"Ah, Sabby," he murmured through cigarette smoke. "You are so young." Her face fell under this accusation until he added, "No, no, my dear. I *envy* you, your ability to believe. Well, then, why not, eh, Amanda, when you come to think of it, why not? While huddling in our elderly corner of the madhouse, why not put on a play for your daughter?"

"Now, Nathan, you have a gloomy attitude on life, as my sister did. I don't see why we have to allow the fact that we *have* been surrounded by more insanity than some people might think was their fair share, get us so run down in the mouth. Why, yes, I think we should do that play. Everyone seems to think it's a good one, and as you know"—we certainly did—"I have always believed in keeping busy. There is nothing that will depress a person sooner than sloth."

So we were agreed, and only waited to tell Leila. She was

gone a long time. When she did return, she had her own announcement. And she was no longer pale, but flushed down her neck and shoulders. "Mrs. Booter," she said loudly and clearly, "has just advised me that we are no longer welcome at her establishment."

The old waiter grinned with smug delight from the corner where he always watched us eat. "You are dismissed," Mrs. Thurston informed him. His grin spread wider, like a gargoyle's. "Insolence!" she named him, but he stayed where he was.

"For meals?" asked Joely.

"No," Leila said, "we have to vacate the rooms too. She doesn't like what she's heard about us from her brother."

"That pig!" Marlin reminded us.

"She says she believes in decency."

"Why, I certainly hope this lady isn't trying to imply that other people do not believe in decency! Leila, honey, I hope you gave her a piece of your mind."

Joely was pulling on his flames of hair. "We've already paid 'til the end of the month. Double rates too! Plus we're still paying board for Jennifer and Ashton. And they're GONE."

"Thank God," threw in Ronny.

"And she didn't think there was anything indecent about that? Well, shit, why don't we just stay? Let her take us to court if she wants to!"

"No, I don't think so," Leila picked at her cold food. "I said we'd be out by the end of the week. We can make do at my place and at the theater. It's okay."

"But why? Why let her win?" He began polishing his glasses ferociously. "Hypocritical old bag."

"Oh, Joely, come on." Leila put her fork down tiredly. "It's just not worth it. Really. She'll refund the money."

Sabby came over to her with some coffee and sniffled, "Leila, everybody wants to do the play." Mrs. Thurston offered Sabby the handkerchief she kept up her sleeve.

chapter 24

Good and Bad Angels

"Naw, Leila wouldn't just give in. I bet that bitch threatened her, said she was going to bring up all sorts of juicy tidbits about the others." Joely was grumbling in his bed that night. "Drugs, sodomy, knocked-up girls. Bet that place was a voyeuristic paradise for a prurient old bag like Mrs. Booter."

I hadn't been sleeping either. "You like Leila a lot, don't you, Joely?"

"Yeah. A lot more than most."

It was quiet except for the whirring of bugs against the window screen. Then Joely's voice came out at me from the darkness again. "Leila got Margery a doctor. They're going tomorrow. I don't know how she got Ferrell to give her the name of an abortionist."

"I thought they were going to get married."

"They didn't want to get married."

"Oh."

"It must have been rough for Leila, the way she feels about all that. And God knows how Margery must be feeling. And Marlin. Aaahhhhh, boy." I heard him turn over to beat a hollow into his pillow. I lay there. How would I feel in Marlin's place, how did Marlin feel? Time and a thousand past failures dragged through my mind. My crotch itched. My back hurt. I knew I had only so long to escape by sleep before need forced me on my feet and up to the john.

Ten minutes later, I was feeling my way along the walls upstairs. There was a light under Leila's door, and when I came back from the bathroom, she looked out.

"Devin?"

"Yeah?"

"Are you okay?"

"Yeah. What are you doing up so late?"

"Trying to wind down, I guess. I'm reading some plays."

"Which plays?" I stood whispering in the dark, the light behind her hurt my unaccustomed eyes.

"*As You Like It.*"

"Really?"

"Wouldn't it be nice if things were that way? I mean, as we'd like it. Everybody gets reconciled. And we all sit down for a big, joyful feast."

"*King Lear's* closer to the way things really are."

"They're worse. Not many of *our* Lears ever stay out in the storm long enough to understand anything. Well, I'm sorry to bother you. Good night, Devin."

"Good night. Try to sleep."

Her door closed. The thin angle of light swept past my bare feet. I felt like I was walking around in a dream, strange and impalpable. What in hell was *that* all about, standing in the dark at 3 A.M. exchanging literary criticisms through a bedroom door? What in the world was Leila doing up reading Shakespeare in the middle of the night when everything was falling apart and she ought to be asleep? I wanted to go in and ask her, but I had chosen distance and disapproval and had kept to them until now—mostly because I didn't know how to get back.

Then, during the night something happened to all of us, as if a mountainous Puck had come along and sprinkled impetus over our wills. Mrs. Booter's eviction, like a foreign invasion, had filled us with tribal fervor. After a summer of collective indifference, we woke up ready to do a play. And with no more reason than we had ever had in the last months of calamities, everyone woke up happy. Upstairs, Mrs. Thurston persuaded Nate to eat an egg.

Then she sat down to write her dry cleaning plant and extend her extension of her leave. In the backyard, Maisie and Davy giggled. For love's sake alone, Sabby had overcome her terror of the freeway on-ramp and was driving by herself into Boulder to Xerox copies of *All My Sons*. Marlin and Margery left with her. At the boarding house, Suzanne, Pete, and Ronny packed up the company's belongings under the suspicious eye of Mrs. Booter. Joely and I would take Pete in; the children would sleep with Leila so Suzanne and Sabby could have their room. Ronny and Seymour would use Mittie's office at the theater. Things were tight, but what did we care! Why, when Margery and Marlin got back from the abortionist, we could move Mrs. T into bed with Wolfstein, and let them have hers. So there was a letter for Marlin from his draft board in Dayton, propped up on the mantel! It would all work out. There was a bright golden haze on the meadow, and the corn was higher than Mrs. Booter's eye, and God was in his heaven winking over the circle of mountains that morning.

The silver linings, of course, had clouds. As Joely and I were setting out for the theater, a Porsche pulled up in the driveway. From it slid a man in his early thirties, expensively hip, Carnaby Street mod, in a soft leather jacket and love beads by Tiffany's.

"Peace," he urged glibly, like a campaign sign. "Is this Spur Debson's place?"

"No, it isn't," I let him know quickly. But I was wrong.

"Yeah, he's out in back—far end of the yard," Joely told him.

"What are you talking about? Spur's not out there." Of course, then it occurred to me that Spur would have to be *somewhere*, so why not where we were?

Joely pointed out Leila's old wooden trailer, her gypsy wagon with its red roof and window and its two red-hubbed tires at the end of the backyard among a group of aspens. There, from its roof, flew one of the little shat-upon American flags.

"Far out," grinned our guest, reaching in his car for a soft leather Gucci briefcase. We waited until he had knocked on the wagon, been told through the shut door to go fuck himself in a gas chamber, and then, amazingly, been allowed inside.

The next morning, our spirits were slipped into another of fortune's slings. Since the day when Sheriff Booter had first thrown the Mexican flower ladies off his streets, Leila had been following quietly behind him—out of the same impulses, I suppose, that she followed those trucks to retrieve abandoned chickens—campaigning to rescue them. Now she gave her second speech before the town aldermen, asking them to grant street- vending licenses to these three old women. They said they knew what she really meant: she meant license not just for flowers, but license for hippies to sell dope, free love, protest marches, anarchy, and Eugene McCarthy posters. She said no, she was speaking only as a local businesswoman whose establishment had been, in the past, income-producing for Floren Park, and as such she wished to remind them that street vending added local color, and local color, like picturesque old Mexican women singing, "*Fiori, por favor*," amid pots of bright blossoms was also income-producing for a town whose only business was tourists. They said they thought they knew what sort of local color she had in mind, and did she or did she not know there was a guy out on the streets selling filthy feces. She said she did not know. (For she evidently hadn't run across Spur in the last week.) She concluded her speech by reminding them that they, she felt sure, were the last people who needed reminding of the rights of the individual. Then she thanked them for their time, and they thanked her, and she left, and the next day most of the local businesses canceled their ads in our playbills and on our street parade posters.

All morning, Sabby answered the office phone, sobbing between calls at this latest assault on Leila as Navajo jewelry, Austrian sportswear, Japanese restaurant, Danish toys, mountain landscapes, and trout in plastic bins rang up to ring off. Most gave no reason, but the lady at Western Outfits, Mrs. Booter's cousin, was jubilantly blunt, telling the blushing Sabby that after what she'd heard about her and the rest of her hippie friends, she wouldn't dream of having her name associated in print with such trash.

Leila didn't give up, but went down Main Street, store by store, to ask why. Some of the merchants she had shopped with summer after summer looked sheepish, but no one changed his or her mind. I stood behind Leila and listened to their excuses.

On the other hand, Mr. Ed Hade, owner of the largest car dealership in the state, did not want to cancel. In fact, he might even take out a full-page ad. He might, in fact, be willing to sink some money in the theater: what else was money for but to shell out. "Ain't that so, little lady?" he puffed at Leila from his tan vinyl chair in his office at the rear of his indoor coliseum of Cadillacs and Buicks. "Maybe you and me can make a deal, what you want to bet? You've always looked to me like the kind of girl that knew what was what."

"What did you have in mind, Mr. Hade?" Leila agreeably asked.

"What did I tell you, she's smart, ain't she?" He was asking not me but the air, so I kept my eyes on the fake-paneled walls lined with bowling trophies, and Shriner citations, and the photographs of his fat children. "Oh, well, now, this isn't what you'd exactly call the best time and place for talking over a deal, now is it?"

"It's fine with me, but of course if you're busy, we'll come back tomorrow." She sounded like a charity booster for the D.A.R.

"Well, I was thinking more in terms of you and me getting together tonight over a drink or something. Informal-wise."

But Leila just smiled. "I work nights. You know: put on plays. You should come one night. Bring your family. We're pretty good, aren't we, Devin?" She touched my arm.

"The best in town," I told him, but he glanced over me without seeing.

"How about afterward?" he pressed.

"I don't think so, Mr. Hade. My mother sits with my children, and I like to get back home with them as soon as possible." She smiled again, "Devin and I will be glad to drop by here tomorrow, though."

"Sure," I echoed dutifully.

Hade's chuckle was forced. His thick arm, matted with freckles and reddish hair, leapt out and hugged Leila quickly. "Huh. Huh. Huh. I don't believe you're quite catching my drift."

"Oh, I think I am," Leila sweetly replied. "Please call me about the ad, then. Devin." And I sailed in her wake out the door.

"Creep," I muttered, remembering with pleasure the way the Marine had slammed him into the side of the bar that night.

"Oh, he's no different than most. No better. No worse."

"Leila, what are you going to do? I mean, maybe you can keep the theater going without Bruno, but you can't keep going without ads. That's half your income."

"I know."

"And Bruno's going to buy the place and close it down anyhow."

"Not just yet," she said.

• • •

Turning off Main Street into the Arcade, we saw Rings Morelli walking toward us with Kim. She was wearing long chandelier earrings of green glass and looked misplaced in sunlight—unnatural, like a painted metal cutout. I had never seen her except through the dark smoke gauze of the Red Lagoon Bar, where (since Tanya's departure) she danced alone. Morelli nodded his head and said, "Mrs. Stark," as they passed. She nodded back, and said hello to Kim.

"'Mrs. Stark'?" I mimicked. "How does he know you?"

"Mr. Morelli? He owns the big dance hall on Main Street. We're in the same business. Entertainment."

Someone else in the entertainment business was coming out of the streetcar diner: Spurgeon—carrying two large valises full of his merchandise. Beside him, smoking a blue cigarette and talking briskly, was the Porsche/Gucci hippie. By all reports, during the past week, Spur had been doing a booming business. Like a carpetbagger

with his big valises, he kept on the move, one intersection ahead of
the good sheriff Booter, whose trained nose had undoubtedly caught
a whiff of Spurgeon's trafficking in public obscenities. Joely said he
used to think Spur's plays were pure shit, but he must have been
wrong because Spur couldn't even give those plays away, and pure
shit was clearly a bestseller. Indeed his turnover was rapid. College
kids on their way through to the purity of mountains, teenage runaways, guru-followers, summer-of-love-ers, all were eager for Spur's
emblems of Amerika. Even some older tourists bought the flags and
rockets on the suspicion that poop art might be pop art of an Andy
Warhol fashionableness.

"Spur!" Leila called.

"I hope," I threw in quickly, "you're going to ask him to start
paying rent. He can afford it."

"Rent?"

"He's living out there in the backyard in your gypsy wagon."

"Are you kidding? He didn't ask me."

"Surprise. Surprise."

We walked over. Gucci's grin shot out at Leila.

"Spur, are you using my trailer? I wish you'd let me know,"
she said for openers.

"Okay, babe, okay, everything's cool, I'm splitting tonight."

"That's not what I meant."

"Moving in with my partner here."

"Partner?"

"Well, ah"—Gucci gave a deprecatory smile—"friend, really.
Vic Falz."

We all shook hands.

"Are you interested in Spur's work?" she asked.

"Yes, indeed," he promised us.

My God, was somebody going to produce one of those awful
plays? Not even Leila had been willing to do that. Maybe he collected folk art. Political art?

"You must be very happy, Spur," she turned to say.

But Spurgeon, ever the Beau Brummel of etiquette, was
already striding away up the Arcade, a suitcase under each arm.

Leila called after him, "Wait a minute, Spur, okay? Could I talk to you for a second?"

"No sweat," he yelled. "You'll get your bail money back."

"It's not that. I'd like you to—"

"Later, chick, okay? I gotta go. Let's go, man. Bustville!" And he was around the corner.

"Nice to meet you," his partner told us, and rushed after him.

"Boy, Spurgeon must have radar." I pointed out Deputy Maddox closing behind him the door of the shooting gallery at the other end of the Arcade. He must have been in there practicing his aim in case there were any more public disturbances in Floren Park.

"Can you believe that guy?" Leila laughed.

"Spur? No."

"The other one—Mr. Falz. If this is for real, it's got to be those stupid posters or something. *Nobody* would seriously consider putting on *Napalm* or *Dachau*, but, you know, he does look like a producer. The *Hair* kind. In the sort of theater-in-the-round where the cast strips and runs out and feels up the audience. So all the Long Island lawyers can get their rocks off on the bouncing boobs."

"What would Mr. Hade think of his 'little lady' if he heard you talking like that?"

"Mr. Hade *assumes* I talk like that. And that is why he wants me to have a little drink with him 'or something.' So he can get *his* rocks off listening to me talk like that."

"But you don't talk like that in front of him."

"Oh, he probably thinks we only do it after dark."

I laughed and put my arm around her, and we left together to bring her children home from their day camp.

• • •

The next day Leila cooked breakfast for twelve people with her mother, talked to Wolfstein about Arthur Miller, swept and made beds, drove me to the Laundromat with Mrs. Thurston, told stories to Maisie and Davy as she drove to the grocery store, the hardware store, the thrift shop, talked to the kids at the McCarthy campaign headquarters, talked to a plumber and to the realtor about the stopped toilet at the house, fixed lunch for twelve people with her mother, discussed a set for *All My Sons* with Joely and me, drove the kids to day camp, drove Pete Barney to Dr. Ferrell's to renew his asthma medication, drove with me and Sabby to Boulder to pick up posters from the printer's, stuck them up in the part of town where summer school students were drinking beer and buying records, drove back to Floren Park for a rehearsal reading and casting of *All My Sons*, talked to the flower ladies about their rights, served to ten people the spaghetti she'd made while fixing breakfast, showed Sabby how to make up her eyes, picked up the kids from day camp, went to the theater, got into her costume, and performed the lead in *The Fantastiks* to an audience of twenty-seven, accompanied by Pete on the piano, went to the Red Lagoon Bar, had a drink with Kim, and was joined by Dennis Reed and Suzanne, searched for and found Wolfstein slumped in a corner booth and brought him home, studied the part of the mother in *All My Sons*, and fell asleep.

"That child is simply going to drop dead in her tracks, and it won't be long," Mrs. Thurston warned me.

We were in the lobby putting Cokes in the freezer and setting out a few candy bars. There were no longer enough customers to warrant the bright, popcorn-showering machine of the Fitzgerald era.

"Yes," she nodded fiercely, "Leila Stark is a fool, killing herself to no earthly avail. Trying to prove…well, you tell *me*, Devin, honey, because the Lord knows *I* fail to understand her motivations. It appears she is under the impression that she can keep this fool theater running, when it's as clear as the sky," she dropped her voice to an audacious whisper, "that not a soul gives a good goddamn."

I think if she had pulled up her dress and shined her buttocks at me, I couldn't have been more surprised than by this profanity.

"Well, Devin, I'm sorry," she added in response to my shock, "but I swear to the Lord I just get so exasperated, I could weep vexation. Just look at her trotting all over creation and annoying the law officials of this town—whom, honey, she is in no position to antagonize—all on account of those three pitiful old Mexican women that ought to be in a county home in the first place. Just yesterday, 'Leila, darling,' I asked her, 'what are these *flower*-sellers to you? Surely you have problems enough of your own.' 'Mama, they're *people*,' she says to me, as if I had insinuated they were anything else. 'They have a right to earn their livelihood.' 'Why, I don't dispute that for a minute,' I told her, 'but, darling, are you going to go sit out on the sidewalks with them and make sure they are allowed to earn it? Are they worrying about *your* livelihood? Of course they aren't! Never crossed their minds once!' Oh, Devin, why doesn't she use the head on her shoulders and call Bruno up and say, 'Your grandchildren and I will be on the next plane to Portland, Oregon, Bruno. *The next plane*. Now, you just go out and find us a nice little house and start making arrange- ments for me to get myself a college education, and you set aside a trust fund for Davy and Maisie so those blessed children can get themselves a college education too.' If she had an inch of sense, she'd be on the phone to that man right this minute. Of course, I *can* see the temptation of keeping this theater open pure and simple to spite Bruno Stark because my truthful opinion is he's just the sort of puffed-up Mr. Own-the-Whole-World that it's almost your moral duty to pull up short. But we have to face real- ity, Devin, and Leila cannot support herself and her babies even the way she lives...out of Salvation Army bins, and Mexican food with no nutrients in it, and the Good Lord knows where she got some of those rags she's dressing that poor little boy and girl with...even so, you cannot make a living by putting on amateur dramatic performances that nobody cares about. I supported two husbands"—she wrung the two Coke bottles in her hands by their necks as she evoked those deserters' memories—"*and* a child, *and an* invalid sister—even if it was purely psychological in Nadine's case—and I know what I'm talking about."

"Yes, ma'am." I handed her some more bottles. "But I don't think Leila's planning to keep the theater open after this month. She knows the Menelades are selling it to Mr. Stark."

"Yes, and he bought it for pure spite, just so he could shut the door in her face." She slammed down the cooler lid. "No, not *this* theater, Devin. Leila Stark is planning to open her *own* theater, coming right back to North Carolina, where I have to make my living and hold up my head, and starting up her own theater in the woods, if you can believe what my daughter has been telling me. And this one isn't even going to charge! 'Free for People,' she advised me. And I suppose everyone concerned is going to sleep on the clouds and eat daisies!"

"Is that true?"

She gave me a look, sorrowful and suffering as a Puritan in Drury Lane and went backstage to show Sabby how to hem up a costume properly.

Mrs. Thurston's news made me happy, and I couldn't figure out why. Somehow I felt like a decision had been made about *me*, though, of course, it had nothing to do with me at all.

I thought about it, looking at the painting of Leila faded on the floor, and the portraits of our company lining the lobby wall. Jennifer and Ashton, who were gone. And Mittie. And the Buddy Smith from Omaha who had never come because he'd gone to Vietnam.

The door opened and Marlin and Margery stood there.

"Hi, Devin, how's it going?"

"Fine. How 'bout you?" What could I say? How was the abortion?

"You two look tired. Want a Coke?" Somehow, they looked older too.

"Well, Devin," Marlin told me as he handed Margery her Coke, "Old Uncle Sam gave me the finger. You can bless that busted ear and knee and psyche of yours."

"Oh, shit. That letter from your draft board. We were worried about that."

"Yeah. Joely gave it to me. Can't say it was much of a

surprise. Low grades in a low-grade school."

"I'm really sorry, Marlin. What are you going to do?"

The door opened again, and Leila hurried in. "Sabby said…" She stopped, and with her face intent with question, stared at Margery. Margery smiled, then grinned, then shook her head and ran over and hugged Leila. "I couldn't do it," she said. "We couldn't. We got all the way there, and then we couldn't. We didn't want to."

"Oh, Margery…I'm glad."

"So give me a cigar," Marlin said to me. "I'm going to have a baby. Then give me another cigar. I'm going to get married."

"Well, congratulations," I said. "Wait'll Joely hears."

"A Canadian baby," he added.

"We're leaving," Margery explained.

"Oh, Margery, are you sure?" Leila took her hands.

"Yes, we've thought about it a lot. What if Marlin went over there and got killed? I'm sure. This is what I want to do." She smiled again. "Do you think I'm going to risk their dropping a bomb on an expectant father?"

Decisions—that's what made them look older.

chapter 25

Absence

Because the leads were theirs, we gave a final performance of *The Belle of Black Bottom Gulch* the next night, and for the last time, Margery was the Belle and Marlin was the Hero who saved her from being robbed, seduced, foreclosed upon, abandoned, nearly raped, practically frozen, and almost bifurcated by a cardboard buzz-saw, just as it had happened when I had looked in from the lobby that first night in Floren Park. Twenty-six people came.

"Seems like all we've ever done this summer is say good-bye," Sabby sighed.

I poured her another glass of wine from one of Leila's half-gallons. It was midnight, and everyone sat in the Belle's lowly cabin on the stage to say good-bye to Marlin and Margery, to offer our commiserations at their exile, our best wishes for their nuptials, our blessings on their baby. Everyone thought they were very brave to give up their country, though no one thought much of the country they were giving up. Everyone was scared for them, and they were scared for themselves, but no one knew what else they could, or should, do. It was an insane choice to have to make, and if you had told us at the prom, or midterms, or sit-ins that we would have to make it, it wouldn't have made sense.

"It shouldn't be happening," Leila said. But it was.

Seymour counted the profits. "Sixty-five dollars tonight. Best in a while."

Leila gave the money to Marlin and Margery. "It's your play," she said.

Then Verl walked in on us out of the darkness.

"I've been trying to reach you," Leila said.

"So have I. Verl, where have you been?"

"Been in a little trouble," he said. Verl had been arrested at a demonstration of draft-card burning. Leila moaned when he told us.

"Verl!" I yelled at him. "Why did you burn your stupid draft card? You're a C.O.! You're one of the few bona fide C.O.s around! He's a Quaker," I went on yelling at everybody else. "He's always been a Quaker. His father's a Quaker. His grandfather!"

He stretched his long legs up onto a box on the stage. "Devin's giving me sort of a dramatic entrance here, isn't he? How's everybody doing? How's Mr. Wolfstein? Any more wine, Leila?"

"Verl—all those articles you've been writing for that paper, I bet they've got you on some sort of list. They're going to rake your ass over the coals," I told him.

"Maybe not. A couple of us went in on a good lawyer." Then he told us his court date wasn't coming up for months, and in the meantime, he was going out to Resurrection City in Washington.

"The Poor People's march?" Joely scoffed. "What for? You missed it. That movement was over when they shot King. What did Resurrection City manage to accomplish except to give each other the runs and sit in the rain listening to old fogies like Reverend Abernathy try to steer his mules right down the middle of every issue. You think the government's going to listen to *them?* The place to go is Chicago. The Democratic Convention. That's where I'm going as soon as we finish up here."

This was the first any of us had heard about it. Next thing we knew, Sabby Norah would be telling us she'd decided to run guns for the Weathermen.

"You think the Democrats are going to listen to you?" Marlin asked. "Yippies and hippies and skippies and potheads?"

"They're going to have to listen," Joely replied solemnly.

"Play the piano, Pete. This is a wedding party," Leila said. Pete played, "Here Comes the Bride," and Sabby cried.

Outside, the sky was strewn with stars that gleamed outlines of the mountains. Now the long heat wave was over, and the night was cold. Verl and I sat down by the creek's edge to talk about how he'd been, how I'd been, why he'd let himself get arrested, why I'd thought I'd never get over Jardin. My concerns seemed silly to me now beside his, or Margery's, or Marlin's, or Joely's, or Leila's, or just about anyone's.

"Now, now," he chuckled. "Don't start feeling sorry for yourself for being shallow."

"Boy," I laughed. "You just never let up, do you? Well, just wait 'til you make a mistake!"

"Make them all the time. Like Dennis Reed. Misjudged him. Thought he was one of the good shallow people. Like you. He's a total sleaze."

"Thanks. I guess."

He leaned on my shoulder and stood up. "But some people, now, I'm right about, right from the start." He slapped my arm. "Take it easy, hear?"

I watched him whistle off to his old battered Triumph.

Back in the theater, Seymour stood beside Pete's piano and in his clear, high voice sang "Taps." On the stage, everyone sat in a circle, their arms crossed, holding hands. "Day is done, gone the sun." Holding hands, just like in some kids' camp before all the lights go out.

chapter 26

The Wanderer

"*Yow!* YOW! YOW! Cool it, lady, cool it! HEY! WATCH
OUT! YOU CAN'T DO THAT!!" It was Spurgeon's voice.

"GET OUT OF HERE THIS MINUTE. March yourself
off this property before I lose my mind. This is an outrage! AN
OUTRAGE!" That was Mrs. Thurston.

Joely and Pete and I leapt from our beds and raced outside.

"HEY, YOU CAN'T DO THAT! That's private property!
That's ART, you Philistine bitch!"

In the backyard, Mrs. Thurston's quilt-robed rear end pro-
truded from the door of Leila's little trailer, and Spur's rockets,
flags, coils, and buttons flew out around her while, from behind,
Spur jerked at her legs. Maisie and Davy, with their underpants
around their ankles, stood by peacefully watching. When Spur
finally pried Mrs. Thurston out of the door, her face was wild with
anger, she had my fishing rod in her hand, and with it she began
at the same time lashing Spur's artworks and Spur's legs, face,
and arms. Like Samson with his ass-bone, she laid into her foe,
beating those rockets and coils as if they were swarming snakes.

"YOW! YOW! YOW!" Spur jumped. "You're crazy! You're
NUTS, LADY! You're going to get yourself SUED, destroying
private property!"

"SUED! HA!" Mrs. Thurston's eyes roared flames, and her
arm never faltered. She drove Spur leaping before her, slashing

with the rod at his calves, all the way down the drive and out onto the open road. Righteous fury gives one the psychic edge (as Spur himself should surely have known), and this time Amanda waxed full of it, not to be withstood. The rest of us just gaped.

Jerking up the children's underwear, she marched them furiously into the house. They bawled in confusion as they went, while from the other side of the street Spur yelled, "This house is an asylum! Moronic cretinous nest of vipers! Spider cunts! Read *One Flew Over the Cuckoo's Nest!* BIG NURSE! *Castrators!* Motherfuckingassholemumumumum," he mumbled to a halt, and we went back inside.

Mrs. Thurston was fluttering her hand over her heart as she tried to keep herself from hyperventilating. So beside herself was she that she hadn't realized her lacquered wig was halfway around her head so that it looked like her French twist grew out over her right ear.

"Have a glass of water," I told her.

She took three slow breaths. "Thank you, Devin, if you would be so kind." We could hear Maisie and Davy crying on the front porch. Mrs. Thurston sipped her water. "You boys," she said, "will have to pardon my behavior just now."

"No, no, it's nothing," we assured her.

"I have always been a rational person, believed very highly in rationality"—we all nodded vigorously—"but there comes a time when even a stone would rise up and speak its mind against Spurgeon Debson."

"Yes, ma'am."

"I thought I had seen the worst that man could do. When I heard that he had bitten and relieved himself upon the county sheriff, I thought I had seen the worst. But that was before this four-year-old child informed me that she could not do her potty in the bathroom because, 'Grandma, Davy and I save our'"— she wrenched up her face and spelled out the word like a sentence of death—"'our S-H-I-T for Spur. We work for S-H-I-T power.'"

"I wondered if it was real," Joely said. "I couldn't see how he could be doing it all himself if it was. I thought maybe it was dogs."

"Well, I had not been informed that this...vileness was going on in our backyard. To tell you the truth, I hoped the Good Lord in his mercy had at last spared us the acquaintanceship of Mr. Debson altogether. I don't know why I bothered to delude myself. Of course he was hiding out there! Out there all the time, where else would he be? Or any of the other riffraff she drags in."

Was she talking about us?

"But I did *not* know he was manufacturing manure until I caught sight of those two little children doing their potty in two of my *cooking pans*, and then with their own hands scooping it up and packing it into those contraptions. That he was using those innocent babies in that obscene way. That knowledge I did *not* have. And, I will tell you, Joely, when I saw that going on, I simply saw flashing stars and screamed as loud as a chicken with its head cut off."

Out the kitchen window, I could see that Spur had sneaked back to the trailer, where he was collecting his property as fast as he could, with furtive glances over his shoulder to be sure Mrs. Thurston didn't fly out with the rod again.

Leila, who'd left at seven to drive Margery and Marlin to the bus, pulled up just as Spur finished his packing. We all went out on the front porch to hear what they had to say to each other. "Spur," she began, "I'd like you to apologize to Booter. If you do, he'll let those three flower women—"

But, though she had fed and housed him, Spur was not receptive. "Forget it, chick. I am splitting this rabbit-hole-corn-ball-slime-slop town. Today! I'm moving to Chicago!" Spur pushed past her.

"Damn," Joely mumbled. "Maybe I won't go, then."

"You can't leave," she reminded Spur. "You have to show up for court."

"Taken care of. You think I let these boondock pigs hassle me?"

268 • michael malone

"Taken care of how?"

"I got friends with bread, baby. This is AMERICA. They'd let you bugger their grandmother if you had enough bread to stuff in their ears so they couldn't hear her screaming. That's how." He walked to the middle of the yard, where he could address the crowd: "STAND THERE! Don't think you've driven me off!"

"We daren't hope," threw in Mrs. Thurston.

"Wow, man, I got places to go. This is it! And you plastic Philistine middle-class reactionary college DUMMY-TITS are going to be stuffed up to your honkie necks in MY shit! *This house is coming down!* And ALL the houses are coming down and all the factories and all the banks and all the universities and EVERYWHERE all you napalm-farters go to hide!"

This speech had nothing particularly to do with us; Spur would have said the same to a gathering of Ubangis. Nevertheless, Mrs. Thurston replied, "Young man, the Good Lord has the patience of Job, but I swear if I don't believe that you are just about to wear Him out!"

"The Good Lord can take THAT up His asshole!" Spur dropped his two valises and gave God the finger with both hands, cork-screwing his wrists, raising his arms higher and higher, as high as he could reach on his tiptoes.

Davy was peeking out from behind Joely's legs. "Wave good-bye to a poor one-armed son-of-a-bitch," Joely told the toddler.

"Can I have his dog?" Maisie asked.

"The sheriff got his dog. That was before he was rich enough to buy off the cops," Joely explained to her.

•   •   •

And through it all, we kept working on *All My Sons*, everyone trying for once as hard as they could to do, for Wolfstein, or Leila, or themselves, the best that they could. Everyone, that is, except Suzanne Steinitz, who was angry because Wolfstein and

Leila had given Sabby the role of the fiancée, the ingenue lead. And the only other female part left was a small one—a frowsily sexual, affable housewife who lived with her husband next door to the main characters. (I was her husband; at this point, everyone had to act—some taking double parts; Sabby would also be a child's voice offstage.) Sabby hadn't wanted the big role: it was too important, she said; the girl was supposed to be pretty; she wasn't good enough; she'd ruin the play for everyone else; she'd do the little part.

"Sabby, I'm going to tell you something I've been thinking for a long time," said Wolfstein gently as he sat down, swaddled in a droopy sweater and a scarf on the stage steps beside her. Sabby, who was sure he was about to advise her to stay away from the theater altogether because she was making a fool of herself, began to poke the stems of her glasses through her knit skirt. "You know why I want you to do that part?" She shook her head mournfully. "It's precisely because you *can* do those little parts when they're given to you. And do them right. I've been watching you all summer, Sabby, and you want to know something? You're very good."

She jerked her head up as if waiting for the punch line.

"I've been watching you pretty carefully. Yes, that's right, even through my fog." He waited to stop coughing. "And you've got it. Not just the love of it. But the gift. Oh, clumsy still, and uncertain, and cluttered with banality, but it peeks through— almost in spite of yourself. In *Hedda Gabler*. In *Cat*. The scenes with Cal...yes, it's there. And besotted waste that I am, I still know it when I see it."

As if he had told her she might fly if she wished to, Sabby stared at Wolfstein without daring to believe him. And though I doubt it had ever crossed our minds before that Sabby was especially good at *anything*, I think the rest of us saw then that it was true, recalled how, when we used to talk about the performances, we'd use everyone else's real name—"Marlin was off" or "Ashton overplayed it"—but with her, we always used the *character's* name. That's how well Sabby hid behind the masks.

Well, that speech did it for Suzanne. She wanted her tuition back. This summer was certainly not what she had been led to expect when she applied. It was certainly not what *she* would call a professional training company run by reputable people. She had thrown away an entire summer being surrounded by talentless provincials, unsophisticated, uncivilized, unsanitary barbarians. The owner was dead, his wife was insane, his director was a stupid has-been alcoholic, and the rest of us were pimply, puerile, and boring, boring, boring; and she burst into tears. Leila gave her her money back.

Joely told Suzanne that her speech was the best performance she'd given all summer, and when Dennis Reed didn't show up to take her away as she'd said he would, Leila drove her to the airport.

Rehearsals went on. Wolfstein was playing the blustering father with energy remarkable in someone as ill as he was. Somehow he even made himself look healthy, bulky, and coarse. And the rest of us struggled to keep up with him while he nagged, yelled, coaxed, and trained us into "something that *coheres*, for once!" "Ladies and gentlemen, this time, let's try to do it right." "Again, please." "Again."

We still hadn't figured out what to do about Suzanne's part. Mrs. Thurston was reading the lines, but she was needed to stay with the children and wasn't exactly what the part called for anyhow. She still sounded like Big Mama in *Cat on a Hot Tin Roof*. Joely had canceled his plans to get to Chicago in time for the presidential convention. He figured he ought to stay and see Leila through the play. "I was here for the first one," he said. "I ain't missing the final line."

So that left him and me, Sabby, Seymour, Ronny (who stayed because he was having an affair with Dr. Ferrell's daughter, Bonnie), Pete, Barney, and Leila. Seven out of an original company of thirteen—fourteen, if you counted Buddy Smith.

Late on the night of August 20th, Sabby and Leila were going over the confrontation between the mother and the girl about the son who had been killed in the war. Someone started banging on the door. It was Kim, and with her was Rings Morelli. Kim always came to our plays, but I don't think I'd ever seen him in the theater before. When Seymour let her in, Kim yelled up to the front of the house, "Is Leila Stark here?"

Her eyes shaded by her hand, Leila called back, "Is that you, Kim?"

"Yeah, and Rings here is with me." They walked up to us. "Listen, Leila, 'scuse me for busting in on you like this, but I just found out something's going on, and I thought you oughta know. I don't usually meddle in other folks' business, but you been so good to me and my boy over at the day camp. Well, shit, I think it's lousy, what they're trying to pull."

"What is it? Should we go outside?" Leila jumped down from the stage.

"Naw, it's nothing to hide. Well, they think so."

Morelli prodded Kim in the back with a finger. "Stop gabbing and tell her."

"Yeah, okay. I heard this phone call, Leila. Well, before that I heard Tony and Lady Red arguing. That Mr. Stark, your husband's dad, I guess, he wants this place shut down pronto."

"I already know that. The lease runs out at the end of this month,"

"No, honey, no." She shook her head dramatically. "Now. As soon as he can get it done. Lady Red calls up Sheriff Booter, and they're going to close it down on some kind of town violation—fire hazard, or you know what I mean. They figure they can do it quicker that way than evicting you on a lease."

Joely groaned, "Bastards."

"I just wanted to let you know, Leila. And anyhow, if there's anything I can do to help, I mean, like packing, or watching the kids, or something, you just let me know, okay?"

Leila said, "There is something you could do, Kim."

"Just name it, honey."

And to our amazement, she then and there persuaded Kim to take the part that Suzanne Steinitz had refused to play. Lady Red was closing the bar and discotheque in a couple of weeks anyhow, Kim said, so it was just a question of being out of a job sooner or later. Why not sooner?

"Look here," said Morelli when Kim was through. "I don't know what your plans are, but how'd you like to go into business with me? I'm talking straight, you know what I mean."

Leila smiled. "No. What?"

"A cabaret-type place, see." He waved his arm contemptuously around the theater. "You're never gonna make any dough with this kind of stuff. This is peanuts. No insult intended. I'm sure you do a good job, but let's face it, you can only sell one ticket to a customer a night, right?"

"If you've got any customers to sell them to," Joely added.

"Right. There's no percentage in putting on plays." So far, Morelli and Mrs. Thurston shared the same bleak view of drama in America. "But a night club, now, you can put on two, three shows a night. Sell a lot of drinks. How 'bout it? I'm thinking of expanding out of the dance hall business. You take care of the shows. I'll take care of the business."

"I don't know a thing about night club shows," Leila told him.

"Who gives a damn what's up on the stage?" he pointed out.

She laughed. "Well, I don't think so, Mr. Morelli. But thanks for the offer."

"Look here," he persisted. "The Menelades are pulling out. Now, that place was always strictly peanuts, and look at the dough *they* were raking in hand-over-fist. Why not us? See, I don't like outsiders moving in around here. This Stark guy. What's he planning to do with this property?"

"I don't have any idea," Leila said. "But I doubt he's going to open a night club."

"Well, I don't like it anyhow. I tell you something else I don't like. The way the sheriff's been acting. Now you, I like. You got brains. Business brains, I can tell. But you're decent, too, know what I mean? You've been decent to Kim and the kid. I like that."

"Thank you," she nodded.

Polite as a prince in his bright suit, Morelli nodded back. "If I was you," he went on, "I wouldn't mess with Booter over those old women. Flower-hawking! That's peanuts. You come into business with me. People'll bust a gut to hand over their money, you play it right."

"I'll think it over. Anyhow, thanks for thinking about me."

After they left, we wondered whether there was any point in going on with the rehearsal, since we probably weren't going to get a chance to put the play on if Kim was right and Booter was planning to evict us. "He hasn't done it yet, has he?" Leila told us. "Where were we, Sabby?"

Joely shrugged his shoulders and read Sabby her next line.

When we got home, we found Mrs. Thurston still up in her bathrobe, seated in Mittie's chair, reading *Nicholas and Alexandra*.

"Mother! It's 2 A.M."

"Yes, I know. I could not sleep. Well, I hope you're satisfied, Leila Stark. You and all these *liberal* young people setting fire to our institutions and raving about China, and socialism this and socialism that."

"What are you talking about, Mother?"

I thought Mrs. Thurston must have just been reading about how the Bolsheviks took the Czar's family down into the basement of the Winter Palace and shot them. But it was much more current. "I heard it on the television," she said. "I'll have you know that the Communists have invaded Czechoslovakia with *tanks*. They have simply bullied their way in, just like they always do, and overturned Mr. Doobchick and his entire government. *That*, Leila, is what Communists do."

"Dubcek's a Communist too," Joely put in.

"Oh, that's awful," Leila said. "When? Tonight?"

"I turned on the set, and poor little Shirley Temple Black was there with a microphone in Czechoslovakia, and she was crying right there on television—it was so horrible what the Communists were doing to the people!"

"Stupid. Stupid. Why the hell did they do that? Now! Well, that does it for McCarthy, folks. Damn," Joely went downstairs cursing.

Leila sank slowly down on the couch. "I guess a little freedom scares other people. They think you will want more and more."

"You will," I said.

Later that night, I got out of bed to see if Mrs. Thurston had left anything to eat unlocked. Leila's light was on again. This time I knocked. "Still reading Shakespeare?"

The sheets were still blue; over the brass headpost, the poster of Robert Kennedy was still smiling. Coat hangers were still stuck in the chain strung across one window, but Mittie's clothes had been taken away. She looked up from a large, crumbling cardboard box laid across her lap. Photographs were piled around her on the bed. There were a lot of Mittie. Studio portraits, theatrical poses, Mittie as a child on a pony, Mittie wearing khaki shorts in Israel, Mittie in a cap and gown, Mittie as a Boy Scout. He was always alone, and his smile was always uncertain. We looked silently at them all spread across the bed. "You can see the unhappiness there, can't you, even when he was a child?" There was one picture of Mittie sitting next to his grandmother Strovokov with Maisie standing between his legs and Davy on his lap. Leila set it aside. Most of the other pictures were of the two children. There weren't very many of Leila.

"Do you have any of you when you were a baby?"

She handed me eight yellowing snapshots; they had all been taken on the same day in the backyard of the Earlsford duplex, I thought. Leila was six, and very skinny, and very blond. In most of them she stood shyly beside her uncle, Ethan Clyde. In one colored print, she appeared in the background watching with a puzzled look her stepfather, Jerry Thurston, light a cigarette. There was also, in the box, a full sheet of those little school pictures, twelve of them, each row complete.

"Pretty pitiful, hunh?" she said.

I fished through the cardboard box, took out an old torn photo. "Who's this?"

"My father."

"He's very handsome. He looks like one of those old movie stars from the twenties."

She didn't say anything.

I found a picture that startled me. "Spurgeon? Is this Spur?" It was a guy with a pompadour haircut leaning with a cocky smile against a big motorcycle. If it was Debson, he certainly had changed his style.

She looked at it. "No. That's Link. Link Richards."

"The guy you used to go with? That guy?"

"Yep. My first true love." She smiled. "That makes you my second."

"Leila, he looks just like Spur. I mean it's kind of blurry, but I thought it was Spur."

"You did?" She was making stacks of pictures of Maisie.

"Yeah. Look at it. Look."

She glanced at the photograph, nodded, "I guess so," and went on with what she was doing.

"Well, that explains a lot," I said, though I wasn't sure what.

She closed her eyes, leaned against the brass post. I looked back down at the picture. "Why did you get involved with Spur, Leila?"

"Oh, Devin, I don't know," she sighed. "Mixed motives, I'm sure. When Mittie and I met him, he hadn't gotten so...angry. He wanted to be a playwright, I'm sure that was part of it. That he was *trying* to say something, even if he said it all wrong. And, well, I thought he must be very hurt to be so unhappy, and furious at life... And I guess I was tired of failing at trying to fill Mittie's holes, make him feel safe. I guess I thought I could succeed with Spur. Maybe a part of me wanted to help *him* to hurt *Mittie*. To get back at Mittie for letting me fail him. Selfish—selfish 'goodness.' Thinking I could make up for his not succeeding with the acting, make up for his father. After he was...killed, I think I let Spur move in just to punish myself...to keep reminding me I'd let Mittie die."

"Leila, don't be stupid. You didn't 'let' Mittie die."

"Yes, I did. That night, when Spur was there, when I turned away, I stopped loving him. And he knew it. He saw it. When he hit me, I stopped."

"But that didn't make him die. Mittie didn't even tell you he knew Bruno had quit on the theater. And even if he had, it wouldn't have mattered."

Her eyes were still closed. There was one tear caught in the lashes.

"It's been a rough day, Devin."

I stood up. "Do you know what ever happened to Link?"

"No, he left Earlsford, I guess. Went off someplace—maybe he joined the army…and I don't know what happened to my stepfather, where he went. Or my real father. I think he did join the army. They all just…wandered off, sailed out to sea. Sailed out to see the world I guess. Don't men think they can figure things out by going off someplace they've never been? If nothing makes sense where you are, go someplace else?"

"I guess so, I don't know." Why was I in Floren Park?

"I'm going back home," she said, scooping up the loose pictures to put them back in the cardboard box.

"Yes, your mother told me."

"I think it's time, not space, where you figure things out."

"What does that mean?"

"The past. I want to find out what happened."

"What happened to you?"

"For a start." She reached up to turn out the light. "Good night, Devin. Thank you for saying what you did."

"Don't thank me, please. Try to go to sleep."

chapter 27

Tempest

Kim learned her lines quickly. She was enjoying herself. "I always used to daydream about being a movie star," she told us. "But musicals, you know. I never thought I'd be acting in a *serious* play." While we rehearsed, Mrs. Thurston brought over our food, rounded up boxes from the local stores, even—with *noblesse oblige*—from the ones that had canceled their ads. When we weren't working on *All My Sons*, we packed equipment, costumes, all the myriad residue of Mittie's desire to be an actor. "I'm not leaving it for Bruno to toss on the funeral pyre," Leila said.

Kim and Cary helped with the packing too. "Y'all are being so nice to me," she kept saying.

By the beginning of that week, everyone had his part memorized.

Seymour would play Sabby's outraged brother. Ronny was the idealistic son. Pete Barney would take tickets and seat people and run the concession stand and work the lights. Everyone would be stagehands when they weren't onstage. Joely would run the production. Somehow, Wolfstein had wrestled wholeness out of all the pieces of our talents, feelings, voices, gestures. "I'm proud of you," he said the night of the dress rehearsal, said for the first time that summer. "I didn't think I could do it," he added, for the first time, too, I imagined, in a long while.

We argued out approaches. "If you read it that way, Nate, it elicits sympathy for your character, doesn't it? I mean, the audience is going to feel sorry for him."

"The man is not *evil*, Joely."

"Bull."

"No, no. Don't be so hard and self-righteous. It's the easy way. Try pushing your compassion where it *doesn't* want to go. Extend it to a man who loved his wife, who loved his sons, who tried to give them everything he had been taught to think they ought to want and have…a house, a nice yard"—he held his arm out to the set now put up on the stage—"security. This is an uneducated man who feels inferior to people like his son, but he's the one who gave the son a chance for an education. All he has to offer is his success."

"A man who purposely, callously sells machines that are no good, that fall apart and kill people—for *money*. For a fast buck, Nate!"

"Yes, you're right, Joely, he wasn't strong enough to be stronger than what he had been taught to think he was supposed to do: succeed. But he wasn't bad enough, either, to be able to live without his son's respect… He fell, he *morally* fell, and if you live out your life without ever falling once, you'll be a rare man, Joely, and without need of others' compassion… Excuse me, I think I'd better go lie down."

I took his arm. "Are you okay?"

"Yes, thank you, yes," he coughed. "I'm just going to lie down in the office for a minute."

"He's not okay at all," Sabby said anxiously. "I think Dr. Ferrell ought to see him. Do you think he'll be all right for the performance tomorrow?"

On the phone, Dr. Ferrell said we should bring Wolfstein in on Friday. He told Leila also that if he saw Ronny Tiorino with his daughter again, and if his fifteen-year-old daughter was doing what he didn't want to find out she was doing, he was going to have the book thrown at Ronny. It was the first time we'd heard Dr. Ferrell take a serious attitude toward almost anything.

"Well," called Joely from his bed that night, "there goes the last of the gang that was getting any this summer! Good old Ronny hung in there as long as he could."

"Yeah," I said. "Sure hasn't been a summer of love."

"Come on, now. I didn't have any runaway wife at my fly either."

"Awh, one night. That's all. Big deal."

"Is that all it was? Well, don't knock it, kid. At least you're good-looking. What I've mostly had is the old personal hand-job. My person, my hand."

From his mattress on the floor between us, Pete giggled.

I laughed. Joely laughed. And Pete said, "What about Seymour and Sabby?"

"Them?" Joely snorted. "Forget it. Sabby screwing?"

"On the other hand," I said, "nobody thought she could act either."

I dreamed that Verl and I were sitting on the creek bank talking, and he told me Leila was over on the other side of the water past the woods. He said she wanted to talk to me. I didn't want to go over there because that was where Mittie had gotten killed. But Verl said I ought to. When I got halfway over the bridge, all the woods were on fire. The trees were shafts of flames. So I started back. But he kept waving his arms at me, telling me to go ahead, go ahead. "You're crazy," I said. "I'll kill myself." "No, you won't," he kept saying. "Go on. Go fast." I ran. I could feel myself on fire—my hair seared, my face burning. I kept running. When I came out on the other side, I wasn't hurt at all. My face, hair, clothes, shoes were just the same. I was in a meadow, and Leila was picking some of the periwinkles Verl and I had seen in the field that first evening when we drove into Floren Park. She didn't notice me, and then the dream faded.

• • •

That morning, I got up before the others and walked down to the creek. I took my notebook with me so I could reread what

280 • michael malone

I had done. The poems to Jardin seemed—maybe it was because
I was outdoors in cool, new air off the sharp mountains—like an
old, embarrassing diary. Verl had been right, just too kind—they
didn't even have technique. I tore them into small squares, let
them fall to float either to the Atlantic or the Pacific, whichever
it was.

•   •   •

"We need to get the keys to this place, boy."
"Well, sir, I don't have them. You'll have to see Mrs. Stark."
"You reckon she's at home this time of the morning?"
"Yes, sir. I'm going back there now."
"Why don't I give you a lift, boy?"
I didn't want to ride in Sheriff Booter's car again. When
I'd seen him in front of the theater on my way home from the
diner, I had tried to cut a wide arc around the parking lot. But
he'd spotted me. With him was a plump and sour man in a
short-sleeved white shirt with a thin tie who carried a clipboard.
"That's okay, thanks, I can walk." I started to do so.
"Hold on. We got to go out there anyway. Most folks run-
ning a business gits it open before ten o'clock. You think she'll
be at home?"
"Yes, they're probably having breakfast."
"Having breakfast?" he chuckled and gave his associate a
broad wink. "Ten o'clock and they're having breakfast! Think
they can git their street clothes on by noon?" The other man
forced an unenthusiastic smile that quickly was canceled.
"We generally stay up pretty late," I explained.
"I bet you do, I bet you do," Booter wisecracked. He seemed
to be in a very good mood. "Doing all sorts of things, I wouldn't
mind wagering." He told the plump man, "This young man's
ridden in my car before on a previous occasion. Strange, isn't it,
he don't seem too eager to accept my hospitality. I been good
to you, son. You know that, and I know that. Don't we? I could
have come down hard, lot harder than I did. You'd been in

Chicago, or one of those mean southern towns, you'd-a been in a lot worse fix. Isn't that so?"

"Yes, sir."

"So you just take a seat in this car here, and we'll go on up and wake up your friends in case they're not down to breakfast yet. How about that?"

I got in the car.

Maisie ran out on the porch and yelled back inside, "Mama, Devin's arrested. The police got him!" The company gathered on the porch to see. Fortunately, everyone was decently dressed, no one was shooting heroin, or screwing, or protesting the war, and Spurgeon was gone.

"Good morning, Gabe. Mother, this is Mr. Booter. I believe you met last month."

"Yes. Mittie's accident. How do you do, Officer?"

"I'm doing fine, ma'am. And you?"

"Fine, thank you. It's gotten a bit chilly, hasn't it? I do believe this summer is just about coming to an end."

I climbed out of the back seat of the patrol car.

"Was Devin lost, Gabe?"

"Uhhuhhuh," he gave her a chuckle. "No, this boy just came along for the ride. He likes riding in my car. That right?"

I went up on the porch so I could face him with the others.

"What can I do for you?" Leila asked politely.

"Well, now," he strolled up to the bottom step, propped his boot on it, while his friend stayed in the car, scowling down at the ditch beside the road. "Mr. Bipple here, from our department of safety regulations, needs to take a little look-see at your the-ater, Leila."

She smiled. "What seems to be the problem?"

Booter smiled too. "Why, we don't know there is a problem. We just have to do these little checks regularly to make sure there *ain't* a problem."

"I guess Mr. Bipple must have missed us last summer when he did his regular check-up. And the summer before, too."

"I guess he musta." Booter's grin got wider. "Lot of folks been checking into the town statutes lately. In fact, our mayor called *me* in just the other day over a little notification he'd gotten from a lawyer regarding one of our statutes." He bent and lazily picked some grass out of his boot toe. "'Course the mayor was kinda surprised that three old Mexican biddies that can't read or write or even speak English worth a damn had gone to the trouble, not to mention the expense, of hiring a lawyer to send that little notification outlining my abuses of their legal rights. Our mayor's a nervous kind of person. He don't like people getting upset with him. He likes things peaceful." He stared at Leila, who just looked back at him politely and waited. "So I happened to come across a couple of statutes myself that folks had gotten slack on, had let 'em slide over the years. Safety statutes regarding public places. Seemed to me somebody ought to look into things right away before we had some kind of bad accident here in Floren Park. We can't risk people getting burnt up and blowed up while they're here to relax and enjoy themselves. It's bad for business."

Mrs. Thurston drew herself taller. "I certainly do wish you had thought of that a month ago, Mr. Booter, before you and your associates allowed several dozen boxes of Fourth of July fireworks displays to be left sitting unattended in the middle of a public field where they could explode on an innocent passer-by." Well, Mrs. Thurston had not, like Spur, "bitten" the sheriff, but she'd gone a lot further than I would have thought likely in her criticism of a law official.

"Now, whether or not any '*innocent* passers-by' were involved in that particular incident you're referring to ain't been proved, ma'am," he grinned evenly. "But I agree we got to be more careful in the future. So let's you and me go on down, Leila, and take a look around the place with Mr. Bipple here."

Maisie and Davy burst into tears, as if they thought their mother were being taken to the Tower. They had become more and more reluctant to be separated from her as the summer passed. I went, too, to see injustice done. Mr. Bipple discovered, in forty minutes' time, thirty violations of the town safety regulations—fire hazards, electrical hazards, sanitation hazards.

They pasted CLOSED and CONDEMNED on the doors with a printed explanation of the violations violated. We were shut down.

"As of when?" Leila asked.

"As of now," the sheriff let her know.

"Look," she said, "I've got posters up, tickets have been reserved." It was true about the posters, we'd put them up in Boulder. But nobody had ever *reserved* a ticket, even in good times. Leila's quickness impressed me.

"Well, take them down. And unreserve them."

She walked him back to his car. I went with them. Maybe, like Maisie and Davy, I was afraid he was going to take her away.

"Gabe, you think you're really being fair? I know the Menelades told you to close the place, and I know my father-in-law told them to tell you."

"Look here, honey. Don't tell me what you know. I think I've been *more* than fair. More! Have I been riding you hard? Did I or didn't I look the other way when that crazy husband of yours got himself blown to smithereens? When your boyfriend was selling shit, and your pals were peeing on each other?"

Leila's head turned away from him. As if filmed in slow motion, I saw the gold swirling of her hair.

"I let you stay in my sister's place despite all the drinking and sex, and I wouldn't be too surprised if there was drugs. But you just went too far."

Her head jerked up. "When was that, Gabe? When I tried to help three old women keep the right to sell their flowers on your fucking street?"

"Don't you curse at me, young lady! Look here, you went over my head, rubbed mud in my face. I don't like it when people I'm good to stab me in the back."

"Neither do I, Gabe. Neither do I."

"Christ Almighty, why didn't you come back to me about it? I didn't realize you were so fired up about those Beaners. Maybe we coulda talked. But with that freak out on my streets—"

"Gabe, it's the principle! And none of this is the point anyway. You know that. Even if I hadn't called the lawyer, you'd still
be closing me down. How much did Bruno tell the mayor he was
going to invest in Floren Park?"

The sheriff's face bulged purple, "Are you accusing me of
being *bought*? Well goddamn..." All of a sudden, he turned on
me. "This is none of your damn business! Git the hell out of
here! Christ Almighty, I let him off too!"

"Are you all right, Leila?" I asked.

His face turned a darker purple. "You think I'm going to
horsewhip her? Police brutality, is that what you think? You
punk college kids, somebody *ought* to horsewhip you! Git out of
here before I make up my mind to do it!"

"It's okay, Devin, I'll be inside in a minute." So I left them.
It was funny. Booter was acting as if she'd hurt his feelings.

"Well, what are we going to do?" Sabby asked.

"There's nothing we *can* do," Pete told her mournfully.

We sat around the living room after lunch. Though no one
really had known why we were doing *All My Sons* in the first
place, when the theater had clearly already folded, most of the
company was gone, and Wolfstein was too ill to be working—still,
once Booter told us we *couldn't* do it, everyone, even Ronny, was
despondent.

Leila put more logs on the fire for the weather had been
turning cooler each day. "Nate, put this blanket around you.
Maybe it's all for the best. I don't think you ought to leave the
house today, anyhow. It's stupid, I suppose, letting something
that counts so little get so important."

"No, it counts," Wolfstein said hoarsely. He put down his
coffee. His hands shook out a cigarette, and he fumbled for his
lighter in his old bathrobe pocket.

"Nathan, don't!" Mrs. Thurston stood up, then sat down.
"Oh, Good Lord, why shouldn't you? Go ahead." She smiled
back when he grinned at her. The grin was like a grimace in his
emaciated face.

"Well," he began, speaking slowly and carefully. "What is surprising, my friends, is that, after all of it, after making such a botch of my declining years, now, when I was fairly certain I had lost the slightest capacity to care in the slightest about…anything at all, that now, I should be given—that your 'Good Lord' should give me, Amanda—this most improbable chance to… care very much." He coughed through his laugh. "Improbable, you must admit, ladies and gentlemen, out here in a Rocky Mountain resort, with a half dozen young folks performing Arthur Miller in an old rollerdome. And I tell you, too… I like it more than anything I've done…in a long while."

Leila smiled across the fire at him. "Since *The Good Years*, Nate?"

"Yes, since then," he answered softly.

That was the first time, I think, that any of us had known it. That Wolfstein had—"My God, of course," Joely said—directed *The Good Years*, the movie about World War II that had won so many awards. And when I later looked him up in a book of film criticism, they said in a footnote that in the fifties he had appeared before the House Un-American Activities Committee, that he had been praised by the committee as a "model witness" and a "true patriot," and that he had made no other movies after that. Leila had said once that Nate was dying from self-contempt. It must have been then, with that betrayal of his colleagues, that he had simply quit on himself. That was the thing for which he could not forgive himself.

"Yes," he said, as we all watched the fire flame up, "it's too bad they've stopped us. But we did well. Leila, as your mother would put it, we did make an effort."

"Maybe," I offered. "Maybe we *could* do it anyhow. Why not? We could just go in, lock it up behind us, and do it anyhow. Even if we don't have an audience."

We were all quiet, deciding.

"Devin, yes! We could do it just for us!" Sabby burst out. Everyone looked at everyone else, then all together chortled aloud.

"Call Kim," Leila told Ronny. She sat up, started lacing her blue leather sandals on.

"You know it's illegal, Leila. Your performance license has been revoked," reminded Wolfstein.

"Had you rather not do it, Nate?"

"Ah, dear," he pulled himself up on Sabby's arm, "if even *Amanda* agrees that at this point I might as well smoke, then surely I might as well spend a night in jail."

"I would certainly hope," Mrs. Thurston replied, "that after you young people have exerted yourselves to the extent that you have, that the public officials have got better things to do with their time than to go around arresting college children."

"Tell that to Mayor Daley, Amanda," Joely said. "I was listening to the news. There are ten thousand cops out on the streets of my hometown today arresting college children."

chapter 28

Intelligence

The sun set behind the circling mountains, and down in their valley, night fell with almost a frost, then a slow, cold rain. One by one, throughout the afternoon, we had come quietly into the theater. After dark, Mrs. Thurston, dressed in her flowered summer frock, a hat with roses on it, and even her white gloves, drove up in the battered Austin and brought Wolfstein, Maisie, and Davy crowded beneath her umbrella into the theater.

From Slough Lane, Kim—a plastic raincoat over her costume, which she and Sabby had chosen—brought her son, Cary. "I told Lady Red tonight I quit. She docked me the week's pay I'm due, but I said to her, 'Fuck you, Red, add it to my liquor bill.' Kim gave a rich belly laugh. "Listen, Leila…Rings, you know, he wonders if you'd mind if he came and saw this play. Told me he'd never seen one in his life, and said if I was going to keep on yapping about being on the stage, he might as well come see this one when nobody could catch him doing it."

"Sure, of course," Leila laughed.

"I told him I didn't think you'd mind. And he's going to bring along a couple of friends of his too, if that's okay. They'll come to the back door at eight."

"You like Rings a lot, don't you, Kim?"

A blush livened Kim's dough-white cheeks. "Tell you the truth, honey, I'm crazy about him. Thing is, you know, I've been

slammed down pretty hard in the past. But this time I think it's
gonna be okay."

Leila pressed her hand. "I hope it works out for you."

"Oh, me too, Leila, me too. We're gonna try and make a go
of this nightclub idea. Guess I never will get to California."

"What for, anyway?" Leila smiled. "Let me help you with
your makeup, why don't you?"

"Mother of God," Joely muttered as we went to check the
lightboard for Pete. "Seymour's getting a little carried away,
nailing all the windows shut! And did you see those friends of
Morelli's? Looks like we're under the protection here of some
sort of local underworld! Life! Life!" He laughed and jerked on
his hair 'til it stood out like a halo of fire.

Seymour hurried into the booth. "Somebody's knocking on
the front door! Joely! What'll I do?"

"You don't have to whisper, Seymour. There's nobody around
but us lunatics. Go look through the blinds and see who it is."

"I did. It's seven kids. Look like college kids. Maybe they'll
go away. Couple of other people did when they read the sign.
It's raining harder."

"I'll go see," I told them. I went out the stage door in the
back, around the creek side. They were still there. Three girls
and four guys, about my age or younger, huddled under our narrow awning. "Can I help you?" I asked.

One of the girls, in blue jeans and a sweatshirt like my own,
answered for them. "We came to see the play. There was a poster
in the U.C. Student Union that said you were doing *All My Sons*
tonight?"

"'Starring and directed by Nathan Wolfstein'? Is that true?"
A guy asked suspiciously.

"Yes. But we've been shut down, They revoked our permit."

"Awh, shit," they said. "Can you believe it?" "What for?"
"We came all the way from Boulder!"

I looked around the parking lot. No one was near the cars
but a couple hurrying out of their station wagon and covering
their two children with their panchos. People were rushing into

the Arcade. Over the shadow of mountains, the lightening pulsed in the sky.

"Come on around this way," I told the students, starting back toward the creek.

"What for? Are you opening then?"

"It's a private benefit," I told them, and led them through the stage door.

"See," said the guy who'd asked about Nathan, "a couple of us are film majors, and so when we read that, we wanted to check it out."

•　•　•

"Shit, well that's it!" Joely peeked through the box office curtain. "It's Tony Menelade." It was 8:00, and we had just bolted the front doors from the inside. I looked out with him. Tony was gesturing at his chest with both hands and shaking his head vigorously. He motioned for us to open the window. The rain splashed off his hat.

"I think he's trying to tell us something," I said. "Open the window a minute, Joely. What do you want, Mr. Menelade?"

"Is Leila here? I called the house."

"What did you want to see her about?" I asked him.

"About all this." He waved, I suppose, at the placards condemning us. "It's none of my doing, you know. It's my wife owns the place, and once she sold out to Mr. Stark, and he said he wanted the plays stopped right away, you see. I didn't have anything to do with it. I mean, I'm sorry it happened this way. It's her. There's nothing...I just wanted to apologize to Leila, that's all." He looked at us earnestly.

"Come on around to the back, Tony. You can talk to Leila back there." Joely motioned him with his head to go around the side. With a furtive look toward the bar, Tony did so.

At 8:15, the house lights dimmed on Mrs. Thurston seated with Maisie, Davy, and Cary in the front row, center. Nearby in a group sat the seven summer school students from the

University of Colorado. Off to the side, Tony Menelade hunched down in his chair. And in the back row, one left, one center, one right, sat Rings Morelli in his bright blue suit and his two friends—both wore ties and looked very ill at ease.

"Who's that sitting by herself?" Seymour asked as we looked out at the house from behind the main curtain.

"Bonnie Ferrell. She came in with Ronny," Sabby explained. "One. Two. Five. Six. Seven. Fifteen," she counted the house as she always did.

"Why, that's not bad at all for a week night," Joely joked. And hand over hand on the rope, "Here we go, folks," he called, as he always did, and raised the main curtain.

"I'm so scared, I could pee in my pants," Kim whispered.

Leila squeezed her arm. "I am too, every time," she said, and then walked out on the stage.

We huddled in the wing.

"Sabby, you're gorgeous," I told her.

"Isn't she?" Wolfstein smiled.

"Oh, it's not me," Sabby blushed. "It's Leila. She made me up so I'd look the part."

"You look the part," Seymour said.

"You're on, Nate," whispered Joely.

When Wolfstein made his entrance, first one, then the rest of the college students began to clap. The noise cracked sharp and loud as a storm in the empty theater. He stopped, startled, then slightly bowed. Sabby burst into tears.

"Stop sniffling, Sabby. Blow your nose," Joely told her.

By the end of the first act, we all agreed we were doing the best we had ever done. "Y'all are all so good," Kim kept saying. "I just hope I'm not messing it up for you."

"Oh, you're doing wonderfully well," Sabby promised. "Just can I say one thing? Just a little thing I always find helps me. When you don't have any lines, but you're there on the stage, you know, Kim? If you concentrate on what the other people are saying, like you really would, I mean, then I think it helps."

"I got yuh, kid," Kim told her. Sabby beamed; she was a

teacher now of all Wolfstein had taught her.

So far, the outside world had left us alone. We took only a five-minute intermission (the concession stand was closed) before Joely rang the bell, the lights went down, and the curtain went up on Act II.

We were even better in the second act.

"Who would have thought that old geezer could get his voice to project like that. It's amazing. He's not even coughing," Ronny whispered.

"He's drinking brandy," Joely said.

"He shouldn't be doing that," Leila frowned. "Look how flushed he is."

"He's okay."

"No he's not," she shook her head.

At the second intermission, Mrs. Thurston announced she was serving doughnuts and coffee to anyone who would care for them. Rings Morelli and his associates sat on the lobby chairs with her saucers and cups on their laps, her miniature doughnuts on paper doilies in their hands, staring silently ahead, while the seven students stared at them in polite puzzlement. Once her guests were settled, she brought "a little refreshment" backstage for us too.

"That Amanda!" Joely chuckled.

"Hey, Verl's out there!" I hadn't seen him come in.

I went down the aisle to where he was standing, rain still shining in his black curls.

"How long have you been here?"

"Oh, a little bit after you got started. Mrs. Thurston let me in. I'd called the house. You're doing fine up there."

"Hell, I'm the worst of the bunch. It's been a long time since the senior play."

"The girlfriend, the sister."

"Sabby?"

"She's good, isn't she? And Wolfstein. I didn't know he was an actor."

"This is a one-timer."

"I heard about all the shit, the sheriff and all, from Mrs. Thurston. Looks like Leila didn't let it stop her, though."

"Not much can," I agreed.

"It's interesting what you're doing up there."

"What do you mean?"

"Like when it takes place. I mean, in 1940 our fathers were *sons*. And they didn't wanted to accept what we don't want to accept."

"Yeah, well, but they *did*, though, didn't they? Aren't they the ones that own the companies and build the planes now? And when we're the fathers, we'll be the ones building them and saying, 'But I did it for *you!*' when our sons spit in our eyes! And their sons spit in theirs, and then go out and build planes too, until finally the last sons blow it all away."

"Boy, you just don't have no faith at all, do you?"

"Who's changed it, Verl? Who's made a difference?"

"Everybody."

"You're the one they've just arrested! And you still think 'the big change is gonna come.'"

"I suppose I figure the only way I can be, just me personally, is to keep *wanting* to see it happen. It's not happening now, though, you're right." He looked sadly off toward the stage. "Did you see what's going on in Chicago tonight?"

"No. But I guess they gave Humphrey the nomination."

"They're beating the kids. They're really beating them this time. Clubs. Mace. Some of the delegates tried to get the convention called off, but the whole place has gone crazy."

"You know what Mrs. Thurston says, 'lock, stock, and barrel'? The whole world ought to be committed to an insane asylum lock, stock, and barrel." I had to get backstage. "Let's have a drink after the show, okay?"

"Wish I could. I'm leaving right about now, taking a plane out of Denver."

"Tonight?"

"Yeah, there are some people still in Washington from Resurrection City I want to get a chance to talk to before they leave. Mostly church people…the left wing of the church, I guess you'd call it."

"*Can* you leave?"

"Oh, hell, yeah. They won't get around to our trial for three or four months. Then we'll appeal. Question is now, can I leave *after* my trial! Listen, I'm gonna go backstage and say good-bye. Stay here a second, okay?"

I had finished my coffee when he came back down the aisle. "I'll be in touch. You too, all right? Are you going back to Earlsford?"

"Yeah, I think so."

"Then what?"

"I'm not sure, but I tell you one thing, I'm not going to carry any more signs, or sit down, or march, or yell any more slogans. I mean, you can have your five hundred thousand students and workers holding hands and singing songs in the streets of Paris all you want, but it's over, Verl. You say you don't want to preach, but you do. I don't."

"Lots of different ways for people to make a difference. Preaching and teaching, remember? Write me."

"Same address?"

"I hope so." We laughed, and then he squeezed my shoulder. "Well, the summer's over. You stuck it out here. I wasn't sure you would. Leila just thanked me for bringing you over. She said you'd helped her get through it."

"Shit, I just made everything worse."

"Why do you want to think so, you jerk?" He cuffed me.

The house lights dimmed, the bell rang, and our small audience moved back from the lobby to their seats.

"Good luck, Verl."

"Take care of yourself," he said in his slow, quiet voice. I held out my hand, he, his. We shook hands solemnly. "You too," I said.

When I got backstage, I looked from behind the curtain. He was still there, leaning over the back rail, watching. Onstage, Leila, as the mother, talked to the girlfriend about her two sons—one whose death she cannot accept, the other whom she

294 • michael malone

fears will be destroyed if he learns the truth of his father's perfidy. Somehow Leila had stripped her youth away, broken her youth on sorrow and knowledge, so that now she seemed in her carriage and in her face to be that mother of those sons. And so I could see how she would be when Davy was as old as this woman's dead son. I felt an ache quicken in me, a stir that rushed through my body in a heaving wave, so that to let it out as quickly as it came, I had to sigh aloud.

I turned aside and looked back out into the audience. The door to the lobby was closing. The light on the floor thinned to a line, then went away. Verl had gone.

We told Wolfstein about the students in the audience. "Twenty-five years later," he whispered, shaking his head with a faint smile. "My God."

The play moved to its end.

"Well, this is the big one, Joely," Wolfstein said, handing back to him the towel he'd been wiping his face with. His hair was as wet as if he'd just showered.

Joely nodded seriously. "You've got 'em in your pocket."

Sabby put her hand on Wolfstein's forehead, "Nate, you've got a fever. You're burning up."

He took her hand and kissed it. "I'm fine, sweetheart."

Onstage he begged his outraged son to understand why he'd done what he'd done. Beseeched him, cursed him, begged him to forgive, to love. Let the son throw the money in the sewer if he thought it was dirty. But why ask him to go to jail? Didn't everybody do it? Should the whole goddamn country go to jail? Joely, Ronny, and I stood together in the wing and listened to the son say, no, no I cannot accept what you've done.

"Something's the matter. Did you hear that? Nate didn't say 'Tom,' he said 'Cal.' He just said, 'If Cal was alive…And he's shaking!'" Frowning, Joely put his hand on the curtain rope.

"He's supposed to be shaking," Sabby said. "He's supposed to be in despair."

"You're right, Joely," I said. "I heard it too." And the revelation exposed seemed too intimate for strangers to overhear.

Wolfstein's face was scarlet, sweat ran down his thin hair, and he was holding onto Leila's arm as his living son read him the old letter from his dead son. The letter saying he knew what his father had done, and, knowing, wanted to die.

Joely started waving for Someone to lead Wolfstein off, but I stopped him. "Let him finish, he's almost finished."

We caught him when he came offstage. Joely and I half carried him to the small dressing room behind the wing, laid him down on an old couch that seesawed on three legs. I pulled his shirt loose and took off his shoes. His breath sounded like the rasp of a bird. He was trying to talk. "Get him some water!" Joely stuck a coffee cup under the faucet.

Onstage, I could hear Leila and Ronny and Sabby ending the play. "Are you trying to kill him?" Leila asked the son. While I held Wolfstein's head, Joely put the glass to his mouth. He whispered something.

"What?" Joely asked.

"Gun," he rasped.

"Crap! His suicide gun! He's right, it's supposed to be going off!" He ran out. I counted to ten. The shot fired. Wolfstein spoke so faintly I couldn't hear him until I put my ear against his mouth. Even then the words were slurred and strangely mispronounced. "Not like...last time."

"What Nate?"

"*Hedda...Gabler.*" His eyes smiled.

"No. A lot better than last time."

"Cold," he whispered. I pulled off my coat and jerked all the costumes from the clothes rack to cover him with. His hands were chilled white; the veins stuck out. I put my hands over each of his and rubbed them; I kept rubbing them back and forth, but they didn't get warmer.

Joely was back in the room. "Call Dr. Ferrell," I told him. He ran out.

Wolfstein breathed, "Curtain?" and tried to lift his hand to motion toward the stage.

"It's okay," I said. "Ronny's on the curtain. Everything's going fine." Wolfstein did not cough or even tremble. He lay quietly, patiently, just as we had placed him, as if he were waiting to understand what he was feeling.

I heard the applause. The fifteen people clapping. Someone, one of the students, called out "Bravo!" and Maisie repeated it, "Bravo!"

Wolfstein's hands tightened under mine.

"We finished it," I said.

The corner of his mouth lifted, then he closed his eyes. Frightened, I squeezed hard on his hands, and his eyes opened again. Horribly, one of his eyes had rolled up toward the eyelid. He didn't know it, and that helpless vulnerability of his not knowing terrified me.

"Nate? Nate?"

Finally his finger moved beneath my hand.

Leila was there. She caught her breath silently when she saw him, but then came quietly over to the couch. Behind her Sabby and Seymour stood in the door.

I moved aside and she sat pressed against him. "It was true," she murmured. "It was a true thing, Nate. We did it. I'm grateful." She did not ask him, or me, how he was, but sat for what seemed forever, but was less than a minute, with a look that was somehow more valuable than a smile, a look almost as if they were soldiers together, and almost as if they were old, old lovers.

And the eye that could see looked back at her with a long, grave intensity. Then a word fell softly from his mouth on a breath that rasped in a slow sigh to its end.

"What did he say?" She turned to me.

"He said, 'Thank you.'"

chapter 29

The New Wound and the Old

"Those guys from U.C. are asking if they could talk to Mr. Wolfstein. Good God, what's the matter?" Pete pressed into the room that was crowded with everyone's disbelief.

"It's Mr. Wolfstein," said Seymour, his voice flattened by shock. "I think he's dead."

Near the couch where Nathan lay formless under the heap of costume rags, Leila stood, her arms around Sabby, who sobbed out no after no in endless shuddering heaves.

Joely snarled his fingers through his hair. "Where the hell is Ferrell?"

"Devin," Leila said, and gestured out toward the theater.

I took Seymour and Pete out with me, past Maisie and Kim's son chasing each other through the aisles, and Kim talking to Mrs. Thurston, who still sat in the front center row with Davy asleep on her lap.

"Mr. Wolfstein isn't feeling well," I said to the seven students waiting politely in a group at the rear of the theater. "He's resting now. But he thanks you for coming."

"Oh," they said, disappointed. "Okay."

"Well, maybe," the filmmaker added, "sometime he might have time to come over and talk to our class for an hour. I'm sure everybody would really appreciate it. Well, anyhow, would you give him my number?" He scribbled it on a corner of his program.

"I'll tell him," I nodded, as I tried to lead them to the lobby, where Seymour was unbolting the doors so Tony Menelade could get out.

"Thanks," he was mumbling. "Tell her I said thanks, okay?"

"He's here. There's Ferrell!" Seymour called.

The headlights snapped off, hiding the rain again. A door slammed. His raincoat wet against his pants legs, the doctor came in with his bag. Now, I thought, maybe it will be okay.

"Where is he?" he asked without stopping.

"Backstage." And the lobby door swung shut behind him.

"What's the matter?" Tony asked.

"Why is my father here?" Bonnie Ferrell and Ronny hurried out into the lobby.

"Mr. Wolfstein has..." I began. And then the unlocked doors flew open on the rain and Sheriff Booter and Deputy Maddox, in glistening yellow slickers, stared at all of us.

"Well, now, looks like a little party's going on here! A little surprise party that we wasn't invited to, Jimmy."

"Sure does, Mr. Booter, looks like—"

The sheriff cut him off. "Seems like nobody around this town knows how to read too good, don't it? 'Course maybe they just don't know how to read *some* words yet. Maybe they never got as far as the Cs, is that it, Tony? You know that word, C-O-N-D-E-M-N-E-D? How 'bout C-L-O-S-E-D?"

"Look here, Gabe, I just dropped over here to speak to Mrs. Stark for a minute." Menelade tried to go around Booter out the door, but the sheriff stopped him with a raw, wet hand.

"Well, you know," he nodded agreeably, "I had the exact same idea in mind. Except I guess I wasn't expecting to find so many *other* folks out paying social calls on Mrs. Stark, seeing how the weather's so bad." He addressed the puzzled students. "What you young people doing here?"

"We came to see a play," one said.

"That so? Not supposed to be any plays being put on here. You know that?"

Rings Morelli had come silently out of the theater. A blue line of smoke twisted toward us from his thin cigar. "Sheriff," he nodded.

Booter caught his surprise and quickly hid it. "Good evening, Rings. I didn't realize you were a fan of the thea-tur too. But maybe there's some other kind of entertainment been going on here I just haven't had a chance to check into yet."

"Don't think so, Sheriff," replied Morelli smoothly. "A couple of us thought we'd get together to pass the time, that's all. You know how it is, Sheriff, this hole being so deadbeat. Hard to find something to do on a weeknight."

"Something like public performing without a license and trespassing on condemned property maybe? Couple of you found that, for starters, looks like."

"That's right, Sheriff. They coulda gone and played bingo together," Maddox proudly echoed his chief's sarcasm; he kept his hand on his gun so we wouldn't jump him.

"Shut up, Jimmy," Booter said pleasantly.

Morelli shook his head. "Afraid you're wrong there, Sheriff. Nobody sold any tickets here tonight. Nobody bought any either. Just came over to see my girl enjoying herself."

"They're our guests," I added. "We invited them. They're helping us."

Booter looked at me scornfully. "Son, you got no right to invite folks. Now, nobody sells tickets to a riot either, but that don't mean the folks that shows up aren't likely to get themselves into a little trouble."

"Listen, can we go? We've got to drive all the way back to Boulder," one of the now-nervous students asked hopefully. They had edged around the door that Tony Menelade already stood in.

Booter appraised each of them slowly, then, satisfied by their intimidated squirms, he nodded. "You young people here are liable to arrest on a charge of unlawful assembly." He waited. "I'm going to let you go now, but before you come to this town again, I want you to sign up over at your college for a course in reading print. I guess you ain't had a chance to take that one yet," he smiled, "what with all that marching around and setting fires. Okay, you can go on too, Tony, 'fore your wife locks the place up and you got to sleep out in the rain."

Maddox, recovered from his humiliation, risked a snicker. And without arguing, grateful to be reprieved, Tony and the students pressed together through the doors out into the rain.

"See how nice I can be," Booter turned to me, "when people don't—"

From behind the lobby doors a cry wailed sharply, "Oh, Dear Lord." It was Mrs. Thurston.

"What's going on?" Booter snapped hurriedly, then from the inner doors Ferrell came, rolling down his sleeves. "Where's the phone?"

I pointed at the box office entrance.

"What's going on, doctor? You got some trouble here?" Booter wanted to know.

"Got a dead man back there."

Seymour sucked in his breath as though he'd been hit, while adrenalin rushed through me.

"Who?" snapped the sheriff. Maddox jerked erect, ready.

"The old guy. Wolfstein. I'm calling Fletcher's."

"Jimmie, go to the car, call Saul Fletcher. Tell him to get his ambulance over here. Go on, Jimmie!" he added, as the deputy appeared reluctant to miss anything by leaving. "Killed?" Booter then asked.

"Not by anyone else."

"Shit. Another one of those suicides!"

Ferrell looked annoyed. "No. Natural causes, Gabe. His heart stopped."

"Hospital?"

"No. No, he's gone." Booter started back inside with him, as Ferrell snapped at his daughter, Bonnie who slunk behind the concession stand. "Get out there in the car and stay there!" The door shut.

Bonnie looked up at Ronnie, who told her, "I guess you better do what your father says."

•   •   •

"For Christ's sake, Gabe, enough's enough. I don't have time now to play games," Leila told him. But the sheriff arrested us anyhow.

After Saul Fletcher Morticians came on his crepe soles through the rain and helped Dr. Ferrell arrange Nathan on a wheeled stretcher, which they slid quickly through the opening of the black hearse, and after the doctor drove his daughter away, the rest of us were taken too. Leila, Kim, Sabby, Mrs. Thurston, and the children in the patrol car with the sheriff. Joely, Seymour, Pete, Ronny, myself, and Rings in a van that Maddox brought over.

"Your two pals?" I asked Morelli.

He was leaning easily back against the side of the smelly van, still smoking. "Business," he explained. "They couldn't stay for the end. Went out the back." He added politely, "They thought it was real good, though."

There would have been more of us crowded into the sheriff's waiting room, but Mrs. Thurston had simply refused to take the babies out into the rain again, telling the sheriff tersely that he would have to drag her and the children physically across the wet lawn of the courthouse if he wanted her in there. He left them in the patrol car. The rest of us waited silently to be charged. The magistrate released us without bail, told us to show up for a hearing Friday, the 30th, the day after tomorrow, told us Maddox would drive us home, told us he was sorry our friend had died, and maybe we'd listen to the sheriff next time.

"Hick town. Hick law," Morelli summed up on the sidewalk. "What else's he got to do to feel big? The mayor pushes him around, he pushes you."

At home we sat silently in the cold living room, Leila quiet in the old corduroy chair—like before. Finally, Joely absently reached over and turned on the little television set. A voice spoke dryly behind blurred pictures of a frantic, moiling crowd loud with screams of, "Hell, no! We won't go!" and shots of smoke and reeling signs scrawled, "The Whole World Is Watching," "Welcome to Prague." A blurred picture of, as Verl had said, chaos. The voice said, "However, those charges have been vigorously denied by Mayor Daley, who has repeatedly defended the actions—"

"Oh, turn it off, Joely darling. Dear Lord, child, *turn it off!*" Mrs. Thurston left the room, her white gloves pressed to her eyes.

chapter 30

Return

Leila spent Thursday trying to find someone Wolfstein belonged to. He didn't seem to belong to anyone anymore. She called each number in the initialed address book we found among his pills and drink glasses beside his bed. Of those she could reach, most had not seen him in years, though they were sorry he had died. His former lawyer was sorry too; his former banker; his former insurance agent. The former superintendent of his former apartment in Los Angeles was sorry.

"Jesus!" Joely said. "He didn't have *anything*. I mean, he was living at point zero, Devin."

"It must be we don't know where to look," Seymour said. "Everybody's got, you know, something. A family or friend or money or something."

Leila called Calhoun Grange. They said he was filming a war picture in Spain.

"Do you think he'd come?" I asked her. "I don't think he thought Nate was his father."

"I don't think he gave a good goddamn one way or the other," Leila replied, her hand still on the phone receiver. "Good old Cal, he just doesn't care." She stood up. "I hate people who don't care. And I hate the fact that they seem to be the ones who win. Because it's easy if it doesn't matter. It's all so easy."

"Why bother to call him, then?"
"I want to make it a little harder."

• • •

Friday morning it was still raining, when, accompanied by
Rings Morelli's Denver lawyer, we appeared before the magistrate, who found Leila guilty of violating Section 2B of local
statute 35, fined her a hundred dollars, then suspended the
sentence. Charges against the rest of us were dropped, and we
were released. After all that, that was all. Rings's lawyer knew
the mayor, and the mayor knew the magistrate, and Rings said
Sheriff Booter probably wished he'd never gone to so much
trouble just to be mule-headed. If he'd done it to save face, his
plan had backfired. Of course, he was sure Booter'd still be sheriff
twenty years from now, and still a horse's ass, too. We thanked
him for helping out. "Forget it," he said. "If Kim here wanted to
play that stage part, I sure wasn't going to let a couple of hicks
put her down, you know what I mean?"

"Thank God for love," Joely said.

At home Leila received a telegram from Spain: SORRY TO
HEAR ABOUT NATE. FINE TO SEND BILL TO BERT SILVER. GREAT
COUNTRY OUT HERE. HOW ARE THINGS THERE? GREAT, I HOPE.
YOURS, CAL. Bert Silver was Cal's agent. His name and address
in Los Angeles were enclosed.

That afternoon we buried Wolfstein in the small plot
behind the Chapel of St. Lucy's, where I had found Leila and
Verl the night Mittie died. Saul Fletcher fixed Wolfstein up in
a nice casket and sent the bill to the name and address in Los
Angeles Leila had given him.

So we stood together for the last time of the summer, there
across from the rich dark mahogany of the silver-handled casket
that Leila had chosen for Cal to pay for. On the other side stood
a small, very old priest whom none of us had ever seen before,
except Leila and her mother—one or the other or both of whom
had persuaded him first to perform the ceremony, and then to

receive the body of Nathan Wolfstein, who had said he had no religion, into his graveyard.

The rain was only mist now as we stood among all the roses and carnations and lilies and chrysanthemums Leila had bought for Cal to pay for. The old priest lowered his head, saying with us, "Forever, Amen." And Leila pressed her hand against the casket top and said, "Good-bye, Nate."

"The Lord rest his soul, now, and let him be at peace. Sabby, darling, you walk on back to the car with me, and give me your arm up this hill." Sabby could not stop crying, and Mrs. Thurston held her to her side.

On the way to the airport that night, she sobbed again. "He wrote for me, Leila. Last week. He wrote to Julliard. In New York. He told them they should take me, give me a scholarship. Oh, he can't be dead! Why should *he* be dead?" she cried.

I thought of Leila's light in her room as she read Shakespeare. "...Oh, let him pass!"

"I hope you'll go, Sabby. Be what he knew you could be," Leila told her.

We piled out of the Red Bus at the airport in Denver—suitcases, souvenirs, and all of summer's passage. Ronny, Seymour, Sabby, Pete, and Joely had the tickets Leila had reserved for them. In Chicago, all but Joely would change planes. We drank coffee while we waited.

"Oh, shit, can you believe it?" Joely came back to the booth with his Chicago newspaper.

"Don't tell me anything else," Seymour winced.

"No. No. Listen. Not politics. This is under Arts and Leisure:

The new show Tuesday at the highly successful Gallery of Contemporary Arts on Harriss Street shocked the critics but apparently delighted a crowd of popular art lovers who eagerly purchased the entire collection of so-called "PopPoop Art" on display. The vulgarism is quite accurate, for Spurgeon Debson, the artist responsible (or irresponsible) works primarily in human excrement. Victor Falz, owner of the Chicago gallery (as well as others in New York and San Francisco), said that he was pleased with the public's reception of "a vital new force in modern American art." He added that reproductions of Mr. Debson's sculptures (?) and poster designs (?) would soon be available. *Caveat emptor.*

"I don't believe it!"

But we saw the picture. It was, in fact, Spur. He stood beside a giant version of the plastic rockets we had seen him making in Floren Park, and the smiling Gucci-Porsche modster had him in a warm embrace.

• • •

The players walked away, straddled with knapsacks, dragging suitcases, shoving boxes ahead of them. At the end of the gate they turned. We had said each kind of good-bye, promised to write, to remember, until the last; they had told Leila their plans, asked her advice, hoped she would not lose touch. She said she wouldn't, and I think they knew it was so. Sabby cried.

Joely raised his arm, made a V that turned into a fist, then to a wave.

"Blow your nose, Sabby," I yelled, and they were around the corner.

I offered to do some more packing at the theater.

"It's midnight, Devin. Just come on home. We'll do it tomorrow."

I told Leila I didn't think I could sleep, so she dropped me at the parking lot. "Go on to bed." I asked her to promise, and she waved as she left. Her face was gray.

People still came and left the Red Lagoon Bar, but the Red Lagoon Theatre was dark, a long dark shape beside the creek. The lock popped as I turned Leila's key. With a squeak that cut loudly into the quiet, the door opened. I was scared and ran back to prop the door ajar when it shut me in the black space of the lobby, so dark I couldn't find the light switch that I had turned on a hundred times.

In the box office, I found a flashlight that would get me down the shadowed side aisle to the lighting booth. From there, I made my way backstage. Behind the curtain, the stage was still set for *All My Sons*. In the costume room, the tie I had taken from Wolfstein's neck was still on the floor. I went to the scene shop and started to pack up the paints, tools, nails, brushes, that somehow had been collected and put to use over the summer. When my fingers began hurting, I realized how cold I was. And hungry. Still cold and hungry, though Wolfstein was dead. Back in the lobby, I found a white sweater, dusty and soiled on a shelf of the concession stand. I put it on. There were some of Mrs. Thurston's miniature doughnuts on the counter still. I ate them. They tasted like dust.

From the wall, the bright shine of our pictures reflected the lights. We all looked out with the same smiles we had had in June and in the pictures, would always have. Mittie and Nate, too, who were already dead. And Buddy, who had never arrived. I brought a box over and took each of the pictures down, pressed each smoothly on top of the one beneath it. I took them off in the order in which they had left us. First Mittie. Then Jennifer Thatcher and Ashton Krinkle. Last I took me, and Leila, and Maisie and Davy, and Mrs. Thurston, and laid us on top, and closed the box.

That left the portrait I had painted of Leila on the wood floor. I knelt down to look at it, wet my palm with spit, tried to wipe it clean. It would be nice, I thought, to keep, but there was no way to save it. I couldn't even get it clean now, after three months. I kept rubbing the arm of the sweater across the paint, harder and harder. Then all of a sudden, I burst into tears, and, like Sabby Norah, cried. I kept thinking, "This is crazy," but I just couldn't get myself to stop. I fell to sleep, still crying.

"Wake up, Devin."

The light from the opened doors shined sun bright in my face.

"Are you awake? It's me. Leila. It's morning."

chapter 31

Liking Life on My Own Account No Better, I Form a Great Resolution

"I must have fallen asleep."

"I guess so," she smiled. She knelt over me, and I felt easy just to stay there, the sun coming between us into the room. "You must be pretty sore sleeping in the cold on the floor all night."

"No. I feel good."

"You took the pictures down."

I leaned on my hand to look at the empty squares of darker felt on the wall. "I took them down in order."

"In order?"

"Of when people went away."

"Oh. Where did you find that sweater?" She touched my arm. "It's Mittie's."

I sat up. "Oh, I'm sorry, Leila. I'll take it off. I got cold. It was over behind the concession stand."

Her hand closed softly on my sleeve. "Don't be silly. He…" She brushed her hand across the shoulder. "It's fine." She stood up and then walked quietly around the room in her long white robe of loose woven linen, the small leaves embroidered green about her wrists and throat, her hair like goldenrod moved in the light, Leila Dolores. Leila D'Or.

"Leila…" I began. My voice faltered.

"Your mother called this morning. I talked to Fitzgerald."

"Is something the matter?"

"No, I don't think so. Everything seems okay. Your brother James has gone to France for a month. With his wife."

"Oh." All that seemed so long ago. A remark of Mrs. Thurston's came back to me: "I don't know why I bothered to delude myself." It seemed applicable.

"She wants to know what your plans are."

I looked past the door at the mountains where fall had already touched scattered aspen. "First, to go home."

"I told her I'd bring you, tomorrow."

"Leila…"

"How would you like to take me to lunch, Devin?"

"Sure. Help me up." She gave me her hand.

• • •

In the parking lot a large sign was stuck in the dirt to tell us that by August 1969, there would be on this site a Memorial Shoppers' Mall tastefully designed to blend with the environment, and that Mr. Stark with certain other investors would be responsible. A ski shop, a liquor shop, a gourmet shop, and a record shop already planned to be there. The Red Lagoon Theatre, as a result, was gone for good. Nor the Red Lagoon Bar, which now announced in magic marker: "Closing in Two Weeks."

"I don't think he was trying to punish *me* so much," Leila said, "Though in a way he does blame me. I think Bruno hates this building itself. He wants it destroyed for destroying Mittie. He wants there to be no more acting. Because Mittie insisted he could be an actor, and Bruno couldn't stop him from wanting to. And now he's dead."

"Do you think he really loved Mittie?"

"Oh God, yes. I think he loved Mittie like his own arm. And if you cut off your own arm because it won't do what you want it to, or if you lose the arm, it's painful. It must be agony."

"But don't you think all parents do that? See their kids that way? Extensions of themselves?"

"They have to give it up. I'm sure going to try to just let Maisie and Davy be."

I took Leila along the road winding beside the meadow up to the restaurant Verl had brought me to that first evening. Cervantes. The proprietor brought a carafe of wine to set beside the clay pot of wildflowers that turned toward the slant of sun.

We sat in silence while Leila looked out the window. Finally she spoke. "There's a hummingbird. They're so small. Don't they ever perch?"

"Well, they have to sleep."

"Maybe they don't sleep. Maybe they just die. Devin, thank you for this. I think I was...tired."

We ate our lunch.

"Kim told me she had a letter from your friend 'Tanya.'"

"Don't rub it in, okay?"

"She wondered if Kim could send her some things she overlooked when she left the cabin—rather quickly, you may remember. And she said she was bored."

I supposed she had been bored in Floren Park too. And me? Something occurred to me. Though I had wanted to, had figured I would sooner or later, I had never slept with Jardin. Then I couldn't, and so the possibility froze into desire, desire nourished, aggrandized by imagined loss. Tanya, without knowing or caring, melted the fantasy.

"You ought to thank that lady," Leila said, startling me. She must have been inside my head, following beside my thoughts. "I gather you got it out of your system," she said, as if to explain her magic, "from what you told me when I came to bind the wounds."

"Leila. I love you," I heard myself say.

"I love you too, Devin."

"I feel...like it was when..."

"Love's old sweet song," she smiled.

"No. I'm serious. I've always been in love with you."

"Don't be silly," she said, but gently.

"No. Listen, please. It's true. It's always been true."

"Oh, Devin. *You* tell the truth. Last month, when you went around here sulking and snarling at me thinking God knows what you were thinking, were you in love with me then? Or last year? Or the year before? Did you sit up in Cambridge and say to yourself, 'I love Leila Beaumont, whom I haven't really thought about recently, but nevertheless…' Confess. Were you?"

"Listen," I protested. "I've been a jerk."

"Now, that," she smiled, "may *be* the truth. I confess it crossed *my* mind once or twice over the summer. Tell the truth, didn't you hate me for a while there? You even stayed away from Maisie and Davy, and I *know* that you care about them."

I flushed in the hurt of her condemnation. "I…I thought you were sleeping with, with Spur, and then Cal…"

"How about Nate, and Gabe Booter? Jesus, no wonder you and that Dennis Reed got along so well! Oh, I see, and so you waltzed off to share your own purity with that fragrant lily, the chaste Tanya? Is that it?" She laughed, "Oh, Devin!"

My face and ears tightened with the rush of blood.

She stopped laughing. "Oh, I'm sorry. I shouldn't be facetious. God knows I've screwed up enough myself."

"No, you haven't. No."

The owner brought us more coffee.

"But I do love you, Leila. I know you can't believe me now. But *someday* you will. Even if it takes years. Someday. I promise you that."

She looked quietly at me. "All right," she said.

"You could make me be the best I can be."

Palm first, she pushed her hand out. "No, not that way."

"Why?"

"That's the one thing I've managed to learn this summer. *You* helped me learn it by what you said about Mittie. I did think if I just loved enough—Mittie, or Nate, everyone—I could make them be the best they were, hold them up so they could reach the dream." She frowned. "And when they didn't, I had failed. I

had been too selfish, or impatient, or tired. I had failed in understanding to Mittie. Had failed in concern for Nate. I had forgotten to feel their pain for an instant, and in that instant, they had
died. And so it was *my fault*, see? If I had loved them better, they
would not have died. Talk about arrogance. Whew! Love is not
enough. Like you said, you can't make people be. You can only
let them be. You can just hope."

"No, you can *help*."

"I have to help myself now."

"And Maisie and Davy?"

"If I help myself, they will learn how. I hope."

The owner brought me the bill.

"Can I still come home with you?"

"With me, not for me."

"No, for me."

She smiled. "Okay."

We walked to the van. "I know that's where I want to be,"
I told her. "Home."

"Do you know why?"

"I think so."

"Why?"

"I want to stay in a small place and teach a small thing.
Teach children like Maisie and Davy. Not Verl's teaching and
preaching, but mine."

"You know what's ironic? That's what my mother told you
you ought to be doing the first day she came out to Floren Park."
We both laughed and climbed in the van.

"But you always said you didn't think it would do any good
to teach. I thought you said the craziness and the ugliness will
never go away, will only change its clothes. You said the only
thing to do is laugh and grow roses."

"I say a lot of things, don't I?"

"Let's go home."

chapter 32

The Beginning of a Longer Journey

"When did you decide?" Leila asked me.

"I've been thinking about it for a while."

"Because of the play and Nate?"

"Because of everything, I guess."

"Do you think it's going to do any good, then?"

"No, I don't really think it will at all. But I *hope* it will. Verl told me Wednesday night that the only way he could be was to *want* change to happen. I do want it to happen."

We put the last armful of logs on the fire. Mrs. Thurston was in the kitchen sanitizing the plastic dishware that had come with the house because she believed that people should leave a place not like they found it, but better.

I showed Leila the letter I'd gotten from Professor Aubrey on Wednesday, for it formed a part of my resolution.

Dear Devin,

As you see, my somewhat Nabokovian pilgrimage across this country of theirs is ended, and I'm home in Cambridge where I belong. Your friend, Ashton, left us after a week of traveling, having struck up acquaintanceship with a collective of young artisans near Santa

Fe. Randolph, too, decided that he preferred San Francisco to puttering among the ruins of Aztec kingdoms, so I learned gradually to rely on my own tattered Spanish, and the rather greedy assistance of native guides. So much, I think, for field trips at my advanced years. For the rest, I will write of Mexico looking out over the Charles, as Gauguin painted Brittany cottages sweltering in Tahiti.

I was delighted to find your letter waiting here on my return, and was particularly charmed by your description of the southern mythos and that long vainglorious line of artifice from Poe onward that so many of our expatriate boys have inherited. But Devin, your recent note distressed me. I am very sorry to hear you won't be coming back to Harvard for graduate school. I urge you to reconsider. Let me put my slight leverage into the machine.

Yes, I agree. Mankind is mad. The wonder is we all cling with such persistent desperation to even the paltriest of lives in this very mad and sad universe where Someone has so indifferently dropped us. Even those of us who should know better.

But given that we do, to the last spasm, insist on life, why not—in the wait—choose what little of grace and beauty has been saved for sharing in the last few strongholds; cloisters, rather, where like can sit (hide, if you will) with like-minded men, to admire, to understand the best of this bloody world? To teach the brightest about the best is, Devin, a most appealing way to pass the time. Why not come back?

Cordially, D.C. Aubrey.

"Did you answer him?" Leila asked me.

I folded the letter and returned it to my pocket. "Yes. Yesterday."

"Well, what did you say? No, I hope."

"No."

"I'm glad. I don't think it's enough to pass the time, even gracefully."

"I told him I was going to work for a certificate to teach in the elementary schools at home. I told him that I wanted to start a lot younger."

"Good," she asked, rising from the fire to pour more Chablis in her old coffee mug.

These were really the reasons why.

In 1968, which was the final year of my Harvard education, the North Koreans took the spy ship, USS *Pueblo*, which was not supposed to happen, and the North Vietnamese took the Tet offensive, which was not supposed to happen either. We let them keep the *Pueblo*; it was not supposed to be a spy ship.

In early April, which was when a nervous policeman gave me a glancing blow on the side of my head in a Harvard hallway and Professor Aubrey told me to stay out of politics, we had our twelfth major political assassination since 1963, when Verl and Leila and I graduated from high school and President Kennedy was shot. The one in April of my senior year was Dr. King. This one, the magazines said, was with a 30.06 caliber Remington pump rifle on the balcony of the Lorraine Hotel. And so, in 125 cities across the land, there were riots "because," as one looter said, "they killed what's-his-name." Then, while my classmates and I studied for exams in the library, 46 people were killed and 2,600 people were wounded, while 155,000 people (and the 55,000 people sent to stop, or shoot to kill, maim, or cripple them), destroyed, the magazines said, several hundred million dollars' worth of private property and free enterprise. After which, all the politicians and presidential aspirants, and their wives, went to Dr. King's funeral, where they jostled for seats with all the famous athletes, and all the famous movie stars, all of whom we got to see together on our television in my Harvard dormitory. If the assassins had been better organized, as Joely said later, they could have flown over the church with a bomb and put an end to America as we knew it. But they didn't.

And so, while I fell in love with Jardin while she fell in love with my older brother, George Romney stopped running, and Reagan and Rockefeller couldn't decide, and Eugene McCarthy ran and Johnson quit and Robert Kennedy ran and McGovern ran and Kennedy got shot and Nixon won.

Governor Wallace's wife, Lurleen, who was also the governor, died. Then Governor Wallace ran again. He said he was after all the overeducated ivory-tower folks with pointed heads looking down their noses at the people. He was right. Professor Aubrey was. James Dexter was. I was.

Robert Kennedy said, "Men are not made for safe harbors." And he was right, too.

That summer, while I ran out of schedule and took a long time to find something better, Robert Kennedy died, and Mittie died and Wolfstein died, and Leila's Aunt Nadine, and the Buddy who had never come to Floren Park because he had been drafted died too. And over five hundred American soldiers in one week of May died because the peace talks in April in Paris had nothing to do with it since, Leila's radio said, in the next three months we dropped 670,000 tons of bombs on our enemies anyhow, the ones we were having the peace talks with.

And in the one week of June after Robert Kennedy died, while the Shriners met in Floren Park, over two hundred American civilians died because they shot each other, because there were across the land two hundred million mortars, revolvers, shotguns, rifles, machine guns, bazookas, derringers, hand grenades, and pistols (one was Mittie's), with which we had killed seven thousand of us on purpose, and three thousand by accident, and almost killed one hundred thousand more, while ten thousand of us (like Aunt Nadine) just killed themselves. So really Buddy'd been safer in Da Nang, Wolfstein'd been safer in the Pacific, because in the past century we had killed two hundred thousand more of us with private guns at home than in all our shoot-outs overseas, where that summer on the shores of Vietnam, U.S. F-4 Phantom jets bombed the USS *Boston*.

And that summer, the Dow Jones Industrial Average told us on the radio it was 923.72 in the July heat. And Fitzgerald told us that the IBM quarterly profits were 213 million dollars. And Joely told him that our National Defense Budget profits, though, were in the billions, so that we could give 39 percent away to private corporations where they worked in metals like Mittie's father did. Because, while we had already spent eighty-five billion dollars on the war, we had a lot more money left.

And that summer, while Leila put on her play and Mr. Nixon said he would bring us together, while Dr. Spock, my sister's guide, who had raised us all, and Father Berrigan, and Reverend Coffin, and Verl, and many of my classmates went on trial for objecting to the war, while Margery decided to have her baby in Canada, while in Miami, the week that Bruno Stark's helicopter came down on us, a five-hundred-foot-long elephant waved above Convention Hall, where the Secret Service, the Border Patrol, the F.B.I., the I.R.S., the F.A.A., Military Intelligence, the Bureau of Narcotics, Army Demolition, the City Police, the Highway Patrol, the County Public Safety Board, the Conservation Patrol, the State Beverage Department, the Marines, and the USS *Fremont* protected Mr. Nixon (in a former men's sauna atop the Hilton Plaza) and Mr. Rockefeller (in 720 rooms of the Americana) from a mild delegation of Cubans, a mild delegation of Elder Citizens, and from an elephant in a purple tutu dancing through the streets—until Senator Hatfield could endorse Mr. Nixon (whom Calhoun Grange had endorsed for Ed Hade), and Mayor Lindsay could second the nomination of Mr. Agnew. And across the land, Marcuse taught the new philosophy at San Diego, and Verl and Joely didn't believe we had already lost, while in Joely's hometown, Chicago, below the windows of the Conrad Hilton, where Mr. Humphrey promised to bring us together, the army and the national guard and twelve thousand policemen, who were there to preserve order, clubbed, beat, and gassed hippies, yippies, anarchists, Maoists, New Leftists, runaways, Black Panthers, dissident Democrats, delegates, campaign workers, newsmen, photographers, passers-by, clergymen, Abbie Hoffman, a member of Parliament, a cripple, Hugh Hefner, and each other; while Senator Ribicoff and Mrs. Thurston couldn't believe it was happening. And while Spurgeon Debson became a celebrity, and Sabby told us Richard Burton gave Elizabeth Taylor a $305,000-ring, I decided to go home.

chapter 33

A Light Shines on My Way

"Leila Stark, I certainly hope I am not going to have to resign myself to your driving down the public highways all across America with a cigarette hanging out of your mouth and a bottle of wine stuck between your legs," called Mrs. Thurston from the back seat of the Red Bus where she sat in her travel suit and white gloves surrounded by suitcases, boxes, clothes, records, toys, a poster of Robert Kennedy, and Wolfstein's golden Oscar we had found in the back of a dresser drawer.

"I'm not sure this junk heap is going to make it all the way across America," Leila laughed. "But if it does, yes, Mama, you're going to have to resign yourself."

"Well, I frankly doubt a soul would believe so, but I honestly did make an effort to raise you right. But, of course, people are going to Think the Worst. They always do."

We jostled down the gravel road and turned onto the street toward town.

"Look and see if the gypsy wagon's still there," Leila called to Davy.

"It's still there!" he squealed delightedly from the mattress on which he and Maisie sat in their pajamas looking out the back window at the bouncing wooden trailer hooked behind us.

"And why in the Good Lord's name we are choosing to begin a journey of this nature on a Sunday, in the dark of night, instead of at a decent hour, is more than I could tell anyone who asked me. But naturally it is not surprising because you can be sure the stranger a thing is, all the more likely to look for us there."

"We're leaving because, Mama, today is September the first. And on the first, our leases all ran out. So we're going home. And get some *new* leases. Aren't we, babies?"

"Yes, Mama," they yelled.

"Aren't we, Devin?"

"Yes, ma'am," I yelled.

"Aren't we, Mama?"

"Oh, Leila, Leila, honey, you are a pure and unadulterated fool. Why, you could be sitting in a house of your own and attending college in Portland, Oregon, this very minute." Mrs. Thurston snapped her door locked, leaned forward to snap down Leila's. "Well," she added, "at least somebody had the sense to fry up some chicken and make some hard-boiled eggs, and I've also got some potato salad here, if anybody wants it, so at least we'll be able to *eat* like rational human beings, even if every last one of us ought to be committed to a lunatic asylum…"

"Lock, stock, and barrel, Mama! Lock, stock, and barrel."

The first night of a cold, quick fall rose up behind the mountains and pulled the sun down with it as we drove in the chill out of Floren Park along Main Street past Navajo jewelry next to Western Outfits next to Hade's Buick next to the Nixon headquarters, next to the Memorial Shoppers' Mall, next to whatever would be next.

Above Main Street a bright new banner was fluttering.

FLOREN PARK WELCOMES VETERANS OF FOREIGN WARS
SEPTEMBER 4–8

So they would be back. Sam Midpath and the fat Bobby. And their friend Artie. Maybe Jerry Thurston would be there. And Brian Beaumont. And Bruno Stark. Maybe Marlin's father would be there. And mine. Jostled in the crowded streets with Sheriff Booter and his deputy. All our fathers. And maybe it would make sense to them.

We'd be home by then.

Night took Floren Park, hidden safe in its low valley, as Leila's old school bus wound around the road circling the bright ring of mountains that climbed up to see the stars.

About the Author

Michael Malone is the author of ten works of fiction and two works of nonfiction. *The Delectable Mountains* is one of his earliest novels. Educated at Carolina and at Harvard, he has taught at Yale, at the University of Pennsylvania, and at Swarthmore. Among his prizes are the Edgar, the O.Henry, the Writers Guild Award, and the Emmy. He lives in Hillsborough, North Carolina, with his wife, Maureen Quilligan, chair of the English department at Duke University.